Praise for Alisa Sheckley writing as Alisa Kwitney

TILL THE FAT LADY SINGS

"If Milan Kundera, Tama Janowitz and Dr. Joyce Brothers had collaborated on a book, they might have come up with this imaginative and quirky first novel."

—MAXINE CHERNOFF,
The New York Times Book Review

"A lively novel and a compulsive read, which is saying a lot—and it taught me a thing or two, ..
more."
—..N

"Subversive, revolutionary . . . it's great!"
—CAROLYN SEE, *Los Angeles Times*

"A delicious confection, as tart and spikey as a lemon meringue pie." —LAURIE MUCHNIK, *Newsday*

"Bright and funny and remarkably poised."
—*The Boston Globe*

"A cool, funny, stylish, and very original look at life and love in Manhattan, by a remarkable new writer."
—ALISON LURIE

"Hip, contemporary, Alisa Kwitney is also a stylist: funny and wonderful, witty and philosophical." —KIT REED

"*Till the Fat Lady Sings* is an engrossing satire of the New York female intelligentsia." —NAOMI WOLF

"An immensely poised and well-crafted performance, which kept me smiling to myself throughout."
—PHILLIP LOPATE

FLIRTING IN CARS

"This exciting tease of a novel will set your heart pounding like the best love affair. Smart, funny, sexy—I loved it!"

—PAMELA REDMOND SATRAN,
author of *The Man I Should Have Married*
and *Suburbanistas*

"*Flirting in Cars* is a modern-day fairy tale about finding happily-ever-after where you least expect it. I couldn't put it down."

—KAREN QUINN,
author of *The Ivy Chronicles* and *Wife in the Fast Lane*

"Alisa Kwitney's cross-cultural love story is intelligent, funny, and sexy." —THELMA ADAMS, *US Weekly*

SEX AS A SECOND LANGUAGE

"The romance between Kat and Magnus is, except for the CIA part, true-to-life and achingly bittersweet. Kwitney even gives them one of the sexiest scenes involving two forty-somethings since *The Thomas Crown Affair*."

—DEBRA PICKETT of the *Chicago Sun-Times*

"An engaging and intelligently written comedy—with a few genuinely titillating sex scenes."

—*Publishers Weekly*

"*Sex as a Second Language*, Alisa Kwitney's smart, sassy, sexy tale of the single mom who brings in a spy from the cold and warms him up, is funny and emotionally true, a great read!"

—JENNIFER CRUSIE, bestselling author of *Bet Me*

ON THE COUCH

"Less concerned with embarrassing pratfalls for her neurotic heroines than many of her chick-lit sisters, Kwitney still wants them to find love, and not a little bit of sex. The single girl here is Marlowe, a Manhattan psychologist

with divorced parents providing her with distant affection and a trust fund. Joe is the NYPD detective with more crime smarts than tact. . . . The relationship is fitful, playful and exciting, then cold and hostile, swinging wildly about as each tries to figure out what game the other is playing, all the while trying to find the killer to boot. Kwitney deserves credit for not throwing out illogical roadblocks, and there's a refreshing absence of stock best-friend characters."
—*Kirkus Reviews*

"A teasingly good read. Sexy, sassy and a little kinky. A different take on Manhattan life—more handcuffs than cocktails."
—CAROLE MATTHEWS, *USA Today* bestselling author

DOES SHE OR DOESN'T SHE?
"Alisa Kwitney is my guilty pleasure."
—NEIL GAIMAN,
Hugo Award–winning author of *American Gods* and *New York Times* bestselling author of *Coraline*

"Witty, charming, funny and real, Alisa Kwitney brings a fresh voice to Chick-Lit and Romance!"
—CARLY PHILLIPS, *New York Times* bestselling author

"Sharp, sassy, and sexy."
—JENNIFER CRUSIE, *New York Times* bestselling author

THE DOMINANT BLONDE
"Her search for the perfect boyfriend and the perfect hair-color is delightful. It belongs right up there with all the legally and naturally blonde bombshells of our time."
—LIZ SMITH, nationally syndicated columnist

BY ALISA SHECKLEY WRITING AS ALISA KWITNEY

Flirting in Cars
Sex as a Second Language
On the Couch
Does She or Doesn't She?
The Dominant Blonde
Till the Fat Lady Sings

GRAPHIC NOVELS BY ALISA SHECKLEY
WRITING AS ALISA KWITNEY

Destiny: A Chronicle of Deaths Foretold
Vertigo Visions: Art from the Cutting Edge of Comics
Sandman: King of Dreams
Token

THE
BETTER
TO
HOLD
YOU

ALISA
SHECKLEY

Alisa Sheckley Krishley

DEL REY

BALLANTINE BOOKS • NEW YORK

The Better to Hold You is a work of fiction. Names, characters, places, and incidents are the products of the author's imagination or are used fictitiously. Any resemblance to actual events, locales, or persons, living or dead, is entirely coincidental.

A Del Rey Mass Market Original

Published in the United States by Del Rey, an imprint of The Random House Publishing Group, a division of Random House, Inc., New York.

DEL REY is a registered trademark and the Del Rey colophon is a trademark of Random House, Inc.

ISBN 978-0-345-50587-3

Printed in the United States of America

www.delreybooks.com

9 8 7 6 5 4 3 2 1

This one's for Mark,
who feeds me,
keeps me sane,
and reminds me that I say
there's no way I can make
my deadline every year.

ACKNOWLEDGMENTS

I wrote this book five long years ago and was helped in my research by a lovely young veterinary intern at a large teaching hospital of veterinary medicine in Manhattan. I've lost the intern's name, and the hospital asked me to lose theirs when I mentioned werewolves and mad scientists. But thank you both all the same. More recently, one of my local vets at the Pine Plains Veterinary Practice, Dorraine Waldow, helped me sort out my (fictional) sedatives.

This is the first novel I've written using the name on my birth certificate; I'd like to thank my father, the late, great science fiction writer and grand master of irony Robert Sheckley, for all the writing advice he gave me over the years.

My mother, Ziva, believed in this book from the first, but I might never have taken it out of its drawer if Neil Gaiman hadn't prodded me by asking what had become of it, and if my marvelous and motivational agent, Meg Ruley, hadn't believed in it and helped find it a home. Liz Scheier, my editor, inspired me to go back into this world and helped me to realize how much larger and more complex it really was, and Holly Harrison kept me from getting lost, freaking out, and forgetting how everything tied together.

Kim Canez and my son, Matthew, have braved snow, rain, ticks, mud, snakes, and a very aggressive fawn to go dog walking with me in the woods, which is vital when writing a wolfish book; Liz Maverick and the rest of my bat guano posse helped keep me a prisoner of

Starbuck's until it was written. Last but not least, a special mention for my wolf-loving daughter, Elinor, who slammed her pinky finger in the car door just as my agent was telling me about Ballantine's offer, thereby sealing my fate in blood.

PART ONE

ONE

●○○ There are many different Manhattans. Which one you happen to live in depends partly on geography and partly on perception. I live on the Upper West Side, in the midst of an eccentric animal kingdom.

In my Manhattan, people like their animals big: aristocratic hunting dogs with wide, soft mouths, overfed guard dogs and pit bull mixes, sled dogs that have kept the look of a wolf about them. These are large animals for large apartments: six-room prewars, with a couple of children and possibly a weekend home in the Hamptons. Nobody has time to go jogging with the dog anymore, and the nanny refuses to pick up feces from the sidewalk, so a walker is hired.

Elsewhere, on the East Side, are toy breeds with their adorably hydrocephalic heads. The owners are older; the children have grown up and been replaced by skittish canine midgets with the appeal of perpetual infancy. Downtown are the elaborately designed fashion victims, entrancingly ugly breeds with faces wreathed in wrinkles, their noses squashed up between their eyes. They are dragged behind their fit and fabulous owners, panting from their deformed jaws.

And then there are the exotics: lizards, parrots, rabbits, the odd squirrel monkey or de-glanded skunk. I don't usually see these outside of work, but then, they're not my specialty: They belong to someone else's Manhattan. So I suppose I was a little startled to see the man with the baby barn owl on his shoulder, although not as surprised as the other subway riders.

The man had a quality of alertness about him that didn't quite seem to match his appearance. He had that look you get from sleeping rough: T-shirt not quite clean, the worn cotton molded to his wiry chest. I noticed that the man's eyes were a pale hazel, almost yellow, as he kept moving his gaze around the subway car, careful not to make eye contact with anyone. I wondered where he had found the little gray bird, which had sunk into itself, but stopped myself from asking him. Most people think they're rescuing owlets when all they're really doing is stealing the baby on its first day out of the nest. My friend Lilliana can explain this to people and they'll frown and say they had no idea, but when I open my mouth, people tend to get red in the face and become defensive.

The little owl huddled closer to the man's neck and he reached back and patted it, shifting his other hand from strap to pole. A blond businesswoman sidled away and I saw the man notice.

Then, for a moment, the man met my eyes, a half-smile on his lips, as if he had something amusing to impart. I turned away from him, because I don't approve of people wearing animals as accessories. Particularly wild creatures, which are far more delicate than you might think.

I knew this because we get the odd raptor at the Animal Medical Institute. We're the only veterinary service in the New York area that caters to exotics, so we're pretty much the only game in town if your anaconda loses its appetite or your parrot breaks its foot. We're also the only place in the tristate area that can do dialysis on cats and the best place to give your dog chemo.

But somehow I didn't think the raggedy man was taking his little pal in for a checkup. I was wondering if I owed it to the owl to intervene when the subway screeched to a stop and the doors opened. There was a reshuffling of bodies and I realized that the person pressing against my back had gotten off, giving me room to breathe again. Reflexively, I lifted my hand to adjust my pocketbook strap, only to find that there was no pocketbook there.

I felt a moment of disorientation. Was it possible that I'd left home without it? Had it fallen to the floor? And then, on the heels of these thoughts, the realization: Someone had stolen my bag. I said it out loud, half in disbelief, just as the subway gave a hiss and a jolt, the doors closed, and the train began to move again.

I looked around, wildly, as if I expected the thief to still be there. But of course, whoever it was would have gotten off the train. Around me, people were watching with various degrees of sympathy, alarm, and disinterest. I met the raggedy man's eyes and he gave a little shrug as if to say, Sorry, but it wasn't me.

A heavyset woman with a vast ledge of a bosom patted my shoulder, and there were murmurs from the other women and some of the men. "What happened?" "Somebody stole her bag." "Didn't you feel anything?"

I shook my head. "I didn't feel a thing." I felt a rising panic as my fellow passengers checked their own bags and briefcases and wallets. But they were fine, while I was suddenly stranded without money, credit cards, cell phone, and keys. I tried to remember how much cash I'd been carrying. Crap. I'd just gone to the bank yesterday after work.

"They carry knives," said a thin teenage boy, his oversized jeans hanging off his hips and revealing white boxers. "They just cut right through the strap, and bam—emergency surgery on your finances." He looked at me with mock concern, aglow with his own cleverness.

For a moment, I suspected the cocky boy of being the pickpocket, and then I turned, feeling the owl man regarding me with heavily lidded eyes and a cynical half-smile. He knew what I was thinking, and I could hear his judgment of me as if he'd said it out loud: racist. As if the color of the boy's skin had anything to do with my momentary suspicion.

Flushed and embarrassed, I turned away. I realized with a clench of anger that the man had been observing me for a while—he might even have witnessed my being robbed without bothering to warn me. My heart pounding, I felt a wild urge to accuse him. He met my eyes as if he could read this thought as well, and then the subway lurched to a stop. Without actually making a decision, I found myself pushing through the crowd to get off.

On the subway platform, I tried to think things through. I was already going to be late for rounds, but I couldn't wait till lunchtime to cancel all my credit cards. And whoever had taken my bag had my house keys along with my address. I had to tell my husband to change our locks.

Reflexively, I reached for my cell phone before remembering that of course, I'd lost that, too. I made my way back to the station agent, who was hiding behind the Plexiglas, pretending to be deaf.

"I'm sorry," I said, trying to keep the note of hysteria out of my voice, "but my purse was just stolen. Do you think I could borrow your phone to make a local call?"

"I'll make the call for you," said the woman, apparently thinking this was some elaborate ruse to bilk the MTA. Maybe I should have gone for more hysteria. I told her my number and waited as she lethargically dialed my home.

"Nobody's home." She regarded me with blank indifference.

"He is home, he's just sleeping the sleep of the seriously jet-lagged. Can you please try again?" My husband had just come back from Romania last night looking ill from fatigue, a good fifteen pounds thinner than I'd ever seen him before.

The station agent stared at me for a moment, as if weighing her options. In the end, she redialed the number, using a pen to protect her inch-long nails.

Hunter, I prayed, please wake up and answer the phone. I hadn't been expecting him for another week, and had nearly jumped out of my skin when he walked in the door as I was eating day-old Thai food from the carton with my fingers. He'd been sick with a stomach bug, he'd explained, and had changed his ticket. No, he didn't feel up to giving me the details just yet, and yes, if he needed a doctor he'd call one. His tone implied we were having an argument, and mine implied I hadn't noticed.

I'd gone to bed at eleven and actually fallen asleep fairly quickly, an unusual occurrence for me. I had no idea when Hunter joined me, but at three A.M., when I woke up, he was on my right, snoring lightly from his attractively once-broken nose. For a moment I had wished him gone again, so I could pamper my chronic insomnia without restraint—turning the lights on, surfing the television, eating breakfast cereal in bed.

Then he had spooned his body around mine, a rare intimacy, and I had felt his warm breath on the back of my neck. Savoring the closeness, I had remained motionless while my left arm fell asleep and he began to snore again. I hated to bother him now, and knew he'd probably be irritated at first, but he'd understand once I explained what had happened.

"Still not home," said the station agent, hanging up the phone. "You want to talk to the police about the theft of your personal possessions?"

"No," I said, disconsolate. "Could you just let me back through the turnstile so I can go home?"

The station agent buzzed me through and I retraced my steps in a sort of daze, making my way to the downtown platform, then to the crosstown shuttle, which took me back to the West Side, where I could catch the Broadway local. It took me three trains and forty minutes during rush hour to get to work each day. Most of my fellow interns had taken housing near the center, but Hunter hadn't wanted to give up our brownstone apartment on the Upper West Side.

Wishing that there were some way to call my team to let them know why I was so late, I emerged from the subway and headed for Riverside Drive. An unseasonably cool wind was whipping in from the water. It had been the coolest summer in over one hundred years, and now fall seemed ready to bring the curtain down on a lackluster performance.

As I quickened my pace to a jog, I felt a twinge of cramp low in my left ovary. I was about twenty-five days into my cycle, but I'm not all that regular; I'm one of those women who skip months, then get their periods every three weeks for a while, then start going into a six-week cycle. Still, I felt that sort of warm looseness in my abdomen that usually heralds the start of things.

My gynecologist said that I might find it difficult to become pregnant. I told my husband this last year and he said, It's probably for the best. I should explain that there is a history of mental illness in Hunter's family: His mother's sister became schizophrenic at the age of nineteen and his mother committed suicide when he was a teenager. Hunter is moody, the kind of moody people expect from writers, but he always says he's not sure he should have children. He spent most of his adolescence wondering if one day madness would explode in him like a time bomb; and I think he worries that if we had a baby, he'd spend the next twenty years waiting to see what might detonate in his offspring.

I suppose I'm ambivalent about becoming a mother. I'm not sure I have the vocation for it, and I think my own mother is a good example of what can happen if you have a child without one. I mean, Mom wasn't quite in the "Mommie Dearest" league, but she did like making scenes. Maybe it's something to do with being a film actress. Perhaps movie stars, even "B" ones, shouldn't propagate.

In any case, my schedule wouldn't allow for a baby. I had this year of internship to get through, a residency to apply for, and a husband who was away more often than he was home.

Nervously checking my watch, I turned the corner on Eighty-fourth Street and finally reached our building.

Hunter and I had spent the past four years living in one of those modest turn-of-the-century mansions that had been subdivided into small apartments, so that the whole structure is like one big dysfunctional family. We lived on the second floor, in the only apartment without a bricked-in fireplace. But we did have a balcony of which we were inordinately proud, even if it was barely large enough to accommodate two chairs and a portable mini-barbecue.

What our building didn't have, of course, was a doorman to let me in. I buzzed our intercom repeatedly, to no avail. I tried the friendly couple of middle-aged men in the garden apartment first, and then the angry family who had the nicer duplex above us. Also not at home.

Great. Sinking down onto a floor littered with Chinese take-out menus, I blinked back tears of frustration. Clearly, I should have just gone on to work, but now I was here and unless Hunter let me in I didn't have the money to get back to the Animal Medical Institute.

Of course, I could hike a few miles across the park,

but I was probably going to get my period today. Call me prudish, but I don't feel comfortable going up to other women in a quest for pads or tampons. I don't even like sitting in a stall talking to another woman, particularly if there's going to be any grunting involved. I blame my mother. She was so intent on my not being ashamed of my body and its functions that she instilled in me a fiercely beleaguered sense of privacy.

And Hunter was in there. All I had to do was rouse him out of his coma. Feeling more than a little desperate, I pressed all the buzzers one last time, then went outside and shouted "Hunter, it's me" at the top of my lungs while searching around for a rock to throw against our window.

And then, looking up at our balcony, I thought: I can just climb up there. Not by going straight up our building—the first floor was faced with 1940s flat yellow brickwork, which didn't offer a hand- or foothold. But the Victorians who'd designed our neighbors' place hadn't worried much about crime. Whoever had built the entrance had arranged foot-long concrete rectangles into a pattern around the black iron-and-glass doors, giving the house a vaguely medieval look. Right under their first-floor terrace was a little black iron lamp, a perfect handhold. Their terrace was only two feet away from ours.

A twelve-year-old would have seen this in an instant. Most adults stop looking at the world as something that can be climbed, unless they're of the breaking-and-entering persuasion.

But back before I sold my soul to the Animal Medical Institute, I used to do some rock climbing at the Chelsea Piers gym. I'm good at anything that requires methodical attention to detail, and I actually got to the point where I was developing a few muscles in my legs and rear, and was looking a bit less like a loaf of white bread.

Then AMI accepted my application for an internship and I lost all semblance of a life.

The only obstacle to climbing the ten feet to our balcony was my outfit. Hunter had always said that he had never known a woman who spent as much money on sacks as I did, but I like comfortable clothes in rich fabrics, the sort of thing you could wear to a medieval fair and pass as a rich guildsman's wife. That day I happened to be wearing my Eileen Fisher wide-legged pants in soft brown cotton paired with a deep gold cotton tunic, not ideal for scaling the facades of buildings, even small ones. I tucked my pant legs into my socks and looked around to make sure no one was watching. Luckily, ours is pretty much a block of opera singers and older people, so the police don't cruise by too often.

It was almost as easy as I had thought. The footholds were generous, almost two inches wide, and I was about twelve feet up, right under the balcony, when I reached the lamp. It was bolted in, solid enough to step on. I suppose I looked like one of those graceless little girls you see in the playground, heaving their sturdy little bodies up the monkey bars, but I got myself over the wrought-iron terrace railing. There was only one bad moment, where I had to balance on the neighbors' railing before jumping over the two feet onto our balcony. I was about to step over when I heard a dog barking.

I looked down to see an overexcited dachshund with a dapper old man attached. The man looked familiar, and I realized he lived in our building. You couldn't have come home two minutes earlier, I thought sourly.

"And what do you think you're doing, young woman?"

"It's my apartment," I said. "I live here." His dog kept yapping.

"I should call the police!"

"Please don't. I'm Abra Barrow, your neighbor in 2B."

"Wait a minute, don't I know you?" He pointed his finger up at me. "The girl. The actress."

"The vet. I'm a vet. My husband didn't hear the phone, and I lost my key."

"The what?"

"The key! Lost the key!"

"Thickey?"

Another old man, thinner and bearded, joined the first. "What's she doing? Breaking and entering?"

"Nah, nah, it's her apartment. Husband trouble."

"Hey! You! Girl!" The bearded man sounded angry.

"Look, it's really okay . . ." I started to turn to face him better, lost my grip, and reached over to grab the railing of our balcony. Unfortunately, this left me in the awkward position of having my feet on one building and my hands on the other.

"Get your leg over! Your right leg! These kids don't know how to climb trees, is the problem."

"As a boy, I climbed trees, houses, barns. In Ukraine." The dachshund gave a little bark of agreement.

I stepped over to our balcony, then turned back to the men, who had now been joined by an elderly woman in a fox-trimmed winter coat.

"I'm safe, you guys. Thanks."

"Next time ask us, we'll let you in. Sidney has all the keys to the apartments in that building," said the bearded man. I waved. People think the city is big and impersonal. The suburbs, where I grew up, are big and impersonal. The city is a patchwork of tiny provincial villages without clear borders, each with its own yenta, postmodern revolutionary, and idiot.

From the street, I heard the old woman ask, "What's that girl doing up there, Grisha?"

"She's a veterinarian. With husband problems."

Maybe *I* was the town idiot.

I tried our window. Thank God, we'd left it open. I

shoved the glass up another foot and climbed inside, and for a moment I stood in our living room, feeling very good about myself. I was the prince scaling Rapunzel's tower without a hair rope; I was Robin Hood sneaking into the Sheriff's stronghold.

Then, with a start, I realized how very unsafe my apartment was. During the three months that Hunter had been away, I had often left the window open. Until that moment, it had never occurred to me that I was within harm's way whenever harm might take a notion to come find me.

But if a modestly athletic twenty-nine-year-old woman could climb up here and break into her own apartment, then it didn't take a big bad wolf. Anyone could get in.

Distracted by these thoughts, I didn't immediately notice the strange sounds coming from the bedroom. My initial thought was that Hunter was having a nightmare. He kept uttering little panting groans, punctuated by a soft whimper that sounded almost like a dog's. I walked toward the bedroom thinking, Maybe I should wake him. Then I heard the rhythmic slapping sound of flesh, and a chill of gooseflesh traveled down my neck. That wasn't the sound of Hunter having a bad dream. That was the sound of Hunter on the brink of orgasm.

TWO

◑○○ My first reaction was a prickle of embarrassment and a tingle of desire. Then Hunter's breathing
picked up and I thought, Wouldn't he be surprised if I
just walked in there now?

I didn't assume, in that first moment, that there was a
woman in there. That came a half-second after, when I registered the fact that Hunter had shown no interest in making love to me this morning, despite our not having seen
each other for three months. But he had been sick. And I
had been expecting my period, which is not something
Hunter enjoys. I hadn't mentioned that I was due, but I'm
pretty sure Hunter would have noticed the box of panty-
liners I'd set out in the bathroom. He had a journalist's
knack of always spotting the one thing you wish he'd miss.

There were quick, fleshy slapping noises from the
bedroom, and I listened for the sound of a second panting voice. Nothing. Of course, some women are pretty
quiet. I've learned to make my breathing more audible
when there's something going on that I like, even though
it feels a little fake. Hunter once told me I made love like
a nun in wartime.

He said it teasingly, of course.

There was a slight grunt, nothing theatrical, and then
silence. I waited a moment in the living room, noticing

the thick layer of dust on the Mexican pottery. I hadn't cleaned under the couch in a long time, either.

"Hunter?"

Silence.

"Hunter?"

Rustling sounds. "Abra? Is that you?"

"It's me." I stood there, waiting.

"Of course. Wait a moment—" More rustling sounds. "Yeah, come in, come in."

I walked in to find Hunter sitting upright against the cherry mission headboard, pale blue sheets pulled over his lap. He hadn't bothered to close the shutters. There was the faint sea-smell of fresh semen in the room. He was still breathing hard enough that his pale chest showed the deep pattern of ribs on the exhale. His dark brown hair had grown long enough to fall in his eyes and over his neck, and his brown eyes looked darker, sunk more deeply into his face. But he was a handsome man, even when looking wan and disheveled.

"I didn't hear you come in." Said with no embarrassment.

"That's because I climbed in through the living room window."

"Trying to catch me with another woman?"

I just looked at him.

"All right, let's try again. Why didn't you just use the door?"

"I didn't have my key. A pickpocket stole my bag and you weren't answering the phone or the buzzer." I tried to keep my voice from sounding prim and accusatory. The way I felt.

"You're kidding. Poor Abra." He gave me all his attention as he said it, and I felt myself being dragged back into the force field of his charm. Hunter has this way of listening to you so carefully that you realize that most of the people you talk to are really just waiting their turn to speak.

"I'm not kidding."

"And you really climbed up the front of the building?" Hunter reached for his watch on the bedside table and strapped it on.

"Actually, I climbed the front of the building next door and came over the balcony."

"Good Lord." Hunter shook his head, admiringly. "And I suppose you worked out that this was the most logical course of action?"

"I needed to get some . . . things."

"That explains it, then. By the way, your pants are kind of torn."

I bent to inspect the damage, wondering how to segue into my next question. "Um, Hunter, is there—there isn't anyone else here, is there?"

Hunter laughed, his head nodding forward, as if he were embarrassed to meet my eyes. "What, you mean hiding in the closet? No, Abra." He looked up. "I'm sorry about the phone. I thought it was one of those telemarketers." Hunter patted the bed. "Come sit down."

"I have to cancel my credit card and checks."

"You can do that in a minute. Come over here and sit down. I can see you're upset."

I sat down beside him, and he wrapped me in his arms. He wasn't even sweaty. The people in Hunter's family didn't seem to develop as many body odors as the people in mine. As he held me I noticed that all along the top of our low dresser, Hunter's wallet had hemorrhaged business cards, loose change, dollar bills, and cigarettes, breaking the neat ranks of my perfume bottles and enameled jewelry boxes.

"You okay, 'Cadabra girl?"

I nodded into his shoulder. "Hunter." I tried to think of a way to put this. "Is it me?"

He stiffened under my hands, then slid away. "It's nothing to do with you, Abs. I'm just—it's been a difficult couple of months."

It had been three months, actually. Back in early May, I'd been lying on the plastic chaise lounge we'd wedged sideways on our balcony, reading a brochure on Block Island. No cars in summer, just like a little Nantucket close to home. My internship at the Institute began in July; I'd asked Hunter if he wanted to try to get away with me in June. Sounding distracted, he had responded that he'd just gotten an idea for a piece on some mythical Romanian beastie.

This, roughly translated, meant, *I've already bought my ticket and you won't be seeing me again till the last dead brown leaf of summer gets ready to take that final dive.*

Hunter had spent the last few years writing articles for magazines like *Outside* and *Backpacker.* He hoped, I knew, for the kind of career-making story that meant a feature article in *Vanity Fair,* a book deal, movie rights, and full circle to an ongoing gig as contributing editor. All he needed was the right break—his own Everest, his personal perfect storm.

And that was why Hunter was intent on spending the summer with his Romanian-English phrase book instead of with me. It seemed that the existence of Europe's last surviving wolves was under serious threat. Ceauşescu's totalitarian regime, like Hitler's, had possessed a hunter's fond regard for preserving native woodlands. The Romanians figured that wealthy American and European eco-tourists might pay to see the ancient woods where their ancestors once walked in fear of trolls, dragons, and flesh-eating creatures. This was Transylvania, after all, monster country.

And some people will pay good money to see monsters.

So, while the enterprising Romanians were cutting down old-growth forest and setting up boutique hotels, the real wolves' ranges were growing ever smaller. And since wolves are a little less popular with family tourists than, say, a nice elk or eagle, the villagers weren't shy about killing the rogue that went after a local calf or sheep.

If it was big enough, it got called a werewolf.

It was a good story. It was a morality tale with a good dose of irony and a hint of B-movie Transylvanian spice. And Hunter had told it well, sitting next to me on our little Manhattan terrace.

Unfortunately, it was such a good story that my Transylvania-hopping husband barely found time to call me three times in as many months. Once I'd started my internship at the Institute, I'd been able to distract myself with work—I'd been assigned to Malachy Knox's medical group, which was the veterinary equivalent of special ops. There wasn't much time or opportunity to ruminate about your faraway sweetheart.

But now Hunter was back, which filled me with relief and gratitude, and yet also made me want to bark: Who've you been sleeping with? If only there was a way to say this without saying it. Ask it without asking.

"You haven't told me much about your trip yet."

"Abra? You're not going to blow this whole thing out of proportion, are you?"

I turned to look at him. He was clipping his words, getting prepared to be angry, just in case.

"I just want to know why you didn't—why you didn't want—" Me. I left that last pathetic "me" unspoken.

Hunter sighed deeply, pulling me back into his arms. He rested his chin on the top of my head, which hurt. "Oh, Abra, I am so sick and tired and out of my head. I wouldn't have been any good for you. I just needed—I just wanted something quick and easy."

"I can be quick and easy."

Hunter's hands rubbed my back, moved under my shirt, and then skimmed the waistband of my pants. "You sweet girl."

I felt the sting of tears and fought it. "Hunter, I need to make my calls and get to work. I'm going to be late as it is."

"I could make you later." His mouth moved down, found my ear. His breath was a little stale from sleep.

"Hunter." Was this affection, or renewed lust, or pity? With Hunter, I could never tell. His mouth moved down my neck, then he lifted my shirt and slid his hand under my practical beige brassiere.

"God, you've still got the breasts of a thirteen-year-old virgin." This may not have sounded like a compliment, but believe me, it was. Hunter pulled my shirt over my head, and for a moment I was caught in my long brown hair.

"You're never going to cut this, right?"

My hair nearly reaches my waist. "No."

Hunter wrapped my hair around his wrist and tugged. "I've got you—you're my prisoner."

I looked at him with my head back, throat bared. His dark eyes were shining now. "Is that what you want?"

Hunter glanced down at himself. "What do you think?"

We looked at each other. "All right, then."

There was a pause, a beat, and then Hunter let go of my hair and yanked down my pants. "Like this? Without touching you first? Quick and easy. My prisoner."

I watched his eyes. This was real. We hadn't made love in three months. The last time I'd been in his arms, his thoughts had been a thousand miles away, on the trip ahead, on the adventure of the unknown. "No," I said carefully, whipping my head a little back and forth, making my hair move. "No, please, no." In case he'd thought that first no had been real.

Hunter pinned my hands over my head. He was stronger than his wiry frame suggested. "Spread 'em."

"No." How was this really done? With his hands holding my wrists, how could he get my legs apart if I didn't help?

Hunter wedged his knee in between my thighs. "I said, spread 'em."

"No."

A look, almost one of anger, crossed Hunter's face, and for a moment I thought maybe I'd done something wrong. Then he transferred both wrists to one hand, and tried to use his other hand to guide himself inside me. After a moment, he gave up, looked at me again, and said, "Slave Girl, you'd better start listening to your Master."

There was a touch of real anger in me. "No."

Hunter sat back, trying to figure this out. This was a game of domination. How far to go? I was curious, too. And more than a little excited.

What he did next surprised the hell out of me. He sort of yanked me up, threw me on my stomach, and grabbed me by the back of the neck, like you would a cat. I think I was lying on the remote control; something was digging into my breast.

"Hunter—"

Our bed is a high one, and he was standing when he thrust into me. For a moment, I felt just the blunt knock of him at my entrance, and then he started to go deeper, faster, a pace set for his pleasure, not mine. There was the slap of flesh, just as I had heard it from the other room, except this time I was there beneath him. I had wanted this more than I'd let myself know.

"Hunter." But he was beyond hearing, caught up in the chase. He slammed into me with a roughness I wasn't used to, hitting the place high up inside that is just this side of pain. But it wasn't pain. Not really. Because pain doesn't climb, doesn't build and build and . . . Hunter came too soon, with a deep moan that didn't sound like him at all. And then he collapsed on top of me.

Hunter kissed the back of my neck. "You okay, Slave Girl?" He put his hand between my legs. "I was too quick for you."

"No, I . . ." He moved his fingers, and I took a breath.

"There? Is that it? Come on, Abra, let me take you there."

I started to cry then, just a little. I would never be able to lose control this way, with Hunter watching me, waiting for my response. He moved his fingers faster, mistaking my sounds for pleasure.

Cheating him, cheating myself, I cried out my dissatisfaction, and he was content.

THREE

◑○○ I finally arrived at work two and a half hours late. Even though I'd called to explain, I felt conspicuously guilty as I moved through the vast white labyrinth of corridors. I kept wanting to announce to the people I passed in the halls that I'd left home as quickly as I could, borrowing thirty dollars from Hunter and leaving him to call my bank and the local police office. I hadn't wasted a single moment.

Aside from that little aberrant time-out as a slave girl.

I found my medical services group S.O.A.P.'ing a few of the noncriticals. Dr. Malachy Knox, the staff veterinarian in charge of our unit, was holding a limp rag of a cat with the distinctive uremic smell of kidney failure.

"All right," he said, "let's see what we've got here. Now, what does the S in S.O.A.P. stand for?"

Sam rolled his eyes at me: Even the Institute vet techs knew the acronym for Subjective analysis, Objective data, Assessment, and Plan. But that was Malachy's style—he drawled out his questions in his plummy British accent as if he thought we were all a bit slow. Of course, in Sam's case, he might have had a point.

"S stands for Subjective analysis," said Sam. "My opinion? He looks half dead."

"I'd list that as unresponsive." Malachy glanced over at me. "Welcome to morning rounds, Ms. Barrow."

I flushed, realizing that he must not have received my message. "I'm so sorry I'm so late, but my pocketbook was stolen on the train."

Lilliana, my favorite member of the team, gave me a sympathetic smile, while the humorless Ofer pushed his glasses up on his nose like an officious gnome. Malachy just looked at me assessingly, his hands still stroking the cat's abdomen, feeling reflexively for the state of the cat's skin, the size of its spleen, its bowel loops.

As Malachy described what he was doing, Sam kept watching the older man intently as if he were expecting some sleight of hand. Even though Sam hulked a full seven inches over Malachy, and both men wore the AMI uniform of white lab coats and khakis, even a casual observer would have known which one was in charge.

The question of late was whether he would remain so. Dr. Malachy Knox, a.k.a. "Mad Mal," was the Institute's resident rock star, a brilliant researcher with a reputation for thinking outside the box and using unorthodox methodologies. In vet school, I had studied his infamous experiments transplanting the brains of rhesus monkeys, and had been torn between horror and awe at the implications of his work. More recently, he had been involved in isolating the so-called lycanthropy virus, a rare disorder that caused some individuals' cells to behave like fetal or stem cells, rendering them capable of radical shifts in form and function. Despite the name, the virus did not actually turn the host into a wolf—or, at least, that was the prevailing wisdom. Malachy himself would only say that the virus manifested itself very differently in different hosts, and that canid DNA was among the most plastic in the animal kingdom. He also liked to point out that humans and wolves had been associating with each other since the days when our own DNA hadn't yet been fixed in its current arrangement.

I wasn't entirely sure what Malachy had done that

had resulted in his ouster from the research unit and had brought him down to the far humbler position of, as he put it, "shepherding yearlings around." But whatever it was, it had affected his health as well as his career.

Underneath his wildly curling black hair, Malachy's craggy face was pallid and drawn, and where his wrists were visible under his lab coat, they appeared almost skeletal. I knew for a fact that he was forty-six, but he looked a good decade older.

"Well, Ms. Barrow," said Malachy, bringing my attention back to the here and now, "I can only assume that your current state of vague disinterest with our feline patient is the result of your brush with the city's underbelly. Although a countertheory might involve the fact that your husband has just returned from a long trip. He was in Romania, researching the legendary Unwolves, was he not?"

Whatever was wrong with Malachy Knox clearly did not affect his intelligence. He had gotten my message, I realized. He had just wanted to keep me off-balance.

"Yes," I said, "Hunter was looking into the stories about giant wolves."

"I'm sorry," said Ofer, not sounding it, "but what could it possibly matter if her husband is wasting his time looking for vampires in Transylvania? Shouldn't we be concentrating on our patient?" He pointed with one stubby-fingered hand, indicated the limp cat lying glassy-eyed on the examining table.

"Not vampires, Ofer—lycanthropes." Malachy wrote the word out on the whiteboard behind him with a dry erase pen. "Although many people confuse the Greek *vrykolakas* with the Slavic *vârcolac,* the former was supposed to be a sort of undead creature, not unlike a vampire, while I've heard the *vârcolac* variously described as a wolf demon or a wizard with shapeshifting abilities.

The *pricolici*, on the other hand, are large, wolflike creatures inhabited by human souls—Unwolves, or, more commonly, werewolves."

Malachy's blue eyes seemed to glow; I had never seen him so animated. Behind our staff leader's back, Sam pointed a finger at his temple and twirled it, indicating his opinion of Malachy's mental state.

"Of course, I *would* be insane if I believed that, Sam," Malachy said without turning around, making it clear he knew what Sam was doing. "I suspect that what the Romanians have are two distinct genetic strains of the lycanthropy virus. What I wouldn't give to get my hands on some tissue samples." He dragged his hand through his already unkempt hair. "I kept trying to convince the board that I needed a research grant to go to the Carpathian Mountains, but of course all that got derailed."

I exchanged a glance with Lilliana. This was the first time Malachy had alluded to the mysterious event that had precipitated his removal from the research department. "Which was why I was so pleased," Malachy went on, a small smile playing about his thin lips, "when I learned that your husband was going there."

Confused, I stroked the sick cat on the table, and a clump of matted fur came away in my hand. "I didn't realize that you were so interested. I mean—your research is medical, while Hunter's field is more sociological."

"My dear girl, of course I'm interested. Here, hold our patient for a moment." I put my hand on the dehydrated cat while Malachy turned to the computer on a nearby desk and tapped out a few commands. As he waited for the cat's X-rays to appear on the screen, Malachy said, "Not interested!" He gave a derisive snort. "Honestly, Ms. Barrow, did you think that my experiments with the lycanthropy virus had no bearing on my selection of interns?"

I felt as if I'd been slapped. "Are you saying—was that why I was chosen for this group?" I expected him to deny it, but instead, he raised his eyebrows.

"Oh, for Christ's sake. Don't overreact. Ah," he said, as the cat's X-rays appeared on the computer screen, "there we go. Okay, kids, take a look and tell me what you notice." As the others gathered around the screen, Malachy glanced at me sideways. "You're not going to sulk, now, are you? Obviously, you're a gifted veterinarian, but so were many applicants. And unlike Ofer here, you have no background in neurology."

It was as if he'd figured out all of my secret fears and doubts and confirmed them. Worse still, he had confirmed them in a tone of voice so casual it implied that I, like everyone around me, should have been aware of my limited potential. I was the diligent, wonky grind, not the natural talent.

No you're not, said a stubborn little voice inside me. You have talent *and* drive. Don't let him define you. He's British upper class. They excel at only two things: gardening and disdain.

"I graduated near the top of my class at Tufts," I said, my heart pounding in my chest. Nobody was paying any attention to the X-ray, or to the cat, who was seizing this opportunity to attempt to slide off the table. Holding him gently by the scruff, I went on. "My recommendations were glowing. If the only reason why you took me on was because of my husband's research, how do you explain your justification for choosing Lilliana? She's not even a veterinarian."

Lilliana had been plucked from the Institute's social work externship program, which had struck Sam, Ofer, and myself as more than a little peculiar. As far as we were concerned, the social workers were around to keep our patients' owners from asking us questions that really had no answers, and to help them work through their confusion and grief. They weren't supposed to be a part of the medical team, or to be included in our decision-making process. Mad Mal was known for thinking outside the box, of course, but privately I had wondered whether he had chosen Lilliana just for the sake of doing something unexpected.

Still, the moment the words were out of my mouth, I regretted them. Lilliana was brilliant, and my friend. The truth was, she had helped us make good decisions—she was extremely adept at anticipating an owner's reaction and helping us frame our responses accordingly. But I had to know if all my pride in being on Malachy's team was misguided.

"Ms. Jones has a degree in social neuroscience, as well as complete fluency in the facial action coding system. In addition," Malachy said, with a slightly wry expression, "I recall her making a very persuasive argument while I was feeling distinctly under the weather."

"You said something about my counterbalancing your lack of people skills," said Lilliana, including me in her smile.

Malachy rubbed his chin, considering. "Entirely plausible. And, of course, you're an aesthetically pleasing individual. That may have unconsciously factored into my decision." Lilliana had once volunteered that she had a Russian mother and an Ethiopian father. I had no idea what her parents looked like, but Lilli had the kind of subtle, willowy, doe-eyed beauty that charms other women as much as it does men.

Sam cleared his throat. "What about me?"

"What, indeed," said Malachy, not bothering to look in his direction. Sam's mother owned an airline, and, presumably, she had donated heavily to various causes dear to the internship committee's hearts. "Bringing us back to the subject of wolves, we had some excitement with our hybrid while you were out, Ms. Barrow."

It took me a moment to follow this abrupt change of topic. Two days earlier, a hard blond lady with biker tattoos had brought in a very lanky, nervous young dog. She said that she was visiting from out of town, and that her dog, Pia, had been attacked by a pit bull in the park.

I had examined a laceration on Pia's paw, and asked if she had recently been given a rabies vaccine. I added that Pia looked to be at least half wolf, and that there was some discussion over whether that particular vaccine was safe in wolves. Before Biker Lady replied, I added that every state has a different law concerning wolf hybrids: In New York, they're considered dangerous wildlife.

At this point, Pia's owner became very flustered. I think she would have taken her dog back home then, except that the poor animal winced when I palpated her abdomen, indicating possible internal injuries. Biker Lady agreed to leave her dog with us overnight. That was two days ago, and we had no contact number, which was worrisome. Because the Animal Medical Institute is a large teaching hospital, a lot of people assume that we charge discounted rates. We don't.

If Pia's owner had discovered this and realized she couldn't afford to pay us, she might not come back for her animal. And a suspected wolf hybrid was not the kind of dog that could be adopted out. If her owner didn't come back for her, she was going to wind up getting euthanized. And Pia was fine; X-rays had shown that her sore abdomen was just the result of some superficial bruising.

I tried to keep my voice even. "What happened to Pia?"

"According to Sam, she had, and I quote, 'a major freak-out.' He was attempting to get a bone marrow sample from the chocolate lab in the cage next to her, and Pia just started howling her head off."

"Maybe she didn't like your technique," suggested Ofer.

Sam flushed. "Listen, you poison dwarf, I didn't do anything wrong. There's something wrong with that animal, and you know it."

"Of course there's something wrong," drawled Malachy. "She's sick and she's nervous. You will, presumably, have to deal with other nervous canines in the future, unless you plan on restricting your practice to healthy animals."

Malachy gestured to the cat, which I was still holding. "In any case, Sam will take over your patient while you head up to the fourth floor. Maybe you'll have better luck getting the bone marrow sample. Lilliana, you'd better try to track down the hybrid's owner. After Pia's little serenade, we have been instructed to remove her from the Institute within the next twenty-four hours. Now, Sam, let's try again to see if you can spot anything unusual in these X-rays."

Lilliana motioned to me and we left Sam to Malachy's tender mercies.

"So," I said, trying to clear my head as we waited by the elevator banks, "what exactly happened to Pia?"

"I'm not entirely sure. But whatever it was, everyone in the building heard her little call of the wild, and the board responded by letting us know that we are not licensed to treat potentially dangerous wildlife."

The elevator doors slid open and we went inside. For a moment, I just watched as the numbers of the various floors lit up in succession, mulling over Pia's situation. "Lilliana? Do you think Pia's owner intends to come back for her?"

"Absolutely. I told Malachy that there is no way on earth that she is abandoning that animal."

"How can you be so sure, Lilli?" I wasn't challenging her; I was merely curious. Lilliana's gift for reading people was like mine for reading X-rays.

Lilliana furrowed her brow. "It's hard to explain. I

just can tell—Pia's a person to her, not a pet. I was going to ask you: if I help you hold Brownie for the bone marrow test, could you help me scan Pia for a microchip?"

"You must be a mind reader."

Lilliana gave me a startled glance. "I wish." The elevator stopped on our floor, and just before the doors slid open, Lilliana said, "The question is, if she isn't chipped, how do we keep Malachy from taking her home and experimenting on her?"

Until that moment, it hadn't occurred to me that Malachy might try to continue his research independently, but of course, knowing the man, it made perfect sense. I kept silent as we got off the elevator and another group of interns got on, not wanting to be overheard discussing our staff group leader, the mad scientist.

Once we were walking down the brightly lit hallway, I said, "I guess I could take Pia home for a few days and ask my husband to look after her while I'm at work."

"Would he do that?"

"I'm sure he would," I said. "Or, at least, I think he would. He does get a little funny when he's trying to write—doesn't like distractions." Worried that this cast Hunter in a negative light, I added, "But I think he'd be okay taking care of a dog for a few days." Lilliana was silent for a moment, the only sound the staccato beat of her heels on the hard floor. "On the other hand," I said, trying to make a joke out of the whole thing, "if Malachy infects Pia with the lycanthropy virus and she turns human, she could sue him for malpractice."

We rounded a corner and Lilliana nodded to an intern from another group who was walking in the opposite direction. Unlike me, she seemed to know everyone at the Institute. "Pia doesn't have the killer instinct. Turn that dog into a woman and she'll come down with a case of puppy love and follow him around."

"Wait," I said with mock-seriousness, "maybe we

should really examine the possibility that Mal's engineering beast people. Take a close look at Ofer. Check out the monobrow. And what about Sam? You can't tell me he has a full complement of human DNA." I hesitated, then put my hand on my friend's arm. "Hey, Lilli. I'm sorry if I sounded like I was insulting you before. When I asked why Malachy had chosen you, I mean."

We stopped in front of the door to Ward B and Lilliana met my eyes. "I wasn't insulted. What did you think about all that talk about Unwolves, though?"

"I think he's gone beautiful mind on us. Let's face it, sometimes making unexpected connections means you're a genius, and sometimes it means you need antipsychotics. And if you start thinking people can turn into wolves, I know which group you're in." I inserted the card key I wore around my neck into the appropriate slot and opened the door to Ward B. "Isn't that right, Pia?"

The wolf hybrid flattened her ears and tried to cram herself into the rear of her cage. Most people expect wolves to be massive, fierce animals with challenging, intelligent eyes and an air of coiled menace. I don't know whether Pia was typical, but she was the spookiest, shyest, most submissive-looking canine I'd ever seen in my life. It had taken all of us working together to get her into a big floor cage alongside Brownie the chocolate Lab and Duncan, the Bouvier who'd managed to get a fork stuck in his cheek while lunging for a bite of his owner's steak.

The Bouvier was no longer in the cage, but Brownie was still there, wagging his tail with indiscriminate Labrador affection. Pia remained supine with her long, narrow head between her paws, wary yellow eyes darting left and right to follow our movements.

I'd seen Yorkies with more pluck. Malachy said it was because in nature, most wolves weren't alphas, so if you chose one randomly from a litter, the odds were better than good that you'd wind up with a very submissive animal.

Not the kind of pet people who breed wolves are looking for, even though nervous animals can be just as dangerous as bold ones. Sometimes more so.

I knelt down in front of Pia's cage and gave her my fingers to sniff. Her fur rippled in unvoiced agitation. "Hey, girl," I said as her muzzle wrinkled in a snarl.

Lilliana knelt down beside me. "That looks vicious, but it means back off, right?"

"In dog-speak, she's telling me she's nervous rather than aggressive. Easy, girl, easy." While I contemplated my next move, I heard a deep, mournful bark from the other side of the wall. It sounded like Duncan, waking up in recovery. Pia scrabbled in her cage, trying to back herself into the corner, and I breathed in deeply, catching a strong smell of antiseptic and the deeper, muskier scent of flesh and fear.

I moved over to Brownie, opening his cage and caressing his big head. "You big lug," I said, feeling guilty at the trusting look in the Lab's big, dark eyes. Even if I wasn't as clumsy as Sam, I was going to have to hurt Brownie. In order to get a bone marrow sample, you have to really screw the drill in to get to the deep tissue. Taking bone marrow is painful, even with a local. But there's always a risk associated with giving general anesthesia, and Brownie wasn't a youngster.

"You know what," I said to Lilliana. "Let's move Brownie next door, so he won't make any sound that upsets Pia."

Lilliana and I slipped the rope leash over Brownie's head and walked him over to the smaller room across the hall. It took all of our strength to lift Brownie onto the table, and I waited for a moment to get my energy back before administering the local and getting the drill in place. Brownie was a big, fleshy boy, and I had to use my body weight as leverage. Once I knew I had the drill in deep enough, I inserted the syringe. "I'm sorry," I said, as the dog whined deep in his throat.

"We're almost done," said Lilliana, her tone almost hypnotically soothing. "Perfect, Abra."

I pulled the sample out and the dog snapped his head around toward me, then licked his mouth quickly as if he'd never really intended to bite.

"I know, boy, I know you didn't mean it." I gave Brownie a last pat before walking around the operating table. I started to lay out glass slides on the instrument tray.

Lilliana shook her head admiringly. "You were in and out. He didn't have time to complain."

"I wish."

Lilliana watched as I placed a drop of blood on each of the slides I'd set out. When we were done, she helped me get Brownie down on the floor. "You know," she said, "Malachy really does respect you."

"Are you joking? He just told me that he hired me because my husband is writing about werewolves. Excuse me," I corrected myself, "*Un*wolves."

Lilliana touched my hand. "I know what he said, but his face told a different story."

"Mal said you'd studied some sort of face reading system?"

Lilliana nodded. "It's called FACS—the Facial Action Coding System. It's basically an index of microexpressions that transcend cultural differences and slip out beneath conscious control. For example, when Malachy was talking about Sam, I saw a flicker of contempt. When he mentioned Ofer's background in neuroscience, his face remained neutral. But when he talked to you, he smiled—just for a fraction of a second, but it was a real smile."

"Hmm," I said as we reached the door to Ward B. "And what did his face reveal about you, I wonder."

Lilliana's eyes sparkled with amusement. "I intimidate him, actually. Hey, I forgot to tell you about the man who came in earlier with a baby owl."

"You're kidding!" I was just about to tell Lilliana about my encounter with the man and the owl on the subway when we opened the doors to Ward B and discovered that the day's excitement wasn't over.

Pia was gone.

FOUR

◐○○ Everyone else went to look for our missing patient. I went to the bathroom.

I'd started to bleed right after Hunter and I made love. Just a little spotting, but I knew I'd need to check on things in a little while. I suppose every veterinary and medical student goes through a hypochondriacal phase. Mine wasn't too bad; I was only frightened of getting rabies from a bite, contracting a little flesh-eating bacteria on a wound, or dying of toxic shock after forgetting I had a tampon in for twenty-four hours.

That may sound disgusting, but let me tell you, after being on your feet for forty-eight sleep-deprived hours, you're liable to forget a lot of things that aren't written on a chart. Which is why I tend to use sanitary pads, messy as they are.

So I opened the door to the bathroom and walked back to the farthest stall—the big, disabled one.

There, crouched beside the toilet, was Pia, the dun triangles of her ears pressed flat to her head. The scruffy owl man from the subway was kneeling beside her.

I think I gave a quick little huff of surprise and squeaked, "This is the ladies' room!"

Pia growled.

"Quiet, now." The man glanced down at the dog, then back up at me with a rueful smile. "Bit of a sissy, this one."

I said nothing, and the man stood up. "Well, now," he said, "I admit this looks a bit peculiar, but I can explain." He ran a nervous hand through his graying auburn hair, which was cut in the kind of close-crop that looks fashionable on a man in a good suit of clothes and vaguely institutional on a man in dirt-stained jeans and a cheap white T-shirt.

"So explain."

Pia growled, low in her throat.

"Hush, girl. This place makes her nervous," he said apologetically.

"Yes, I heard she started howling earlier this morning." I tentatively held out my hand for Pia to sniff, still hesitant to meet the man's eyes. A thought occurred to me. "My colleagues thought she was scared of what was happening to another dog, but I'm wondering if it had something to do with you." Oh, smart thing to say, Abra. What if the man's crazy? I'd forgotten the first rule of New York City: Don't antagonize the crazy man.

"She sure did raise a fuss when she smelled me. Expect she wanted out of here." The man ruffled the fur at the back of Pia's neck. He had a gentle, sure touch and the dog seemed to accept it without too much hunching of the shoulders. "You work here?" He pointed to my white lab coat.

"Yes." Without thinking, I crouched down to give Pia a pat and then realized I had just done something incredibly stupid. Now I had placed myself at this stranger's feet. Worse still, I was crouching in a bathroom stall, and the floor's cleanliness didn't hold up under close inspection. The man was looking at me with an odd, slightly preoccupied expression, his head cocked a little to one side, his nostrils flaring.

Hang on, did I smell? I looked down and continued stroking Pia as if this thought had never crossed my mind.

When the stranger spoke, his voice was so low and soft it took me a moment to register what he'd said.

"I make you nervous."

I straightened up, then realized that I was now standing too close to this man. "Well, a little." I forced myself not to back up, because dogs and serial killers have an instinctive, aggressive reaction to retreat.

"You make me a little nervous, too." I met his steady, amused regard and realized there was something pleasant about his looks. He had the kind of lean, high-cheekboned, weathered face I'd seen in pictures of the Depression.

"And why is that?"

"I'm kind of hoping to make my way on out of here without too much fuss, and you seem the kind of woman not to walk away from a fight."

I brought up my hands reflexively. "I'm not looking for a fight . . ."

"But like I said, you're not one to back down—even from a brick wall, I imagine." As he said this, the man moved so that now he was standing between me and the door to the bathroom stall.

I felt a prickle of alarm at the back of my neck. "Did you follow me home from the subway?"

He cocked his head to one side. "Ma'am?"

I shook my head. He'd come to the clinic: There was no way he could know about my climbing adventure. "Never mind. Listen, I need to know what you're doing here with this dog, Mr. . . ."

"Red Mallin. Friend of Jackie Roberts, owner of this animal." "Friend" meaning *boyfriend*, I assumed. He held out his hand and I took it without thinking. His skin felt unusually hot, and at the moment our palms made contact I felt an odd little jolt of awareness. I realized that we were staring at each other. I wondered if, on some animal level, it was because I'd had sex that morning. Unsatisfying sex, a little voice interpolated. There was something about the way we were standing there that seemed inappropriate. Why weren't we talking? I wasn't frightened of him any longer.

"So, ah, you're Dr. Abra Barrow?" His finger indicated my name badge.

"Yes." My throat was dry, and I cleared it.

"Yes." He seemed discomfited. "Right. Now, I was just goin' to explain—are you wearing something? Some scent?"

"No."

"Ah." He dropped his hand and inhaled deeply, as if trying to collect himself. Red seemed to be growing more nervous, not less, and that made no sense. I watched as a splotchy redhead's blush climbed across his cheeks.

"Well," he began again. I spoke at almost the same time.

"So Pia isn't your dog?"

Red and the wolf hybrid exchanged a complicit glance. "Nope. Jackie asked me to spring her out before she got herself in some kind of trouble."

I remembered Lilliana's half-joking comment about Malachy's wanting to experiment on Pia. Now that I thought about it, it had been a little strange that Malachy had wanted to keep Pia's case, as it wasn't clear that her owner could afford our services. I found myself recalling Malachy's statement that he'd hired me because of my connection with Hunter's lycanthropy research and wondered: Does Malachy have some agenda with this animal?

On the other hand, what was this man's hidden agenda? "So why didn't Jackie Roberts come herself?"

Red had the ability to stand without shifting weight from foot to foot, which was something I liked. It seemed, I don't know, forthright. "Well, she thought I might be able to make a case for Pia here not being more'n a tiny bit wolf. I'm kind of an expert. See? Here's my business card." He dug his wallet out of his back jeans pocket and extracted a cheap white card bearing a picture of a howling wolf or coyote in silhouette. I couldn't help but notice that it matched the tattoo stretched over the swell of his right bicep.

"Red Mallin," he said, as if I couldn't read it for myself. "Wildlife Removal Operator."

I looked at the card, then at him. "So why didn't you go up to the front desk and assert your expertise, Mr. Mallin?"

Red smiled, a little crookedly. "Well, I don't know. Sometimes big-city types don't exactly seem to value my opinion as much as I do."

"What'd you do with the owl?"

"She's still here. Kind of a trade."

I realized that it was mostly the graying hair that made him look older. That and the sunburn. I figured Red might still be in his late thirties. I found myself thinking that he looked like someone you might see on some reality TV shows, announcing that he was leaving his wife, the fat dyed blonde, for her sister, the emaciated dyed blonde without teeth.

"I probably don't want to know, but—where'd you get the owl?"

"Someone's attic. Listen, I swear I'm not some animal broker who goes around selling wild things to stupid people. I just want to bring this little girl back to her momma, is all. Jackie knows how to take care of her right." Red fished a crumpled piece of paper from the pocket of his jeans. "You can call her right now if you want to check me out."

"I don't have a cell phone."

Red looked at me, surprised. "Well, shoot." He appeared to have reached the end of his arguments. "I don't have one, either."

"It's all right. I believe you." The moment I said it, my

stomach did a little flip. But I did believe him. He was scruffy, but he inspired trust, somehow. Pia got to her feet and actually wagged her tail twice, as if sensing the accord between us.

"You hear that, Pia? You're goin' home." Red bent down to scratch behind the dog's ears while flashing me a conspirator's grin.

"Let me check whether the hallway's clear." I left the stall and opened the bathroom door a crack. "It's okay," I said. "You're good to go."

Red paused by the door. "Now listen, Doc, you ever have some critter getting into your basement, go on and give me a call."

I glanced down at the card in my hand. There was an e-mail address and a toll-free phone number. "I live in an apartment."

Red whistled for Pia and she came to heel by his side. The dog—if that's what she was—seemed calmer than I'd ever seen her. She even wagged her tail again as she looked back at me. "See?" Red pointed with his thumb. "She's thanking you, too."

"Go on," I said with a smile.

His hand on the handle, Red turned around. "Sorry about your purse, Doc. I was just about to say something when you turned and froze me out."

"Excuse me?"

"You know, on the train. You gave me one of those 'Don't even think about talking to me' looks and then cold-shouldered me. So I didn't warn you."

I thought about how it might have seemed from his point of view. "I'm always reading people wrong," I said. "If you'd been a dog, I would have known you were all right the moment I met you."

Red's eyes lit with amusement. "Smart about animals and stupid about people. That's what my grandfather always said about me."

"Sounds like my mother talking about me."

"Well."

"Well." We stood there, uncomfortable with the moment. And then Red lifted my hand to his mouth, kissed my knuckles, and left.

I stood there, stunned at the very physical reaction I'd had to his touch. That was a flirtation. I had committed flirtation.

And then I realized that the slight dampness between my legs might not all be arousal. I darted into a stall to check whether I needed a sanitary pad just as I heard someone come into the bathroom.

As I emerged to wash my hands, I saw that Lilliana was tucking her silky blouse into her gray wool slacks. "Hey, Abra. Any luck finding Pia?"

My mouth felt dry. "None."

"Damn. Well, I hope it was her real owner breaking her out, and not some animal control hotshot." She looked at me in the mirror. "Hey, are you okay?"

"Sure," I said, not completely sure why I was lying to my friend, but doing it all the same. "It's just that time of the month."

FIVE

◐ ○ ○ I have always been the kind of person who wonders what things mean. You would think, as a writer, that Hunter would also tend to analyze life, but the truth is, Hunter reports on things. The moral ambiguity of his stories, which allows readers to draw their own conclusions, is what reviewers love about him. Perhaps the readers of *Outside* are tired of the old "hubris in the face of nature" chestnut, which is the point of most of the magazine's articles. With Hunter, you get an art school ending—the pattern of blood on the windshield as the deer limps away, the intricate whorls of the tribal tattoo on the face of a young Maori prostitute.

So there was no point in my asking Hunter what had precipitated the sudden change in our sex life. For several weeks after Hunter's return, we made love every day, and this unexpected second honeymoon chased every other thought from my mind. I didn't spare another thought for my strange encounter with the scruffy, auburn-haired wildlife operator. I went to work on autopilot, not even noticing that Malachy had become paler and weaker until Lilliana pointed it out. There was no more talk of Unwolves and no mention of Hunter's research. Like me, Malachy seemed to be sleepwalking through his days, and Ofer was openly lobbying for a transfer.

But while Malachy was in the grip of some nameless illness, I was drifting in a fugue state of reciprocal lust. Literally and figuratively, I was Hunter's slave girl, in thrall to his attention and his touch. As for my husband, he was autocratic and imaginative and more passionate than I recalled him ever being before, even in the beginning.

I met Hunter eight years ago, during my junior year of college. He was a senior. We were both in the Science Library, cramming for midterms. It was a late afternoon in early November and the sky outside was the kind of pale dark that always makes me feel cold and a little despondent.

I was feeling low for a variety of reasons. I was sleep-deprived, I had gained five pounds, and my roommate had deserted me to go have wonderful sex with a guy in another dorm. I knew it was wonderful sex because sometimes they had it in our room. My mother had sent me a card telling me she was going to volunteer at the local animal shelter for Thanksgiving and I was free to make plans with my father. My father was in Key West with his girlfriend, Moon, running the kind of hotel local people live in, paying by the week. Moon was only five years older than me, but most people assumed she was over thirty because of the dark circles under her eyes. She claimed to be psychic and knew I was a virgin without my telling her.

Which didn't prove a thing: Most people seemed to figure that out on their own.

At first I couldn't understand what the good-looking guy in the fisherman's sweater was doing. He kept looking at me with a frown on his Heathcliffian face, and then checking his watch. I had lost one of my contact lenses and was wearing the blue eyeglass frames my mother thought brought out the color of my eyes. It didn't: My eyes are gray. I figured Heathcliff wanted my seat on the little couch by the window. Or possibly he was waiting for a computer terminal and just happened to be looking at me while he scowled.

When he came over and dropped a note in my book, I looked up into that brooding face and thought, He must need help with chemistry. I unfolded the little strip of paper. It read: Aaggh Midterms Aggh Agggh. Want to go for a cup of coffee at the Student Center?

It was only my certainty that I was a momentary distraction, my utter conviction that no man that handsome would ever be seriously interested in me, that made me appear indifferent. After "Midterms Aggh" I wrote an exclamation point. Then I added, Not yet, must finish chapter. Heathcliff stood next to me, reading my edits as I wrote them.

—In an hour? He wrote.

—Sure. I *was* sure: Sure he'd be gone by then. But he waited the hour, glancing up at me from time to time, and I had lost all semblance of concentration by the time the big clock on the wall struck six.

"Ready?" There he stood, regarding me with a look that was equal parts admiration and bemusement. I felt that he was surprising himself by asking me out. I was so tense that it required a conscious effort not to twitch, blink repeatedly, or keep nodding. As we walked to the Student Center, I listened intently while Hunter told me about his major, his irritating housemates, his plans after graduation, and his dietary peculiarities.

It turned out that Hunter despised cheese. He called it "the corpse of milk," quoting James Joyce. I joked that we would be a terrible couple to invite for dinner, as I was a vegetarian and basically lived on cheese. This sounded as though I assumed he would want to see me again: I burned with humiliation.

"Why are you a vegetarian?" Hunter and I had compromised on a meal of coffee and french fries. All around us, it seemed, thinner, prettier girls in tight black turtlenecks and perfectly tattered Levi's were drinking cappuccinos and reading annotated copies of Mary Shelley's *Frankenstein*. Only one of them wore glasses, the fake little black kind models wear when they want to look intellectual.

"I don't like the idea of supporting the meat industry." I was wearing a navy sweat suit, and my hair was unwashed and rolled into a messy bun on the top of my head.

"All those poor little battery-raised chickens without beaks? All those innocent little overfed veal calves with ulcers on their eyes and hooves too soft to stand on?" Hunter ate another french fry.

"I see you've dated vegetarians before." Before! As if this were a real date!

But Hunter only laughed. He had brown wavy hair that curled at the ends and wonderful dark eyes that sort of drank you in. He sat like an athlete, muscular thighs spread wide; later, I found out that he played soccer for the school team. When he took off his sweater I could see the shadow of his pectoral muscles through his thin white T-shirt. "Hey," he said, "can I ask a personal question?"

"Sure," I replied, trying to hide my nervousness.

"How long is your hair when it's down?"

This is where I was supposed to pull out the pins and dazzle him. "To the small of my back. But it's not too clean right now."

Hunter leaned back and took a swallow of coffee. "I need a cigarette," he said. "Do you want to go for a walk?"

He wants to sleep with me, I thought, but by dawn he'll be back in whatever hellish frat house he lives in and I'll never hear from him again.

"I have to get back to the fishbowl." Which was what we all called the Science Library.

"Bloody midterms." I later learned that his family had

moved to England when he was sixteen. Hunter had managed to retain a sort of Ralph Lauren patina of upper-middle Britishness, which was to grow even more pronounced after we moved to Manhattan.

Outside, on the badly lit path back to the library, Hunter stopped and gripped me by the elbows. I was dizzy with the smell of him, masculine and Marlboro-tinged, with a hint of verbena soap. "Abra. Are you at all interested in seeing me again, or am I just bugging the hell out of you?"

I wanted to sink my teeth into his lower lip and kiss him till there was blood. I wanted to sink down to my knees and bite him right through his jeans. Shaken by the violence of this lust, I took a moment to answer. "Interested," I said.

"Good." A grin flashed over his heavily shadowed face like a light going on. Then he lit a cigarette and became moody and unknowable again. What do you see in me, I wanted to ask. Is it the hair? Do you have a thing for virgins? Months later, I finally worked up the courage to ask him what first attracted him to me.

"Your confidence," he said. "The way you just sat there in your comfortable clothes, completely consumed by your work. The way you didn't seem to need to check your watch like all the other poor slobs putting in their study time. With your hair up, and those goofy big eighties glasses, you seemed . . . I don't know. Like a little nun, perfectly at peace with herself."

When he finally made love to me, two weeks after our first encounter, I was so unused to being touched that I kept laughing. I was so sexually inexperienced that all my erogenous zones were ticklish. I wanted to beg Hunter to be rougher with me, but he was desperately considerate. I'd ridden too many horses as a girl to bleed when he entered me, but there was a little pain as he stretched me.

I wanted to follow that pain wherever it would take me, but Hunter held himself back until the end, and by then there wasn't enough time to catch up.

"You okay, 'Cadabra girl?"

"Mm," I said, secure in his arms. After he fell asleep I touched myself between my slippery legs and conjured images stolen from my mother's old movies: the pretty young witch, writhing in sensual panic with her wrists tied to a stake, as Satan moves in, glistening with red makeup.

The magazines all tell you to be open and frank about what you want in bed, but this presumes a deeper confidence. I never felt completely certain of what Hunter loved in me. All I had to go by was his image of a young woman as self-possessed as a little nun.

My mother used to say that she hoped the sex was good, as he was likely to treat me like crap in the near future. Which was why I couldn't bring myself to ask her about the slave girl business now, even though I was dying to know: Did this mean Hunter was suddenly seeing me differently?

Or did it mean he wasn't seeing me at all?

SIX

◐○○ Eventually, I had to admit that there was something wrong. But it took me a while. Touch-drunk from all the unaccustomed contact, I found myself able to fall asleep and stay that way for the first time since early adolescence. Forget sleeping pills; I'd discovered the real cure for insomnia—sex-induced coma.

Hunter started joking that it was usually the man who got tired out after making love. But I wasn't so much physically exhausted as emotionally satiated. For once in my life, my brain didn't kick into fretting mode the moment I lay down and closed my eyes. It was almost as though Hunter was taking me over by taking control—or maybe I was just learning to surrender.

But gradually, I became aware that there was no one sleeping beside me. Hunter's side of the bed was always empty when I went to sleep and unrumpled when I woke up. I saw signs of late-night feasting in the kitchen—dirty plates piled high in the sink, cardboard take-out containers in the garbage that hadn't been there the night before. For years, Hunter and I had agreed that he wouldn't bring meat into the apartment, but now he was binging after midnight on spare ribs and meatball grinders. To my sensitive nose, there was a faint, persistent smell of dead flesh in our apartment, and even leaving the windows wide open didn't eradicate it. When I

complained, Hunter laughed and said he'd have to remember to leave the garbage outside our front door.

He didn't apologize for breaking our agreement, and I
didn't call him on it. I also didn't ask him why he was
suddenly less fastidious about his person, and mine. He
no longer avoided making love to me when I had my
period—in fact, he reveled in the slippery, transgressive
feel of it. While I had to admit that I liked this aspect of
his newfound earthiness, I was less thrilled with his new
habit of showering only every two or three days. His
shaving became erratic as well, and my husband's dark
stubble left red, raw marks on my face and inner thighs.

At night, I began to have vivid dreams that I could
never quite remember. I knew when I first woke up that
I had been in the midst of some complex drama, but all
the details bled away as I came fully awake. I had vague
impressions, though. A night sky in the country, brilliant with stars, the moon a huge, glowing orb until a
dark cloud passed over it. My husband, pressing me
down on the bed as I whimpered in fear. Malachy in his
white lab coat, holding up a half-dead cat and instruct-
ing Sam, Lilliana, and Ofer that they were going to have
to learn how to kill things. "Start small," Malachy said,
"with something wounded, like this fellow. Then keep
challenging yourself. Go for something bigger. Work together to bring it down." I raised my hand, asking:
What about me?

"You're the bigger prey, of course," Malachy explained, and everyone looked at me with renewed interest: Ah, yes, now we see it.

My inner life, I was discovering, was basically a B
movie. Wouldn't my mother be proud.

Then, after a week of this, I had a dream that felt different from the others. I was back in the subway train.
Pressed up against strangers, I could feel someone rubbing slowly against me. In real life, I would have been

horrified and repulsed, but in this dream, the subtle touch against my back and bottom felt like waves lapping up against me, sensual and impersonal, anonymous and erotic. A male hand gripped my waist, and I thought, This is like that story by Anaïs Nin, about the woman and the stranger on the train, and I gave myself up to the illicit pleasure of it. As the stranger moved in sinuous motions against my backside, I felt my thoughts drifting to this faceless man, and then, without warning, I *was* that man, struggling to hold myself in check and to restrict myself to just this small necessary contact. I could feel my breathing quicken; I was losing control. And then I was back in my own body. I looked up and saw a barn owl perched on the handrail, swiveling its head a disconcerting 180 degrees to give me a long, slow wink. I realized that the man touching me wasn't a stranger—well, not a complete stranger, at any rate.

"Stop," I said, trying to break free from his embrace. It felt as though recognizing him had broken some kind of spell.

"Hang on, sweetheart, I'm almost done," came Red's response. He sounded like he'd been running hard.

"I don't think so," I said, pushing him away. Behind me, I heard a woman gasp.

"He's written all over you," said a woman, lifting my shirt up and peering at my bare back. In the dream's logic, it didn't seem peculiar that his touch had penetrated the fabric of my clothing. It didn't seem strange that I could suddenly see myself from above, my back covered with scarlet designs, like an aboriginal story or a shamanistic spell.

I came instantly awake, alone in the bed. The bedside clock read three A.M., and it was still completely dark outside. Swinging my feet from the bed, I padded down the hall.

"Hunter? Are you up?" As I checked the apartment

for my husband, I wondered why I was having erotic dreams about a scruffy redneck when the only man I'd ever wanted was finally turning to me the way I'd always hoped he would.

But Hunter wasn't home, and though I went back to bed and forced myself to remain there, I didn't sleep any more that night. It was only in the morning, when I stepped into the shower, that I noticed the fading red marks on my back. I knew they were simply the imprint of the wrinkled sheets on my skin, but for a moment, in the mirror, they resembled arcane symbols.

Hunter came home just as I was leaving for work, looking sweaty and disheveled. He had gotten up early, he said, to go running.

To paraphrase Upton Sinclair, it's difficult to get someone to understand something when her marriage depends on her not understanding it. But even I was coming to recognize that a few short weeks after it had begun, my second honeymoon was coming to an end.

Still, I allowed myself to pretend for a little while longer that I didn't know *why* it was ending.

SEVEN

◖◯◯ On Sunday, October 7, I ran out of denial time. Because I wasn't working, there was nothing to distract me from the fact of my thirtieth birthday. Like all birthdays that end in zero, this one demanded a certain amount of attention. I was entering the decade in which life decisions carry the most weight. My mother always used to say, In your twenties, you can have a first career and a first marriage that turn out to be nothing but a footnote later on. In your thirties, however, you are making your adult life. You could remake it in your forties, of course, but still, turning thirty was a very big deal.

Not that I expected Hunter to make a big fuss about the day.

He had established early on in our relationship that he felt birthday and Christmas presents were for children— grown-ups surprised each other by commemorating more inventive, personal dates. Which, to give him credit, he sometimes did—a bouquet of red roses one year to celebrate our first year of shared rent, a pair of silk panties the morning after he'd first seen me drunk.

But birthdays, even pivotal, painful ones, Hunter tended to forget. If you don't need to buy a gift, you don't mark it on your calendar—as simple as that. I suppose, if I'd asked him out to the movies, he would have taken me. But it just seemed a bit pathetic, somehow, like calling in a special favor. Far better to just let things slide by.

I thought I had come to terms with the absence of any special anniversarial treatment—or, as Hunter would call it, any false emotion. So maybe it was just my imagination that he seemed particularly dour that morning. He was preoccupied as he stood by the fussily percolating coffeepot and short-tempered when I asked him if he wanted toast, so I didn't bother to suggest an afternoon movie. Clearly, he was intending to spend this day as he had all the others since his return: searching the Internet for obscure books and articles on wolves, or interviewing Canadians as he worked on his seemingly endless article.

I'm not sure what the deal was with Canada—I guess they just have more wolf people there to interview.

My mother called to wish me happy birthday and asked me to take the train to see her so she could give me her gift in person. She knew about Hunter and his birthday theories, because in a weak moment I had complained about it. And if there is one thing my mother, the former B-movie star, cannot understand, it's putting up with something you don't like.

"Act like you have top billing or you'll never get it," she always said. "If I'd slunk around like you do, I'd still be 'blond vampire girl number three.'"

But I have watched people's faces as my mother launches into one of her tirades, and I think there may be worse things than slinking around dissatisfied. In any case, I said I would try to visit her next weekend. My father called next and told me he'd sent a check, because he wasn't sure what I needed. He spent a while telling me about his girlfriend's crazy ex-husband, and then told me to come visit soon. He didn't mention Hunter.

I knew my work friends wouldn't call me, as they

would see me tomorrow. I had lost touch with my college and high school friends; funny how you never see that in movies—the heroine always has at least two close childhood friends, each a little fatter or crazier than herself. Sometimes there's a third, a gay man who is smarter, more stylish, and underneath more tragic than the rest. I wished for such sidekicks. I wondered if you could put in a personal ad: Straight woman seeks gay man, straight women, for walks in the park, foreign films, impromptu makeovers, well-chosen gifts. No secret competitors, annual migrators, or disappearing acts need apply.

Or maybe what I needed was a dog. Dogs don't wake up one morning and realize that the relationship isn't working for them anymore. Dogs don't lie about what they've been doing, or leave you to go explore other options. Like their wolfish cousins, dogs love for life.

Feeling maudlin, I decided to go for a long walk by the boat basin in Riverside Park, to get my endorphins flowing and work the wobble out of my thighs.

"I'm going out," I told Hunter.

"Aah," he replied, looking briefly in my general direction. Once out the door, I found it hard to move my legs very quickly. I contemplated taking a bus to the park, but then convinced myself that the urge to move would take hold once I got my feet near some grass.

A few runners passed me on Riverside Drive, looking lean and serious in skintight Lycra while I churned along in my gray sweat suit. A businessman with a plastic bag on his left hand waited for his mastiff to defecate. It's moments like these that make me love the city so much: Nowhere else is the natural made to seem so unnatural.

On Seventy-ninth I met a woman I'd gone to high school with in the suburbs. She told me she was writing plays and designing software. She had perfect toes in strappy sandals, and her stomach bulged with chic, designer-sweatered pregnancy.

"Are you married?" she asked me, not waiting for a reply. "I just married a lovely man from a small village in Italy. I can't tell you how happy we are. We got married in the little white church where Paolo was christened and the whole town turned out, all the young girls wearing ribbons. I remember you used to say you weren't going to get married. I always imagined you'd wind up in a big, funky apartment with a lot of cats."

"No," I said slowly, "that's my mother. I prefer dogs."

Mrs. Small Village in Italy threw her head back and laughed. "Oh, that's what I remember about you, Abra. Your killer sense of humor. Let's get together for dinner sometime soon. Here's my number."

I stuffed her card into a pocket and continued walking, passing young lovers in faded jeans, laughing and talking animatedly, their faces turned to each other.

On the way back, I shopped for dinner at the health food store, where I saw a woman in her fifties with stark black hair and oversized tinted glasses. She looked familiar, but I couldn't place her until she ran up and hugged me, explaining that she was my father's old girlfriend Rita, and she hadn't seen me since I'd been in college, and how was the old man.

"He's doing all right."

"Is he with someone? He's always got to be with someone, your father."

"He's with someone."

She shook her head. "I just have no respect for people who have to be in a relationship at any cost."

Rita embraced me again, enveloping me in strong perfume. She gave me her card in case I needed a job or some public relations, and then she finally left me free to examine the onions.

The problem with Manhattan is, everyone comes here

eventually—all your old friends, enemies, lovers, demons.
People you met on vacation in Nepal will wind up beating you out for a taxi. The bully who called you "Dog
Breath" all through first grade will turn up at your local
diner, and will remember you didn't come to his sixth
birthday party, which is where the whole trouble began.
Don't come to the big city to become anonymous. New
York is like Oz: The Wicked Witch of the West turns out
to be the lady who didn't like your dog back in Kansas.

Back in the safety of my own apartment, with no one
to remind me of my failings as a human and as a wife, I
prepared dinner while Hunter remained focused on
whatever he was writing. Because of the roiling uneasi-
ness building inside of me, I chopped and mixed and
measured with more care than usual, the way I did back
in high school when I was first teaching myself to cook.
Our kitchen was really a windowless nook, and from
time to time I found myself gazing out into the living
room. I tried not to look at the taut, defended posture of
Hunter's back as he brooded over his words.

When there was nothing more to do with the vegetarian chili, I made my way through four sections of *The
New York Times* waiting to see if Hunter would finish
up what he was doing, but at three o'clock he was still
hard at work, so I decided to take myself off to the
bookstore. I returned from Barnes & Noble at seven
(having glanced through a few titles in the Help, My
Marriage Is Dying section at the exact moment our
next-door neighbors strolled by, arm in arm, with books
on gardening and Tuscany).

"Want some wine, Hunter?" I said to the back of his
head.

"Mm."

"Red or white?"

"Whatever."

"Or should I just put out some blotter acid?"

"Hah, very funny."

"So you are listening."

Hunter looked up from his computer, and I was reminded of a dog guarding its bone. "I'm almost done," he said. "Two more sentences and then I can take a break."

You would think, from his tone, that he was closing up after an arduous surgery and I was asking him to leave his patient bleeding on the table. Swallowing my annoyance, I opened up a bottle of Merlot.

I glanced up when Hunter pushed his chair back from the computer and shambled over to the dinner table, his mind clearly a thousand miles away.

"Okay, then, I'm here," he said, reading over a page of notes before laying it on the couch. "What's for dinner?"

I served him his chili, so intent on concealing any hint of my own hurt and irritation that the first hint I had of Hunter's hurt and irritation was when he shoved his bowl away with such force that it skidded off the table and bounced against the living room wall.

For a moment, I just stared at the shattered pieces of pottery. Then I looked at my husband over the flame of a thick gold candle. "Mind telling me why you just did that?"

Hunter gave a long, deflated sigh and then buried his face in his hands. He spoke without looking at me. "I don't ask you to cook, Abra, but if you say you're going to make me chili, then for God's sake serve me something I can eat."

"You are aware that I'm a vegetarian?"

Hunter's head came up, and he stared at me from bloodshot eyes. "Are you aware that I am fucking not? You keep saying how thin and tired I look. How sick I am." He snarled out the word "sick" like a curse, then gestured sarcastically to my bowl. "Here, babe, build up your strength with a nice, juicy, red *tomato*. Genetically modified and pesticide-filled, I might add."

I remained calm as Hunter got up, fumbled in his jacket pocket, and extracted a cigarette. I'd thought he'd quit over a year ago. On the exposed brick wall, the sauce was dripping slowly onto a woodcut of a hare.

"Hunter, I don't suppose you feel like telling me what's really bothering you?"

He dragged his hand through his hair. "It's just all this sitting in the apartment day after day, trying to write about nature. I'm a fucking prisoner of the Upper West Side."

"Then why don't you go out more?"

He paused as if weighing his reply against my stupidity. "Abra, I'm writing about wilderness. And yes, I know I can take a walk in Central Park, but somehow after spending the summer in the Carpathian Mountains, crossing a grid of Gap stores and concrete to get to a sliver of toddler-infested grass is not as exciting as it once was."

I looked at him with what he called my nun's face. "So you're tired of living in Manhattan, and you decide to let me know by throwing your dinner at the wall?"

"I didn't *throw* it." Hunter shook a cigarette out of the pack, lit it, and inhaled.

"I'd rather you didn't do that in here."

"It tastes like shit anyway." He ground his Marlboro out on the butter plate.

"Don't ruin the butter," I said, "just because you don't like dairy products."

"Christ, I've got to get out of this place. I'm dying in here, Abra, can't you see that?"

The stick of pale yellow butter was coated with dark ash, a crooked spear sticking out of its side. Why did I even care about that now? My hands were shaking, so I let them hold each other. "Get out of here? Do you mean out of the marriage?"

Hunter examined the palms of his hands as if he could

read his own lifeline. "Maybe. I don't know. I need something to change."

I felt my face crumple, then got it back under control. "Okay, so something in your life needs to change, and you don't know exactly what it is yet. Okay. If something's bothering you, we need to talk about it. Is it the writing? Or did something happen on the—" He was getting his jacket out of the closet before the word "trip" had left my mouth.

"I'm sorry, Abs," he said as he left, "but I just can't do this now."

I leaned against the open door for support. "Are you leaving me?"

"Don't read more into this than there is."

Suddenly I wished I had bought one of those self-help books with multiple choices and single answers. Something with a title like *The Caveman at Your Table* or *How Gone Is He?* I closed the door quietly and leaned my head against it, listening to the sound of Hunter's footsteps as he bounded down the stairs and out of the building.

At midnight my husband returned, reeking of cigarette smoke.

"Where have you been?"

"Out."

I was sitting up in bed, wearing my white cotton pajamas and tortoiseshell glasses. The remains of dinner had been cleaned away long ago: I wasn't the sort of woman to leave the tomato on the wall as a kind of unspoken recrimination.

Especially since Hunter would just leave it there.

"Out where?"

"Movie."

In the background, I was half aware of the television's still reporting the day's disasters.

Hunter threw his clothes off without looking at me

and climbed into bed. I was relieved he didn't feel the need to shower: That's one of the first signs of infidelity, according to *The Six Signs of Infidelity* by Louise Rosegarten. I had discovered this earlier, during my visit to the bookstore. You also had to watch out for a new style of underwear, particularly a switch to bikini briefs. Of course, Hunter already wore bikini briefs. When he wore underwear.

"Which movie did you see?"

Hunter tossed a thick lock of brown hair out of his eyes, like a fractious horse. "*Womb Raider*. Rated triple X. Want to check the times?"

I didn't flinch. "Yes."

Heaving himself dramatically out of bed, Hunter went to the back door and fished the paper out of the recycling pail. He returned to the bedroom, loudly flipping through it till he found the page, then slammed it down on the bed in front of me. We glared at each other until we both started to laugh.

"You didn't really go to this, did you?"

He was still laughing. "Why? Did you want to see it with me?"

The tension lifted, he pulled on his tattered robe before excusing himself and heading into the bathroom. As I waited for my husband to come back to bed, I opened up this week's *New Yorker* magazine and tried to come up with a caption for a wordless cartoon. There was a couple in a marriage therapist's office, being shown a tank of water. Befuddled, I looked up, startled by the chime that meant the computer was being turned on in the living room.

"Hunter?"

No response. For a long moment I just sat in bed, trying to figure out if the monster in the closet was real or a trick of shadows and imagination. Was Hunter really changing toward me, or was he just caught up in some internal drama that had everything to do with his work and nothing to do with me?

I walked into the living room and watched him. After a while, he turned around.

"Can't you sleep?"

"It's my birthday," I said. I couldn't help it: I was asking for special favors.

"Is it? Is it? Christ, what's the date?"

"October seventh."

"So it is. God, I'm all messed up with dates since I got back. So what are you now, twenty-nine?"

"Thirty."

"Well, why don't we have an unbirthday dinner tomorrow. I'll bring you orchids and take you someplace absolutely fantastic, where virgins massage the beef before they serve it. We'll stay up atrociously late, go to some smoky blues bar, and tip the piano man to sing 'Happy Birthday' with extra vibrato."

"Tomorrow is Monday. I have to work."

Hunter raked his hair back with his hand. "Do you? Of course you do. Aw, baby, I'm sorry. We'll find another night. Friday night? We'll do Friday. It'll be even better. Listen, I'm almost done for tonight. Just give me two more minutes and I'll be in. Give you a birthday cuddle."

I watched him turn, begin to work, cast an anxious, almost irritated glance over his shoulder when he saw I had not yet moved.

"Hunter?"

"What is it, Abs?" He was trying to keep the impatience from his voice, with some success.

"You were with someone else, weren't you?" As he opened his mouth to respond, I clarified, "Not tonight. In Romania."

He looked almost relieved, I thought. "In Romania," he said, and I waited for him to continue. But he just left it there, and I thought about all the ways I could interpret those two words. They could mean, Yes, I was unfaithful in Romania, but now I am here and I am with you. Or, There is so much you don't understand about Romania that I don't know where to begin. On the other hand, they could also mean that, in some very real way, my husband was still in Romania, his whole imagination caught up in the adventure of it.

But, no, I was trying to analyze this away. I knew what he meant. "Who was it?" My mind raced through the possibilities. Magdalena Ionescu, the chief wolf researcher, had to be in her forties, too old for Hunter. "Was it a girl in a bar? A call girl? Who was it?" I found myself hoping that he'd been with a call girl, something that moments ago would have felt unspeakably disgusting.

"Listen, Abra—I don't think there's any point in rehashing all the details. It's only going to upset you, and frankly, I don't have the stomach for it. Besides, it's very American, this idea of absolute, uncompromising fidelity, with any deviation punished by an exhaustive cross-examination." Hunter rummaged on the table for a cigarette. "In any case, sex is really the smallest part of what we have, isn't it?" He lit the cigarette and then said, "For Christ's sake, woman, don't just stand there all doe-eyed. Either slap me or get over it. I don't have patience for this victim act."

And then I understood. Not a call girl. Not a random girl in a bar. "Are you in love with her?"

Hunter took a drag on his cigarette. "I don't know, Abra. Probably not in the way that you mean."

At that moment, I think I could have walked straight off the balcony without blinking. Instead, I made myself walk into the bedroom, lay myself down on the bed, and removed my glasses. Turned the light off and tried to sleep, but only wound up staring into blurry space, tears trickling down my face and into my left ear.

I wanted to scream: Tell me who she was! Tell me how

many times! But in a sense, the deeper betrayal was what he'd said afterward. It wasn't his extramarital affair that he felt was meaningless, it was sex with me that felt unimportant. All our passionate games had been nothing more than a distraction for Hunter. And he hadn't said he didn't love her.

I hadn't had the guts to ask if he still loved me. It was like being told I had a potentially fatal illness, and not being able to ask whether or not there was hope.

From the other room, I could hear the steady click of the keyboard as Hunter typed. Closing my eyes made me feel like crying; I kept hearing my mother's voice, telling me all the things that would go wrong with my marriage after the newness wore off.

I put my glasses back on and found the remote control. On Channel 54 I found what I didn't know I was looking for: my mother, her perfectly voluptuous size-eight figure encased in a skintight space suit, trying to kiss a poor man's Steve McQueen.

"I'm not what you think I am," she warned him as she wrapped her arms around his neck.

"Baby, the way I feel right now, I don't care if you're really a five-headed barbatrid from the swamplands of Venus."

"Well, in that case . . . kiss me."

I settled back under the covers as my mother consumed her prey.

EIGHT

◑○○ The decision to take a sick day and go visit my mother was something I began to regret before I had even arrived. All the way to Pleasantvale, I kept rethinking the moment of sleep-deprived weakness when I had made the call to work. Surely it would have been better to go in and lose myself in rounds before receiving the obligatory birthday card and cake at lunchtime. But once I had made the call, I couldn't unsick myself, and the idea of staying home all day to be ignored by Hunter felt too much like self-inflicted torture.

So I took a cab to 125th Street and waited for a train on the high, rickety platform, along with a loud young mother with two small children, a middle-aged man carrying a biology textbook, and a suburban matron in her early sixties—folks who couldn't be bothered to go all the way downtown to Grand Central.

"My daughter said this station was safe," confided the white suburban matron in her Burberry raincoat, "but I don't know." She patted her lemony hair with one hand. "It seems very run-down, don't you think?" To our left, the mother screamed at her children: "You go near that edge and I'll kill you!"

"Bill Clinton thinks it's safe," I said. "He has an office around here."

"He can afford to."

I laughed. "I'm going to see my mother in Pleasant-vale. That's scarier than anything you're likely to meet around here."

The woman smiled, revealing coral lipstick on one tooth. "I'm sure she'll be very happy to see you. I'm on my way to see my younger daughter's children." She pulled a stack of photos out of her wallet. "Look, that's the three-year-old in the Easter dress I bought her last year; she's got lovely dimples just like my daughter had. And that's the five-year-old; she takes after the father's side—they all have that hard-to-manage Italian hair."

The train arrived, saving me. I moved far back, away from the chatty lady in the expensive raincoat. There was no way to explain to her that my mother would not be happy to see me. My mother was not like other mothers: Cats and dogs were her dimpled favorite grandchildren, and I was the unfortunate inheritor of my father's bad genes.

Of course, if I'd said my mother's name, the lady would probably have gone into verbal overdrive. As Piper LeFever, my mother made six films between 1974 and 1979, the year I was born. She'd appeared in *Beware the Cat!* (as the youngest of three sexy witches terrorizing a small village in medieval England) and *The Harpy* (as a morsel for a big vulture), and had made quite an impression on one reviewer in *Lucrezia Cyborgia* (as a dangerously beautiful alien in a skintight space suit). Her first starring role had been in *Blood of Egypt* (as a mousy librarian who is really a powerful priestess of the ancient Sect of Anubis), which was followed by *Satan's Bride* and *El Castillo de los Monstros*, her last movie. *El Castillo de los Monstros* was my father's big break. Only twenty-five at the time, he replaced Domingo Santos as director after my mother drove the man to a nervous breakdown. My father, who is Spanish, knew how to handle temperamental women. He made my mother pregnant and finished the picture right on schedule.

I'm not exactly sure why my parents left the West Coast, or even whose idea it was to buy a splendid Spanish-style house in Pleasantvale, thirty minutes from Manhattan. I guess it must have been one of those rare decisions they came to jointly, without arguing. In any case, it was a strange sort of place to grow up in, a great fanciful villa modeled on El Greco's house in southern Spain, smack-dab in the middle of a resolutely working-class neighborhood. The house, which was built in the 1920s, had come first, and the neighborhood had grown up around it like the forest of thorns around Sleeping Beauty's castle.

At first there was enough room for two warring spouses, a suit of armor in the formal dining hall, two wolfhounds, and a wandering tribe of cats, not to mention a Roman fountain in the central courtyard. But then Dad's career as a director died completely with the ill-fated mid-eighties television series *I Married a Werewolf* and the arrangement soon became unbearable. The fact that the show was about a henpecked husband married to a temperamental lycanthrope may also have had something to do with it. Reviewers called it a misogynistic *Bewitched*.

Already the proud owner of six cats, two dogs, and a ferret, my mother decided to turn our house into Beast Castle, a nonprofit organization for housing unwanted animals. Like Brigitte Bardot, Piper LeFever likes to say that she gave her youth to men and her mature, wise, nurturing, unselfish prime to animals.

My father likes to say that he gave his youth to Piper LeFever, which was like living with an animal.

At the Pleasantvale station, I got up, smiled wanly at the chatty lady, and began walking the familiar suburban route backward through time. It takes only ten minutes to walk to my mother's house—five to cover the town's tiny commercial center, five to make your way past the run-down houses that border my mother's property. I walked past the pizza place, the dry cleaners, the deli; I passed two small, fenced-in yards and the stationery shop where lotto tickets were sold. Every step felt like it took a year off my life—twenty-nine, twenty-eight, past the sensible age of twenty-five when insurance companies will let you rent their cars, past twenty-one and the right to have white wine at a restaurant, back before the legal age to vote, to have sex, to smoke a cigarette.

Nothing but a thin line of sidewalk now, the grass growing too long around the pavement. There were the same old lovely maple and pine trees and a bit of broken glass and empty beer cans to mark my way.

I was somewhere around fifteen or sixteen, anxious and rebellious, when I arrived at the curved black iron gates of Beast Castle: An Animal Refuge.

NINE

◑ ○ ○ I rang the doorbell and a young woman opened the door, holding a shivering Chihuahua. She had long, blond, stringy hair and was thin and serious in an Indian batik skirt.

"Yes?"

"I'm here to see Piper LeFever."

"She's busy. If you have an animal you can't take care of, you can leave it with me." Her voice dripped scorn. She must be a real hit with the customers, I thought. Would anyone adopt an animal from this person?

"She's my mother." I tried another approach. "Here, do you want me to look at that dog? I'm a vet." The shivering Chihuahua had clear fluid dripping from its nose.

The young woman stepped to one side. "Oh, you're Abra," she said, with an emphasis on the second word. I had a sense she'd been expecting someone more impressive. She cuddled the little dog closer to her small breasts. "I'm Grania and this little fellow is Pimpernell and he has a cold. Yes, you do, little sniffle-up-a-kiss."

I walked in and inhaled the familiar tang of cat urine. All the chairs had been thoroughly shredded. There was a bulging bandage of rope covering one leg of the antique French mirrored table, but clearly, no cat had taken to this improvised scratching post. I took off my cotton sweater and stared up at the skylight, which was spotted with bird feces. "God, what a mess."

Grania bristled. "Our funds barely cover the cost of feeding and maintaining our animals," she began, but I held up my hands.

"I'm not criticizing you. This place is vast, and my mother has always been a slob," I said. "When I was a kid, it took a team of cleaning women to keep her from trashing the house. Here, can I have a look at the little guy?" I held out my hands for Pimpernell the Chihuahua.

"It's just a cold," said Grania.

"In this case, I think you're right. But sometimes, with these big foreheads, the nose becomes a pop-off valve for their brains."

The blond girl stared at me. "What do you mean?"

"Fluid drains from the brain. Does he act neurologic— you know, inappropriate?"

Grania looked down at the shivery little animal with a frown between her eyebrows, apparently considering what the appropriate behavior for a three-pound dog might be. "I'm not sure. He runs in circles sometimes, when he's excited."

"That sounds normal." I took the little creature in my arms and it fixed its pop-eyed imploring gaze on me, shivered, and licked my nose. "Hey, you *are* kind of cute."

"Is he all right?" Grania seemed a little jealous as Pimpernell gave me another wet kiss.

"I should probably run a test on the fluid, but yes, I think he's all right." I smiled, realizing that a good four minutes had gone by without my thinking about the fact that my husband had been having sex with another woman. Except that now I had just thought about it again.

"Wow, Pimpernell likes you."

I turned. It was my mother, coming down the long staircase with one hand on the heavy wood banister, her purple velvet caftan flowing behind her and her long blond hair three shades brighter than the girl's. On the carved bottom of the banister was a great, rheumy-eyed Persian, one of several cats I could see sprawled around the foyer now that I was paying attention.

"Hi, Mom." She kissed me three times, once near the left cheek, twice near the right, like some sort of Russian noblewoman.

"You look bottom-heavy in that. Why do you keep wearing khaki pants? You need something dark below."

"These are comfortable."

My mother pulled back, looking me over more carefully. "You've started plucking your eyebrows. I like that, but you need to get someone to show you how to do the arch better. Your left side is thinner than your right."

"You look good," I said pointedly, to remind her what good manners were. Actually, she had gained at least ten pounds and her hair was too bright.

"I'm fat. But as the French say, there comes an age where one must choose between one's face and one's derriere."

"She thought that Pimpernell might be leaking some kind of brain fluid," said Grania.

"Oh, please, you were always a hypochondriac, and now you have a license to practice it." My mother took the Chihuahua in her sturdy arms and cradled it. "Have you met Grania? Abra, this is Grania."

"We've met."

"Grania has her BA, but she's taking science courses and applying to vet school. So smart, this girl. Barely even has to study—not like you, holed up with your books for weeks on end. She's a natural student."

Grania snorted and gave me a complicit sort of smile,

as if she already knew how my mother's mind worked, and why.

"When you're not around," Grania said, "she tells me about how fantastic you are with the animals, and how you either have practical intelligence or you don't."

"And I do?"

"According to your mother."

My mother huffed, her giant purple velvet breasts expanding. "Well, it's true. Abra has practical intelligence. Grania has a better head for facts."

"Mom, just stop."

The lavender-shadowed eyes widened in surprise. "Stop what? I'm just stating what I observe."

"You don't *have* to state anything. You weren't injected with Sodium Pentothal." Grania took Pimpernell back to her room, promising to get me a sterile sample of his nasal fluid.

I followed my mother to the kitchen, down the elegant Spanish-tiled hallways with their dark wood accents, accompanied by the piercingly strong smell of tomcat piss, a sour and musky smell that no detergent or perfume can conceal.

In the corners, cats stretched and yawned, gathered themselves and watched. The dogs were kept outside in the kennel, so long as the weather remained mild.

"So," my mother said, "what can I get you?" The kitchen was the one room that didn't look like an old Spanish grandee's house. It was just your typical unrenovated 1970s kitchen—yellow walls, brown linoleum, avocado stove, about fifty animal-shaped magnets holding up photos, vets' bills, schedules and shopping lists.

The only thing it had in common with the rest of the house was the tang of feline urine. "Anything. A sandwich."

"I can make a little curry? Something with tomatoes?"

My mother was a terrible, highly experimental cook. "Just peanut butter would be fine." I watched my mother's plump, be-ringed hands preparing my food. "Grania seems nice. Does she work here often?"

"She's my lover," my mother said, in that particular blend of matter-of-fact and dramatic that soap opera actors tend to employ.

"Ah."

"Does that mean you disapprove?"

"It's just an expression of surprise."

"You're surprised I have a woman lover? A young lover?" My mother handed me my sandwich. I looked down at it in surprise.

"You forgot the jam."

"There isn't any. Look, Abra, if you have something to say, get it off your chest."

I took a bite of the sandwich, too used to my mother's dramatics to take this seriously. "Do you have any juice?"

The refrigerator door slammed open. "I suppose you won't deign to tell me what you're really thinking. Here's your juice."

"Thanks." I drank and wondered: What was I really thinking? That it always had to be about Piper LeFever, I suppose. Even on my birthday. Even when I was having a bit of a crisis at home. My mother never really noticed what was going on with me.

"God, you really have a talent for making things unpleasant, Abra."

I raised my right eyebrow. "I don't think it's me doing it, Mom."

"Well, it may be time for some therapy, then." She reached into a drawer and pulled out a flat gift box, wrapped in shiny purple paper. "Here. This is for you. You probably won't like it, but I saw it and thought, That would look fantastic on Abra."

I opened the box and pulled out a deep black and purple crushed velvet gown with lots of corset-type laces and hanging sleeves, the kind of thing Morgan le Fay might have worn for a dark faerie's night out. "Wow," I said. "It's . . . amazing."

"Handmade. But you'll never wear it."

"It's just—I don't really have anywhere to wear it *to*, really . . ."

"Try it on."

"Now?"

"Go on, Abra, make your mother happy."

I took off my shirt.

"And the bra. You can't wear a bra with that."

I took off my bra.

"Look at those breasts! Why you wear a bra at all is beyond me."

I slipped the dress on over my khakis and turned around. "What do you think?" I felt ready for Halloween.

"Wait a minute." My mother tugged the dress down until the sleeves exposed half my shoulder and the neckline barely covered my nipples. "There. Take a look at that."

I went into the bathroom just as a cat stalked out of a litter box, and looked in the mirror. White skin, long dark hair, breasts about to fall out: I looked like a gypsy wench. "Thank you so much for my present," I said, over my shoulder.

"Don't expect Hunter to compliment you on it. Your husband prefers you when you look like a little nun, Abra, or hadn't you noticed?"

I had forgotten how perceptive my mother could be. Maybe she might have something to say that would help me out.

I followed her back into the kitchen, pulling the dress over my head. "Mom. I have something I want to say to you."

"I knew it. You're strung out about this. Listen, Abra, Grania is the best thing that has happened to me in years, and I won't have you waltzing in here and handing down judgments."

"Mom." Just as the dress came off my head, leaving me naked from the waist up, Grania appeared. She didn't so much as look at me as I yanked the fabric up over my breasts.

"Piper, we talked about this."

"I'm not having her insulting our relationship."

Grania turned to me as I pretended to be unself-conscious about putting my brassiere back on. "I'm sorry if this was a bad time. I told her not to do this on your birthday." She held out a vial. "And I brought the nasal fluid."

"Thanks," I said, but my mother, a professional scene-stealer, would not be gainsaid.

"She's over twenty-one, and if you would just take the time to get to know her, you'd see that—"

"Mom. I don't care about Grania. I'm glad you're happy. I wanted to talk with you about something else."

My mother's eyes narrowed in suspicion. "What is it? Is it Hunter?"

I glanced over at Grania, who held up her hands as if in surrender. "Hey, I'll leave you guys to it. Just let me know about Pimpernell, okay? I love that little guy."

When we were alone again, my mother said, "So? What's the bastard done now?"

"He cheated on me, Mom."

She held out her arms, and I came into them. "How did you find out? Did he lose interest in sex? Or was he suddenly more interested?"

"Mo-om," I said, embarrassed.

"More interested, I see."

I pulled back so I could look in my mother's all-too-knowing eyes. "The thing is, I asked if he loves this other woman, and he said . . . he said, 'Probably not in the way you mean.' " I collapsed into my mother's meaty shoulder, sobbing. She smelled of smoke, which reminded me of Hunter.

"Typical. He screws another woman, and instantly plays it so you're the one on tenterhooks. Oh, Abra, when are you ever going to take a stand in your marriage?"

I sniffled, knowing she was right, knowing I was being weak and pathetic. "I just don't want to lose him," I admitted. "Do you have a tissue?"

"Here."

I blew my nose. "I don't know what to do, Mom."

"Well, Abra, I just hope you're not going to catch some disease from that man. Because in my day, men just fucked you over when they slept around. Now, they can kill you with it."

Trust my mother to find the one thing to make me feel worse. "I'll have to go get tested, I guess." A great chunk of despair forced its way up my chest and throat, emerging as a sort of broken moan.

My mother sighed and lit a cigarette, watching me get myself back under control. "Here. Do you want a cigarette? Don't look at me like that—sometimes it helps." She shook out the match. "Why you want to keep him with you, I'll never understand. He's a bastard."

I gave a little hiccup of a laugh. "You just think all men are bastards, Mom."

"It's a safe assumption."

"God." I folded the tissue and blew my nose again. "How my father stayed married with you for ten years, I'll never know."

"You talk like he's such an angel. Remember who left!"

"Mom, you were having affairs right and left. And you hounded him all the time. I remember when I was ten you actually had a fight where you said he was personally responsible for the subjugation of women in Spain."

"He was a filmmaker. There's a responsibility there. Besides, he said a lot of shit about me."

"Mom, you gave him an ulcer. He didn't give *you* an ulcer."

For a long moment, my mother and I just looked at each other. Then she pushed herself off her chair. "Listen. I don't want to tear your father down. You want to believe he was the injured party—"

"He had to get a restraining order!" I hesitated. "Whose idea was it to get divorced, Mom? Yours or his?" They had always claimed it was mutual, but suddenly, I wondered whether that was the case.

My mother took a deep drag of her cigarette. "I suppose it was me. I couldn't put up with the cheating anymore. And I was tired of playing tit for tat."

"Oh." I took her hand, touching the amber of one of her big silver rings. "Do you know, I saw one of your movies last night, Mom."

"Which one was it? *Blood of Egypt*?"

Her role in *Blood of Egypt* was my mother's favorite. I am named for Abra Cadabra, the deceptively mousy librarian. "No, Mom. *Lucrezia Cyborgia*."

My mother stubbed out her cigarette. "I had an affair with that spaceman, you know. Dan Daimler." There was a distant cacophony of feline yowls in the background. "So if you're up watching Dan making out with me, then you're not sleeping again."

"Do you think I should leave him, Mom?"

I expected her to say, Damn right, but instead, my mother's face softened. "How about I get the cards out?"

I took another tissue and wiped my eyes. "You know I don't believe in that stuff, Mom."

"But that stuff believes in you, Abra."

"Not this again."

"You keep saying you don't remember, but I'll never

forget it. Standing outside the château, insisting you wouldn't set foot inside."

"I was six."

"Pain, you said. Someone in there was in great pain, and they couldn't get out."

"I'd never seen a château before. To me, it probably looked haunted."

"And then when we came back the next day, in broad daylight you crouched right down—"

"Oh, God, please, not that again . . ."

"And told the landlady her dog was hurt . . ."

I buried my face in my hands. "I was a kid. I must have heard someone talking about the dog."

"You didn't speak French, Abra. And Madame Broussard said, Hurt where? And you put your hand right into that animal's huge mouth . . ."

"Mom, can I change the subject?"

"And there was a tumor the size of a lemon. Honey, don't you see that you've closed yourself off from this part of you?"

"No I haven't. I stick my hand in dogs' mouths every day."

"But you ignore the instincts that brought you there." Every time I think my mother might honestly have some advice for me she goes into her psychic phenomena spiel. According to her, this is the big talent I've neglected.

"Mom, about Hunter . . ."

"Think about him while I get the cards out."

I sighed and watched her shuffle on the kitchen counter: badger, owl, turkey, squirrel.

"What are these?"

"Medicine cards. Native American. I did a reading for you last week and I saw magic in your future. And deception."

Her fingers were deft, as if she'd been practicing a lot.

"Mom, I've asked you not to do my tarot without permission. It's intrusive."

Ignoring me, she laid the cards out on the Formica, a shield of owl, turkey, coyote, and raven.

"Oh, yeah? Which tribe? The crystal-gazing holistic Zuni merchandiser's clan?"

"Don't be flip. It's inspired by aboriginal wisdom. Don't snort at me, please."

"Mom, it's just some New Age nonsense."

"Sh. Think about your problem."

"No."

"Okay, here it is again. Owl in your recent past. It's an omen. Magic is coming your way. Deception."

"I don't want to do this, Mother."

"Wait a minute, this one's new. Coyote, the trickster. The universe is about to play some kind of practical joke on you."

"I'm going to leave now."

"No. Wait. Here's the wolf card reversed. Contrary medicine. Something negative. Usually wolf is a guide, but in this position, it could mean—" My mother glanced up at me, then swept the cards up in one swift movement, as if trying to erase whatever message she'd seen there. Despite myself, I felt a little uneasy.

"What?"

"You need to look beneath the surface of things, Abra. You need to wake up to whatever's really going on between Hunter and you. And you need to be careful."

"Gee, thanks, Mom! What a great birthday treat." I sounded like a whiny adolescent, a sure sign that I had stayed too long in my mother's presence.

My mother reached out a hand and held it on my arm for a long moment. "Baby," she said, "I'm scared for you. The wolf's not a good character to have as an enemy."

"I thought you New Age types adored wolves."

"Abs, I'm not New Age, I'm middle-aged. And you can

laugh all you want, but I think that husband of yours is dangerous. Remember when you first brought him home, and I told you he was flirting with me? I knew then he wasn't a moral person." She flung back her head, tossing her long, dyed blond hair as if she were still the defiant young star of some overwritten drama. I could feel it coming, the big, closing line. "I don't think he really ever loved you, you know. Not as an equal."

I was so mad I could have slapped her. "You never stop, do you? Everything has to have a starring role for Piper LeFever."

"Abra—" She reached out again, and I jumped back.

"Don't touch me. I am so damned tired of your theatrics I can't stand it. I'd rather go back to Hunter's brand of abuse than have your poisonous comfort for one more minute. I hope you do a better job of mothering Grania, because you sure are not going to get another chance to get at me."

It took me two hours to get home. When I walked in, Hunter was lying on the couch and smoking a cigarette, a dark cloud of smoke over his head. "How's your mother?" He was still wearing his jeans and his cheeks were dark with stubble. There was a cup of cold coffee half spilled over some papers and on the wood floor.

"Fine." I busied myself pulling off my coat so I wouldn't have to look at him. I never know how to behave after a big fight. Should I be haughty? Conciliatory? I feared that in my indecision, I usually wound up coming across as vaguely schoolmarmish.

"Did you ask her advice?" Hunter pulled himself up to gaze at me, his chin resting on the wood back of the couch.

"No." I fought the urge to look at him, fussing instead with the straps on the old backpack I'd been using since my handbag was stolen.

"Did she give it anyway?"

"Of course."

Hunter continued regarding me. "You do realize that I didn't know you'd taken the day off till someone named Offal called you from work."

"Ofer. Oh, God, you didn't tell him I was out, did you?"

"I said you were asleep and not to be disturbed."

"Thanks." My hand was on the doorknob to the bedroom. I was ready to just have a bath and get into bed, even though it was barely six o'clock.

"Anytime." I went into the bedroom and put my backpack on the dresser along with the paper bag containing my mother's gift. There was a woman's handbag resting on the lace doily where I keep my perfume bottles. Expensive, supple leather, a shape so seductively elegant you knew it had to belong to someone who wore stockings instead of panty hose. I opened the bag up and saw a leather wallet, also expensive. I felt the beginnings of an anger white with fear.

"Hunter." I came out holding the handbag as if it were a bomb. "I just found this in our bedroom."

"Did you?" He was back on the couch, reading something again. A book on medieval wolves.

"Yes, Hunter, I did. Now, are you going to tell me whose wallet this is?"

"Why don't you just look inside and find out."

I opened the wallet and took out a driver's license. Abra Barrow. Me. Hunter had gone and replaced all my cards. My eyes filling with tears for what felt like the hundredth time that day, I held the wallet to my face and sniffed the distinctive smell of new and expensive leather. Then I saw the designer name on the handbag and realized what it must have cost. This was more than a casual gesture; this was an engagement ring's worth of caring. In that moment, flooded with unexpected hope, I knew that I would do whatever it took to make my marriage work.

"I have just one question, Hunter."

"Go ahead."

"Are you sleeping with the owner of this handbag?"

Hunter finally put down his book and smiled. "Well, as a matter of fact," he said, reaching out to me, "yes."

TEN

◐○○ Nobody would eat at the Animal Medical Institute's cafeteria by choice. The room is dark as a basement, the food is greasy, and the long, grim picnic tables look ready for a fresh shipment of cadavers. But we interns work about ninety hours a week, and the residents don't fare much better: It's hard to believe there's an actual city out there with restaurants in it.

"I'm starving, but the spaghetti looked like a breeding ground for bacteria," said Lilliana, carrying two strawberry yogurts and an apple on her tray. "Where do you want to sit?"

"You choose." I had selected two large chocolate chip cookies and a container of skim milk. Looking at my friend's tiny waist in her chic straight black skirt, I wondered whether I should switch to yogurt, too. Not that it would really help; Lilli was the kind of woman who wore heels and matching French-bra-and-panties sets, and I was not. As much as I wanted to keep my husband, I knew I wasn't capable of undergoing some dramatic transformation at this late date.

"I guess we might as well join the boys," said Lilliana, searching the crowded room for a free table.

I looked around and spotted Sam, who waved us over, winding the spaghetti on his fork with sloppy enthusiasm. Ofer, who had brought his food from home, was using a toothpick to eat meatballs out of a little Tupperware container. Sitting a little apart from them, Malachy seemed to be lunching on tea and saltines while reading from a pile of files.

"I've heard a rumor," said Lilliana while we were still out of earshot, "that the board's trying to remove him from the Institute completely."

I didn't ask where she'd heard this; the unlikeliest people tended to confide in Lilliana. It was uncanny. If she'd been standing next to the chief of staff for two minutes at the cafeteria, she probably knew more about the man than his secretary did. Give her half an hour, and she'd know more than his wife. But Lilliana would never expose her sources.

"Do they want Mad Mal out because of his health?" I wondered aloud. "Or is his health getting worse because he's on the way out?"

Lilliana shrugged. "I don't know. Either way, he looks awful." Lately, Malachy's cheekbones were so prominent that he looked positively cadaverous.

"Shoot," said Lilliana as we reached the table, "I forgot something. You sit, Abra, and I'll be right back." I put my tray down as Lilliana returned to the food servers.

"Ms. Barrow." Malachy nodded at me. "Did you get the rads back on that golden retriever yet?"

"No, but the bloods are in." I took a sip of my milk. "I don't know where to go from here, though. The owner's pretty much tapped out."

Malachy tapped his chin thoughtfully. "So chemo's not an option, regardless of the diagnosis?"

"Not with us. Maybe the dog's regular vet can work something out."

"You feel up to making the call?" His voice, I thought, was almost kind.

"I can do it."

Malachy raised his eyebrows. "You do know it's Mrs.

Rosen? The lady who thinks we should give her a discount because we're a teaching hospital?"

"I'll explain it to her."

"Well, then," Malachy said, "I suppose that the only thing left for me to say is . . ."

"Say happy birthday," said Lilliana, reappearing with a tiny, perfect chocolate cake on her tray. There was just enough room for the big 3 and 0 candles.

"Oh, Lilliana, thanks." I blew out the candles, and Sam said, "What did you wish for?"

"What all women wish for—true love, happiness, a pedicure."

"I can help you with part of that," said Lilliana, handing me a beautiful print of an Impressionist garden, along with a gift certificate for a day spa.

"Of course, I'm tagging along," she said, peeling her apple in the European fashion.

"With knife skills like that," said Malachy, "you are truly wasted in social work."

I rolled my eyes. "Oh, just stab him, Lilli."

Ofer's card featured a wolf wearing a woman's dress, looking at Little Red Riding Hood with a kind of embarrassed smirk. The caption read, Really, Red, it's not about the clothes.

"I was a little worried you might be offended by this," Sam admitted. His card displayed the waxed chest of a muscular young male model, and contained an unfunny joke about older women.

"Very cute, Sam. Thanks." I wondered why I had the reputation for being prim. For some reason, I thought of Red Mallin, Wildlife Removal Operator. *He* sure hadn't thought of me as prudish.

Lilliana took a look at Sam's card. "I'm sorry, but this is not a ladies' man, if you catch my drift."

"Yeah," said Ofer. "Real men don't wax and pluck and dress up in designer clothes."

"Yeah," said Sam, his voice dripping sarcasm. "They call those real men 'bears.' You know, big, lumberjack-style men. Very popular in the gay community."

Malachy handed me his card last. It was very plain, with just a pressed wildflower on the cover, and inside, he had scrawled: We need to discuss something.

I closed the card quickly and stared at him, a cold wave of fear hitting me. Was he going to suggest terminating my internship?

Then Malachy stood up, nearly dropping his files. I re-acted quickly and caught them, but some of the papers still tumbled out. "Thank you, Ms. Barrow," he said. "I don't suppose I could impose on you to leave this little gathering a bit prematurely?"

Swallowing back my fear, I followed him to the eleva-tor banks. We didn't speak as we went down to the base-ment level, where Malachy had been given a small office when he'd lost his position on one of the major research teams. I hadn't actually been inside his office since my initial interview last spring.

The elevator doors slid open and Malachy said, "Af-ter you." I waited for him to precede me down the hall, noticing how unsteady his gait seemed as differ-ent scenarios played out in my head. Ms. Barrow, you are the only intern I can trust with the news of my im-minent departure. Ms. Barrow, I have come to the re-alization that you are not really qualified to be on my team. The only thought that I instantly dismissed was that my austere boss might be coming on to me in some fashion.

As we walked past a number of offices and turned a corner, I began to realize that Malachy was taking me somewhere I hadn't been before. This section of the cor-ridor was darker, the fluorescent lights flickering over peeling paint and the occasional broken chair left in a corner.

"Dr. Knox," I said, because we never called him Malachy to his face, "where are we going?"

"Here." Malachy stopped in front of a door at the end of the long hallway. Handing me the files he had been carrying, he fumbled with a set of keys.

"I don't understand what's going on here," I said. "Are you letting me go from the group?"

Malachy cursed under his breath as his trembling hands prevented him from inserting the key in the lock. Amazed at my boldness, I put my hand over his. His skin felt like ice.

"Please," I said. "Are you kicking me out?"

Malachy turned to me with a scowl. "No, I'm not kicking you out, you foolish girl. I'm taking you in here to show you something that could get *me* kicked out if anyone knew."

"But why me?" I said, almost too surprised to speak. "Why not the others?"

"Because they are not in close personal contact with someone who has been exposed to the lycanthropy virus. Damn," Malachy said, dropping the keys to the dingy concrete floor.

Well, Abra, I just hope you're not going to catch some disease from that man. The memory of my mother's voice ringing in my ears, I bent down to retrieve the keys. "Which one is it?" My voice sounded strained and unnatural.

"The bronze."

I opened the door, revealing what appeared to be a small, dimly lit laboratory. In one large cage, there was a Dalmatian, in another a German shepherd. Both dogs appeared to be asleep, but the fact that our appearance hadn't wakened them let me know that they had been sedated. A third cage stood empty, and I thought of Pia, the wolf hybrid. A stainless steel table in the middle of the room was equipped with restraints, and I also noticed a small refrigerator, a Bunsen burner, a centrifuge, numerous vials, a microscope, and what appeared to be a kitchen blender.

"I thought you were no longer involved in research," I commented, trying to sound offhand. The truth was, my mother wasn't completely wrong when she called me a hypochondriac, and all of my husband's recent erratic behavior was running through my mind.

"Officially, I'm not." Malachy shambled over to a computer that looked at least ten years old. "But I couldn't just abandon my work to a bunch of incompetent wankers, now could I?" He tapped a few keys and an image came up on the screen: the familiar image of human DNA, a double helix. "Do you know that human chromosome 17 shares linkage with canid chromosome 23?"

I shook my head. "Not specifically, no." I knew we were all mammals, and that we shared a common ancestor if you went back far enough, but I'd never delved too deeply into genetics.

Malachy tapped out a key and a segment of DNA removed itself, turned upside down, and then was reinserted. "This suggests that at some point, there was a mutation—an inversion, probably."

Behind me, the Dalmatian growled as it fought off the effects of its sedation. "Dr. Knox," I said, trying to call his attention to the animal.

"But wait. Look what happens when you reshuffle a few more genes." On screen, the DNA began to shift and recombine. "There you go—the sequence for canid DNA."

"But that's at the genetic level," I said, suddenly grasping his point.

"Exactly," said Malachy. "I always suspected that the lycanthropy virus could affect cell function, and I surmised that there might even be some shift at the level of the nuclear DNA, so that one cell would start looking and acting like another kind of cell. But it took me a while to understand that the change was taking place in the mitochondrial DNA."

I looked at Malachy, suddenly wondering if, in fact, his illness was muddling his brain. "If you're telling me that my husband could have been infected with this virus, I'd like to know exactly what you think that means." Because at the moment, every werewolf movie I'd ever seen was running through my head, ending, disconcertingly, with an image of my husband turning into Jack Nicholson.

Malachy raised his eyebrows. "My dear girl, that is what I'm trying to find out. No one knows precisely how mitochondrial and nuclear DNA interact, but clearly, it's complex. All I can say is, there's a genetic factor, and then there's an environmental factor. But I do think it would make sense for your husband to pay me a little visit."

I could just imagine how that suggestion would go over. "I don't think—" I began, but we were interrupted by a long moan from the Dalmatian.

"Blast. I'd better check on him. What I really need, of course, is a pure wolf specimen." Malachy knelt down awkwardly to open the cage door, and before I could react, the Dalmatian rushed him, snarling and going for the throat. I tried to reach for the animal's legs, to pull him up off-balance, but I couldn't move fast enough. I could see blood, and Malachy's hands were raised, trying to block the dog's head.

"Telazol," Malachy shouted, "in the fridge." I opened the small refrigerator, grabbed the syringe, and plunged it into the dog's flank. The Dalmatian lashed its neck to the right, releasing Malachy as it reacted to me, the new threat. Growling, the Dalmatian curled its upper lip as it prepared to pounce.

"Oh God," I said, knowing the sedative was not going

to take effect in time. And then the dog was on me, his front paws pressing down on my shoulders, and I couldn't help it: I closed my eyes. There was a sharp crack, and I screamed as the full weight of the dog came down on my chest. I looked up, and there was Malachy looming over me, except that for a confused second he didn't look like Malachy at all. His eyes seemed to glow with an eerie, phosphorescent blue-green light, and he looked bigger, wilder, stronger, his arms grotesquely attenuated, as if he had stretched them out from across the room to break the Dalmatian's neck.

But that's impossible, I thought, and then I passed out.

"Jesus," someone said.

"Is she bleeding?"

I was wondering the same thing myself as I came back to consciousness with Lilliana and Ofer and Sam standing around me. It's very disconcerting to be the victim of a medical drama; I think that when we watch this stuff on television, we all tend to identify with the doctors and nurses, the ones standing on their feet with all their clothes on and their skin intact.

"Okay, someone help me pick this guy up and get an IV going," said Ofer.

Lilliana knelt down to stroke my hair. "Abra, you okay?"

I tried to nod as Ofer and another intern lifted the dead dog off me.

Malachy crouched down beside me. "I'm sorry," he said, his voice softer than I had ever heard it before, filled with regret. "Did he bite you? Did he break the skin?"

I looked up at him, remembering that strange, distorted glimpse of him that I'd had before I'd passed out. Shock, I thought, but couldn't help wondering: Had Malachy used himself as a test subject? If so, he certainly hadn't turned into a wolf man.

"Your jacket is ripped," I said, realizing that Malachy's lab coat had been shredded, as if he'd worn it through a cyclone.

"Irrelevant. Show me where you're injured," Malachy said, and I realized I hadn't answered his last question.

I met his eyes, understanding why this was his paramount concern. "He didn't bite me."

Malachy looked so relieved that I caught a glimpse of what he must have looked like when he was younger, softer, more capable of emotion. I found myself wondering if he ever had been in a real romantic relationship, or if science was the only passion that had ever moved him. Perhaps this secret underground laboratory was the place where his truest self could emerge. And then I realized: Malachy must have called the rest of the team down to help me. Which meant it wasn't a secret anymore.

For the rest of the day, people kept coming up to me and making bad Dalmatian jokes. Want a fur coat, Abra? Just say the word. I tried not to think about the wolf card, reversed. Did a Dalmatian attack count? Or was this some divine coyote practical joke? That's the problem with tarot cards: Anything can mean anything.

Sam walked by me in the hall. "You okay now? Not seeing spots?" I pretended an exasperation I did not feel. But all of us were pretending, really. Underneath our facade of normalcy, we were wound tight with the tension of not knowing our fates. By the end of the day, we heard the official confirmation: Malachy Knox was no longer employed by the Animal Medical Institute.

We hadn't seen our teacher since the EMTs had arrived, crowding into the lab along with Mr. Simcox, the cadaverous head of administrative affairs. We'd managed to convince the emergency medical technicians that I didn't need to go to the emergency room, and then Mr.

Simcox had summoned two guards to escort Malachy from the building.

Something about Malachy's unruffled demeanor suggested to me that he'd managed to cram some files into his briefcase while Simcox had been distracted.

"You'll all be fine," he said, nonchalantly removing his torn lab coat and pulling a tweed jacket off a hook on the back of the door. His bony arms, I noticed, protruded from the frayed cuffs of his shirt as if the sleeves had shrunk—or his arms had grown.

As the guards herded him out, Malachy added, "They'll just assign you all to other teams."

"But Dr. Knox," said Sam, "what's going to happen to you?"

Malachy shocked us all by grinning with real amusement. "To tell you the truth, my boy, I haven't the faintest idea." And with that, he left us, whistling under his breath and swinging his briefcase with surprising vigor as he walked out of our lives.

ELEVEN

◑○○ I am in the AMI cafeteria and Lilliana hands me a straw basket. "You have to bring this to Malachy, Abs. He's not at all well."

"Where is he?"

Lilliana points to the basement corridor. "Down there. But just go straight to his laboratory and don't open any of the other doors."

"I promise." Then I am in my own apartment and I open the door to our bedroom to find Hunter masturbating with what appears to be a piece of liver. Just like in *Portnoy's Complaint,* I think. At this point, I understand that I am dreaming.

"Excellent! You've brought more food," says Hunter. "Is there any meat in there?"

"It's not for you," I explain. "This is work-related." I back out the door and I'm in the basement again, walking toward Malachy's laboratory. There's a young woman crouched in a corner, holding her stomach as if she's in pain. She's wearing a red hooded sweatshirt that conceals her face, just like in that sixties movie, what was it called, *Don't Look Now.* Recalling the film's ending, I immediately suspect the child of being a homicidal dwarf.

"Are you all right?" I ask, cautiously.

"No, I'm not all right," says the girl, pulling back her

hood. She has a winsome, pointed face, and she seems angry and frightened. "Look at me! Look what he did!"

"You look fine to me," I say, and then I see that the hands peeking out of her sleeves are the hairy paws of a wolf. "Oh, you poor thing."

"No, no, I'm supposed to be a wolf," said the girl. "He did this to me!" Not knowing what to do for her, I reach into the basket and hand her a sweet roll.

"Thanks," she calls after me, gobbling it up with canine enthusiasm. "Oh! Hey! Don't let him take his clothes off!"

Unsure if she means Malachy or someone else, I nod my head. When I reach the door to the lab, it turns into the front door to my mother's house. My husband opens it. He is wearing my mother's purple caftan.

"Hunter," I say. "Where's my mother?"

"I am your mother now," he says.

"No, you're just wearing her clothes. What have you done with her?"

"I have incorporated her into my being, so I can be everything to you. I don't have a mother, so why should you? You don't need anything or anyone else but me."

"That's a little extreme, isn't it?"

"Just hand over the goodies." I lay the basket on the table, and before I can stop him, Hunter pulls off the caftan. I protest, remembering the wolf girl's warning, but suddenly Hunter is on top of me, and he's a wolf, his fangs inches from my throat. I close my eyes and feel his dead weight collapse on top of me.

"You can open them now," says a familiar, Texas-flavored voice. I look up and see Red Mallin, Wildlife Removal Operator, dressed in a plaid lumberjack shirt and carrying an ax. He looks subtly younger and handsomer in this dream, just like an actor who's gone from a bit part to a starring role.

"I think you're getting better lighting," I say. Then,

taking in the lumberjack shirt and remembering Sam's comment, I add, "You're not a bear, are you?"

"Different animal entirely. Come on, Doc. Open your eyes now."

"They are open. I'm looking right at you."

Red leans close, and I can smell his breath. It's nice breath. It smells like he's been chewing mint leaves. "You've got to wake up, darlin'." And then, as if he can't help himself, he puts his nose in my hair and takes a deep, snuffling breath. I pull back when I realize that his nose is cold and wet. Of course it is—he's a wolf, too.

I open my eyes and wake up.

For a moment, I didn't know where I was, and then I realized that I was in my own living room. I must have fallen asleep on the couch. After a long and surprisingly sympathetic talk with my mom, I'd sat down to watch CNN until Hunter returned.

It had been comforting to talk to my mother about the Dalmatian's attack and Malachy's dismissal, but the person I really wanted to tell was my husband. Now, barely able to shake off the vividness of my dream, I turned the set off, feeling wide awake and more than a little unsettled.

It was one A.M., and Hunter wasn't home yet. He had said that he might go to a late night café to write, and not to wait up for him, so I wasn't even entitled to be mad. I filled the kettle with fresh water and set it on a high flame.

There was a good chance my mother was still awake. Better than good. But despite the ease of our earlier conversation, I was reluctant to expose more of my marital problems to her.

When she'd first met Hunter seven years ago, she'd flirted with him. I didn't really blame her: She'd never met any of my boyfriends before and had no idea how to behave. When she realized Hunter was laughing at her, she became his sworn enemy.

"I suppose you like my daughter because your own mother is somewhat lacking," she said, chopping kidneys for the cats.

"Interesting insight," said Hunter, looking at my mother in a manner even she could not misinterpret as favorable. "Do you think it's something Abra and I might have in common?"

After Hunter graduated college and our weekends together grew more and more infrequent, my mother began to call him my ex-boyfriend. As in, "that ex-boyfriend of yours I never liked."

Most of our friends assume that Hunter and I had been together since college, but the real story was more complicated. After I graduated, we moved in together, but we had stopped sleeping together, and Hunter began calling me his roommate. I think he wanted me as protection in case his landlord decided to evict him while he was away in Anchorage or Pulau Pangkor or Goa. I worked at various animal shelters, saving money and applying to veterinary schools, while Hunter came and went, sometimes for months at a time. My mother asked me what the hell I thought I was doing. I told her we were friends now. What was wrong with sharing an apartment with a friend?

So I mailed out the bills while he was away and provided protection from clingy girlfriends when he was in town. His girlfriends always asked me for advice, then never took it. I told them to act as if they were his friends, not his lovers.

And then I went off to Tufts for four years. When I graduated, I came back to New York to visit Hunter and we got drunk and wound up having energetic sex all night long. It was so much fun. I'd forgotten how sex could be like that, like a game of Twister—left foot on red, right arm on blue, now you go here and whoa!

We got married a year later, on the gray day after Valentine's in City Hall. I tried not to let on how surprised I was; there's really no dignified way to ask a man why he has proposed to you. There were no guests. We asked another couple on line to be our witnesses. I wore a plain light beige silk dress that had looked great in the shop but made me look stern and matronly when I put it on; Hunter wore jeans and a sweater. Our honeymoon was one unbearable weekend in his family's grand Victorian ruin of a house in Northside, New York. His mother had committed suicide when Hunter was a teenager, but his father was there, unexpectedly; he kept saying how funny it was that we had just gotten married. There were a lot of loaded comments about the proud Barrow lineage and a debt owed to future generations, and it took me a whole day to understand that Hunter's father was under the mistaken impression that my parents were rich. Awkwardly, I explained that neither my father nor my mother had the money to help renovate the house. Even if the tower room was in danger of falling into the basement. Even if the 1920s radiators hissed like cats but didn't give off much in the way of heat and the grimly shadowed upper two floors still had gas lighting.

Even if it was the heritage of my future children.

"Oh, well," Hunter said. "Maybe we could just kill your mother and move into the El Greco house."

In the end, it was his father who financed us while Hunter wrote and I applied to AMI's internship program. But my mother never got over her conviction that Hunter wasn't to be trusted.

Steam was beginning to whistle in the kettle and I removed it from the burner. I had just poured boiling water into my mug of powdered cocoa mix when the phone rang.

"Hello, Abs."

Not Hunter. My mother. Stupidly, I'd just taken a sip of cocoa and started choking on my reply.

"Hello, hello, are you all right?"

"Sorry, Mom. I just burned the tip of my tongue."

"Honey, what is it?"

I broke like an eggshell. "Oh, Mom, Hunter's not home yet. I haven't even had a chance to tell him about what happened at work." Or about the possibility that he had caught the lycanthropy virus; I'd neglected to tell my mother that as well. "I'm worried Hunter's getting ready to leave me."

"Is that all? Baby, I'm more worried he's not."

I thought about hanging up, but instead I told her about my dream.

"Are you sure that Texan guy was also a wolf? The cards included a wolf and a coyote."

I thought about that. "I think he was really this man I met. I think it was one of those mental puns—you know, all men are wolves."

"You met a man?" My mother's voice was suddenly bright with interest. It was so easy for her to go off point.

"A wildlife removal operator, Mom. As in, kills the squirrels hiding in your basement." At least I assumed he killed the animals he removed, although, remembering the owlet, I wondered.

"Oh. Well. But if he's attractive, at least sleep with him. The big mistake you make is letting Hunter have all the power. I'd just feel so much better about your relationship if I knew you were cheating on him from time to time."

On that note I did hang up.

TWELVE

◐○○ I knew I was in trouble as soon as I saw the restaurant. It was the kind of place where one person fills your water glass and another removes your used dishes, and neither is the waiter. The hostess who showed me to my table was slight and gamine in a black evening dress with no bra. She gave Hunter a sympathetic smile as she gestured to my chair with one elegant little hand.

"Hunter," I said, "you didn't warn me that we were going somewhere this nice." I'd thought we'd have my deferred birthday dinner at one of those casually trendy West Side places where it's chic to be underdressed. Instead, Hunter had managed to book us at one of those East Side places where terrifyingly thin women make a career out of eating squab. My husband, who had dressed up in a pale pink, button-down shirt and black jeans, was the only man not wearing a tie, but on him it looked deliberate and stylish. The other male diners were florid-faced and stout, drinking scotch and lecturing their ash blond, stiletto-shod companions.

I, on the other hand, was trying to remember not to touch my hair, which was on that knife's edge between passably clean and suspiciously shiny. I was wearing Lilliana's too-small spare black sweater because a terrified Lhasa apso had defecated on my lavender cardigan right before lunchtime. I'd also borrowed some lipstick, but it hadn't helped matters much. Fatigue was making my contact lenses feel like scouring pads and I was getting a nervous rash on the right side of my forehead, near the scalp. All in all, I wished I were at home, eating tomato soup out of a can. But my husband and I had a date, so there I was, like a boxer struggling to stay in the fight.

"You look great."

I raised one eyebrow.

"Mm. Just like a Victorian nanny." Hunter pulled out my chair for me, beating the waiter to the job. Or was it the busboy? Whoever the man was, I thought he glared at us as Hunter sat back down. "Ah, there you are. Gin and tonic for me, champagne cocktail for the lady." The mystery server gave a polite nod, possibly recognizing Hunter as one of those rare diners who immediately assumes the dominant role.

"I look like a Victorian nanny? How is that?"

Hunter grinned at me. "The hank of hair barely restrained by a tortoiseshell spear. The flare of nostril. The haughty arch of unplucked eyebrows."

"The furry legs?"

"Thankfully, you are not Victorian in all respects."

I put my hand to my chest. "Stop, I'm getting a swelled head."

"Don't fish for it—you know you're beautiful. And, as I was going to say before you interrupted me, it's the air you have of something deliciously repressed." You know you're beautiful, he'd said, so matter-of-fact. I inhaled a deep lungful of happiness, the inverse of a sigh. The real waiter came with our menus, and Hunter thanked him.

"My name is Pascal, and I'll be your server tonight." I noticed that Pascal seemed to approve of Hunter more than he did of me. I couldn't really argue with the guy:

Hunter had recently gotten a haircut and it fell in smooth waves around his high cheekbones. He looked expensive and dangerous, like he could drive a Porsche while dismantling a bomb barehanded. Barehanded, as in missing the thin silver wedding ring he usually wore when he wasn't out in the wilderness courting disaster.

"You're not wearing your ring." I'd bought it as a joke at a flea market, sure Hunter would refuse to wear anything other than a watch. To my surprise, he'd taken to it, saying he liked the idea of being branded.

"What? Oh, that. Must've got out of the habit of wearing it. I'll put it on when we get back home." Hunter reached for my hand across the table, but just as I placed my palm over his, Pascal returned with the drinks.

"Monsieur. Madame." My hand was released so abruptly it just sat there for a moment on the table like a dead fish. "I'll be back to tell you the specials."

I sipped my champagne and looked at the menu, which was printed on parchment and vellum, like a wedding announcement. To my surprise, there seemed to be nothing offered that did not contain some dead thing in its ingredients. Salad of fresh greens with goat cheese and crisp apple-cured bacon. Duck and mushroom ravioli. Even the vegetable soup had pork wontons in it.

"Hunter," I said, "there's nothing I can eat here."

"Hmm." Hunter looked up at me. "There's salad and stuff. Cheese."

"It all has meat in it."

"For God's sake, Abra, we're not in college anymore. You don't have to be such a purist. Just pick the bits you don't want out."

I stared at him, thinking of the Dalmatian. Drop eye contact now, I thought, to avoid the lunge. But instead I attacked. "I don't think it's very considerate of you to pick a restaurant that doesn't have any vegetarian dishes, Hunter. Especially when you're supposed to be taking me out for my birthday."

There was a pause, and then Hunter reached over the table for my hand. "You're right. I'm sorry, Abs. I just heard about this place from a friend at *Vanity Fair*, and I thought . . . But, you're right. Do you want to leave?"

Unfair, I thought. He knows how I hate making a scene. And leaving here would entail a little drama worthy of my mother. "No," I said. Grudgingly.

Hunter scanned the menu. "Here, what about the sautéed mixed vegetables and some, ah, julienned potatoes?"

Two side dishes. "Fine."

Pascal returned to recite, in a bored, distracted voice, the roasted duck and turnips, parsleyed veal, and braised rabbit with mustard and calvados. He said all the names in French, slowly, and gazed at us challengingly, as if daring us to request a translation.

I gestured for Hunter to go first. He considered things for a moment. "Is the *Ragout de Lapin* good?"

"Excellent."

"I'll have it."

"Very good, sir. And for Madame?"

I examined my limited options one last time. "I suppose . . . I guess . . . I think I'll start with the cream of sorrel soup, and then when my husband is having his main course"—I couldn't bring myself to say "rabbit"—"you can bring me the, um, sautéed baby artichokes." I closed my menu and handed it to Pascal.

"And that will be all, madame?"

I met his gaze. "That will be all."

"Perhaps, if I may suggest, the shrimp and eggplant tart?" In case I had been intimidated by the lack of English translation, I suppose.

"No."

"The mushroom and prosciutto toast?"

"I'm a vegetarian."

"Ah. Aha. I understand." His tone implied that, in his opinion, I was suffering from a self-inflicted disease. "Do you wish the soufflé for dessert?"

I wished to leave as quickly as possible. "No, thanks." Pascal looked at me as if he were planning to spit in my soup. Then he gave Hunter a sympathetic little nod, and went off to tell the chef to stick a little bunny corpse in the skillet.

And then we were alone together, Hunter and I, and I realized that the evening had acquired a kind of portentous heaviness. The low murmur of the other diners seemed to fade away. The clink and chime of glasses and cutlery was replaced with the pounding of my heart.

"Abra," Hunter said, making a helpless little gesture with his hands. A how-can-I-put-this gesture.

I wanted to stop this. Whatever this was. "You're not going to propose, are you?"

Hunter dipped his head and then looked up at me, a rueful light in his dark eyes. "In a manner of speaking, yes. Propose something. Ah, Christ, Abs." Hunter took a swallow of his gin and tonic. "You must have noticed I'm not very happy."

Striving for composure, I found my professional you-have-several-treatment-options voice. "Is it the writing?"

"It's work, in part. I haven't figured out the exact story I'm going to do, but Christ, Abs, I found something back there, in the Transylvanian Alps."

"Not a werewolf, I assume." Ha, ha.

Hunter did not smile. "If you feel you have to make a joke out of everything—"

"No, no, I was just teasing. Start again. You said you found something . . ."

"Well, you know the woman I was working with,

Magdalena Ionescu. The wolf researcher. Born right near the forest, totally untraveled outside of Eastern Europe, but so smart about the wolves—Abs, the time I spent tracking with her was like nothing I've known. She was like—she was almost animal in her instincts. Uncanny."

My mouth went dry. Why had I thought Magda too old to interest Hunter? "She's the one. Oh, God, why are you telling me this here? So I won't make a scene?"

Hunter took in the look on my face. "Oh, Christ, Abs, it's not that. Yes, I slept with her. Yes, she made a big impression on me. Changed me. But I'm married to you. I love you."

"Tell me what you have to say." I was holding on to my diamond wedding band as if it might be pulled off by a sudden howling tornado. By whatever Hunter would say next.

Hunter leaned forward. "Abra, when I say she changed me . . . Christ, I don't know how to explain this so it doesn't sound like I'm mad."

"It's the lycanthropy virus, isn't it? She infected you."

I'd surprised him. Maybe even shocked him. "How did you—"

"Malachy Knox. My former teacher. He was doing research, and he knew about your trip. But Hunter, I'm not sure I really understand what this means."

Hunter was silent for a moment, as if mentally rewriting a prepared speech. When he finally spoke, his voice was low and a little urgent. "Here's the thing. You have to have a genetic marker, passed down on your mother's side. There's no reliable test, but one thing Magda said was a likely indicator was schizophrenia in the mother's line. When the virus is introduced into an individual with the right genetic makeup, it can create a complete realignment on the cellular level." Hunter gripped my hands. "Do you understand what that means, Abs? I don't have to worry about developing my mother's illness anymore." He took a breath. "I don't have to worry about going mad."

The mitochondrial DNA, I thought, passed down the mother's line. But Malachy hadn't suggested that inoculation with the lycanthropy virus might be a cure for anything, let alone schizophrenia. Striving for composure, I extracted my hands from his and took a sip of my champagne cocktail. "So what happens now?"

Hunter tossed back the rest of his drink, then signaled the waiter to bring another. "I don't know yet. It varies from individual to individual. Most people just develop a few lupine characteristics—improved hearing, a keener sense of smell, some muscular and skeletal rearrangement."

"Copious body hair?"

Hunter ignored my feeble attempt at humor. "Magda says that full body morphing is very rare. In her family, she's the only one who can do it. But I can already feel the difference in me, Abs." He leaned backward, his arms along the back of the chair. I could see a businessman staring, and I thought: I can see the difference, too. You've lost your mind.

"So you think there's a possibility that you'll be able to change into another shape?" I used my best professional voice, the one that revealed absolutely nothing of what I was thinking or feeling. "A wolf shape?"

Hunter seemed so excited I half-expected him to jump out of his seat. "It's a slim chance, but yes, that's what I think—hope—might be happening to me."

I drank down the rest of my champagne cocktail too quickly, swallowed the wrong way, and started coughing.

"You all right, Abs?"

I nodded, still coughing. As I used the corner of my linen napkin to wipe my streaming eyes, I sorted through possible responses to Hunter's pronouncement. My first instinct was to find a politic way to suggest seeing a psychiatrist. Assuming that there was a politic way to suggest seeing a psychiatrist. Maybe I could ask Lilliana for a referral. But then I thought about what Malachy had told me in his lab. I wasn't going to buy the idea that a human could shapeshift until I'd observed it in a controlled experiment, and then had someone else repeat the experiment to verify results. But still, the whole idea of recombinant DNA had sounded pretty far-fetched until someone had succeeded in getting human genes into bacteria and producing insulin in a petri dish. Whatever else might prove to be true, I had to accept that my husband had caught a rare virus, and that its effects were not fully understood.

And then another, more disturbing possibility intruded.

"Can I catch it? What happens if you don't have the right genetic makeup and you're exposed?"

"Oh, baby." Hunter reached out and took my hand in his. "Nothing happens. Nothing happens to ninety-nine percent of the people who are exposed to the virus. And it's not contagious unless it's active in your system, and you're in wolf form. I don't even know yet if anything will happen to me."

The waiter brought Hunter's second drink, and Hunter gulped it down as if it were water. "Ah, Abs, I wish you could have seen the Carpathian Mountains. But I don't have the words. Here, it sounds ridiculous. Too sentimental. There, it seemed—it was all right to use words like 'timeless' and 'primal.' It wasn't forced. It wasn't false. There was a beauty to the landscape that made the heart lift. There was something almost supernatural about it—a magic of place. I would walk up a rise and see the world falling away. I would put my hand on a tree so old it felt like it had a soul."

"It sounds wonderful." To my credit, my voice didn't crack.

"It was."

There was a lull in the conversation, one big enough to drown in. I said nothing. Fear returned, raising the small hairs on the back of my neck. Someone, not Pascal the waiter, brought me a tray with my soup on it.

"Hey. Wait! Bring us this wine, will you?" Hunter pointed to a selection from the wine list. He'd already finished his second gin and tonic, and I thought: He's not just charged up. He's manic.

"So you want to go right back there? Is that it?"

Hunter tore off a piece of bread. I thought of that ridiculous commercial for a candy bar that suggested sticking the chocolate in your mouth whenever you needed time to come up with a story. Hunter crammed the bread in his mouth but spoke anyway. "I want to be in a place where I can fulfill whatever potential there is in me."

I cleared my throat. "And exactly where do you find this kind of a place?"

"Magda says that wherever there are remnants of old forests, wherever there are still legends of beast men and magic, that's where I will have the best chance of becoming . . . complete. It has to be an old forest, and there has to have been a long history of humans interacting with the wild. She calls them borderline places . . . crossroads between more than one reality."

Now my credulity was stretched past the breaking point. "I'm sorry, are you saying that *magic* is a catalyst for this virus?"

"Magda showed me that a belief in science and a belief in magic don't have to be mutually exclusive. There are just different kinds of truths, Abs. Old places—wild places—she says they can unlock things inside of us, just like art can. Or poetry."

According to this version of reality, I understood, I was the passionless, literal geek, while Magda was the lyrical sorceress. I didn't bother trying to argue my case. Instead, I thought of Hunter hunched over the computer, passionately frustrated, and realized what his sudden sexual hunger had been. A tantrum. A venting of pent-up emotions that had nothing to do with me. My soup was growing cold; I stirred it, but couldn't force myself to taste it. "So you're leaving me for that woman. Magda."

"No, Abs." Hunter smiled, and for the first time in our relationship, I thought about his mother's mental illness, and how much of it she might have passed down to her son. "Right in Northside, where my family's house is, there's old-growth woods. And legends about werewolves dating back to the early settlers. Hell, some stories probably come down from the Indian tribes who lived there." Hunter tore off another hunk of bread as Pascal the waiter arrived with the wine. Hunter continued his discourse, oblivious as Pascal went through the ritual of uncorking.

Visibly irritated by Hunter's disregard of him, Pascal poured the wine into my glass first. "Madame?"

"It's fine," I said, barely tasting it.

"Great, thanks," Hunter told Pascal, not looking up at him. Then he threw back half the goblet in one huge swallow. "Anyway, that's where I need to be." Hunter leaned forward, fingers drumming on the table, longing, no doubt, for a cigarette to hold.

"In Northside? You want to live in that big old house in Northside?" I was still trying to get to the buried body in this conversation. He had given me the name of the other woman; he had told me he longed to be back in Transylvania. I couldn't quite believe that Northside and myself were anything but a poor substitute.

Hunter drank his glass of water down, audibly swallowing. I had never seen him display such poor table manners. As he wiped his mouth on the back of his hand, I wondered how drunk he was.

"I don't want to work for Magdalena. In her territory, she's boss. I want to make my own way, Abra. And Northside is as good a place as any to start. Ever since he remarried and moved to Arizona, my dad hasn't spent any time there, and he says he'd rather have me looking after it than the caretaker he's got now. I can write there, and do research. I'll have space, and nature around me. And it's only two hours from you. We can visit each other."

This, at least, made sense. I didn't entirely believe he loved me more than he loved this other woman who had so captured his imagination. But I did believe that he would not choose to be a follower, not even for love. I drank some wine, slowly. I wanted to slow Hunter down, slow everything down. The hum of other people's meals and lives and celebrations seemed to be growing louder. I took a deep breath. "When are you leaving?"

"I'd like to leave in a week." Hunter paused, as if he'd just noticed that we were having different conversations. And that only his was happy. "Abs? Abs, why are you crying?"

"Because I thought you were leaving me."

"Oh, sweetheart, no," said Hunter, misunderstanding. "I'm not leaving you. This is just like one of my research trips. Except I'll be able to see you more often. Oh, Abs, come on, cheer up. I love you, woman." He leaned across the table and kissed me on the lips. "Now, cheer up! I command you."

"Oh, God, I'm sorry." I started to laugh, tears still running down my cheeks. I never make scenes in restaurants. Well, except for that day. At first, the relief was so great that I felt a great surge of appetite and began to eat my cold soup, started tearing great chunks out of the bread and stuffing them in my mouth. It was only after-ward, when we began to discuss the details of his move over his rabbit and my artichokes, that I realized what had happened.

I'd been so braced for news of an affair, of some final break, that I'd felt relieved when Hunter had said that all he wanted was to move to Northside. And he, misin-terpreting my tears of relief for tears of sadness, had tried to reassure me that we weren't really separating.

But the truth was, we were, because we would not be living together for some time. When a marriage is as generous with distance as ours had always been, it can be hard to distinguish a real parting of ways. But as Hunter and I went over the details of relocation—how much money was to be allocated for city expenses, how much for Hunter to purchase a car, and so on—it hit me that we were, in effect, negotiating a breakup.

I looked at Hunter, who had finished amputating the rabbit's leg and was now happily chewing on a chunk of its thigh. "I suppose we won't be seeing too much of each other over Christmas this year."

"You'll get time off for good behavior, won't you? And we'll see each other most weekends."

I didn't have most weekends free, though; I had only one day, at best. And I didn't have a car. The nearest train stopped forty minutes from Hunter's family's house. That made it an almost three-hour commute. One way.

Hunter reached for my hand. "You could always come with me."

I felt as though I were having an operation and people were pretending my internal organs weren't hanging outside. "But I can't."

"So we'll see each other whenever we can. Don't worry." Hunter signaled Pascal the waiter for our check without asking if I wanted dessert. When we got home,

I discovered that my mascara had smeared from crying, giving me raccoon eyes. Liquored up and elated over his new future, Hunter went straight to bed for a change and fell asleep almost instantly, facing the window, probably dreaming of escape.

At three A.M. I stopped watching him.

THIRTEEN

◐○○ Once I admitted it to myself, it was all I could think about. My marriage was being restructured and relocated. My husband was letting me go. And while my moods were swinging wildly between depression and anxiety, I tried to act as though I were at peace with Hunter's decision.

I didn't want to drive him away any faster than he was already going.

Maybe it would have been better if I'd let myself rage at him, but I was too frightened. I don't fall in love easily. I don't even fall in like very often. And I'd given so much of myself to Hunter that I didn't know how much of me would be left when he was gone. I wouldn't even be able to console myself with sleep, the way other depressed people do. I would sit up with the furniture, watching my familiar things become shadowy and strange the way things do when you pass the witching hours of fatigue and solitude and are still awake.

And there was nobody to tell this to. My father, who remembered Hunter as a cocky twenty-one-year-old with a goatee and a lot of unexamined ideas about American cinema, wholly disapproved of my husband. It was the one thing he and my mother agreed on, although my father believed it was in poor taste to say anything more than, "Well, you know how I feel on that subject." The way he said this, however, implied a loathing so deep and pervasive that it defied language. For a while, my mother tried imitating him, but then she couldn't stop herself from going on. And on.

As for female friends, well, I couldn't see turning to Lilliana. We had only been friends for a few months, but I could already tell that in Lilli's version of reality, men were easier to come by than career opportunities. My situation was a bit different. During my college and postgrad years, when most women meet more eligible partners than they will at any other time, I had encountered only three men who were interested in me: a brilliant math and music major with poor people skills, a good friend going through a bad time, and Hunter.

I couldn't confide in Malachy or Sam or Ofer, and Malachy, while he knew about my husband's exposure to the lycanthropy virus, was of questionable sanity himself. Too much time had passed to call my small crowd of high school friends.

I began trying to find a way out: There had to be a cure. Hunter had said, "You can always come with me." But that wasn't a real option, not unless I wanted to give up AMI and everything that gave my life meaning.

Except for Hunter, of course.

The next day I called in sick and went to the bookstore. I was looking for An Answer, but of course there were lots of Answers: *Letting Loose, Holding On, The Leap of Faith, Making Him Want to Change, Making Change Work, Changing the Way You Love, Understanding the Alpha Male.*

I picked up this last, figuring it had been misfiled: Surely Alpha Males belonged in the animal category? Could there be a special self-help section for Women Who Loved Lycanthropes? According to this author, though, we were all animals.

Is your mate an Alpha Male? Take this test.

1. Would your mate describe himself as
A) A team player
B) One of the guys
C) A highly autonomous individual with leadership capabilities
D) Your lapdog

2. When confronted with a major life choice, does your man
A) Ask your advice
B) Ask an expert's opinion
C) Tell you and the expert what's wrong with both of you
D) Pant and whine

3. When driving, if cut off by another car, does your mate
A) Curse and yell
B) Pursue the offending vehicle very closely and then swerve off at the last possible moment before impact
C) Physically assault the small dog sitting in the other driver's lap
D) Shake uncontrollably, often losing control of his bladder

I assumed that anyone who answered D) was probably a shih tzu. There were a few more multiple-choice questions designed to ascertain if the woman reader was an Alpha, Beta, or Gamma Female. I was an Alpha, just barely, because of a high score of autonomy (willing to see a movie alone, does not need mate's advice to select clothes). As an Alpha Female, however, I needed to work on "asserting my right to submit."

Do not think of submission as surrender. Instead, think of it as a choice—an assertive female knows she is strong enough to submit when it serves her needs. Traditionally, women have understood that their greater emotional intelligence, often called intuition, actually makes them stronger than men—strong enough to back down. In any pack, you will see that the Alpha Male is dominant over the Alpha Female, with the exception of the period of intense initial sexual courtship and the postpartum period. At these times, the male caters to his mate; otherwise, the female uses her enhanced social abilities to hold the family unit together.

It was pseudo-scientific bull. It was absurdly atavistic. And I couldn't put it down.

If you, as a woman, decide that you desire to hold on to your mate with the long-term goal of producing viable offspring, you should understand that you will need to know when, and how, to submit. If during moments of key pack decision-making (when to move to a new hunting ground, for example) you assert your will, you will be setting yourself up as rival, not mate. Be aware of your enhanced capacity for emotional compromise, and remember that there will also be times (postpartum, for example, or during enhanced periods of sexual connection) when you can expect your man to submit to *your* will.

I finished reading the book at home. Hunter was out, buying a secondhand car. He came back in the late afternoon, and threw his keys and briefcase on the table.

"Success?"

"Success."

"What kind?"

"Ford Explorer, three years old." He pulled out the purchase agreement to show me the particulars: CD player, front air bags, enough miles on it to qualify it for early retirement.

"It's been driven a lot."

"Yeah, but it's in great shape, and it has a sunroof."

"That won't mean much if it's in the shop all the time. Did you look at a *Consumer Reports*? And didn't those cars have something wrong with the tires?"

"Christ, you sure know how to take the fun out of things. It's a fucking car. Don't make a doctoral project out of it."

I picked up my book. "Fine. It's going to be your car, you're going to be the one driving it. It won't really affect me at all."

"Oh, so that's what this is all about. You're going to start laying some guilt trip on me about going. Look, I've already said you can come with me if you want—"

I put the book down to glare at him. "Which you know I can't do!"

Hunter turned away from me and began looking over the purchase papers. "Well, that's not my fault. I don't see you giving up your work to be with me, so don't ask me to do it for you."

We talked again, at seven-thirty, to decide what to order for dinner, and ate separated by walls of paperwork. At twelve Hunter went in to bed without saying good night, and I took the opportunity to cry, shave my legs, and apply a facial mask. In all the women's magazines it says to pamper yourself when you feel low. It worked only in the sense that I felt I was doing something. My face had dried into a brittle shell and I was scrubbing the dead skin off my heel when I became aware of Hunter, standing in the bathroom doorway wearing nothing but faded plaid pajama bottoms.

"Do you know it's almost four in the morning?"

I nodded, trying to hide the pile of my callused skin.

"Hey, what is this shit you're reading?" The book.

Which I had been carrying around all evening. "Alpha Males are notorious for ambition, energy, drive, and promiscuity. Does your man sound like an Alpha male? Do you want to know how to hold him?" Hunter looked at me, absolutely gleaming with mischief. "I'll show you how to hold me, darling. You use your right hand. No, seriously, what do you need this crap for? Smart girl like you. By the way, do you know your face is beginning to crack?" He came forward, hitching up the waistband of his pajamas. He stopped an inch away, his chest broader and hairier than it had been in college. I felt as if all this were already part of the past.

I leaned forward into him, and his hands came up to stroke the back of my head. "Is this the end, Hunter?"

His hand lifted my chin. "It's the end of this phase of our lives."

"Is it the end of us?"

He didn't answer right away. In his silence, I thought about the fact that I had old friends and work friends, but no friend close enough to cry on. No friend other than Hunter.

"I hope it's not the end. I don't mean for it to be, Abs. So come with me."

I wrapped my arms around his waist. "What if I said yes?"

Hunter looked down at me. "Is that what you want?"

I couldn't tell if he wanted me to say yes or not. I thought of my mother, histrionically holding my father responsible for the subjugation of all women. In the middle of the night, at the top of her voice. I thought of the emptiness of having nothing but my work and the city, no one to care if I was in the apartment when it was burgled. Having no one to touch me anymore. Somehow I knew that if I let Hunter go, it would be a very, very long time before anyone would be touching me again. I would become a highly qualified veterinarian and eventually go into a successful Manhattan practice, and there would be nothing much to go home to, not even a dog.

Or one of us could sacrifice something. Like me, the one with all the emotional intelligence.

"It's what I want, yes. I want to go with you, Hunter. If you want me to." Relief flooded me. Oh sweet surrender. No more fighting to stay afloat; just cut the anchor and let Hunter pull me along.

Hunter leaned forward, examining me closely, taking in the glow of my happiness, which was threatening to become tears. "Hmm. I'd kiss you right now, you know, but you're likely to flake off on me." He looked down at the pile of dead skin in the bathtub. "Yes. Quite a lot of flaking going on here."

"I'll wash my face."

"I'll dispose of the corpse." He gathered up the disgusting waxy bits of skin in his hands and dropped them into the toilet. "You see that? With my bare hands, too. True love, darling. Nothing less."

There were no more jokes after that. We made love slowly, carefully, like two people made of glass. I fell asleep wrapped in his embrace.

When I told the board that I was leaving, they were very polite. They seemed to feel that I was having some wild overreaction to Malachy's departure, and warned me that they could not guarantee a place if I decided to reapply. Sam was sweetly befuddled at my decision, while Ofer, predictably, dripped scorn.

"I can't believe you're going out into the sticks to watch some old guy castrate bulls with his bare hands," he said.

"I'll miss you, too, Ofer."

Lilliana, of course, knew just the right thing to say. "You know I've got your back," she said. "And if this is what you want, then I'm happy for you. I'm just going to miss you like hell." She came with me when I used the day spa voucher she'd given me as a birthday present, and we gossiped about Malachy.

"Actually," she said as we sat side by side, having our feet scrubbed, "I e-mailed him."

"You're kidding! What did you say?" I pressed a button to stop my chair from vibrating so I could hear her better.

"I asked him if he knew what he was doing next. He said he was looking into renting facilities upstate, where it's cheaper." Lilliana leaned back as her pedicurist told her to put her feet back in the mini-Jacuzzi. "Mm, if I ever get rich, I think I'll buy one of these chairs for home. Hey, maybe Mad Mal will move near you and you can go into business together."

"Assuming I'd want to. Besides, Lilli, the man was not exactly the picture of health," I pointed out. "For all we know, he could be on his deathbed." But then I remembered that distorted glimpse I'd had of him just before passing out. Maybe he was fighting off his ailment. Or maybe it was mutating into something else.

"Somehow, I think Malachy's got a lot of fight left," Lilliana said as her pedicurist removed her right foot from the water. Mine followed suit.

"I don't suppose you'd ever leave Manhattan, Lilli."

Lilliana grinned. "If I did, where would you stay when you came to visit? Do you know what hotels cost in this city?"

"Hey, nice color," said my pedicurist as she began to paint my toenails. I had brought polish from home: All things considered, I figured Wolf Whistle Red was appropriate.

After that, I was at loose ends for a few days. For the first time in my adult life, I didn't have a plan, a schedule, a place to be. It felt as though the laws of nature had been suspended. On my last day of work, I walked out of the Animal Medical Institute into the uncomfortable heat of late September. "Indian summer," the weather report had called it this morning.

I had walked half a block before I realized I was still wearing my white coat. Folding it and draping it over my arm, I turned around one last time toward the East River. There I saw the ghost of a half-moon still hanging low in the sky, like some Shakespearean portent of wild spirits and mad kings.

Or like a low-budget movie warning that lunacy is waxing near.

PART TWO

FOURTEEN

◑○○ On the day we moved, with two weeks still left to go on our lease, I already felt nostalgic for the city. This condition had been building steadily, and on D-day I woke up and actually started to cry when I heard a jackhammer start up on the sidewalk below.

When you've lived in Manhattan, no other place feels quite as real: It's the solid, looming presence of all those high stone buildings, not the aristocratic skyscrapers but the solid middle-class structures of fifteen stories or so. They make all those two-story suburban houses look like flimsy stick-and-straw affairs, something a wolf could blow down. And then there's the fame factor, which makes Manhattan seem so oddly familiar, even to Belgian factory workers and Lancastrian sheepherders. You see this one narrow island everywhere you go—in print ads, on television, on multiplex screens—the quintessential city: noisy and glamorous and dirty, a village packed tight with avant-garde toddlers, mentally unstable artists, businesslike Europeans, marginal actors, hopeful immigrants from Haiti and Ohio, drug dealers, cat collectors, the unapologetically successful and the walking wounded—one layer overlapping the other, the uncivilized center of the civilized world.

And I didn't want to join the ranks of the deserters, claiming to still love the city's energy and culture but frightened off by muggings or wildings or blackouts or terrorist bandits. Like there's safety somewhere out there in a small town, like no child ever disappeared on a cricket-filled summer night, on a bike ride home from church. At least in New York, hearing the worst about human nature is never a complete surprise.

Think of your favorite urban myth. Stolen kidney? Crispy fried rat? Radioactive subway? Chances are, when you imagined it happening, you imagined it happening in Manhattan, with smoke billowing from manhole covers, and rude pedestrians yelling across broad avenues, and gray and brown pigeons teetering along as yellow taxis shot past.

In those final days, I went to museums, the Empire State Building, Bloomingdale's. Halfway through the Planetarium space show, when my seat began to vibrate like a rocket ship and the whole Milky Way galaxy receded until it was no more than a distant spot in an alien sky, I began to choke back tears. My home, I thought. The known universe.

Of course, you don't think about these sorts of things unless you've just arrived, or are on your way out. With my job already gone, leaving a gaping, empty wound in my days, I had time to sit around and notice things. I realized that in the country I would need a car to get a tube of toothpaste and began to miss being able to walk everywhere even though I hadn't left yet. I began to feel as if Manhattan were a lover I was giving up to save my marriage.

As if to torment me, Manhattan pulled out all the stops as I prepared to depart.

A few sidewalk maples had begun to turn yellow and there was a briskness to the air that made you want to look at all the new clothes in the shop windows, lovely deep purples and oranges and deep wine shades, like a dark glass of rich burgundy after a summer of acidic whites. The grinning faces of death had already been put out on display in all the stationery and drugstores along Broadway, and as I walked down the aisles of my local supermarket I watched as child after child pressed the button on the snarling zombie display.

While a small army of Israelis moved our belongings into one of their huge Samson Movers trucks, I had a last breakfast at Barney Greengrass, sitting alone at a table for two while a pair of old men argued politics over platters of sturgeon and belly lox. I had promised my doctor that I would eat fish from time to time to keep from becoming anemic, and so I sat there with my whitefish salad, feeling a little drunk from all the salt and protein. My father, born in Barcelona, loved fish. Especially the skinny oily ones with heads and tails.

"Don't become a vegetarian," he'd told me the summer I stopped eating meat. "Vegetarians are boring."

"I just don't want to eat corpses anymore, okay?"

"This is your mother's fault. In Europe, children grow up seeing that chickens have feathers. You pluck them, you cook them, you eat them. Here everything's stripped and cleaned and wrapped up like a piece of candy, and by the time you kids figure out that what you're chewing used to have teeth of its own, you're shocked."

"I'm not eating these shrimp, Dad."

"Crayfish."

"Whatever. I just feel it's hypocritical to eat something that used to be alive, unless you're willing to kill it yourself, like aboriginal peoples do."

I still remember my father's smile. "So kill it yourself. You *need* a bit of killer instinct to get along in this world."

Fourteen years older and less sure of my reasons for not eating meat, I spread a last schmear of eyeless, toothless fish salad onto my bagel and checked my watch. It was time to go change my entire life.

Hunter, who disdained anything with scales, had said he would meet me outside. He arrived only two minutes late, looking wonderful in faded jeans and a white fisherman's sweater. The haunted look had left his face, and he had begun to shave and shower regularly again. In fact, he seemed ebullient these days, energized by the prospect of our move.

"Ready?"

I folded up my grease-stained copy of *The New York Times* and hooked my arm in his. "Ready," I said.

As we made our way toward our car, I felt the first, faint stirrings of excitement. This would be a new beginning for us. An adventure. Couples who had adventures together lasted. I would join a country practice and become a partner within a few years. I would know everyone in town by name and my children would go to kindergarten in winter along a snowy path marked by deer prints.

Hunter squeezed my hand with his bicep. "You're quiet, Abs."

"Thinking happy thoughts." At Eighty-third and Amsterdam, a skinny, dark-haired woman strode past walking an aristocratically anorectic borzoi, a husky, a standard poodle, and two shih tzus. She hailed a man in a knit hat, who was walking a rottweiler, a golden retriever, a Yorkie, a wrinkly shar-pei, and a lamblike Bedlington terrier.

Jut as we passed, the rottweiler and the poodle started barking, followed by the Yorkie and the shih tzus. The Bedlington terrier wrapped itself around the man's legs, cringing, while the retriever and the husky joined in, the former yodeling low, like a hound, the latter giving a long, low wolflike howl.

"Je-suz, Candy, pull them back," said the male dog walker, struggling with the tanklike rotty. "Your monsters want to eat my babies."

"They're usually so calm, even the pood—argh, down,

boy! Poodle," said Candy, hauling with all her famine-thin, gym-toned might. But the aggressiveness of the big French dog seemed to have inflamed the husky and borzoi as well. They yanked and leaned their full body weights against their leashes, struggling to break free.

"Well, that was a Manhattan moment," Hunter said, laughing and guiding me along the sidewalk, away from the dogs.

"Maybe I should stay, in case they need help," I said, looking over my shoulder.

"Not our fight, Abra."

As Hunter led me gently but firmly away, I realized that the dogs had already begun to calm down. Only the husky and the little Yorkie still barked, and they didn't seem to be warning each other off.

Perhaps it was my own guilty urban conscience working overtime, but they seemed to be directing all their canine territorial rage at Hunter's departing back.

FIFTEEN

◐ ○ ○ In most of Jane Austen's novels, it is the flighty, shallow, venal people who long for town amusements; thoughtful, feelingful people possess the internal resources to enjoy the quiet pleasures of the countryside.

I have to admit that I'm thinking more of the films than the actual novels, as I haven't read a Jane Austen novel since I was sixteen. But I always mean to, especially right after I see some great BBC production with a firm-chinned actress charging resolutely through muddy vales in a soggy Empire-waisted gown.

But it's one thing to admire the rolling green English downs while somebody photogenic stomps across them and another thing altogether to be confronted with the reality of being stuck in a house in the middle of the woods.

Of course, like most things you suspect you'll grow to regret, it didn't seem so bad at first.

"Well, what do you think, Abra?" Hunter threw an arm around my shoulders as we looked at our new home. Nestled between yellow and red maples, its path carpeted with a fragrant windfall of pine needles, the Barrow family house appeared suddenly as you turned the corner of the path, just like something out of a fairy tale. Ivy covered one wall. The rest of the house revealed itself in sections: the flaking dragon-scale ripple of roof;

the lonely, steepled tower; the twin slitted attic windows that gazed down at the grim, willow-shrouded entrance. All along the north side of the house, which never got much sun, you could see damp, spongy sections of wood and the larger holes that announced the presence of small armies of vermin.

In bright October sunlight, it appeared to be no more than a ramshackle old mansion. But as I recalled from my previous visit, when winter arrived and shadows claimed it before four o'clock, it was a house straight out of one of my mother's films.

"I guess it needs some work," I said.

"Want me to carry you over?" Hunter indicated the threshold.

"I'm too heavy."

"Hey, I'm not going to beg you."

I lifted my arms and he bent and grasped me below the knees, pausing once to adjust his grip.

"Can you get the door open like this?"

"Possibly." Hunter struggled with the old lock for a long moment before putting his back into it. After a moment, he put me down. Lifting and turning the key simultaneously, he managed to get the rusty mechanism to work.

"Needs some oil."

"All right, Abs, get back here. We'll do it right." He lifted me again and held me against his chest for a moment. The inside of the house was musty and dark and for a moment Hunter was in shadow as he bent his head to kiss me.

I wrapped my arms around him and kissed him back, more deeply, inhaling the nicotine and wool scent of him as he released my legs so I was standing in front of him.

"We have a lot to do, Abra." His hands slid mine down, away from his neck.

"Of course we do. Right." I took a deep breath and

looked around at the vast, dim foyer, where a stained-glass window cast a weak greenish light on the heavy oak grandfather clock and worn Turkish rug. That was it in the way of furnishings, except for a low wicker couch, which boasted a selection of 1970s paperbacks, including *A Man's Guide to Fishing* and *Nurse Angelica's Dilemma*. Nurse Angelica was clasping her head in one sharply manicured hand, as if her head were hurting her badly. I knew how she felt.

I could sense the vastness of the house around me, the rambling maze of rooms and back staircases and strangely outfitted cold pantries unrenovated since the days when women worse corsets through pregnancy. In my previous visits, I had gotten lost exploring and found myself thinking of things I usually associate with my mother—mysterious cold spots, strange breezes in airless rooms, sinister sounds from behind the walls.

"This house has a lot of history," Hunter once had told me, pointing out where a Barrow grandmother had died in a cedar closet and rotted, undiscovered, for two months.

Now this was my home.

And Hunter had disappeared.

Heart thumping, I made my way out of the foyer and through the blood red walls of the dining room. From there, I creaked over rotting floorboards into the sadly derelict kitchen, where heavy old clawfooted furniture gave way to bad '70s linoleum and rusted beige appliances.

"Hunter. I wondered where you were." I tried to lower my voice and sound collected.

"Just checking the food situation." Hunter closed the refrigerator door. "There isn't any."

"I could do a shopping run . . ."

"In a little while. The movers should be here pretty soon, so maybe we should do it after they're gone?"

Hunter didn't bother to wait for my answer. He seemed restless and oddly energized, rummaging through cabinets, opening and closing drawers, as I hovered nearby. Glancing over his shoulder, he said, "Do you think you could get started on straightening things out down here while I check out the rest of the house? You wouldn't want to cook on that range till you've had a chance to clear it off."

Of course, I wanted to look our new home over with him; but I had seen it all before, hadn't I, and we would want to be eating here this evening.

"No problem."

"That's my girl." Hunter planted a kiss on my forehead and walked away. Halfway to the curving back stairs, he paused and turned. "You okay with this?"

I lifted a cut-crystal bottle of olive oil off the counter. The cork stopper was half chewed through, and in the largest part of the bottle a dead mouse lay curled, its little mouth opened in a bucktoothed frown. "Fine."

"I'll be right back to help you, Abs."

After I disposed of the mouse outside, I tried to get rid of some of the dust with an ancient mop and an equally aged can of pine cleaner. Despite my best efforts, I seemed merely to be stirring the dirt around, creating a dazzling display of dust motes in the still air, so I tried to crank open one of the old-fashioned windows, breaking off the handle in the process.

After an hour spent sorting out the kitchen utensils, I had found a few usable plates and cups (which all, oddly enough, had Peter Max '60s psychedelic patterns on them), two flimsy frying pans with peeling no-stick, and an extremely heavy enameled cooking pot. The only silverware I had discovered was a fine Edwardian bone-handled set.

There was a hibernating frog in the dishwasher.

Hunter still hadn't come back down by three, and the

movers were nowhere in sight. I paused at the foot of the stairs. "Hunter?"

No reply.

"Hunter?"

I made my way up the stairs to the second floor, where there were four small bedrooms, two on each side. "Hunter? Are you up here?" Even though it was still full daylight, I found it hard to see. There were no overhead lights, as Hunter's mother had not wired for electricity here. According to Hunter, she had believed the Edwardian gas lighting on this level to be charming. Unfortunately, I could not hear the slight sizzling sound of the jets without worrying about the possibility of asphyxiation, fire, and explosion. Not necessarily in that order.

In the first bedroom, which was furnished sparsely with a single bed, a small table, and a picture of fruit, I heard the sound of wheels on the pebbled driveway. Looking out the small eyebrow window, I could just make out the front end of the small yellow movers' truck.

I walked up the last flight of stairs to the attic, which was half finished and stretched from one end of the house to the other. It was drafty and dark, and I could see parts of the kitchen from an unfinished section of floor. Hunter was tapping away at his laptop, one navy and yellow striped leather sneaker braced on a beam, worn jeans stretched tight over the long muscles of his thigh. As I came up behind him I could make out the words *A steep and hilly silence* before he looked up and caught my eye.

"You know, Abra," he said, his voice filled with excitement and pleasure, "I kept thinking that I was stuck working on this article. But I wasn't really stuck at all. I think the real problem was that this isn't just an article. I think what I have here is enough material for a book."

Well, I thought, what had I been expecting—a declaration of his love and gratitude? Swallowing back my disappointment, I said, "The movers are here."

"Be right down." He turned back to his computer.

Mentally counting to ten, I managed not to sound as irritated as I was feeling. "I didn't mean to disturb you, but maybe you could finish that a little—"

"Of course. Just give me a moment to save what I'm working on."

I walked down the stairs and felt his eyes on my back for a moment, and then I heard the soft tapping of his fingers on the keyboard, typing faster than before. The sound of my feet on the stairs made an odd, rhythmic counterpoint.

When I opened the front door I could see the movers arguing in front of their truck.

"What I tell you? 'Skunk Misery Lane,' " said the taller mover, who had a large, bald head and a tattoo of the Egyptian eye of Horus on the back of his neck.

The smaller mover, who wore old-fashioned glasses and a lank blond ponytail, said something in a language that sounded like bad French. Hebrew, I assumed.

"Hello," I said.

"It's his fault we are late," said the bigger man. "He was reading the map."

The slender, intellectual-looking mover looked completely unapologetic. "You say to us one hour on Taconic, yes?"

"My husband was the one who talked with you."

"But this is not one hour. I say to Ronen, if we keep on, we're going to need a passport for Canada."

"Itzik," said the larger mover. "Shut up."

Itzik walked around to the back of the truck. "It gets pretty cold up here in winter? Minus ten degrees? Minus twenty?"

The bald mover shook his head and said something in

Hebrew. For a few moments the men concentrated on wrestling the couch out of the truck. From time to time they barked commands at each other while I watched, feeling helplessly protective of my furniture.

"Can I help you?"

"Just get the door for us."

Ronen and Itzik were finished and gulping water out of chipped porcelain cups by the time Hunter came downstairs.

"How's it going?" He stood and looked at the movers and then at me, running his hands through his hair, which, for some reason, was damp with sweat.

"It's all done," I said.

"Except for you pay us," added Ronen.

"Right. I'll get my checkbook."

I came up behind Hunter. "You need to give them a big tip. What have you been doing up there?"

Hunter continued writing out the check for the movers. "I had to finish something before I lost it." He walked around me in order to hand the check to the larger mover. "There you go."

Ronen looked the amount over and then tucked it into his back pocket. "Great, thanks, Itzik, *yallah,* put down the cell phone."

"I'm trying to reach Ari at the office."

We all waited.

"There's no signal," said Itzik, staring down at the phone and then punching a few buttons. "No, nothing." He looked up at us. "Can I use your house phone?"

Hunter shook his head. "It's not turned on yet."

Itzik looked up at Ronen and they conversed briefly.

"Okay, *nu, yallah,* we have to go," Ronen concluded, and shook my hand. "I wish you luck here," he said to me. "Goodbye," he said to Hunter.

It had somehow gotten to be almost six and the shadows of the trees were lengthening as I walked the movers back to their truck. The trees here were not like the neat little trees of my suburban childhood. Here the pines and maples and silver beech grew into one another, tangled at their roots, encircled by thorny hedgerows, cluttering the sky with their interlocking branches.

"You need to get someone to garden this place," Ronen observed, heaving himself up into the driver's seat.

"Yeah, there's too many trees here. Better watch out for that tick disease," added Itzik, polishing his glasses on his shirt. "Limb disease."

"Lyme disease," I said. "It's the wrong season, though. You're kind of afraid of the country, aren't you, boys?"

"Hey." Itzik smiled. "If you like ticks and skunks, good for you. I'm a city boy."

Ronen was trying the cell phone. "Still out of range," he said. "Ari's going to have a fit."

As they began to pull away I could hear them arguing over whether to order from a kebab house or a Mexican restaurant when they got back.

I turned to face the house, and it seemed to have gotten darker in the few moments I'd been standing outside. In the city, this was rush hour in the subways: Out here I could feel an intangible shift, a kind of ratcheting up of tension, as all the twilight hunters began to grow more alert.

I entered the house, which was still dark. "Hunter?" I flipped a light switch and nothing happened. "Hunter, where are you? Haven't you contacted the utilities guys? We don't seem to have electricity." I felt stupid for not checking earlier. Hunter was so irresponsible about these things, and I hadn't even seen to the bedrooms upstairs to figure out where we would sleep. "Hunter?"

I found him staring out on the back porch, watching the yard grow dark.

I wrapped my arms around his waist and he seemed startled, but then turned his attention back outside.

"We don't have any electricity. No light, no heat. Did you bring a flashlight?"

"In the car."

I thought about lodging a complaint or ten about how he'd gone about this move, but something about the vast stillness of the encroaching night stopped me. We were all alone out here. I didn't want to fight with Hunter now. "Well, don't you think we should head out and see about getting some dinner? Or do you just want to stand here for another hour?"

"Dinner?" Hunter turned to me and smiled, so happy and excited I could see the whites of his eyes and his teeth gleaming. "Sure. Oh, Abra, wait till you see what I'm working on. This place is bringing something different out of me."

"That's great."

Hunter put his arm around me and inhaled the darkening air, and I tried to stand quietly beside him so that he wouldn't notice that I was just tired and apprehensive and not excited at all.

SIXTEEN

◐ ○ ○ The problem with moving to a new place is, you lose your antennae for trouble. In New York, I could immediately pick up on the kind of places where I was not welcome. I knew which cheerfully homey midtown Irish bars were unreceptive to orders of white wine and where newly trendy neighborhoods bled into no-man's-land. No matter how distracted I got walking across the park in springtime, I never forgot that a few blocks north the Upper West Side turned into a place where you could get yourself exorcised by a voodoo priest.

But in Northside I was a babe in the woods.

Moondoggie's was a flat, one-story building set in a parking lot in the middle of nowhere. On three sides of the restaurant there were hulking dark mountains, rustling trees, and a clear and starry sky that seemed much higher and colder than the one that curved over Manhattan. Directly in front of Moondoggie's Bar and Grill, however, floodlights on the roof picked up the presence of three Ford trucks, a jeep, some teenager's broken-down Camaro, and a gleamingly new Land Rover.

"This looks good," said Hunter, and I pulled my cardigan over my shoulders and tried to believe him.

Inside Moondoggie's we found ourselves in a little foyer, which separated two distinct kingdoms. To our right, dim pink lighting, round checker-clothed tables,

and pictures of tropical sunsets laminated on wood; to
our left, a dark and shadowy bar and a huge fireplace,
the kind medieval barons might have used to roast whole
pigs and unruly peasants.

Hunter turned to me. "Where do you want to sit?"

I looked to my right, where an old couple sat in a corner, cutting up something white and creamy. I looked to
my left, where a big man in a flannel shirt glowered at me
from his heavily bearded face. "I think the dining room,
don't you?"

Hunter looked at that menu, which was chalked on a
blackboard propped on a chair. The white stuff was probably fettuccine Alfredo. "Are you sure? We could just
have some burgers at the bar."

"Um . . ."

"Soy burgers, whatever." He sounded exasperated.

I glanced at the bearded man, who was inhaling his
beer. A barmaid worked the taps under the sad-eyed aegis
of a decapitated deer. "I don't think they serve soy here. It
doesn't bleed enough."

But Hunter was already walking over to the bar. The
barmaid, the bearded man, and about a dozen shadowy
shapes watched him as he sat down on a stool by the
counter with the studied unself-consciousness of a journalist on location.

The barmaid, a strawberry blond in her twenties, continued filling a mug of beer. "Drinking or eating?"

Hunter looked at me, pointedly. I walked over to him,
feeling like an obedient dog—heel, girl—and he turned
back to the barmaid.

"Both."

She handed us menus. "Don't worry, ma'am. We have
veggie burgers. Right here." One sharp pink fingernail
pointed it out. I blushed a little, realizing she'd been listening in on our disagreement.

Hunter smiled at her, and then at me. I could tell he

thought she was attractive. She had the bright, hard prettiness of a beauty contestant. "See, Abs, what'd I tell you. Now, uh—What's your name?"

"Kayla."

"Well, Kayla, we'd like two beers. Was that a Guinness you were pouring? A Guinness, then. And something light for her."

Kayla slanted a look at me, thinking things over. "Amstel okay?"

I agreed that it was. She served it with an afterthought of lemon. Hunter's Guinness was much more of a production and involved a lot of angling of the mug beneath the tap, bringing the foaming head to the point of disaster, letting it settle, bringing it back to the tap again. In order to serve it without spilling, Kayla leaned way over, her breasts brushing the counter.

Hunter ordered a bacon burger, "so rare it's still got some moo," and I ordered a veggie burger and fries. We looked around us before settling on watching the fire in the elaborately casual way of couples who have nothing to say to each other that will not start an argument. The bearded man beside me hunched himself over a little clay bowl and spooned chili into the general vicinity of his mouth.

"Dr. Barrow? Abra?"

I turned, so surprised at hearing my name spoken that I forgot the usual reflexive smile you give to people you're not sure you know.

It was Red the Wildlife Removal Operator, standing in what appeared to be the same dingy white T-shirt and jeans, holding a bottle of Budweiser by the neck and looking at me with more open warmth than I would have expected from a good old boy in a bar.

"What're you doing here? Hold on, now, you remember Jackie. Jackie, this here's the doctor that helped me out with Pia." He indicated the frowsy dyed blonde just behind him. I did not really remember her and understood from her smile that the feeling was mutual. She was wearing a pink airbrushed deer sweatshirt and smoking a cigarette between stiff fingers.

"Hi, Jackie."

"Hi."

"I'm Hunter. Abra's husband."

"Glad to meet you." We all shook hands with extreme awkwardness. Hunter and Red looked at each other, smiling in a way that didn't reach their eyes. I felt a prickle of tension at the back of my neck, the way I sometimes did when I put the wrong two dogs together at work.

"So, what're you doing in Northside?" Handshake over, Red hooked his left thumb into his belt loop. He was still facing Hunter, but I got the feeling he was speaking to me.

"Actually, what we're doing here is moving—we've just moved into Hunter's family's house."

"No kidding. Whereabouts?"

"It's the old farmhouse set back on Skunk's Misery Road."

"That so?" Red shook his head in a very cowboy way, and if he'd had a hat, I got the feeling he would have tipped it back. "Well, small world. That just about makes us neighbors."

Kayla arrived with Hunter's food and I tried not to watch her serve him, breasts flat against the counter. She handed Hunter his bacon cheeseburger, which was dripping blood onto his plate just as he had ordered.

"Ketchup?"

"Nah, just hides the flavor." He smiled at her. She smiled back.

"I'll get your veggie burger right away," she reassured me. I didn't ask why it had taken longer to cook than meat. Of course, Hunter's meat was almost raw.

Red put a hand on his girlfriend's shoulder. "Come

on, Jackie," he said. "We should leave these nice folks to eat in peace."

"Hang on a second. Didn't you just say you're my neighbor?" Hunter sounded casual as he took a bite of his hamburger, but his eyes narrowed. "As far as I'm aware, though, there aren't any houses near ours."

Jackie cleared her throat, her eyes darting back and forth between the two men. "Red's been building a house up in the woods by your house. Been working on it all summer."

"You're building your own house?" I suppose it made sense: Red had the look of the kind of man who wouldn't be able to tell you what the House Judiciary Committee was or who wrote *The Portrait of a Lady*, but who knew how to build a house from scratch, wire it for electricity, and install a septic system.

"Just a bit of a cabin."

Kayla the barmaid finally brought me my veggie burger, which was cold. She asked Hunter how he liked his hamburger and he gave her a thumbs-up. Then he turned back to Red, all trace of friendliness gone. "And just exactly where is your land?"

Red sketched a map with his finger in the air. "Here's you, here's Old Scolder Mountain. Up to the north here, behind your barn—"

"There isn't any barn."

"Yes there is, it's just gotten a bit swallowed up by the woods back there. You walk due north up your hill and back beyond the barbed wire, you'll see it—too run-down to fix now, though. Anyway, you go on up the hill—"

"In the forest?"

"Yup, you can walk it or if you've got a four-wheel drive you can use the road I've been clearing up till about here." Red wiggled a finger and then walked his pointer and index past the point of no return. "From there, you walk about a half a mile to the building site."

Hunter pushed his plate away and leaned back on his stool. "I thought that was still our land, all the way to the Murdock farm over on Oak Ridge."

"Well, now, when old man Murdock died last winter his kids sold me a parcel. Here, you got a pen? I'll show you on a napkin."

"You don't happen to have a survey map showing exactly what bit?"

I put my hand on my husband's shoulder. "Hunter—"

"I'm just curious. I thought there was three-acre zoning around here."

Red looked up from his napkin. "There is."

"Then I don't exactly understand where my land ends and yours begins."

I laughed, weakly. "God, Hunter, we've only just arrived here. There's no need to get so—so—"

"Territorial?" Hunter gave me a very unfriendly smile. An I'm-going-to-yell-at-you-in-private smile.

"Man's got a right to know which side of the fence to piss on." Red gestured with his chin, something between a nod and a bow. "I'll get you a map. I'll even walk you around the boundaries." He paused. "Tell you a little about the town, if you like. Some interesting folklore about Northside." This last seemed directed at me, but Hunter intercepted it.

"I'm not exactly a stranger, you know. My family and I spent summers here while I was growing up."

Red hooked his fingers into his belt loops. "Know where it got its name?"

Hunter made a dismissive gesture. "It was the north side of some settler's property, I guess."

"Nope." Red was clearly enjoying himself. "You know the old stone church at the edge of town? Well, the graveyard out back was getting awful crowded, 'cause all the townsfolk wanted to be buried out front, where the sun kept things bright. The poor and the evildoers got stuck on the north side—that used to be called the devil's side, you know. In fact, the church even has a door in the north wall, and they open it at baptisms and communions, to get rid of troublesome spirits."

Was I ever a long way out of Manhattan.. "So you're saying that the town got named after the bad end of the graveyard?"

"I guess it was kind of a bad town to begin with. I know for a fact that a bunch of so-called witches escaped here during the ruckus in Salem. Seems Northside has a long history of being desirable to the undesirables."

"It's true, you know," said Jackie. "My great-great-great-grandmother was accused in Ipswich, and she managed to get herself here." She smiled a little crookedly. "Seems the Ipswich witches never got quite the reputation the Salem ones did."

"Probably too hard to pronounce," I said, and Jackie laughed, an attractive, deep, smoky sound.

"Funny I never heard about all this before," said Hunter, patting his breast pocket for cigarettes.

"Well," said Red equably, "even some full-time residents don't know the history. But even nowadays, the town gets its share of unusual characters. Take the sheriff, for example—"

"Actually, I'd rather not." Hunter shook a cigarette out of its pack. "Small-town gossip doesn't interest me."

Red's mouth tightened fractionally, but he nodded with better grace than I could have mustered. "Sorry, friend, but you can't smoke in here. Used to be we got away with it, but nowadays we're health-code-compliant."

Jackie started to say something, but Hunter wasn't paying attention, and he spoke over her. "You sure do volunteer a lot of information—friend." He stuck his cigarette behind one ear, but his tone was borderline offensive.

"Which is just what we need," I cut in. "I feel completely at sea here, and I, for one, know nothing about the town." I gave Hunter a warning look. He was acting so boorish that I felt implicated: Oh, look, there's one of those wives who get browbeaten by their overbearing husbands. On an impulse, I turned back to Red and said, "Why don't we make it dinner. You can both come over"—I dipped my head to include Jackie—"and, uh, fill us in on the neighborhood." I didn't expect them to accept, but I figured the offer might make up for Hunter's belligerence.

There was a half-beat of silence. "Well," Jackie said. "That's nice of you to say, but . . ." She looked at Red for guidance. Red looked at Hunter.

"How's Friday sit with you?"

Hunter, who hated it when I invited people over without checking with him first, smiled with all his teeth. "Friday's fine by me. Abra's going to be doing all the work, anyway." He finished his Guinness and instantly Kayla was there, asking what else he needed. "Thanks, honey. Can I get another? Great."

I looked up and Red glanced away from me, as if he hadn't meant to be caught looking. "So it's a date? Friday?"

Again, his gaze danced away from mine. "If it's all right with Jackie."

"Fine by me." She sounded miserable. "But it really should be *me* inviting *you*. I sure owe you one. Seeing as how you helped sneak Pia out and all."

"How is she doing?" I thought about my glimpse of Malachy's laboratory, and my crazy dream of a wolf girl.

"She's acting kind of funny, actually. Scratching at herself. Her fur's coming off in clumps."

"I'd be happy to take a look at her," I offered, thinking with relief that it sounded like something I could treat with a shot of cortisone. "Just bring her over. I'm not working yet."

Red put his hand on my shoulder. "Now we're going to owe you two favors, Doc."

To my surprise, I didn't want to shrug off his hand. "Well, given the state of our house, I may just call on your services."

"Hey, Texas," said Hunter, abruptly shifting to a falsely hearty tone. "Quit flirting with my wife and have a beer." Hunter handed a bottle over to Red.

"Well, thanks." Red drank his beer as a bright tide of color washed over his cheeks and neck.

"Tell me something, Texas." Hunter took another swallow of beer, making Red wait. "Do I know you from someplace?" I wondered if my husband might be getting drunk, or if something else might account for this sudden shift in mood.

"Don't think so. No."

"Your eyes—there's something familiar about you. Hey, you don't have any relatives in Romania, by any chance?" Hunter took another bite of his burger, a thin trickle of juice escaping from the corner of his mouth. "I was just in Romania for three months, and you remind me of someone I met there."

"Family's pretty much all Irish, with a bit of Mohican and Mohawk thrown in on my mother's side." Those were New York tribes; I wondered how he'd come by his Texas accent.

Hunter shook his head. "It's the damnedest thing. You just remind me so strongly of—" He inhaled once, sharply. "Maybe it's just your cologne."

Red took a swallow of beer, set the bottle down. "Or maybe I just stink. You said you been in Romania lately?"

"Yes."

"Studying wolves?"

Now it was Hunter's turn to frown. "How'd you know that?"

Red tipped his head back to give Hunter a considering look. "Let's just say you have a certain—air about you. And what else is there to do in Romania? Adopt orphans or study wolves."

A little of the tension left Hunter's shoulders. "I guess."

"Not so many wolves around these parts. Coyotes, though. And bear."

"Do you trap them?"

Red nodded. "Sometimes."

"Kill them?" There was something aggressive in the question. I watched Jackie regarding my husband with trepidation.

"If I have to. Listen, Jackie, I think maybe you and I should be moving on." Red put his arm around Jackie's shoulders, and I felt an odd twinge of jealousy. It wasn't that I was jealous of Jackie for having Red, but rather that I wished I were the one whose man was being reasonable and protective.

"When do you have to kill wild animals, Red? When they wander into someone's backyard?"

"Hunter!"

My husband didn't look at me. "You ever kill a wolf, Red?"

"Once. Up in Canada."

"For any particular reason?"

"Yes, he was fixing to attack me." Red dropped his hand from Jackie's back and addressed Hunter in a flat, reasonable voice. "Listen, I understand that you being a wolf . . . researcher and all, you might have some prejudices against my profession. But I am not some deranged old Wild West trapper. My grandfather taught me the Mohawk way. I respect the wolf. I respect nature."

"Do you?" I watched Hunter and didn't understand

what he might be feeling. His question seemed loaded. I had never seen him take such an active dislike to anyone.

"Do you doubt it?" The two men held each other's gaze for a long moment, and then Red broke away to shake my hand. "Goodbye, Doc. Hunter. See you Friday."

Jackie smiled at me unhappily. Like me, she was probably wondering why Red had accepted the invitation. Doubtless, he viewed it as some sort of challenge. "You want me to bring anything, hon?"

"No, no, just yourselves."

I watched them walk away through the crowded bar, stopping once or twice to talk to people they knew on the way out. "Why were you acting like such an asshole, Hunter?"

Hunter took a long swallow of beer. "I thought he was interesting. That was a good idea, inviting them over for dinner." As Hunter put down the money for our meal, I felt another strange prickle of tension, the way I had when he and Red had first confronted each other. I looked up to see Hunter smiling at Kayla the barmaid. He'd left her a large tip.

Outside, I could smell the remnants of a light rain. Wisps of fog clung to the headlights of cars.

"Wow, look at that."

"Look at what?"

"The moon."

I squinted. "You can't see the moon tonight."

"Can't you?" Hunter unlocked the car and shrugged himself into the driver's seat. "Maybe I just feel it, then."

"So what's it feel like to you?"

"Feels like it's growing." I laughed, thinking he'd made a joke. But when I looked at him he wasn't smiling.

On the way home, the fog thickened until all we could see was the stretch of road directly in front of us. Hunter honked the horn an instant before I saw the doe leaping from the side of the road, ears pricked, eyes red marbles in the glare of our headlights. If it had been me driving, I probably would have hit it.

Hunter swerved around it as if he had known it was there all the time.

SEVENTEEN

◖◔○ There were small raccoons in the walls. Or enormous mice. Of course, the proper term for enormous mice is "rats," but I felt better not thinking about rats a few feet from my head while I slept. Not that I was sleeping much, as I lay in bed listening to the frantic skittering of busy rodents. The pitter-patter of little feet, I thought, but Hunter wasn't around to make the joke to: He was up in the attic, thinking deeply about wild Romania.

In the mornings I sometimes found little corpses near our porch: mice with long, thin noses. Voles? Moles? A squashed frog, one eyeball popped out. A tiny lump of heart, a threadlike trail of viscera attached. I cleaned them up, because my husband had always been the more squeamish of us.

"Hunter, did your family used to have a cat that got loose?"

"Not that I recall."

It was probably a feral cat. Or a neighbor's dog. I remembered hearing there were foxes around, even coyotes. But a wild creature wouldn't leave all the remains so close to human habitation, would it?

"A little project for you, Abs," Hunter said, pouring himself a cup of coffee. "Solve the mystery."

But it didn't bother me enough to want to set traps, so

I did nothing. I figured I could ask Red if there was anything painless I could do when he came to dinner. Like lay down a barrier of salt, or get a dog. I quite liked the idea of a dog, maybe even a puppy.

Hunter did not. "You'll be out working, and I don't want to be stuck here all day with some bulbous-headed, lop-eared, obsequious mutt for company."

That week I spent most of my time in the car, trying to get my bearings. It seemed to take me an hour to get anywhere on the winding, nameless back roads that meandered through endless cornfields and cow pastures. On a search for an electrician to wire the upstairs, I found a good used-book store and spent the next few days rereading books from late childhood: *James and the Giant Peach; The Lion, the Witch and the Wardrobe; Julie of the Wolves.*

But the nights seemed endless. We didn't have a TV in the bedroom. There was a small, old black-and-white console downstairs, but it didn't get anything other than one grainy station in Poughkeepsie. I found I missed the friendly blond newscasters and the weather maps, and I felt a little lost without even the possibility of stumbling onto an old movie at four in the morning.

Something about the size of the house intimidated me into staying in the bedroom, anyhow. I couldn't even bring myself to go downstairs to the kitchen to fix myself a bowl of cereal. On our sixth night, I made it halfway down the staircase before the creaking floors and ringing silence did me in. I went back up, then past the bedroom to the attic, where Hunter had been holed away for hours.

"Hunter?"

He looked up with a false smile. "Abra. How're you doing?" His gaze had returned to his computer.

"I'm . . . getting used to things. You coming down?" I tried to make it sound like an invitation.

"In a while." Hunter sighed and met my eyes again. "I am busy, Abs. You knew I would be when you agreed to this. I mean, I came here to work . . ."

"No problem," I said, already moving away. "I understand."

"In another week or so, when I've gotten into this project—"

"Sure, of course." I almost yelled the words at him, then went to our familiar bed in its alien setting and cried. There were other people's things in here: someone else's ugly oak dresser, someone else's fragile wicker chair. On the wall, a tattered sampler attested to some luckless child's skill with a needle. I sat up, drying my eyes, and the windowpanes rattled twice, hard. Storm coming. Growing up in Pleasantvale, I had looked forward to storms. They gave you an excuse to huddle inside with a book, free from the responsibility of having to play outside with others. Living in the city seemed to blunt the impact of most storms; Lilliana, who'd grown up in Manhattan, said she'd never been frightened of lightning, even as a child.

I pressed myself closer to the window and saw that the wind was whipping through the leaves, ripping some off their branches before they'd even had a chance to change.

I could hear the howl of it, because there were no cars, no voices, nothing else to drown out the wind. This was nothing like the suburbs. This was nature, raw and unsentimental, liable to reach down from the sky and zap you. I suddenly felt very vulnerable in my cotton nightgown with my bare feet cold on the wood floor.

Oh, now that was self-pity at its excruciating worst. That was the kind of melodramatic, whiny complaint that I would expect to hear from my mother. What was happening to me here? Opening up my closet, I slipped my feet into the furry Dalmatian slippers Lilliana had bought me as a leaving present and grabbed my baby blue terry-cloth robe off the door hook. I was not going to turn into some neo-Victorian neurasthenic. I was going to go down those stairs—creak, creak, creak; I pounded my feet down extra hard—and through that kitchen, and I was going to open that back door and walk the hell out into that dark and stormy night. Because I was not afraid of a little wind and rain. And then I was going to walk back into the kitchen, make myself a bowl of Corn Pops and milk, and I was going to eat it while watching the black-and-white weather in the living room. Because I was not afraid of some heavy old furniture.

There was a clap of thunder and the Victorian lights flickered in their sconces, but I just kept going, one furry slipper in front of the other.

The moment I opened the back porch door a gust of wet wind slapped me in the face. The next gust went in a slightly different direction. I stepped out under the overhang and lifted my chin so that I could feel the rain. And then I heard it, a howl above the howl of the wind and the crackle of electricity in the air. It was a high, clear, undoglike sound, and I realized, with a leap of excitement, that I was probably hearing a coyote.

And then I heard another howl, lower, stronger. No, not stronger. Closer. I looked up, back at the house, and realized that Hunter had stuck his head out the tiny attic window. It was a good wolf howl. That Magdalena woman had taught him well.

I went back inside and picked up the old black rotary phone to call my mother, but this was not Manhattan: The line was dead.

EIGHTEEN

◐○○ "Hope we're not too early, Doc," Red said the minute he walked in the door. His gaze flickered over me so quickly I almost thought I'd imagined it: down to green-sweatered breasts, back to eyes. I'd left my hair loose down my back and worn mascara. I could tell he approved.

"No, you're right on time." He kept his eyes on mine while I spoke, but it looked like he was making an effort. He was wearing an old sheepskin jacket that still had a lot of sheep left in it.

"Wanted to get going before the sun was down so I could walk you around the boundaries in a bit of light." As Red spoke, he kept glancing away, and I realized with some surprise that I could see a bright splotchy flush like a crude handprint on his cheek.

I'd made him blush.

"That sounds great. How are you, Jackie?" Red was helping his girlfriend out of her hideous horse-printed jacket. They had brought the cool fall air in with them, along with a strong smell of cigarettes.

"Doing fine. Here—for housewarming." She handed me a small package of guest soaps shaped like little lambs.

"Oh, thank you so much for thinking of that. Here, I'll take your coat." The cigarette smell had soaked into the wool; I moved it as far from my face as possible.

"Wow." Jackie looked around at the dark Victorian foyer with its green-and-yellow stained-glass window and whistled. "Always wondered what it looked like in here. Used to know Harvey, the old caretaker."

"So you were aware that this place is a mausoleum. Red? Can I take your coat?" He was sniffing the air distractedly. I wondered if something had gone wrong with the chili.

"Oh. Sure. I was just—do you have a dog?"

"No. Why do you ask?" I hung Jackie's coat up in the hall closet, wondering if he was going to tell me I needed one for protection.

"Because some people keep their animals penned up, you know, when guests come, but Jackie and I are really dog people, so there's no problem with us." Red removed his coat, revealing a flannel shirt with the sleeves rolled up over the bulge of his small, hard biceps. I could see only half of his coyote tattoo.

"Nope, no dog here," I said, hanging his coat on a hanger. "I haven't really had time to take care of one. Until now, of course. In fact, I've been thinking about getting one." I turned to Jackie. "You never brought Pia over," I said. "Is she getting better about not scratching?"

Jackie shook her head. "No, she's still itchy. And she can't seem to settle down at night. I thought about bringing her along today, but she gets so weird about new places and people, I figured I'd better leave her at home."

"Would you like me to come over and check her out?"

Jackie smiled, revealing a smear of lipstick on her front tooth. "I'd really appreciate it."

"Well, my veterinary skills are a bit more advanced than my cooking. I hope you guys like chili."

"Oh, no, it smells great. Just great. You know us Texans, we like our chili."

"I'm sorry if it's not quite right. I'm not used to cooking with meat. There's also one without."

"Oh, meat for me." Jackie smiled even more broadly, and there were deep lines in the leathery skin of her face. I found that I liked Red all the better for not caring that his girlfriend was not perfect or young.

"Another carnivore," I said. "Hunter will be thrilled. I'll go upstairs and tell him you're here."

"Anything else I can do while you're up there, Doc? Chili need stirring?"

"No, thanks, Red. Everything's taken care of."

Jackie pulled a pack of Marlboros out of her pocketbook. "Jeez, I can't quite recall the last time you offered to help *me* in the kitchen."

Red looked at the cigarette Jackie was lighting. "Maybe we should go on outside a moment with that, Jackie."

Jackie lifted her eyebrows. "All right, mind telling me what's got you turning into Mr. Manners?"

"Oh, listen," I said, "it's getting cold out: If you want to smoke in here, that's okay."

Red was looking at Jackie. "We don't want to impose."

"No, it's no—"

But Jackie wasn't looking at me, either. "No, no, I wouldn't dream of insulting our hosts." She slammed out the door. Red looked at me for a moment in silent apology before following her.

Well, this was going to be an interesting evening.

I hurried upstairs with the lamb-shaped soaps. I'd left Hunter in the clawfoot bathtub, but when I looked, he was gone, and a damp towel was flung over the toilet seat.

"Hunter? Hunter, they're here." He'd been so surly about having Red and Jackie over that I half-wondered if he'd gone back up to the attic to write. If so, I wasn't going to argue with him. But when I came downstairs, ready to make an excuse, Hunter was already out on the porch, smoking a cigarette with Jackie. He was standing with one hand braced against a support beam, looking muscular as he loomed over both our guests. He must have gone down the back stairs. He waved when he saw me, and I realized he was wearing a short-sleeved shirt.

"Hi, I was just checking to see where you—aren't you freezing in that?"

Hunter laughed, and I realized that Red had taken off his flannel shirt and was wearing short sleeves, too. Maybe it was a macho thing. "Tell you what, Abs," he said, taking another drag on the cigarette. "What we need is a drink to warm us up."

"Of course. Um, Jackie, what would you like? We have vodka, gin, um, I think there's some beer, red wine . . ."

"A Bloody Mary would be great."

I said I'd check if we had tomato juice. I started walking back into the kitchen.

"Abra."

I turned back to Hunter, who was smiling as if he'd just won a bet.

"Yes?"

"You forgot to ask Red what he wanted. And I'll have a gin and tonic."

"I'm sorry, Red. What can I get you?"

"Any old beer you have is fine for me, Doc. Can I help you bring stuff out?"

"If you like." I went into the kitchen feeling somehow diminished, as if I were a little girl pretending to be a hostess and I'd just been found out.

Red stood with a kind of muscular stillness and watched while I found the gin and vodka. "Can I help get the glasses?"

"Over there." I pointed and he opened a cabinet door, revealing nothing but plates. "I'm sorry. Maybe there. I'm still getting used to it here."

"Shh." He came up next to me, as if he were going to take me in his arms. I could feel the deep frown between my eyebrows turning into a headache.

"I'm just—it's all a little overwhelming. Moving. Don't worry, I'm not going to cry."

"All right."

I took a deep, sharp breath and Red moved and then checked himself. I could feel his yearning toward me like a magnetic field drawing me in. So this is what it's like, I thought, to see yourself larger than life in somebody else's eyes. What my mother had always known. What Hunter knew. I took another breath. "I'm okay."

A muscle flexed high in his jaw. "I can't. Touch you. He'll know."

"What do you—"

"I'd like to help you."

"I'm fine now," I said, turning my back to him. "I think the drinks stuff is over here . . ."

"Don't pretend. It's dangerous to pretend." Then he did touch me, taking my shoulders in his hands and gently turning me to face him. We stood there in silence. His hands were warm, almost hot. I felt a reluctance to move away, which was odd, because in general I'm not a touchy-feely sort of person. But he had a reassuring air of quiet calm: Despite the heat of him, I felt as if I could just sink into him, like a lake. I cleared my throat.

"I think you're imagining something that isn't—I'm not pretending anything."

"Aren't you? Things are exactly how they've always been between you and your—Hunter."

"That isn't really any of your business." The worst possible response: I might as well have said, Well, actually he's beating me and shackling me in the basement at night. "Look, I didn't mean that to sound the way it probably did. Hunter and I are fine."

"Good." His hazel eyes were set deep and almost triangular in their sockets, so that he looked pained even when he was smiling. "Glad to hear it. And you're right—it's none of my business. But you helped me. Back in the city."

"I didn't do much of anything."

"Still, I'm beholden to you. Pia is a very special animal." His hands were still on my shoulders. "And I think you're in a bit of trouble yourself, now."

"Look, we've just made a major life change and maybe I seem a little tense because of it. I'm sorry if my husband seemed a little edgy the other night, but he's probably feeling the tension, too." As I said this, something inside my temples pulled taut and began to throb.

"You think maybe I'm not seeing things as they are?" Red's fingers slid down my arms, and he shook his head. "Maybe."

"It's not that you're not an attractive man, Red, it's just that—well, you know. I'm married, and you're— you have Jackie." This was purely to spare his feelings: It seemed unfair not to make some noise about him being appealing on some level, after he'd made his own feelings for me so painfully apparent.

"Jackie's not my girlfriend. Hasn't been for a while."

I wonder if *she* knows that, I thought. "Oh. Well, good. So you're friends. Which is what I hope we can be— friends."

Red's chin snapped up. "You think I'm trying to say I've got some kind of *crush* on you?"

Now I could feel myself blushing, a burning on the back of my neck, my cheeks. "I'm sorry, I thought . . ."

Red laughed. "Hey, don't go all schoolgirl on me, Doc. I'm not saying I'm not attracted to you. 'Course I am. Just like you're attracted to me. But that's not what I've been trying to get at here . . ."

"I am not attracted to you!"

He raised one eyebrow.

"I don't mean to hurt your feelings, but I am not attracted to you."

Red stepped in, dipped his head, and breathed in once, hard. "Yep," he said. "You are."

The mounting tension in my head made it hard to concentrate. "Listen, I don't know what has given you the impression that I like you in that way, but I don't. You're a nice man, but—"

"Your head hurt?" Before I could move away, his hands had slipped up into my hair. The touch of his fingers against my scalp was perfect and precise as he located what must have been acupressure points. Suddenly I felt a burst of heat at the crown of my head, and then the pain was gone, and the flush swept down from my temples to my breasts, to my belly and groin. Without thinking, I leaned against him. His voice was no more than a whisper beside my ear.

"We have to stop this. Before he smells us."

What was he saying? It made no sense. But I no longer wanted to stop. It was as if Red were two steps ahead of me, knowing my reactions before I was aware of them myself. Was I attracted to him? I couldn't bring myself to pull away. I felt the fine tremble of his fingers. "Smells us?"

His fingers contracted in my hair.

"Are you expecting your period?"

"What? No!" I stepped away from him abruptly.

"You get these headaches often?"

What was he now, a doctor? "Not usually, no."

"Your husband getting headaches, too?"

"I don't think so. No." But would I know if he were? "Listen, thank you for the, ah, head rub, but I don't really need medical advice. If I do, I'll go to a doctor."

"If you've got what I think you've got, I don't think the doctor's gonna be much help to you."

I put my hands on my hips, suddenly angry. "And what do you think I have?"

"Well, for starters, an unfaithful husband."

My heart gave an uncomfortable little flip. There was

no way he could know that. "He was just flirting with that barmaid." I turned away from him, opened the cabinet, and took down four glasses. "That doesn't mean anything."

"Okay, fine, have it your way," Red said. "But in about two weeks, you'll be calling me in for help."

I took the unopened bottle of tomato juice and a bottle of tonic out of the cupboard. "I have no idea what you're talking about."

"Only thing is, by then it won't be so easy to deal with."

I fixed Red with a look that would have stopped even my mother. "What won't be?"

"Your little wildlife removal problem."

It took me a moment to make the connection. Then I remembered that I had planned on asking Red what could be done about the visits from the local fox or whatever it was that was leaving little gifts of viscera on my doorstep. "How did you know I have a problem?"

Red looked at me carefully. "What's it been? Small stuff? Mice? Voles?"

"Yesterday there was a baby rabbit."

"Anything inside the house?" His voice was sharp, almost angry.

"No, but I wanted to ask you if there was anything I could do. Short of laying traps. I don't want to kill anything."

Red rubbed his jaw. "Christ." He sounded frustrated.

"Well, I'm sorry, but I don't."

"Look, if you want my help, you can't set conditions. You have to let me decide what has to be done."

"Then forget it," I said, pouring a measure of gin into a glass. I wasn't giving up any more control. "It's no big deal, anyway."

"Maybe." Red moved so that his arms were braced on the wall, trapping me between them. "And maybe it's bigger than you think, Doc. Sometimes small prey are just the beginning. Like if it's a—a young bobcat or coyote, just learning how to hunt." Held captive, I stared up into Red's face and felt an unfamiliar sense of power. I could let him kiss me, I thought. I could let him touch me, press himself against me, I could let him do anything and everything and I would still remain the one in control.

Acting on impulse, I bent and took a nip of his hard bicep. He sucked in a sharp breath. "I don't like traps and poison, Red." I ducked under his left arm and reached for the red wine. "If we have a predator around, I'll get a dog." I struggled with the cork and it got stuck with the corkscrew halfway in. So much for my woman-of-the-world act. But my hands were still shaking. I couldn't believe that I'd just bitten the man.

"Here, let me do that." Red took the bottle and uncorked it with three twists of his wrist. He poured it for me as well, with a waiter's precision. I wondered if he'd worked tables at some point in his life. "Listen, Doc, don't think adopting some cute little puppy is going to solve anything. One morning you'll wake up and instead of dead squirrels and mice, you'll find Fido belly up and missing a few organs."

For a moment, as I sliced a lemon for the Bloody Mary, I thought of telling Red about Hunter's condition. But even if, theoretically, some people infected with the lycanthropy virus could change into wolf form—something I found hard to swallow—and even if my husband proved to be one of the rare cases, he was still my husband. I'd known Hunter since we were just on the cusp of adulthood. I'd known him drunk and sober, elated and morose, at his best and at his worst. I knew that no matter how disinhibited by alcohol or illness, he wouldn't do anything to hurt me.

Keeping my voice very even, I said, "And why are you

so sure that it's not just a fox or some neighbor's cat?" I added a dash of Tabasco to Jackie's drink.

"Because it doesn't *smell* like fox or cat, that's why."

Jesus, him and the smells again. I'm not a great nose, myself. To me, the wine in my glass smelled of fruit and old socks, as all wine does to me, no matter what they say about a faint aroma of plums and wood smoke and an aftertang of vanilla.

"So I won't get a dog," I said, stirring Hunter's gin and tonic. "And if the baby rabbits start turning into lambs and fawns, I'll call you."

Red shook his head, opened his mouth, then closed it. "Fine. Have it your way. But do me a favor: Contact me before the bodies start piling up."

I took a sharp breath, then, because it seemed to me that Red knew exactly what he was talking about. Or rather, whom he was talking about. "Until then, it's not your problem, okay?"

"Maybe not," he said, "but things are about to change." I emptied a jar of nuts into a bowl and handed Red a bottle of beer from the fridge, along with Jackie's Bloody Mary. He walked out of the kitchen, so skinny in his stiff new jeans that I felt a moment's distaste: What had I been thinking, and why had I bitten him like that?

It wasn't until I followed him out onto the porch that I recognized the tune he was whistling under his breath: *Peter and the Wolf.*

NINETEEN

◐○○ It was getting embarrassing. Every two minutes, it seemed, Hunter stopped, stepped behind a tree, and relieved himself.

"And so you're saying that just beyond the tree line there is one boundary? Hold on a moment." Hunter's hand was already at his fly.

"Hunter," I hissed. "This is the third time. Can't it wait?"

But his back was to me. "Must be all that coffee I had while I was writing," he said, up against a fir tree. "Sorry." Beyond him the woods dipped into a valley, spread out into cornfields, climbed into the soft lavender blur of the Catskill Mountains.

"Hunter," I said, sounding like somebody's maiden aunt, but by then he'd come back.

Hunter paused. "You're not offended, are you, Jackie?"

"Long as it's not on my rosebushes, you can do whatever you like, wherever you like."

Hunter beamed at her, full-frontal charming.

"Actually," Red said, "maybe I'll take a moment, too." He walked a little ways off from all of us, right about where Hunter had been, and I found myself thinking about what he was doing. I felt Jackie watching me.

"Men," she said.

"Marking their territory."

"Hey," said Hunter, "it's not like I'm peeing on some-body else's lawn. A man has a right to pee on his own land, doesn't he?"

Jackie and I laughed at that.

Red came out from behind the trees. "What's so funny?"

Jackie lit a cigarette. "You guys acting like a couple of dogs."

"Well, hell, I won, then. Last dog to pee on the tree owns it."

Hunter came up to clap Red on the shoulder. He was a good head taller. "Try to tell that to the tax man."

Red cocked his head back to meet the younger man's eye. "Maybe I'll just bite him."

"That sounds like tempting fate."

"Well, fate's a bitch, and you can't let her run you."

"Oh, look, Abra," said Jackie, flicking her ash, "an-other pissing contest."

"Come on, you guys, before it gets dark."

We walked. The air began to buzz with insects and the sun gentled and dipped. As we got deeper into the woods, nearer Red's house, the shadows darkened and multi-plied, and the mosquitoes hummed their approval.

"I'm getting eaten up," I complained.

"You should try smoking," said Jackie.

"Mosquitoes don't like cigarettes?"

"They like pot, though." Red smiled, his teeth a flash of white.

"I used to walk here when I was ten or so," Hunter said. "I'm sure this is Barrow land."

"Sh." Red froze. "Deer."

I couldn't see anything in the dappled twilight. "Where did you see—"

There was a thrashing in the underbrush somewhere above us.

"Wow," I said. "How many was that?"

"Three."

I turned to Hunter, his eyes still focused on something I could not see. "That's incredible. How could you see that?"

"That's what Magdalena was teaching me. Tracking."

"What were they? Could you tell?"

I watched as Hunter looked past Red, considering. "Two does? A fawn?"

"Very good." Red's voice held a note of respect. "Somebody taught you well."

We walked in silence for another two minutes, until I stumbled over a rock. The sun was sinking behind us, and I realized how dark it was getting. "You know, it's getting a little hard to see."

"Ow," said Jackie, walking into a thorn. "Can't you boys do this in the morning?"

There was a rustle in the leaves, and both men turned to it.

"Raccoon," said Hunter.

"Fox," corrected Red.

"I've had it." Jackie started stomping off down the hill, tripped, then set off again. "Goddamnit," she said as she slid on something and fell with a thump.

"You'd better follow her," I told Red, in case he had any idea of continuing on with Hunter.

Red looked at me. "I guess." He loped ahead, catching up with Jackie in four paces. I saw their shadows touch: Presumably, he had taken her hand.

I stumbled a bit myself as I walked through the darkening woods, though I couldn't help but notice that I didn't trip half as often as Jackie. Or that when I did, Hunter was not around to help me catch my balance.

His footing was perfect, and in a few short strides, he was gone, leaving me to pick my way home on my own.

TWENTY

◐ ○ ○ All through dinner Hunter drank too much and interrupted me. Red would look at me and say, "How do you like the country?" and before I could get my mouth open, Hunter would jump right in.

"Oh, you have to understand that Abs is a suburban girl. Nature, to her, means a quarter of an acre of lawn and a problem with raccoons. This is all a bit overwhelming, isn't it, sweetheart?"

Or else Jackie would compliment the chili, and Hunter would start in on all the many lentil and tofu dishes he had suffered through over the years, and how nobody ever talked about how a healthy diet made you pass gas like a leaky fuel tank, and how goddamn healthy was that to breathe in, he'd like to know.

There was a moment when I realized that I would have done better to have gotten drunk myself: I would then not have had to sit and notice the expressions on Red's and Jackie's faces. I had lost face that evening; I was a wife with a disrespectful husband and now everyone knew it. Halfway through the dinner I also realized that I had somehow served myself a bowl of the meat chili and began to break out in a nauseated sweat. Dead flesh. I had eaten a corpse. I'd probably catch mad cow disease and die, a twittering idiot with a sponge for a brain. I pushed my half-empty bowl away from me.

"Let me help clear," said Red, and working at opposite ends of the table, we began to stack the dishes and carry them into the kitchen. With the evidence gone I began to feel better. Hunter and Jackie were deep in some discussion from which I caught the words "thigh," "breast," and "hormones" and the sentence "Letting it hang for a while to get really ready." I had thought they were discussing meat production, but it sounded an awful lot like they were talking about sex. As I walked into the kitchen, I realized that Jackie, though not pretty, possessed a certain air of sexual confidence a man might find attractive.

"You okay?" Red asked as I deposited the silverware in the sink. He had already started washing the disgustingly encrusted chili pot.

"Yes, fine. Leave that and I'll serve the fruit."

Red's eyebrows pulled together. "Hang on, are you going to throw up?"

I didn't really know. My headache had returned. I closed my eyes for a moment and felt Red's hand on the back of my neck.

"Okay, not doing too good. Let's get you outside." He led me onto the porch, where the air had turned blessedly cool. I took a deep breath and felt marginally better. Red was fumbling with something that rustled in his hand.

"What are you doing?"

"Rolling you a joint. For the nausea."

I had never smoked marijuana. In fact, I had a bit of a phobia about drugs, after a bad experience as a child during one of my parents' wild parties. But something about Red made me feel safe, and I was flattered that he thought of me that way, as someone unquestionably counterculture.

"Here. Just a drag or two."

"I don't think so."

"Sorry, Doc. I didn't meant to—shoot, I always forget

how most people feel about weed. My grandfather always thought this stuff was safer than alcohol, so long as you didn't use it more than once every few months. He thought it helped get into a certain kind of trance state, and . . . I'll just put this out."

"No," I said, grabbing his wrist. "Wait. Is it strong? I once ate a tab of LSD by mistake and . . ." I shivered at the old memory. "I don't like losing control."

"This here's no stronger than a glass of wine. I grew it myself." He held it out and I took a drag, inhaling the distinctive, sweet smell and it was just like eleventh grade with the four of us sitting in Josie's bedroom, two girls and two guys, except Fred and Shawn weren't guy-guys, they were members of the science club, like me. In February they had discovered pot, which they said made everything so very slow and funny, and stopped you thinking about tests and senior year and colleges. It also gave Josie terrible munchies. She had started to gain the weight that would stop her from sleeping with almost every boy she met.

I had never been tempted. I had remained an outsider, even among the outsiders.

"Hey, Doc," said Red, "you okay?"

I handed the joint back to him and wandered out onto the cool grass. There were a lot of stars out there: They looked fake, too brilliant and numerous, like something you might see in the Planetarium right before the lasers and "Freebird" started playing. I walked over to a large oak, then knelt down at its trunk. Red came to sit down beside me.

"What are you thinking?"

My mouth was too dry. "That it's getting cold out here."

"That's what the animals are thinking, too." Red took another long pull on the joint, then offered it. I declined. "Lie back, if you want."

"The grass is too cold." My tongue felt like it had been coated in something gluey.

"Use my arm."

I laid my head back on his arm, my heart pounding. I knew I was misbehaving, but I didn't care. Red had said that Jackie wasn't his girlfriend, so I wasn't being unfair to her. And wasn't I entitled to this small taste of another man's company, since my own husband had helped himself to so much more of another woman?

There was a three-quarter moon, its missing quadrant a thin membrane of mauve, like the shadow beneath someone's eye. There were so many stars I could see the patterns they made—not the constellations, I didn't know those—but triangles, cat's cradles, webs of light.

"What animal do you see up there? Right there, above you?" Red pointed, and for a moment I stared at his arm, rounded with muscle, steady, thick-wristed, with long, rough fingers that looked capable and strong. Then I looked back up, but I was aware of him now.

"I don't know. A dog? There's its mouth." I pointed, then let my hand fall. I wanted him to take my fingers and warm them. I wasn't thinking clearly.

"Dog or wolf?"

"Dog, I guess. Wolves are bigger, aren't they?" I turned on my side. His face, not as handsome as his body, was close to mine.

"Mostly." Our eyes were so close now that when I tried to look at him, his features began to blur. "My grandfather would have said the animal you see is your helper."

"Is there a big difference between wolf and dog?" His skin seemed to radiate warmth.

"The Mohawk think so."

"What's your animal?"

Red looked as though he were making up his mind about something. "Can't you guess?"

"Fox?"

"No."

I thought about it. Something clever and resourceful. But trustworthy. "I can't come up with anything. You're kind of a mixture of things." Animals in legends were either clever or honest. You never got both in the same creature.

"That's what my grandfather said." Half in shadow, Red's long, high-cheekboned face seemed different somehow. His nose was very big from this angle, and I told him so.

"Is it?" He caught my hand. "What else do you see?"

Triangular eyes, deep set, hazel gold even in the dim light from the porch. A faint sheen of down high on his cheek. If I let my eyes go out of focus, he almost looked as if he were wearing a stylized animal mask. Dizzy, I let my head fall back on his arm. "Mmm," I said, meaning to say something more like, God, that pot hit me hard. I felt myself drift a little, in the cool whirling night next to a surprisingly warm body, beneath the twinkling dogstars. I could feel the rapid rise and fall of Red's chest, as if he were panting.

"And what exactly is going on here?"

I looked up to see a great shaggy bearlike figure looming over me, and gave one of those embarrassing short screams you can't keep from making when surprised, even after you know who it is that just startled you.

"I think I fell asleep," I said, which was almost true. I realized how bad this must look. Jackie's expression was sour and closed, but Hunter's was oddly amused, as if he'd caught me in some silly drunken pratfall. His stubble was so dark he looked like he'd grown a beard in the short time we'd been outside.

"I was just telling Jackie that this is where we find you guys in each other's arms." Hunter held out his hand to help me up.

"You caught us just before the mad, passionate rolling-around part got started," Red said, and Jackie snickered.

"In your dreams, Red. This girl's too smart for a scruffy old hound like yourself." There was a note of satisfaction in Jackie's voice.

Red grinned at me. "They don't believe me."

I made myself smile back. "Gee, I wonder why." And, of course, put like that, it did sound highly improbable. But not impossible. Would there have been a rolling-around part? I could tell from Red's elaborate air of relaxation that he thought he knew the answer. But did I?

Hunter slung his arm over my shoulders. "Come on," he said, "let's say good night to these folks and get you to bed."

I don't remember them leaving. I don't remember going upstairs. All I can recall, in blurred snatches, are memories of what came after. Naked in the darkened room on the bed with Hunter kneeling on the floor beside me, his hair cool and slippery between my fingers, his teeth sharp against my inner thighs, his mouth a shock of intimate heat. His rubbing his face against me like an animal covering itself with scent; his surging up to cover me, penetrate me, then withdrawing and crouching down again, as if truly meaning to devour me, as if this were where his hunger had truly led him.

Drunk and stoned and drifting through it all, I forgot to worry that this was something he was doing for my benefit, I forgot to care about him becoming put off by something I did. For the first time since we'd moved, my husband was making love to me. Pushing myself against him, I rode the lapping waves of pleasure until they crested, became pain, then built slowly to pleasure again.

Just before sleep, I curled my arms around him as he moved inside me, and imagined it was Red, imagined it was some stranger, because the play of muscles beneath my palms seemed fluid, seemed to ripple in and out of its familiar forms, as if sex had unloosed Hunter down to his bones.

And in my dreams, I think, he took me again.

TWENTY-ONE

◑◯◯ The next day, Hunter acted as if I'd been rather cute, drinking too much and actually smoking grass. A regular bohemian.

By suppertime the joke had worn thin. "I still can't believe you fell asleep on a guest," he said. "Not that I think Red minded too much. I don't need to start worrying about that guy, do I?" We were sitting at a table in Moondoggie's, waiting for the pretty strawberry blond waitress to serve Hunter's loco steak and my vegetarian wrap.

"You don't need to worry," I said, just as Kayla arrived—I remembered her name just as she warned Hunter his dish was hot. She dimpled, he winked, and I wanted to throw the pitcher of beer on the pair of them. Of course, Hunter wasn't worried. I knew my husband well enough to surmise that all his light, chuckling good humor was masking a gut-deep relief that I'd been caught in a somewhat compromising position, as if that exonerated his own betrayal.

I wanted to confront him, tell him that thought and action were two entirely different things, but of course, I couldn't, not without him questioning just what was going on with Red. And I didn't know what was going on there. I'm not sure I wanted to know: As long as I didn't need to examine myself too closely, I could keep my knowledge that there was a man in the background, desiring me. Maybe there was a little bit of my mother in me, after all, because I didn't want to give that up. I didn't want to pursue it, but I didn't want to lose it either.

I excused myself to go to the ladies' room, then stared at myself in the mirror. There were dark circles under my eyes. Compared with Kayla, I looked ancient. I reapplied some light rose lipstick and emerged to find our waitress pressing something into Hunter's hand.

I didn't say anything until we were in the car. "What did she give you, her phone number?"

"She was giving me change."

"Change from what?"

"Christ, you've become a bore. You know how much I hate this sort of thing." Hunter flipped on the radio and Mick Jagger sang about how some Siamese cat of a girl was under his thumb.

I turned my face to the window. I was angry; he was angry. We didn't speak for the rest of the ride. In fact, we barely saw each other for the rest of that week, as he disappeared upstairs to write his book and I went off in search of a veterinary practice that did not require its practitioners to be familiar with the south ends of cattle and horses.

"In my day, young lady," said one grizzled local vet, "you didn't become a vet unless you had large animal expertise. Until a few years ago, we turned you city kids back if you couldn't stick your hand up a cow blindfolded and tell which month she was in." I went along on one house call and had a horse step on my foot. No one asked if I was all right, and the owner just kept saying, "You're damn lucky she didn't kick you." The Northside vet, who could not move the left side of his face, muttered something about my not being "right for this sort of a practice" and added, under his breath, something about "silly girls who would break like matchsticks." I considered suing him for sexual discrimination, but then had second thoughts when I noticed that he was missing three of the fingers on his right hand, and that one of his eyes was made of glass.

As I was leaving, a trim gray-haired woman walked in carrying a large birdcage. The cage was covered by a black cloth, and whatever was inside was making a strange cackling noise, sounding more like an old witch than a bird. The woman gave me a furtive look as I passed her on my way out, and the moment I was outside, all the shades were drawn shut. Perhaps it was an owl, I thought, feeling curious. But it hadn't sounded like any owl I'd ever heard.

It seemed that all my training and work at the Animal Medical Institute were deemed interesting but useless, somewhere between having the dubious cachet of owning a designer T-shirt and the equally dubious advantage of speaking Italian. That is to say, an asset in Manhattan, pointless in Northside.

I was told I could volunteer at a local animal shelter until something opened up—had I ever heard of Beast Castle?

"That's not local," I pointed out. "That's nearly back in the city."

Unspoken, but clear nevertheless, was the sentiment that that's where I belonged, too.

In Manhattan, I would have known how to distract myself—taken walks, window-shopped, gone to the movies. In the country, these things seemed like possibilities, if distant ones, but I couldn't bring myself to actually pursue them. Nevertheless, after four days of consecutive rejection, I decided to give myself a day off from the job search. I went out into the garden and watched chipmunks argue amongst themselves. I drank cup after cup of coffee. I listened to the wind rustle the trees, knocking off the last few crab apples. I considered calling Lilliana, but when I picked up the receiver, I got a busy signal. The electrician and telephone guy had come to wire the upstairs, and now Hunter claimed to be doing research through the Internet. I say "claimed" because he was suspiciously secretive, hiding the screen when I came into the room.

I went back into the kitchen and for fifteen minutes I did nothing but stare at the dust motes dancing in the air, until I realized I had better start with something closer to home. Like unpacking.

The truth was, besides a few articles of clothing and toiletry, I hadn't really moved into our new house. And it had been almost a month—long enough for me to see how little old ladies wound up living in labyrinths of old magazines and empty soda bottles. I was more than a little overwhelmed by the prospect of unpacking boxes of books and clothes and old college papers and possibly the skeletal remains of a woolly mammoth—God only knew what Hunter had buried under a top layer of bubble plastic and tissue paper.

In those last weeks in the city, while I'd been at work, Hunter had packed our apartment as if the secret police were pounding at the door, indiscriminately throwing my medical textbooks in with his thrillers, my underwear with his sneakers. The guys from Samson Movers had answered a last-minute emergency cry for help and had done a slightly better job, wrapping each dish in white paper, pointing out in contemptuous Middle Eastern accents that even a weight lifter cannot move five boxes filled with thirty hardbacks each.

For the first few weeks I had emptied a few boxes at a time, usually getting lost in college papers and childhood photos so that hours passed in a fugue of nostalgic depression.

But here I was now, on the outs with Hunter, jobless

and without immediate prospects, miserable to the point where the next step down was sure to be a doozy of a drop. So it was time to buck up, pull in the reins, get moving. There was no dignity in my wallowing around in regret, living like a refugee. Besides, it was altogether too Piper LeFever. I was Abra Barrow: practical, sensible, methodical.

I turned to confront the battalion of boxes in the spare bedroom.

I made three piles—throw out, file, and ask Hunter, when I came across a file marked "Old Letters From Hunter" (my handwriting). There was correspondence from our earliest phase of dating:

My Sensual Nun,

I am imagining you in the Science Library, all neat and tidy in something with lots of buttons up the front, reading up on your anatomy in one of the big leather chairs while hordes of nervous freshmen lust for you from afar. How I long to distract you.

As for myself, I am discovering why it is imperative to break in hiking shoes before the big trip. Did you know ticks seem to prefer pubic hair? For the first night here, I just thought I was growing new moles.

In any case, my tulip, remember to use the lotion I gave you for your little hands and feet, and then give your wonderful pert breasts a massage, too, and imagine it is me.

I will be popping blisters, and wishing I could call.

                              Much love, Hunter

P.S. It is actually quite strange being alone for all this time. You don't quite realize how much of your mind and time you fill with conversation, whether real or fictional (books, television), until you have to contend with real silences.

And there was a letter which, from the date, was something Hunter had written but never sent me from Romania:

Abra,

This trip has been one of the most astonishing, heart-wrenching, painfully wonderful experiences of my life. I wish I could find a way to make you understand the change this time in Transylvania has wrought in me, but how can I talk about a transformation that is still taking place? Magda, the senior wolf researcher here, says that this fever is something which I must allow to pass, but I know in my heart that I can never return to the banality of the life I led back in New York.

Which leads me to the difficult task of asking you to call ~~our accountant~~

There was also a note, in a strong, sloping, European hand:

Remember not to rush the change. Give it the autumn. Possibly even the winter. Then call me when you are sure.

I didn't need a signature to guess who'd written it, or when. Magda. The other woman who, Hunter assured me, was not the reason for his strange moods, his sudden desire to move to the country. The other woman who had seized hold of my husband's imagination and held it still.

Call me when you are sure.

He hadn't chosen me over her. He hadn't even chosen Northside over Romania. This Magda had told him to wait, until, presumably, she could judge just how much of a wolf he was. And like an obedient dog, he was waiting.

Heart pounding, I put the letters back in the file, replaced them inside a box, and stood up, the blood leaving my face in a rush. I walked out into the garden and realized that autumn was already past its peak: Last night, while I'd been sleeping, a strong wind must have blown all the red and yellow maple leaves off their branches. I walked up the hill past the torn barbed-wire fence, the air cool even through my light oatmeal sweater. Prickles caught on my black wool skirt as I made my way through the tall grasses, and I felt the tears on my cheeks as I walked higher and higher on the hill, the sky soft and gray with clouds.

I am good with directions, even when I don't admit to myself that I know where I'm going. My feet found the path Red had shown us, no longer shrouded in shadow because it was early in the day and the trees were growing bare. I trudged along the carpet of leaves and pine needles until I saw the cabin we had not reached, a rough log structure set slightly off the ground. Please be home, I thought. Red was the only person I could imagine talking to who would not make me feel like a fool. When someone wants you, they do not look at you with pity.

I walked up to the door, knocked three times. No reply. I knocked again, said "Hello?" Then tried turning the knob. Red's door was unlocked, but as I walked in, I saw that he wasn't home.

You learn a lot about a man from seeing where he lives. Hunter's dorm room in college had been so bare that it hardly seemed anyone lived there at all. And, of course, he hadn't—Hunter had made his home in other people's dorm rooms. Red's cabin was much the same: a bachelor's abode, minimally furnished. I got the feeling most of Red's living was done elsewhere. There was a bed, covered with a woven Indian blanket, and a game of solitaire laid out on a plain pine table with two chairs.

There was a sheepskin rug and a small CD player, a milk-crate bookcase with a few old Elmore Leonard westerns, a small camping stove and a few cans of beans. I turned on the CD player and J. J. Cale sang in his grizzly voice that he might not be able to read or write, but he could make love to me all night long. Sounded pretty good to me.

I heard a sound and whirled around, but there was no one there, just the creaking door opening and closing in the breeze. I sat down on Red's bed and there was a musty, unwashed lanolin smell from the wool blanket or the sheepskin rug. Funny how much wet wool can smell like a big dog.

I wished Red were here. I suppose I wanted comfort. Advice. A sop to my ego. I wanted to be wanted. But Red was off somewhere, removing wildlife, or making Jackie happy.

Still sitting on his bed. I leaned over and saw that, along with the westerns, Red's bookshelf held *North American Medicinal Herbs, Call of the Wild*, and *Cosmopolitan*. Hmm. I opened the magazine—it was September's issue—and saw that it was bookmarked to the article "Why Good Girls Like Bad Boys." The subtitle, which Red had underlined in red Magic Marker, was, "He's kind, sincere, even wants a commitment—so why does he bore you to *tears*?"

Poor Red. The answer was right there in the bookcase—one dog-eared copy of Jack London's classic, one herbal textbook, and a lot of yellowing "man's got to do what he's got to do" novels. He was a beef jerky and white briefs kind of guy. And while I knew I wasn't exactly sophisticated myself, I knew the difference between single malt scotch and Tennessee whiskey, the difference between columnist and essayist, between an elegant transition and a quick dissolve. I wanted to be loved, yes, but I also wanted a man who wouldn't need the end of the movie explained if it didn't end with the hero walking off into the sunset, bad guys vanquished, girl in tow.

Red was clearly in the category of Jack Daniel's and columns on the fine sport of fishing, jump cuts and sunsets, everything pretty as it faded off into the long distance shot. Maybe if he'd been Hunter's age or even younger, I'd have felt otherwise: He'd have had time to change, grow, mature differently. But despite that surprisingly boyish air he had at times, Red seemed to be in his late thirties, maybe even older. He caught vermin for a living, and he lived without electricity. You just can't *Cosmo* obstacles like that away.

I put the magazine down the way I'd found it and noticed, for the first time, the bows and arrows in the corner. They looked metal-tipped and serious, like something you'd use to take something down, not to shoot at a target. I didn't see anything else that looked like a trap, or like poison, which surprised me. How did Red make a living if all he used was a bow and arrow?

I took one last look around and saw something peculiar: The game of solitaire was laid out in a sort of shield pattern, and the playing cards were painted with animal faces. They looked like the tarot deck my mother had used. There were some of the same animals she'd seen in my spread—owl, coyote, wolf, and also something that looked like a wild turkey. Boy, I hoped that wasn't me. What had she said? Owl, coyote, wolf—magic coming my way, something about coyote the trickster and wolf the guide.

Wouldn't you know that the first man to flirt with me would turn out to be as nutty as my mother?

I felt guilty leaving without writing a note—it made it seem as if I'd been spying. But I didn't see anything to write a note with, so I removed a dog card from the pack and laid it on Red's pillow before smoothing the blanket back down. I hoped Red wouldn't mind that I'd been there, but at least this way I wouldn't be deceiving him about anything.

God, I hated deception. I walked back down the hill, calm enough now to have a fight.

TWENTY-TWO

◐○○ There is one sure way to find out who has more power in a relationship. Start a fight. Start a fight with all the righteous grievance on your side. See if your partner, who should be cringing and apologizing, or at the very least listening, winds up going on the offensive and attacks you for invasion of privacy and a lack of trust, and then accuses you of transferring your own feelings of insecurity over not having a job onto the relationship. Then, when you try to bring the conversation back around to his behavior, see whether or not your partner cuts off your response by saying, "I'm just too mad to finish this right now." If you find yourself looking at your partner's departing back, your rage turned into a deep, painful, roiling unhappiness, then guess what? He's top dog.

I walked upstairs to the attic and informed Hunter that I had found the letters. He heaved a deep sigh and half-turned in his chair. On his computer screen I could see an instant message from someone.

"Oh, God, we're not starting that again, are we? Christ, Abs, maybe you should go back to the city and go back to the Institute. You really are falling apart out here."

"I can't go back." My voice was a whisper.

"Then go find something else. Do something before

you drive both of us crazy, sitting around the house all day long."

"I haven't just been sitting around."

"You didn't even start unpacking the boxes till today, you don't have a job, you don't cook—"

"I'm looking for a job, in case you haven't noticed, and I cooked last night, but you said you didn't want—"

"I mean cook real food."

I took a deep breath. "Listen," I said, "we are not talking about what I am or am not doing. I came up here to discuss those letters. And Magda."

Hunter nodded slowly, as if hearing something he had always suspected proven true. "I know what this is. This sudden lack of trust, this new need to be in my face twenty-four hours a day. You've lost your own direction. But you're going to have to work this out for yourself. You can't hang on to me every second, hoping I can give your life purpose."

"Hunter, that is completely unfair! I found a letter you wrote that seems to be telling me to contact our accountant. Were you thinking about divorce? What exactly happened in Romania? I think this is something we ought to discuss."

"Fine. You stay here and discuss it. I'm heading out." Hunter quickly saved the files on his computer and pressed the button to shut it down.

"No," I said again, louder, standing up. "You are not going to Moondoggie's to flirt with that waitress again."

Hunter's face began to flush with color. His eyes glittered darkly. "You are really intent on pissing me off today, aren't you?"

"So you think this is all my fault?"

"I've had enough of this shit, Abra."

"No, I have!" I ran out the door in front of him, my heart pounding so hard I could barely think. I half-expected him to grab me as I raced down the half-finished stairs from the attic, but he must have been too surprised.

At the bottom, I stopped and glanced up. Hunter was leaning over the railing, looking at me as if he were seeing a madwoman. "Abra, what the hell are you doing?"

"Taking the car before you do." I walked outside without taking a coat, knowing I would find the key in the ignition: country habits. The car was too warm and musty inside, and it took me three tries to move the seat so that I could reach the pedals. I almost never drove. Hunter said he hated to let someone else have control, and it wasn't an issue with me.

We'd never had fights like this before. Before Hunter came back from Romania, we'd never had fights at all. That was one of the reasons he'd chosen me, I think: his calm little nun, his serene and quiet girl, his willing sidekick.

I gunned the engine and took off.

TWENTY-THREE

◑ ◔ ◯ When I started crying too hard to see the road clearly, I parked the car. I'd gotten myself two miles outside of town, to the foot of Old Scolder Mountain. I supposed I'd wanted to walk all along, but hadn't realized it till I'd started driving. It's funny: In the city if you need to walk to clear your mind you just head out your door, and if you need to walk on grass you just turn toward one of the parks. In the country, there is lots more land but it's all No Trespassing.

I was wearing a down jacket that I'd found in the car over my sweater and long black skirt, but my soft leather shoes weren't really made for serious hiking. That didn't bother me half as much, however, as the headache, which had begun as a faint pressure at my temples and was turning into something stronger.

I started walking anyway. I passed two orange markers before I realized I had picked a circular route, not the one that led up the mountain: I backtracked and started the ascent between two brilliant red and gold maples. The rest of the trees were half bare. After five minutes I began to breathe harder. A young man with a beard and a golden retriever smiled as we passed each other, he on the way down. I glanced at my watch: four o'clock. I hadn't realized it was so late, but I figured I had at least two hours of daylight left, enough time to get to the top and back, if I pushed myself.

I walked until I stopped thinking of everything except where to put my feet: on that rock, over that root, between those loose stones. The air had that clean, sharp autumnal feeling of imminence, and my head cleared. Now and again birds chirruped and stopped, chirruped and stopped; some insect made a musical, squeaking sound. I could smell the dust of pine needles and the tickle of cold running water sending up foam, which isn't really a smell, but feels like one. A breeze cooled the sweat drying on my neck and back, and I lifted my hair out of the way and fell into the rhythm of walking upward. It wasn't until I saw the house that I realized I'd lost the trail somewhere along the way.

It was one of those ominously rusted trailer homes, planted in the middle of a weedy lawn. How it had gotten there was beyond me—there was no road wide enough for its wheels. I looked harder, and saw that the trailer was an antique—maybe 1950s, maybe earlier. So it had probably been brought up here decades ago. But someone was definitely living here now: There was a carved jack-o'-lantern beside the plastic doe in the front yard, and a rake lying in a pile of leaves amid a veritable sculpture garden of half-rusted cars, trucks, and washing machines. I glanced back at the No Trespassing sign and wondered whether to simply turn around and try to find the trail, or to ask for help. Just above the trees, the sky was turning a darker shade of blue. I glanced at my watch—four forty-five—and then I heard the low growl of warning.

Shit. I turned and saw just the kind of dog you don't want to see when you're all alone on somebody else's land—a great hundred-pound malamute mix, with some rottweiler or mastiff thrown in to account for the gold eyes, slick coat, and enormous jaws.

"Good dog," I said, but the animal continued growling and circling me, hackles raised. They say a barking dog never bites, but of course, I thought grimly, dogs don't make much noise when they've got their fangs wrapped around your thigh.

I could feel the frightened flutter of my heart—show no fear—and the dog could probably smell it. So I stayed very still and hoped someone would show up soon. Until the second and third dogs showed up, slightly smaller and smoother-coated than the first, and began barking.

"Hello? Hello the house! Anybody home?" As if anyone could hear me over the din the animals were making. As the sky turned a notch darker, a fourth dog came running out, cringing and barking near the shadow of a wheelbarrow. It took me a moment to recognize Pia. Jesus, all these dogs looked like goddamn wolves.

"Pia? Pia? Easy, girl, remember me?" She cocked her ears, and whimpered. There were terrible raw patches of skin on her chest and legs. Oh, Jesus, what was Jackie doing here, building her very own wolf pack? What a very lovely white trash hobby if you couldn't afford an alarm system, and how ironic that I'd been the one to get Pia back to her. I'd learned my lesson: Next time, the wolf goes, and no special favors. If there was going to be a next time.

The other dogs had formed a circle around me, and seemed to be building up to some kind of frenzy. Catching the enraged eye of one, I cast my gaze down and kept it there. Submissive and nonthreatening, that's me. Oh, Jackie, where the hell are you? I tried to imagine her face when she found me, bleeding to death on her doorstep. Guess she'll stop worrying about whether or not Red's interested. And Hunter won't even have to get a divorce. No. Down, thoughts. *Bad* thoughts.

The fifth dog was the first I was sure was not a wolf-dog hybrid. It was a wolf-coyote hybrid. I could tell from the enormous leap that took him from somewhere up on a rise to right in front of me, a leap that a deer might have made, but not a dog. He had big coyote ears and a flat red-gray coyote coat, but his big muzzle said wolf, as in Grandma, what big teeth you've got. Even though he was slightly smaller than the malamute, and a lot leaner, he was clearly the more dominant. None of that domestic tail wagging and barking nonsense for this guy. He took one look at me, hunkered down, and tensed every muscle in his body. *Deep, dark, stinking shit.* I knew I was panting, and couldn't help it. And then I made the mistake of looking up, just to see when my throat was going to get ripped out, and caught the Alpha Male's eye.

Right as he winked.

TWENTY-FOUR

◑ ◐ ○ Dogs do not wink. Wolves do not wink. Not in an intentional, Hey there, it's a private joke between the two of us kind of way. There was something in the animal's eye. A bug. It didn't mean anything. It certainly didn't mean, Don't worry, I won't bite you. So I stood there, waiting.

The reddish coyote-wolf raised its eyebrows and gave a questioning whine.

"What is it, boy?" I whispered. The other dogs had settled down to watch the show, but I wasn't taking any chances.

"Well, hell, I wasn't expecting you, Doc."

I turned, and it was Jackie, wearing a fringed jean jacket and a guarded expression. She came up by the coyote-wolf and patted him on the head, and in the deepening twilight I felt as if she were standing with him somehow against me, like a wife with a husband bidding the unwelcome party guest a firm good night.

"I was hiking," I said. "I didn't know you lived up here. I guess I wandered off the trail."

Jackie squinted at me. "Thought for a moment you might be one of the town kids, come up to catch one of my babies for Halloween. You never know what nastiness people won't think up when they're bored—my friend's black cat got its eyes cut out five years ago."

"I didn't even realize it was Halloween." In the city, there would have been children in the street before sunset, dressed in bright plastic superhero and princess costumes, carrying fake jack-o'-lanterns.

"You're damn lucky the dogs didn't rip your throat out. They don't take to strangers. If Red here hadn't seen you—"

"Red?"

"This guy." She hesitated. "Named him after Red, 'cause of his color. And his disposition. He's a good boy, aren't you, Red?"

The animal lifted his muzzle as his ears were scratched, then looked at me with wise, sad canine eyes.

"Jackie. Are they all wolf hybrids?"

Jackie continued focusing on the animal. Red. "There's a good boy. Yes you are. Who's your mama? Who's your mama?" His tail wagged, but he glanced at me again, one of those guilty dog looks that say, I can't help myself. Sorry.

"Are you breeding them?"

Jackie straightened up, and set her jaw. "No, I ain't breeding them. I'm rescuing them from all the idiots who think they hear the call of the wild and wind up calling animal control."

Picking up on their owner's tension, a few of the hybrids began to make low, rumbling noises. "I'm sorry, I didn't mean to insult you."

"I know you didn't. I suppose I get a bit tired of it, though." She sighed, looking out at her dogs. "Stop it, now." The growling around me ceased as if a switch had been flipped. "Lot of people object to my keeping these guys, no matter why I'm doing it."

There was a rustle of wind and leaves, and suddenly the air was colder, raising goose bumps on my bare arms. I turned to the sound and realized how long the shadows had grown. A true harvest moon, full and tinged with red, was rising up over the shadowy tree line.

"I should be getting back."

"It's too late for that. You won't be able to see the trail."

"But Hunter . . ."

"You can call him. I do have a phone, you know."

I smiled, not sure if she could even see my face. We were standing farther apart than we had on previous occasions. "I don't want to impose . . ."

"It's too late. You'll have to spend the night. I have my jeep parked about a half-mile down on the other side, but by the time I got back it would be pitch black."

"You don't go out at night?"

"Not on Halloween, I don't." She turned and walked toward the trailer and I watched the lanky shape of Red the wolf detach itself from the other shadows and slink off into the night, presumably to join the rest of the pack.

"As long as I'm here, do you want me to take a look at Pia?"

Jackie lit a cigarette. "I wish you would." She brought the slender dog back to her side with a whistle and a snap of her fingers. I examined the animal as best I could without the proper equipment. One thing was clear. She was losing all the fur on her legs and belly.

"My best guess is some sort of skin allergy," I said, "but her abdomen seems to be hurting her as well. I think X-rays would be a logical—"

"Can't do it. Not around here." Jackie stubbed out her cigarette on the ground. "They say she bit someone."

I mulled over this new piece of information. "Maybe I can e-mail my former boss. He might have some idea." Particularly if he had assumed Pia had been abandoned and used her for one of his experiments. But I kept that thought to myself.

"You're shivering," Jackie observed. "Best come inside and warm yourself up."

She opened the trailer door and I was relieved to see a certain amount of light, warmth, and order. There was a table and bench, a sink and counters, a bed tucked into the back. Jackie was unwrapping cellophane from a TV dinner.

"I guess you're hungry. I just have these Swanson things, so they'll have to do."

"I, ah, don't eat meat."

Jackie looked over her shoulder at me. "Macaroni and cheese okay?"

"More than okay. Wonderful. Do you have a mirror?"

"Over there."

I peered at my reflection and was surprised to see that I was not as much of a mess as I'd expected after a day of fighting, crying, and taking a long, impromptu hike: In fact, I looked . . . not bad. Flushed cheeks slick with perspiration, bright eyes, tangled hair. There was a rip in my long-sleeved T-shirt which deepened the vee, showing the white edge of my bra. It took me a moment to put a name to my appearance: wild. I looked wild. I tried to finger-comb my hair into a ponytail and wound up creating a Medusa effect.

"You want a beer?"

"Sure." I turned away from the mirror and slid onto the bench that seemed to serve as both couch and kitchen table.

"It's warm. Ice melted in the cooler."

"That's okay." I took a sip of warm beer and felt as if I were truly having an adventure, even though the only thing I was doing was accommodating myself to someone else's life for an evening, and that wasn't exactly trailblazing behavior. No pun intended.

I looked around. All the plates and cups were small

and stackable, and there was a kind of odd charm about that. It was like eating in Munchkinland.

"You know, Jackie, I've never been in one of these before. Everything's so miniaturized."

"Trailer's old as shit."

"1950s?"

"1970s. Here." She handed me a little cardboard plate with macaroni and cheese, a few carrots, and chocolate pudding, each in its own compartment.

"I couldn't use your phone first, could I?"

"Be my guest." The phone was an old rotary, and Jackie turned on a small color television while I dialed. On the fifth ring, the machine picked up.

"Hello, Hunter? It's Abra. Don't worry about me, I'm staying over at Jackie's tonight. Got lost on a hike, I'll be back in the morning." I kept my voice neutral for Jackie's benefit. "If you want to call me when you get back in, the number is . . ."

Jackie repeated her number into the receiver.

"So don't worry. Good night." I hung up without telling him I loved him, another first, just like the fight.

After Jackie and I had finished eating there was nothing to do, and even though it was not yet eight o'clock in the evening, it felt like midnight. I threw the remains of dinner away and Jackie folded back the benches and suddenly the table was a small bed.

"I'm going out for a cigarette and a pee. I got running water for brushing teeth and stuff, but I hate emptying the toilet out so if you don't mind . . ."

"I'll go outside, too."

We walked out together into a symphony of crickets. There was a scratch and a spark, then the oddly comforting smell of cigarette smoke drifting up into the night. We leaned up against a pickup truck that hadn't been anywhere in a very long time. The moon, just clearing the tree line, was full.

"Want one?"

"No, thanks. No, wait—yes. I do. Thanks." I hadn't smoked a cigarette since junior high, and like back then, I didn't bother trying to inhale. Still, it felt rather satisfying, the whole business of holding something in your hand, breathing in and out, the smoke a perfect punctuation to everything said and not said.

"You have a fight with your husband?"

"Not exactly."

"Then you probably ran away from needing to have one." We leaned back and looked up at the moon. Then Jackie burst into a little bronchial coughing fit, breaking the silence.

"You okay?"

"I know all about you and Red, you know."

I turned to stare at her, but she continued looking out at the night, the cigarette a red eye glowing between her fingers. "There's nothing to know."

Jackie blew out a plume of smoke. "He wants you. You'll wind up sleeping with him to spite that husband of yours. And Red'll get hurt, because when all's said and done, he's not your type." Jackie took a deep drag on her cigarette, leaned back. "You know he's some kind of Indian shaman? Has to apologize for each little critter he kills, offer its spirit something so it won't be mad at him." Jackie looked at the stub of her cigarette almost sadly before grinding it out underfoot. "You probably think that's all a lot of horseshit."

"No, I don't. My mother believes in . . . alternative realities."

"He doesn't have a high school diploma, you know. Just a GED, same as me."

I sighed, realized I hadn't been smoking the cigarette in my hand, and stubbed it out. I wanted to tell Jackie I wasn't some alien New York City snob with designer underwear and subscriptions to avant-garde theater. I wanted to tell her I was book-smart and people-stupid, and book-smart only in a very narrow area. I wanted to tell her I wasn't all that sure of myself, but somehow I felt that she already knew that. And still thought I was capable of hurting Red.

From somewhere behind and above us, one of the hybrids howled, a perfect solitary wail, and then one of the others answered it.

"That's beautiful," I said.

"Mm. That's why I like having 'em around. You can get prettier dogs, you can get nicer dogs, but if you want the music, you got to go for a bit of the wild."

"Do they really howl at the moon?"

"Hey, once a month, don't we all?"

Not me, I thought, not with my irregular menstrual periods. I'd be the wolf out of tune with the pack, the one lagging behind.

We listened as two more of Jackie's hybrids joined in, a blending of inhuman voices that filled the night with lupine magic. I wished the sound didn't remind me of my mother's movies, of werewolves and curses and the pretty maiden about to get mauled. I wished I could just have the pure experience of it, the raw lament of I am here, Are you there, and the choral response, We are here, We are here.

"I need a pee," said Jackie.

"Okay," I said. What are you supposed to say to that, anyway? She tromped off, leaving me alone. I moved deeper into the shadows, and tried to keep my long skirt bunched up and out of the way. I couldn't exactly see what was I doing and in the end, I got one of my shoes slightly wet. I realized I didn't have any toilet paper— did Jackie use toilet paper? Not such a good little camper. I was shaking myself off when I heard a sound.

"Wait," I squeaked, "I'm still peeing!" Why I was so shy of Jackie, I couldn't say. Except, even as I shook out my skirt, I knew it wasn't Jackie.

When I looked up, Red was there, leaning against a silver birch. He looked like he'd been there for a while. His face was pale and miserable, maybe hungover. He was dressed only in ragged jeans, his naked chest and stomach furrier and ridged with more muscle than I would have suspected. The howling tattoo on his upper arm looked smaller now that I could see just how large his bicep really was. I realized I was spending a long time looking at him just about the same time he did: Our eyes met and he smiled.

"Red! Are you okay? Jeez, where did you come from?"

"Well, I was born here. But I spent my formative years in a shitty small Texas border town." His voice sounded rusty, as if he hadn't been using it for a while.

"No, seriously. Were you lurking around listening to Jackie and me?"

"A little."

I didn't know what to say to that. When he looked up at me again, his eyes glittered with some emotion I couldn't quite name: a hint of something complicit, as if he knew a secret which concerned both of us.

"You shouldn't eavesdrop."

"Yeah? Maybe you shouldn't go into strange men's cabins and leave your scent all over their beds. Once boundaries are crossed, it's not so easy to set them back up."

"Sorry. I didn't realize I was so . . . pungent."

"You're not." He grinned rather wolfishly at me and I began to feel uncomfortable. Also warm. "And I like your smell, in case you hadn't noticed."

Time to change the subject. "Jackie thinks you're an Indian shaman," I blurted out.

Red hooked his fingers into the loops of his jeans. "Shaman's a Siberian term, I believe. My grandfather would say calling an Indian a shaman is like calling a rabbi a Jewish priest." He tucked his chin and looked up at me. "However, I did meet an Inuit fellow in Canada. Followed him around for a year and learned a hell of a lot about tracking things that don't always walk on the waking side. But I don't suppose that makes me a shaman."

"What do you mean, on the waking side?" I took his arm, eager to get away from what I suddenly realized was the lingering smell of my urine. "You mean you track things down in dreams?"

"Sometimes. I've had a few dreams about you, Doc."

"You have?" I kept my eyes on the ground as we walked. "What kind of dreams?"

"You should know," Red said. "You were there." Remembering my own disturbingly erotic dreams about Red, I stumbled. "Easy now," Red said, his arm keeping me from falling. "Hunter know where you are?"

"I left a message. But he was out." I didn't know if I believed that one person could visit another in dreams. A month ago, I would have sworn that such a thing was impossible. But then I recalled standing with Red in my kitchen, his certainty that I had wanted him, too.

Red stroked my hand where it rested on his arm. "Your husband's probably looking for you. I'll take you home."

"But it's dark out. Jackie said it's not safe."

There was a pause and we both stopped walking, and it suddenly became a little strange that I was still holding his arm. Red inhaled sharply, nostrils flaring. "Not safe for Jackie, maybe. She's got the worst night vision in Dutchess County. But I can get you home."

"Could you? God, I'd really appreciate it."

I dropped his arm and started to walk back to the trailer. It wasn't until I got to the door that I realized he hadn't followed me.

"Jackie? Jackie, Red's here. He says he can take me home, and if that's all right with you, I'll—"

The screen door flew open and Jackie peered out, the outline of her generous breasts visible in an old flannel nightgown. "Red? You say Red's here?"

"Yes, and since I really don't want to impose, I thought I'd just—"

"Red? Abra says you're going to take her home?" She sounded so incredulous that I was a bit taken aback. Surely it couldn't be that dangerous, could it? Were we going to be attacked by raccoons?

Red moved out of the shadows.

"You sure you're up to it? The whole way? Like that?"

Truth was, I had wondered why he was dressed just in torn jeans, but had been too startled to ask him.

"I can do it. She should be home tonight."

Jackie shook her head. "You're a big fool, Red, you know that? Why not just let her sleep here?"

"You know why."

"Her husband's not about to go looking for her in some shotgun fury, Red. You saw how he was."

My mouth went dry. I found myself watching Red, trying to read his response, but his face was a pale blur in the middle distance.

"That was then. This night could be a different story."

I cleared my throat. "Listen, Hunter's not exactly the jealous type. If you're worried he's going to be crazed that I spent a night out, you're dead wrong."

Red took three steps, and I could see the fine sheen of sweat on his face and chest, despite the chill autumn air. "You never know, Doc," he said. "People change."

"I don't think that's the way he's changing."

"You want to stay here?"

I glanced back at the trailer. "Well, if it's not safe—"

Red laughed, a dry sound, more cynical than I was used to from him. "It's safe with me. Tell her, Jackie. That she's safe going back with me."

There was a pause and I turned to look at my hostess.

She seemed older than she had when we'd smoked the cigarettes. "You're safe with Red, Abra." Then she turned and slammed the door behind her, leaving me alone with her ex-boyfriend, the redneck shaman.

"I don't want to cause trouble between you," I said.

Red made a small amused sound. "It's not you causing the trouble."

"But I don't want to make anybody feel—"

He put his hand on my arm and we both jumped a little. "Shut up, Doc," he said, but with such tenderness that I half-felt he'd said something else entirely. "Let's go." Red plunged off into the night, and I followed him blindly.

TWENTY-FIVE

◗○○ The whole way down the mountain, I walked like an automaton, watching my feet in the moonlight to make sure I didn't trip. Red kept having to stop and wait for me, and at one point, he told me to hold on to the belt loops of his jeans as we shimmied down an embankment. I could feel his awareness of me, and when we stopped at the head of the trail, he was breathing hard.

"You okay?" I put my hand on Red's jaw, to make him meet my eyes, but it was all false, completely false. I knew he was going to kiss me, and I knew I wanted him to. Not to make love to me. But just to kiss me. I hadn't ever had this before, this sense of someone's fierce and specific wanting of me.

"No. Not okay." His hand covered mine, and for a moment he looked at me, a long, steady, unabashed appraisal. "My Irish granny would say this is the night the spirits go out walking."

"Do you believe that, too?"

"Northside's the kind of place that makes you believe. Did you know there's a big cavern running underneath the cornfield on the east side of town? We don't advertise it like some of the other places do, and there's a reason. This place is a crossroads between a lot of different worlds. Let me tell you, being an animal removal operator here is a hell of a lot different than in other locations."

"I don't believe in that sort of thing."

"Then why are you still holding my hand?"

I snatched my palm from his and we resumed walking. Well, he resumed walking, and I resumed tripping. "I can't see anything."

"So take my hand again."

"And feed your ego? I think not. You'll have to beg me before I hold anything of yours." Ouch, that didn't sound quite the way I'd planned.

"It's not my ego that's bothering me, Doc. But you're married. So stop flirting."

"I didn't mean . . ."

"Yes. You did." Red stopped and turned to face me. "And I am so damn hungry for you that you have no idea how little it would take to break me down. But if I were to take you, come inside your body, your husband would kill me."

I looked at the ground, where unseen things chirruped and whirred. "Hunter's not like that, okay? Besides"— my voice was surprisingly steady as I said the words out loud—"I think he's in love with someone else."

Red's hand lifted my chin up. "Then leave him. Leave him and come to me." He grinned, his weathered face almost boyish with it, all sharp hazel eyes and sharper white teeth. "Stay up all night with me—I don't sleep much either."

"How do you know I don't sleep?"

"I spend a lot of time watching you when you're around, and a lot more time thinking about you when you're not. You let things slip, and I pay attention."

"I don't know what to say . . ."

"Well, that says it."

It seemed a long time before we reached my car. I climbed in and started the ignition, and after a moment Red opened the door to the passenger's side.

"I guess I'd better see you all the way home."

"Red, listen—I'm not asking about what you were doing at Jackie's. I'm not ready to get into all this . . . complexity right now. But I will think about—"

"Just drive."

"Want me to take you home first? I know you live close by . . ."

"I can walk from your house."

In the enclosed space the smell of him was suddenly strong—male sweat, sharper than I was used to. But not unpleasant. Healthy. I rolled down the windows to let in the night air and as I started the ignition, the sky flickered white in the near distance.

"Storm's coming," I said, but Red was looking out the window, focused on something I couldn't see. His skin was still beaded with perspiration. "Red?"

The rain came suddenly, a few drops, a downpour, then a solid sheet of water. The windshield wipers could not keep up. The headlights could not illuminate anything beyond the rain. The sky rippled with thunder, flashed with light. I didn't know if I was on the main road anymore. I tuned the radio into the weather band.

". . . and a severe weather storm warning is in effect for northern Dutchess and Columbia counties," intoned the computerized voice. "High winds and lightning and the possibility of large hail. Tornadoes a possibility in the Upper Hudson Valley region around Cooperstown, Milltown, Cedar Plains, Northside . . ." Red shut off the radio.

My teeth began to chatter from adrenaline. "Red? What do we do?"

"Just keep going. You're doing fine. Only another two miles to your house if we take this shortcut." His hand came up to cover mine, and he guided the wheel toward an unmarked dirt road. Thunder rumbled again, and a jagged line of bright white pierced the road, so close to us that I tried to remember how you were supposed to count the distance. I felt that strange disorientation you feel in acute distress, as if you've left the rational world behind, entered some strange new twilight zone where, impossibly, it is suddenly possible that you might die.

Something bounded out into the road, a huge shadow, and I slammed on the brakes and the wheels screeched and skidded and we moved in slow motion toward a tree. I had a flash of how the local papers would report it and then Red turned the wheel sharply and we were back in control, and then we were heading toward another tree, more slowly. Red brought my head down into his chest and shielded me so at the moment of impact I was crushed between the sudden billow of air bags and his skin.

For a long moment we sat there, huddled.

"Abra? Doc?"

I looked up and Red was already unlocking his door and turning to pull me out. "We need to run for it."

But I found myself unable to move. I stood there, staring at the carcass of the deer we'd hit, a stag with a great rack of antlers, his gold hide darkened with rain and blood. No, not a carcass. I brushed the water from my eyes and saw more clearly that his hooves were still faintly flailing, his nostrils dilated with fear.

"Abra."

"We can't leave him like this!"

Red went down on one knee and the deer, panicked, began rolling its head from side to side. With one hand on either side of its antlers, Red yanked the deer's neck savagely to the right. Then he just sat there, chest heaving.

"Red?"

He looked up and his eyes were full of regret and something darker, wilder, more excited. He started to stand, stumbled, and caught me against him. Definitely excited. Despite the driving rain and the dead stag, maybe because of them, I felt an answering heat, a sudden stab of arousal.

Red saw it in my eyes and suddenly he was holding me too hard, his fingers painful against my upper arms, his hips grinding into mine. And I gasped and then his mouth was covering mine, one of his hands moved up to cup the back of my head, the other braced at my waist to keep me from falling over. His teeth were sharp on the inside of my lips, on my tongue. I couldn't catch my breath and I had to cling to the solid strength of his shoulders to keep from going down. And then we were both going down, sprawled in the mud beside the stag's corpse, and I couldn't get enough air to tell Red to stop, please wait.

"Abra!" He drew back, his expression anguished, and before I could think I found myself pulling his head back down to mine, my hips rising to meet his thrust for thrust, thrust for thrust. I was mindless with it. I felt his hands move up under my shirt, covering my breasts, his callused palms abrading my nipples, his mouth slanting sideways, nipping at my throat. Yes. I was tugging at his jeans, trying to get at him, mindless and hungry and acting from some primitive, animal part of my brain.

"Hey now, easy, girl, slow down a minute—oh, Christ."

I couldn't understand why Red seemed to be fighting me, but suddenly the fighting kicked something in me into overdrive, and I was biting Red's neck, licking my way down the delicious muscular indentations of his chest and stomach, my nails raking down the lean length of his spine, finding the surprising furriness of him there too, but I wasn't turned off by this, not when I could hear the rapid thunder of his heartbeat, so fast I knew he'd dreamed about this.

"Abra, wait."

But I was hungry for him, ravenous, my body sliding down his, my face at the bulge in his crotch, my mouth on him through the sodden fabric as my fingers worked at the buttons, he was a Levi's man and there was an ungodly row of buttons to contend with, ah, there, free, the dry heat of his erection in my hand. I heard him shout, Jesus, and his hands convulsed on the back of my head, then released and held me with perfect tenderness as I inhaled the clean, male scent of him, a scent of wood smoke and salt, a drugging, intimate scent of cave and fur. I took him in my mouth.

"What are you doing to me?" His voice broke off, the last word a choked gasp.

What was I doing? This was something I had done for Hunter only a few times, done to please, not something I actually enjoyed. But here with this unlikely man I was out to please only myself, this strange self with strange appetites. Under my fingers, I felt the muscles of his back ripple in a way that seemed both strange and familiar, like something remembered from a dream.

"Stop, Abra, please, before I lose control." He had tangled his fingers in my hair, forcing my head up.

I looked at him. His eyes were no more than shadows, but I could still read him: surprise, desire, and regret, and a steady glow of tenderness that made me smile.

"Take off your pants." I tugged on them, wanting him completely naked, for reasons I didn't completely understand.

"Doc, I can't—you don't want to . . ."

I unlaced his hiking boots, pulling them off. "Now the jeans. Lose them."

"I don't suppose I could just keep my socks on?" He sounded almost desperate.

"Very funny. No."

"Um, the thing is, if I'm entirely naked . . ."

I stood up, folded my arms, and just looked at him, knowing that in the end, he would do exactly what I wanted, because for once in my sexual life, I was in control.

Red swallowed hard. "Oh, fuck it." He was naked in two seconds, his compact body muscular and hairy and surprisingly tanned, as if he had spent time outdoors in the buff. I couldn't help but notice that he was not smaller than Hunter in all respects: Who would have guessed that such a slender man would be so well-endowed?

I went up to him, fully dressed, and kissed him. Our heights were similar enough that I could feel the hard length of him pressed against the vee of my thighs, and then Red groaned and bent his knees, his hands reaching down to cup my bottom and press me more firmly against him. Then he stilled, panting hard, his fingers clenching and unclenching on my hips as he struggled with himself.

And suddenly, I knew that he was too close to losing control, and that I wanted him in my mouth before it was too late. I slid down his body, pressing kisses to his mouth, his muscular chest, his belly. Red's hand's caught in my hair, pulling gently.

"Ah . . . no, sweet girl, that's not . . . a good . . ." His voice trailed off as I bent my head and licked the rounded tip.

"You were saying?" I glanced up and saw that Red's head was arched back, his eyes tightly closed. So I took him in my mouth, tasting the first salty-sweet prelude to his release.

Red made a low, rumbling sound, his fingers still tangled in my hair, but no longer trying to pull me away. Now his touch was a dragging caress, and oh, God, the feel of his hands, combing mindlessly along my scalp, coiling the length of my hair around his wrists. His touch said more about what he was feeling than any words could have. I felt the bone-deep hunger in him, the hunger fed by the fact that it was me doing this. I raked my teeth delicately along his length, his desire became my desire, his ecstasy a wave gathering force. He was moving with me now, faster, his lean hips pumping, and I could taste more of that salty sweetness now, and for the first time in my life, I wanted to swallow a lover down into me with cannibal desire.

"Abra, stop!" I felt his hands trying to pull me away, but it was as if I had become him, as if it were my orgasm crashing at the gate. I could feel his pulsing between my own legs and I was clinging to him, wanting to finish it, and then he groaned, a sound of utter surrender. Suddenly I was flung backward. Shocked and stung, I watched him gasp, hunched over, his face nearly purple.

Oh, God, he couldn't breathe. I'd killed him. "Red?"

"Aaarggh!" Red folded over at the waist, clutching his middle. Was he dying? What was it? Heart attack, asthma attack, epileptic fit? I couldn't think.

"Are you in pain? Red, look at me. Can you look at me?"

In response, he threw back his head and howled, a sound of such primal anguish that it ripped through the storm.

"Oh, God, Red, are you—"

Like all impossible things, it happened quickly. Red collapsed onto his hands and knees, shook his head, and then looked up at me for a long moment. There was no humor in his gaze this time, no challenge, no wink. But by the time he reached the trees, he wasn't a man anymore.

I was so shocked that it took me a moment to realize

that he wasn't running away. Another moment for me to realize he wanted me to follow him.

It was only when I saw the bulky shadow of my house that Red stopped as if at some invisible boundary, his four-legged posture alert and watchful as I stumbled down the overgrown old cow path up to my back door.

TWENTY-SIX

◑ ○ ○ Inside the dark and empty house I found a flashlight and two candles, and then I tripped over the torn and bloody carcass of an opossum in the kitchen. Red had been right about one thing: The corpses were getting larger. I wrapped the naked-faced creature in an old kitchen towel and threw it outside the front door, and sat in the living room, waiting for Hunter to come home.

I'd cheated on my husband. I'd had oral sex with another man. With a wolf man. I'd just seen a man turn into a wolf. Or a coyote. No, I'd made a man turn into . . . whatever it was.

And Jackie knew.

I yearned for a hot shower. For television. For a book to read. For any distraction at all. Instead, all I got were questions. Was I going insane? Had Jackie slipped me a tab of acid in the mac and cheese? I felt my heart race and tried to stop myself from panicking. This wasn't a drug-induced hallucination. This was my life.

Which led me to the question: Where was Hunter, carless, on a night like tonight?

I felt instinctively he was not looking for me. I felt he was off on his own adventure. At Moondoggie's? With that waitress? I wouldn't even have the right to object. He could be in her mouth right now, or his mouth between her legs, and I would be powerless to object, because I had been just as guilty.

Except that now I suspected that he'd never been faithful at all. It wasn't just Magda. If he was sleeping with me and cheating with that waitress, then there was every reason to think he had never really been monogamous. And knowing this changed the shape of our past together. It made my memories of our marriage incomplete.

Well, at least I had one man who wanted me. Maybe Red was right—maybe he would be better for me.

Sure, because a man who was also a dog would be a perfect companion. No, wait, that was crazy. He had gotten scared and run off, and then I had seen a coyote. I was sleep-deprived and high on adrenaline, and I was having some sort of weird mental episode.

Red had gotten scared and run off, and a coyote had appeared and guided me home. That didn't make much more sense, but at least I didn't have to get myself committed in the morning. And wasn't it just like a man to run off the minute you finally decide to let him in?

And then, sitting on my dark couch in the dark house, came a shower of memories. Me at nineteen, still young enough to believe in the magic of transformations; still young enough to believe the magazines when they said the new hair, a prettier you, thinner thighs, better sex, making him want you. I had met Hunter still naïve enough to believe that I was on the verge of inventing a new, happier, stronger self, that in choosing the right college, the right career path, the right man, I might shed the old skin of my old life.

But here I was, in a house that was big and old and alien, waiting for someone who didn't really want me anymore to walk in through the door. When he did, it would be time to leave him and face the prospect of life on my own.

No wonder most people don't leave a marriage without a lover to help them open the door. So comforting, the thought of that lover in the background. Too bad Red couldn't have been a little more convincing in the role.

I fell asleep without knowing I had done so. I wakened partially when the first rays of daylight hit my face from the living room window, but then I closed my eyes again, too tired to move. Suddenly, there was a crashing sound behind me, and I whirled. My heart lurched into a faster rhythm a full half-second before my brain caught up with the information: Front door slamming open. Husband standing there. Naked. And bloody.

"Abra." Hunter looked at me with the strangest expression on his face, a look of rueful embarrassment that did not really go with the deep lacerations on his shoulders and chest.

"Oh, my God."

"I see you're back. Well. That's good." He brushed his hands off on his thighs, for all the world as if he'd just come back from a day's gardening. "I think I'll just take a shower, then."

"Hunter, you're bleeding."

He looked down at himself. "Ah. Yes. The thing of it is, I was out looking for you, and—"

"You're bleeding and you're naked."

Something shifted in Hunter's strange expression. "Abra," he said, and it came out clogged in his throat. His eyes were dark with pain and confusion.

"What happened to you?" My voice was softer than I thought it would be. I pulled a throw off the back of the couch and carried it over to my husband. "Here." I wrapped it around his shoulders.

"I can't remember." His arms came around me and he slid down my body, his face pressed against my belly, as Red's face had been not so many hours ago. "Abra."

"I'm here."

"Don't go."

"I'm here."

His arms convulsed around me, hugging me so tightly that I nearly lost my balance. I stroked his hair, not knowing what to say, guilty and a little repulsed by the sweaty, humid odor of blood and dirt. I couldn't remember Hunter ever going down on his knees before me. His sudden need of me was seductive, and I tried to pull back a little. "Were you—did you drink something?"

Hunter pulled back. "You smell funny."

"*I* smell funny?"

"Like . . ." His brow furrowed. He looked up at me. "Are you leaving me for him?"

"You have some nerve." Now I did try to step back, but Hunter prevented me, holding me even as he stood, his arms moving up to grip my arms. "Where have you been all night? With that waitress? And how about all this past summer? Want to tell me again how it wasn't like that with Magda?"

Hunter inhaled so deeply his nostrils flared. "He didn't come on you," he said harshly. "Did you come on him?"

"No! How dare you!" I yanked my wrists from his grip, my voice coming out very calm and precise and overly deliberate, like the computerized voice on the radio warning about the storm. "How *dare* you go on and on about Red when you—"

"But it means nothing to me!" His face was flushed with anger, and I realized I'd never seen Hunter lose control before. "Fucking some girl when I'm away from home—that's like scratching an itch to me, Abra. You know that, deep down. That's why you never paid attention when I—"

"I didn't know!" I was hitting him with my fists, and

he caught each blow. "I didn't know, you bastard! I trusted you because you'd already had a thousand stupid bimbos!"

"And you didn't care!"

"We weren't married then!" We glared at each other, but I could feel that my rage was burning hotter. He was blocking my fists, but then I started clawing at his already bloody shoulders, and I could feel him flinch. "What about Magda? What about those letters you didn't send? Are you going to tell me she didn't matter?" I stood there, waiting for his answer, before pushing him away and walking over to the window. His hesitation had said it all. "Magda was different, I admit it. But it wasn't what you think, Abs. She was my teacher—"

I sobbed so loudly it was almost a wail.

"And for a little while, I thought it was more. I admit it, okay?" He was beside me now, his head bent forward, forehead touching mine. "I thought—she'd changed me, and I was different. I thought you and I wouldn't work together anymore. But I was wrong. You came up here with me. You gave me—you always give me the space I need to figure things out."

I couldn't look at him. I hated having him so close, but I couldn't seem to move away. "Then why were you out all night with someone else? What was that—another itch?"

I could feel his sigh. His hand behind my head felt sweaty, too warm. We were as close as if we were about to have sex, and I felt real nausea building at the back of my throat. "Abra, last night—I started by looking for you. I was mad you'd taken the car. I hitched to Moondoggie's and started getting drunk, and then—no, it wasn't an itch. It was a fire. Ah, don't cry. Look at me, will you?"

I looked at him. "I hate you," I said. "I want out."

"You don't mean that. Red's just—"

"It has nothing to do with Red. Have your waitress. Have them all. I'm going back to the city."

"Okay." He nodded quickly, as if I'd asked for his agreement. "Okay, you go back. Maybe that's best, a little space—"

"No." I stood up. "This isn't about me giving you room to be single while still staying married. This is about me. Leaving you."

Hunter seemed frozen. "All right," he said. "All right." He seemed to have decided that he was going to be reasonable, calm, no matter what.

"No, it's not all right," I said, crying harder now, and then the nausea became more than a feeling, and I clapped my hand over my mouth and ran for the bathroom, too late.

I threw up on the peeling linoleum while Hunter held me from behind, supporting me until all I could bring up was bile. We collapsed on the floor together, me sitting between his legs. Hunter stroked my hair from my face as I watched a trail of vomit trickle down the sloping floor toward the claw-foot tub. My breasts ached from the impact of landing hard on my tailbone, and I tried to remember when I'd had my last period. Last month, I thought. Which could mean that I was due now, except that I was never that regular, and my premenstrual symptoms had never been like this: savage anger roiling inside me, a violent rainstorm of emotions threatening to break down everything in its path.

"Oh God," I said. "Oh God. I think I'm pregnant."

Hunter's arms tightened around me and he held me without saying a word. The sour smell in the room grew stronger, and still I made no attempt to rise. In between the wood cabinet and the sink, there was a small brown spider sitting on her web. A tiny ant was heading her way. Things you wouldn't notice if you happened to be standing upright, on two legs.

"How far along?"

Hunter's question jerked me back into myself. How far along? A minnow, a tadpole, a salamander, a piglet? How far along the evolutionary scale; did it have that downy fetal layer of fur yet, or a vestigial tail—no, that came later, along with the fluttering movement of eyelids, the possibility of dreams. "Not far," I said, thinking of Hunter's long-standing objections to our having a child. His loss of freedom. My loss of independence. The possibility of his mother's schizophrenic genes getting stirred into the fetal pot. Except that it might not be schizophrenia—it might be lycanthropy.

"Do you want it?" His hand slipped down to my belly as he asked the question, cupping my lower abdomen.

"Do you?"

Hunter's thumb moved in a gentle caress. "Oh, yes." There was something poignant to me about the way he was sitting, naked thighs wrapped around mine, his hand over my womb, holding me safe. "I want my baby in you, Abs. I want it very much."

"I do, too." I was crying. Hunter moved his hand to my chin, lifting it. I let him kiss me, my tears running into our mouths. His hand cupped my jaw, flooding me with tenderness. Until the next moment, when I felt the beginnings of an erection stir against my lower back, and remembered that he had no clothes on. But the man had good instincts. Just before my awareness of Hunter's arousal shattered the moment, he drew back, his eyes so warm with emotion that I felt almost frightened.

"I do love you, you know."

"I love you, too." It was nearly too much, this happiness after that rage. I was not equipped for such highs and lows, and I found myself wishing for my old husband back, the one with the faint air of amusement, the one who treated even the most savage emotions as if they were merely big, tame cows.

"Well, then. Let's get cleaned off."

"All right."

He offered me his hand to help me up, and after a moment's hesitation, I took it.

TWENTY-SEVEN

◑○○ The day after the storm hit, the sky was clear and blue and filled with soft white clouds that scudded slowly by with the breeze. It seemed impossible that a little thing like weather could have knocked down so many trees, but there were two down on our road alone. A road crew removed the trees and the deer and by noon we had electricity again. Triple A towed our car to the town's garage and for three days we had a borrowed pickup truck in our driveway. Red called twice, hanging up when the answering machine picked up. The third time he left a message, asking me to call when I had a chance. I deleted the record of his calls, feeling oddly numb, then listened to my own voice on the answering machine, telling Hunter not to worry. After a moment, I erased that, too.

Hunter and I never did talk and resolve what had happened that night. I was checking the fridge for spoiled food when Hunter surprised me by asking me out to dinner and a movie. He said he was tired of being such a recluse and a bastard. He dropped his chin and looked out from under his floppy dark hair, the dangerous, darkly brooding air he had replaced by something surprisingly boyish and vulnerable.

I should have gone back to my book on Alpha Males and their instincts: how a dominant leader, when it has subjugated its subordinate mate to the point of rebellion, will turn back to the ploys it used for its initial sexual courtship.

I ordered grilled mushrooms and pasta at Tooth and Claw, an expensively renovated old farmhouse. Hunter chose steak tartare and I tried not to wince at the sight of his lips chewing all that raw meat. Instead of seeing a movie, we walked around the village of Rhinebeck, where two of the three little dress shops had the kind of expensive, baggy hippie clothes I like best. Hunter bought me a lavender corduroy jumper and a black-and-white Zuni-patterned scarf. The jumper was one of those roomy one-size-fits-all things that Hunter usually despises, but this time he didn't comment, except to say, "Looks like it might come in handy." Hunter drove back with only his left hand on the wheel. His right hand held mine.

"Are you going to take a test, Abs?"

"What kind of test?"

Hunter glanced over his shoulder at me.

"Oh," I said. "I suppose I should."

We stopped at a pharmacy that stayed open late and I bought something that said it was the number one choice of someone or other. At home, I went straight into the bathroom while Hunter fixed hot cocoa.

"Well? What's the verdict, Abs?"

I walked out carrying the little plastic disk and showed him the plus sign. It was faint, which I supposed was because I was testing so early on, before I had even missed a period.

"That's good, isn't it? A plus? That means we did it, right?"

I looked at him carefully, his handsome Heathcliff face open and excited for once, his dark eyes searching mine for my reaction. I had loved this man for a long time, and now a part of him had taken root in me. It would be an odd moment to close off to him completely.

"Yes," I said slowly, making up my mind. "That's the good sign." The next morning, I made an appointment with a local gynecologist who seemed less certain.

"Are you having any cramping? Spotting or bleeding?" She was a motherly looking woman with gray curly hair and a wide bosom, and I had liked her immediately.

"A little," I admitted. "So I'm not pregnant?" I felt a sense of vertigo, as if I had been spun wildly first in one direction, and now in another.

"Let's retest you in a few days, and then I can tell you for sure." She didn't use the word "miscarriage," but I understood that was what might be happening to me. I put my hand over my stomach and thought, Hang in there, Baby. And then I wondered if that was really what I wanted, after all. But when I returned for my second test, the doctor declared me officially pregnant.

"Although I have to admit, some of your hormone levels are a little unusual. Do you have any rare genetic conditions in your family?"

No, I said, thinking: But my husband's a lycanthrope. I took a prescription for prenatal vitamins, made an appointment to return, and e-mailed my old teacher. I wasn't sure whether or not Malachy had kept the same e-mail address, but I figured it was worth a try. A sweet and motherly gynecologist, I realized, might not be the specialist my condition required.

To: Madmal@optonline.net:
From: Abra79@yahoo.com:

Need your professional advice, for wolf-hybrid Pia—and for myself. I'm pregnant and living two hours from city, in Northside.

He wrote back immediately.

To: Abra79@yahoo.com:
From: Madmal@optonline.net:

So you and Pia are in the same town? Send your contact info and I will attempt the trip. My health a little uncertain at the moment, but I hope to be better in a few days.

Given the circumstances, I decided to accept the inevitable and embrace my fate. That is to say, I agreed to work for my mother. After the first few days, during which I felt uncomfortably like an adolescent impostor, I settled in, and by mid-November I had a routine going. On Mondays, Wednesdays, and Thursdays I went over to Beast Castle to assist with the sick animals and new arrivals. My mother was so happy with the arrangement that she actually treated me like a veterinarian, writing down my instructions, calling me for medical advice. Not to mention paying me money.

Meanwhile, Pimpernell the Chihuahua had stopped eating and Grania found herself unable to pay attention to her classes. She had formed a special attachment to the little dog, and kept cooking it delicacies to tempt its appetite—fried calves' liver, filet mignon, lamb chops. I discovered an abscessed tooth in that tiny yawn of a mouth and drained the pus off, which cured the problem. After that Grania became my staunchest ally.

I was so buoyed by this turn of events that I waited three weeks before telling my mother that I was pregnant.

"You're sure? And you're keeping it? Well, I'll look at the bright side. At least this means your marriage won't last long. Once you have a baby you'll see just what that husband of yours is made of." She made plans to come for Thanksgiving with Grania, then canceled them because she didn't want a seasonal feast, she was on a diet. Instead, my mother said, she was going to take a trip to Antigua, where she could snorkel and lose weight in the sun.

When I told him the news, my father hesitated, then asked if I was happy. He said he'd love to see me—he meant us—over the Christmas vacation.

I got sick in the evenings, but felt amazingly well during the first part of the day. So well that I was a bit surprised, actually—I'd never seen my hair look so thick and glossy, and my sense of smell seemed to have become particularly acute. This was more or less typical, according to my gynecologist. Less common was the new acuity of my hearing, although my eyesight hadn't improved.

Possibly because canids are myopic, I thought, and e-mailed Malachy again: When are you coming? This time, there was no reply.

My old friend, insomnia, still kept me up till three or four most nights, but now I nodded off in the late afternoons for an hour or so, and that little bit of extra sleep made me feel more alert all day long.

With less attention paid to it, my marriage seemed to be doing better. Hunter still disappeared up to the attic to work, but at mealtimes he joined me and made plans for the early summer, when the baby was due. We argued about names and whether or not it was safe for me to ski. We spooned each other in bed, but Hunter no longer wanted to play slave girl games with me. One morning, waking to a feeling of animal pleasure in the drowsy warmth of his body, I turned to Hunter and ran my hand down his thigh.

"Let's just cuddle," he said, stopping my hand, and I rested my head on his shoulder, letting him pet my hair until I fell back asleep.

The hair under my arms and on my legs grew so thick and dark that I became embarrassed. Usually I just shave under the armpits, the hair on my calves and thighs being rather sparse and downy. But now I looked like some kind of yeti, and my curved little lady's razor was not up to the job. I borrowed Hunter's cherished English razor, a really lovely bone-handled affair, and his shaving cream, too. Unfortunately, my foamy fur was impossible to rinse out of the blades, and I wound up feeling like Bluebeard's wife, hiding the bloodied key to the forbidden chamber.

"Abs, darling, have you seen my razor?"

"Ah, yes, isn't it in the bathroom?"

"Not that I can see."

"Why not use my disposable?"

"I suppose if I have to—Abs?"

"Yes?"

"Why is there no shaving cream left in this can?"

So I confessed. "It must be the pregnancy," I explained. "My hormones are going wild."

Hunter stared at his five o'clock shadow in the bathroom mirror. "Perhaps I should just try a beard. What do you think?"

"I think I'd miss seeing your face." I wrapped my arms around his middle and he patted me affectionately, and then stepped away. For a moment, I considered doing something more overt, like rubbing my breasts against his bare back. The hormones weren't just making me feel nauseated and hairy—they were making me feel quite frisky as well. Too bad my husband didn't seem inclined to take advantage. For a moment, I thought of Red, wondering if he would still find me attractive like this. Then I pushed that thought away, reminding myself that it's always easy to romanticize the one who isn't around.

The night before Thanksgiving Hunter's father called and announced that he and his second wife were going to drop by to "use the house" for a few days. It was not clear whether or not they were expecting to join us for dinner, although Hunter did invite them, without asking me.

"They'll probably just drink, darling; you know them. And if you could just stick a bird in the oven, you'd still have all the lovely yammy side dishes to yourself."

"Hunter, even if I were well enough to deal with the idea of a big bird, we're talking about tomorrow. There won't be any turkeys left."

"Sure there will; I ordered one."

And so it came to pass that at nine A.M. Thanksgiving day, I was hefting a turkey carcass into my shopping wagon when I saw Kayla, the waitress.

She was even prettier than I remembered, in a shaggy green wool sweater and faded jeans, her strawberry blond hair pulled back in a high ponytail. I glanced at her and then away, but not before I'd caught her looking at me, first with surprise and then with a fierce, narrow-eyed hatred.

As she came closer, I saw that there was a thin red scar on her mouth which I hadn't recalled seeing before.

"You tell that bastard to keep away," she hissed. "If I see one more dead animal on my front door, you tell him I will call the police."

"I don't know what you're talking about," I said, but I put my hand on my stomach as I said it.

"I don't care if Dan finds out anymore. You tell him that. I don't care if you know and Dan knows or the whole damn town knows, but you tell Hunter to keep the fuck away from me."

My mouth was dry and I couldn't seem to get words past the lump in my throat. "What are you—"

Kayla leaned closer to me, and her pretty green eyes were awash with tears. "He's sick, that's what he is," she said. "And you're sick to be with him."

She walked away, just another woman who'd meant

nothing to my husband, and I closed my eyes for a moment because suddenly the little supermarket was way too bright.

"Are you all right, miss?" The boy in the green apron was looking at me with alarm, and that made me straighten up.

"I'm fine," I said. I left my turkey in the wagon and walked out to the car.

I drove home as if I were eighty-six and extremely fragile, slowing around corners, braking whenever I thought I saw a chipmunk about to race across the road. I have had a shock, I thought, and I am pregnant. I must be very gentle with myself. With my hands at exactly the ten and two o'clock positions on the steering wheel, I made my way past vast landscaped horse farms and mobile homes decorated with cornucopias and Indian corn and cardboard turkeys dressed as Pilgrims. I cautiously cornered a bend which, a month ago, had been lush with a dangerous screen of foliage but was now winter-bare. I drove past the patchy brown grass of dairy farms with their ramshackle silos and red-painted barns, and I nearly ran over a marmalade tabby sitting in the road because I was driving so slowly she must have thought I was going to stop and just wait for her to move. Then I pulled into our driveway, parked the car at an acute angle, and walked out without closing the door.

"Is that you, darling?"

"Depends which darling you mean," I said, following Hunter's voice into the kitchen.

"Did you get the turkey already?"

"No, I couldn't."

"Well, never mind, we'll just have lots of leftovers." Hunter gave me a sort of blithe half-smile and shrugged. "Dad just called. Turns out he's not coming after all. Something about an invitation he'd forgotten at the country club." Hunter was making a pot of coffee in the kitchen. He was wearing an olive green wool sweater, almost an exact match to the one Kayla had been wearing. "Never mind. It just saves us the bother of having to put up with the old sot and his atrocious other half." Hunter raked the dark hair back from his forehead where it had flopped forward, a self-conscious gesture, intended to charm. He'd been very charming these past three and a half weeks, since the test had come back positive.

"I just saw your girlfriend at the supermarket."

"What are you talking about?"

I turned away and walked up the stairs.

"Fine." Hunter turned to go back to his coffee, and for some reason this infuriated me so much I found myself returning to the kitchen. There he stood, the guilty party, calmly reading a newspaper and sipping from his cup, and here I stood, the offended party, heaving in indignation, utterly ignored.

"Please don't just stand there panting," Hunter said, without looking up. "And don't make a scene. Just go away, calm down, and come back when you've gotten yourself together." I stared at him.

"Don't you even care what happened to make me mad?"

Hunter flipped a page of the newspaper, folded it, and then looked briefly up. "Frankly, no. You know me, Abs. I don't like big scenes. We talked about the other-women thing; we handled it. I don't really think it's fair for you to go have a cow about this now."

"Not fair? Not fair? Kayla says you've been harassing her—"

Hunter slammed the cup down, his dark eyes utterly cold with rage. "Don't start with that one. She has her own crazy scenario going, and I don't want any part of it. Just ignore her, Abra. It's what I plan to do."

"Are you still seeing her?"

"I won't dignify that with an answer."

"Are you?" He read the paper as if I had ceased to make any more sound in the room. In the bleak, almost wintry light, everything seemed more ghastly and dilapidated, every vase a receptacle for ashes, every window an unlidded eye. I had gotten used to the melancholy decrepitude of the house, but now I felt that it was part of the problem. Bad furniture, bad karma, bad vibes. I wanted to hurl something against a wall.

"Answer me, Hunter."

"Oh, Abra." He sounded utterly bored and disgusted. "Just grow up."

"I just want to hear you say you haven't seen her since that night." It was insane: I felt anger, but the tone of my voice was pleading.

"I'm not having this conversation with you right now, Abra. In the state you're in, you'll just twist everything around. It's probably hormonal."

Every word he said increased my anguish. I was suddenly very aware of my pregnant state, of how few people had ever really loved me, of how much my life hinged on this relationship being okay. If it were not, then my sacrifice of my internship, my investment of time, my position with my parents that my marriage was healthy, my pregnancy, were all mistakes.

"Please, just tell me you haven't been seeing her. Look me in the eye and tell me."

My husband looked at me, and what he said was, "I will not be dictated to."

I began to cry. Maybe it was hormonal, but I couldn't stop it.

"Please, Hunter."

"Oh, Abra," he said, putting the paper down at last. "Have some pride." If he had held me then, I would probably still have buckled. But he walked away, and it was Thanksgiving, so I packed a small bag and left for my mother's.

TWENTY-EIGHT

◐ ○ ○ My mother, who had spent the past three years begging me to leave Hunter, was not home when I got there. I had managed to forget that she was going to be in Antigua until I rang the front doorbell and discovered the sweet, moon-faced young woman who had been left in charge.

"Hi," she said when she opened the door. "I'll bet you're Abra?" She held out a pale, plump hand bearing three silver occult rings. "I'm Pagan."

"How did you know who I was?" But I already knew. Pagan had all the earmarks of a Piper LeFever groupie—clever eyes, interest in the supernatural, cat T-shirt.

"Your mother said you'd be dropping by to check on Pimpernell and a few of the other sick ones. She also mentioned that she wouldn't be surprised if the holidays brought out the worst in your husband this year." The gray eyes were apologetic.

"Sounds like my mother. And, strangely enough, here I am. Is the guest bedroom free?"

"She said to take the master suite. I've just moved into the guest room."

"There isn't another free room in the house? What about the green bedroom?"

Pagan shrugged. "Not fit for humans. I have a lot of

musical equipment set up right now, but if you want me to move—"

"No, but thanks."

My mother's huge, circular bed had been left strewn with duvets, newspapers, magazines, discarded clothing, jewelry, and cats. For some reason, most of the felines seemed to react badly to me, hissing and arching away. Only a little brown Burmese with a strange fungal growth on his face didn't seem fazed by my presence. He sharpened his claws on the headboard and watched me as I moved around the room.

It took me an hour to organize things and to strip the bed of the faintly musty-smelling sheets and blankets. Feeling like I had to make the effort to be festive, I put on the crushed velvet medieval dress my mother had bought for my birthday and went down to the kitchen. I had started a load of laundry in the kitchen and managed to find a casserole dish when Pagan knocked tentatively on the door.

"I hope I'm not disturbing—wow, you look great. What a dress!"

"My mother's idea. I don't suppose you feel like some anti-Thanksgiving dinner, do you, Pagan?"

"Actually, since you're here—I was going to go tomorrow for just a few hours, but since you are here—" The girl, whom I now realized was really no more than twenty, began to blush.

"Go on," I said, throwing back the long, trailing sleeves of my gown to grate some green mold off the cheddar.

"I'll be back tomorrow afternoon to help with the cats."

"Don't bother." I looked up and smiled at the young girl, who clearly had somewhere better to be. "I can manage for a couple of days." I placed the casserole in the preheated oven and closed the door.

Pagan's smile was radiant. "Oh, you are great. Thanks so much for this, I volunteered before Griff and I—"

"Go on before I change my mind." And then, just as I heard the front door slam, I realized I hadn't asked for any instructions regarding the animals. I raced after Pagan, found out who needed close monitoring and who didn't eat dry food, and returned, only to discover I had neglected to put the grated cheese in the casserole. As there seemed to be no potholders, I used a towel to bring the pot down.

I was about to put the casserole back when the phone rang, but by the time I found the receiver under a pile of old bills whoever was calling had hung up. I returned to my dinner, and, in one of those priceless maneuvers you do when your mind is really a hundred miles away, I put my hands right on that metal dish, straight from the 450-degree oven. The pain was so surprising, I gasped and dropped the dish. I was so discombobulated that it took me a full moment to realize that my elegant medieval sleeves had just swept over the lit burner. My sleeves were on fire.

For a moment I just stared at my hands in their nimbus of flames, and then I screamed and beat at them, and finally I remembered to roll until the flames were out.

Hands. My hands. How badly were they—? Bad. Breathe slowly. Assess the damage. The adipose tissue was exposed; white fat bubbled over the blistered palms. No fabric melted that I could see, but a mess of charred tissue, blackened like bacon at the edges, and, worst of all, no pain. No pain meant serious trouble.

"Oh, God. Oh, Jesus. Help. Oh, Christ, somebody, help!" But the front door was closed, and my hands were in no shape to be opening doorknobs. Think, think. The phone. I knocked the receiver off the hood and bent down, trying to use my nose to dial 911. No good, but-

tons too small. Elbow? Worse. Concentrate, don't panic.
I kicked off my shoes and jabbed with my big toe. Please,
911, please.

"911. What is your emergency?"

"Oh, God. I've burned my hands, third-degree burns,
there's no one here."

"Okay, stay calm now. Do you know your name?"

"Abra Barrow, the Beast Castle Animal Refuge." My
teeth were chattering.

"Good, I've got a unit coming. Are you feeling faint or
dizzy?"

"No. No sign of shock yet, but . . . this is third-degree,
full-thickness burns."

"Okay, okay, stay calm. My name is Helen, Abra. Are
you a doctor?"

"I'm a veterinarian." Was a veterinarian. Oh, God, my
hands, my hands.

"Good, okay, the unit is saying they are only three
miles from you now. Is there anyone we can get to come
to the hospital for you?"

Oh, God, who could they get? Not Hunter, not my
mother, not my father. I had no one.

"Miss Barrow? Abra? Are you there? I asked if—"

"I don't know." I started to cry.

"Don't worry, I'm sure there's someone. A friend, perhaps? Is there a friend who can meet you there?"

"Red Mallin."

"Can you spell that so I can look up the number,
Abra?"

"Red Mallin, Wildlife Removal Operator." I heard the
sound of footsteps. What was the operator's name? I
couldn't remember. "I think they're here," I said.

"All right then, Abra, you hold on, and I'll get that Red
Mallin for you."

The emergency medical technicians came in wearing

white uniforms and huge black boots. There was one white and one black, just like in the TV programs. I looked into their young male faces and had the strangest desire to just close my eyes and surrender to their care. But I stayed upright. "I need an IV of lactated ringers," I said to the black one. "Are you an EMT or a paramedic?"

"My name is Joe, Abra. Try to relax." I stared at his hands as he worked over me.

"I need, I think I need a surgical debridement . . ."

"Don't worry, you're going to be fine," said the white one. I wondered if I had insulted him by asking his partner if he was a paramedic first. And then something cool flowed through my veins and I closed my eyes.

TWENTY-NINE

◖◯◯ I was sitting in the examining room when Red burst in. I watched his eyes as he took in the scene: the sterile, pale hospital green walls and strong overhead lights which make everything, even childbirth, look so much more dire; me looking wild and disheveled in my crushed velvet Witch of Camelot dress, ruined hands held out as if in supplication. For a moment, he looked as if he were going to cry. Then he came forward and knelt at the floor by my feet.

"Jesus, Doc, you okay?"

I held Red's gaze as the startled young intern turned back to my hands. Hazel eyes, so much easier to read than Hunter's dark brown. "Not really," I said. "I burned my hands."

"I know."

"I'm supposed to be taking care of my mother's animals."

"You need taking care of yourself, Doc."

The intern, who had been examining my hands, paused. "How old are these burns?"

"I don't know. Half an hour. An hour." I sniffed loudly, like a six-year-old. "When do I go into the OR?" Red put his hand on my shoulder.

"Lady, these burns are at least a week old. Who treated you initially?"

I stared into the intern's round face. He had large, dark pores and one thick unibrow which stretched across both eyes, making him look permanently irritated and puzzled. "The EMTs treated me about half an hour ago. What are you talking about, a week old? There was exposed adipose, charred tissue . . ."

"Are you a doctor?" The doughy face with its villainous brow looked even more irritated and puzzled than before.

"No, a vet."

"Well." He held out my hands as if they were exhibit A. The flesh on my palms was bright pink, horrible to look at, but still, not anywhere near as damaged as it had been forty minutes earlier. "These wounds show substantial healing, wouldn't you say? More than an hour's worth, clearly."

I stared at my palms, raw with new skin. "I don't understand it. I swear to you, this happened only a short time ago."

"Look, I'm not going to argue with you. I'll just put on a dry sterile dressing and give you some supplies to take home. You'll still need some help with the rebandaging."

"I don't have any help." My voice came out thin and small, embarrassing me. I felt that the intern disapproved of me, and this bothered me, too.

"Abra, where's Hunter?" I turned to the owner of that soft Texas drawl and felt calmer. Red, unable to take my hand, had decided to hold both my shoulders. I couldn't see his face, but I could feel his chest behind my head.

"He's home." The intern wrapped and snipped.

"And you are . . ."

It was lovely not to have to look at him. "Staying at my mother's. At Beast Castle."

Red didn't react right away to the news that my mother was the vampire screen queen Piper LeFever. Instead, he just took a deep breath and said, "I see." Then his grip on my shoulders tightened, and I realized I was crying.

"All right," said the intern, "that's done. So you'll be taking her home? I need to give you some instructions."

I stared at the intern's ear. He was not looking at me anymore. "Wait a minute. That's it? Don't I need IV antibiotics?"

"Ma'am, you may have needed that a week ago, but not today."

I looked at Red for support. "But there was charring, tissue damage, loss of sensation . . ."

"Listen, ma'am, you can wait to speak with the admitting doctor who saw you first, or you can look at your chart—second-degree burns." The intern pulled his latex gloves off with a flourish. "Now, do you want the instructions, or not?"

Red placed one hand on my shoulder, and said, "We'll take the instructions—boy."

I didn't pay attention as the surly intern told Red how to care for my injured paws. As we were about to leave, a tall woman in a tomato red jacket came up to me. Her blond hair had been sculpted into a shape faintly reminiscent of a turkey, and I wondered if this was intentional, as a nod to the holiday.

"Are you Ms. Barrow? I'm sorry, but we weren't able to find a number for the contact you gave us." She checked her file. "Red Mallin. Is there anyone else I can try to call for you?"

I turned to Red, confused. "But someone must have called him."

"No," the woman said, rechecking her information. "We tried, but there's no number available from Information."

"It's okay," Red said, giving the woman an easy smile. "I got here, and that's the important thing. Now, I guess I'd better take this lady home." As the lady in the red jacket frowned in puzzlement, I let Red put his arm around my shoulders and guide me out of the hospital without comment, aware of his head, not so far above mine, and of his lean strength. He half-lifted me into the passenger side of his pickup truck and then walked around to the driver's seat.

"You're not in shock, are you, Doc?"

"I should be. They were third-degree burns."

It is not so easy to lean across the interior of a pickup truck, particularly one with a stick shift. Red managed it, his hand under my chin, forcing me to look at him.

"I know they were, Doc. But by the time that little shitheel looked at you, they were healed up some."

"That's impossible."

"I would have smelled the deep tissue if it had been exposed. You won't be havin' the use of your hands for a while yet, and the rest of the healing's gonna take a mite longer, but you don't have third-degree burns, I can assure you of that."

"Red, burns just don't heal up that way. Especially deep tissue damage. It doesn't just go away."

Red stroked the underside of my jaw with his thumb. "It does when your husband gives you a dose of what your husband did."

A jazzy little jingle from an old public service announcement flashed through my mind: VD Gets Around! No wonder Red hadn't wanted to make love with me that night. And then I realized what he was really saying. "You've known all along, haven't you? About the virus?" Red nodded. "But he said I couldn't catch it. There has to be a genetic predisposition."

His hand came up to the back of my head, and he leaned his forehead to rest against mine. "I guess you're predisposed."

"You know, in all the movies I've ever seen, you can only catch this from a werewolf in wolf form."

Red started the car. "That part's pretty accurate."

"But Hunter never—I've never seen him turn into a wolf, and he sure didn't bite me."

Red looked uncomfortable. "Well," he said, turning on his headlights, "it doesn't have to be blood-to-blood transmission. And if, you know, you were tired or a little tipsy one night . . ." His voice trailed off.

That night, after I'd drunk wine and smoked pot with Red. When Hunter's back had seemed to ripple underneath my touch. I curled up in the seat as far as the belt would allow, my head turned toward the window. "Just take me home."

It was very dark and the headlights cast a weak beam over the winding roads, but Red seemed to know his way. For a moment, I remembered that I hadn't asked Red how he'd known to come to the hospital if no one had contacted him. And then I wondered why an animal removal operator would have an unlisted number. But before I could form any questions, I nodded off, and when I woke up I thought, for a moment, that I was a child again, and my father was carrying me to my bed.

He's really very strong, I thought, as Red settled me down and pulled back the covers.

"I have insomnia, you know. I'm not going to just fall asleep."

Red turned the light off. "You always have trouble?"

I yawned. "For the past few years."

The bed dipped with Red's weight. "Anything help? Hypnosis, exercise, massage, sex?"

"Nothing."

"Maybe you're one of those people meant to stay up most of the night and sleep all day."

I leaned back and found my head on Red's arm. How warm he was. "But I want to go to sleep now. I just know I won't be able to."

"Just lie here and let me rub your back."

"That doesn't work."

Red moved his hand up until it was on my stomach. "Roll over," he said.

I turned, and he pulled my dress up at the same time as he covered me with the sheet. With his hand against my naked skin, he began tracing some sort of letters on my back. "This is silly, Red."

"Shh. Don't try to look. Just breathe. Relax."

I closed my eyes and he traced some foreign alphabet down my spine, to the very edge of my underwear, and then back up again. "I tried to call you. After that night with the storm."

"I know. I'm sorry, Red." I took a breath, then forced myself to say it. "I found out I'm pregnant with Hunter's child."

Red didn't say anything, but his hand stilled for a moment before resuming its slow rhythmic stroking of my back. His touch was soothing in its certainty, and I found myself half-wishing his hand would move lower. Pregnancy hormones, I thought. Not my fault. After a while we left the room and were standing in the forest, and Red was a wolf that kept running ahead.

"Hold on," I said, "I can't keep up with you." But he'd scented a rabbit or something and kept lunging forward, and by the time I caught up with him he'd been sprayed by a skunk and sat with his tail tucked between his legs.

"You really are an idiot, Red."

"You'll never make love to me now," he said, and I put an arm around him, thinking, Oh, what the hell, at least he isn't screwing around.

THIRTY

◐○○ The three little words "I fell asleep" may sound simple to some, but to me they are a rare and elusive delight. Whether it was emotional or physical exhaustion, or the unexpected security of Red's embrace, I slept in his arms better than I had slept in all my years in my husband's bed.

I awoke to find myself curled into a fetal position, my bandaged hands crossed in front of me, my dress balled up around my waist. Red was nestled against my back. I'd read once that the happiest couples slept this way. "Tell If Your Relationship Is Happy From Your Sleep Styles," or some such article. Hunter and I slept on opposite sides of the bed, or else I spooned around him, because he claimed his once-broken nose did not permit him to lie on his left side, facing me.

Red held me with loose possessiveness, one hand across my lower abdomen.

"Red?"

"Mmm." He sleepily pressed his erection against my bottom, and for a moment, without thinking, I pressed back. Then he groaned and woke up, although I could feel him pretending not to.

"Red? I need to go to the bathroom."

"What? Oh. Right." He sat up, tousled and almost boyish with his hair tufted in different directions. He wore boxer shorts, dark red ones. I realized he'd gained weight since I'd first met him, that late summer day in the subway. He was carrying a good fifteen more pounds, all of it muscle now padding his shoulders and ribs.

I walked self-consciously to my mother's bathroom and then confronted the predicament of being without opposable thumbs in a floor-length gown. I don't know how long I might have continued standing there had Red not knocked on the door.

"Need help?"

"No!"

"Sure about that?"

"Oh, Christ, Red, I have no idea how to do this."

Red opened the door, and I was slightly amused to note that his face was scarlet. "I could, ah, lift the skirt."

Now my face was scarlet. "I can't even wipe myself. Oh, God, Red, I can't do this with you here, I need a nurse, I should still be in the hospital."

"I'm a former EMT."

"You are?"

"Couldn't take all the dead children. Seems each July a good ten children would wind up in the bottom of pools and lakes. But anyway, I'm still a professional. Your privates are safe with me."

We both burst out laughing the kind of relieved, embarrassed laughter that lasts too long and sounds too loud. But when you have to go to the bathroom badly enough, in the end, that's all you can think about. "Just help me out of the dress."

He did, looking away from my naked breasts. The dress hadn't left room for a bra. I had a moment to remember that I was wearing ratty cotton panties, and then Red caught my eye. "Anything else?"

My cheeks burned. "Don't look."

Red knelt and helped me out of my panties, carefully looking down all the time. At my panties.

"Leave now!"

Red raised one eyebrow. "What, ah, can I do with these?" He held out my underwear, which looked very small in his large palm.

"Leave them!"

He closed the door, and, after a moment, my bladder relaxed enough to function. I shook myself, flushed the toilet with my right foot, and managed to use my clumsily bandaged paws to get a plush purple towel wrapped around my body. I positioned myself in as ladylike a fashion as I could manage on the toilet seat before calling out.

"Red? Could you—do you think you could run a little bath for me?"

"Sure." He came in, still bare except for the boxers, but wearing a nurse's expression, very kindly and matter-of-fact. He crouched down to reach the bath taps and I admired the width of his shoulders and the lean shape of his back. When he turned to me I found myself looking at the ridges of muscle that ran down his abdomen. I looked up and found that Red was smiling; he'd left his shirt off on purpose.

"Want me to put your hair up?"

I was surprised he'd thought of it. "Yes, please. It takes forever to dry."

Red got my brush out of my suitcase and worked it through my hair in long, sure strokes, holding my hair in his left hand so he didn't pull at my scalp when he hit a knot.

"You're good at this."

"I've worked with horses," he said, and I laughed. "Is there a hairband somewhere—ah, here on the brush handle." He caught my hair in a high ponytail, then wrapped it into a loose bun. In a sort of trance, I found myself wishing he could just go on brushing it.

"Thank you," I said, thinking, Hunter may have loved

my hair, but he never offered to do this. It would never have occurred to him.

"If I had my choice, I'd brush your hair every night of my life," Red said quietly. Then, before I could respond, he added, "Let me help you into the bath, Doc."

I snorted. "I don't think so."

"C'mon, you can trust me, I'll keep my eyes to myself." He held out his hand and grasped me around the wrist, and a little shock of awareness shot through me. As I climbed in I saw that yes, he was looking away, and yes, he was definitely affected. His boxer shorts were standing up in front as if they'd been starched.

I sat down in the bath with a slosh of water and Red moved so that his back was facing me.

"You in okay?" His voice sounded throaty.

"I'm in."

"Need soaping?"

"Now, just how far do your medical services extend?"

Red turned around and I sank lower in the tub. "At the moment, Doc, they're pretty extensive."

"Well, I do have a toothbrush in my bag . . ." And then I remembered something that drained all the humor out of me. "Red, this is probably not an appropriate time for me to be flirting, let alone anything more." I took a deep breath. "I'm pregnant."

Red cocked his head to one side, considering. "Listen, Doc, I don't like to be the one to break this to you, but I'm pretty sure you're not."

"What do you mean you're pretty sure I'm not? I've gone to the doctor. It's confirmed." And then I remembered her concern about some of my hormone levels.

Red crouched down on his heels, so that his face was more or less level with mine. "It's the virus," he explained. "It'll play all hell with your hormones at first, and then . . ." He hesitated, as if searching for the right words. "You don't smell pregnant," he finished, although I had the sense that he'd started to say something else and then changed his mind. "Not to make you feel self-conscious, Doc, but you smell like you're close to the change." He cleared his throat. "Which means, uh, that you're also getting your period."

I cried out in dismay. It was too much, too fast. I'd just been told that everything I'd been building my life around was false, and even though I understood on one level that there was no baby, I felt as though I'd just lost one.

Red moved toward me as if to draw me into an embrace, and I began to flail my arms at him, striking out blindly. Water splashed, wetting his chest, his shorts.

"It's not fair," I kept saying. "Not fair."

"I know, darlin', I know." He knelt beside me, our bodies separated only by the porcelain rim of the tub, his hands stroking the back of my head, animal-tamer hands, calming and wise. But my heartbeat was tripping over itself, unable to slow down. "I'm here. I'm going to take care of you."

"I'm not pregnant," I said, trying to get used to the idea. I recalled the doctor telling me that my hormone levels were unusual. "I never was pregnant."

I felt his hands grow still and pulled back to see his expression. He must have known, or else he controlled his reactions better than anyone I'd ever met.

"Did you really want to be?"

"Yes." But I was looking into his eyes, and know he saw that the truth was more complicated than that.

Red slipped his hands around to cup my face. "Abra," he said, then stopped to take a breath before starting again. "I'm sorry about the pregnancy, because I want for you whatever you want for yourself. But in a way, I guess I'm not sorry, because it might have made you stay with Hunter. And even though you probably know it,

I'll say it anyway. I'm in love with you." Red looked at me with a look of such intensity that I found it hard to keep meeting his eyes. "I've never said this to another woman, Doc—I want to spend the rest of my life with you."

And then, because I didn't know how to respond, I said, "Do you know that my father had a television series back in the eighties?"

Red shook his head, clearly befuddled.

"Well, he did. It was called *I Married a Werewolf*. Pretty ironic, huh?" And then I found myself laughing until tears ran out of my eyes. I guess Red must have thought I was laughing a little too hard, because he started stroking my hair and murmuring to me as though I were crying.

"I went too fast," he said. "I'm sorry, Doc, I rushed you."

"No, no, I'm sorry." I looked at him, realizing how vulnerable he must be feeling. "I remember Halloween. How you—what I did to you, how you changed . . ." I stopped because I was naked in the bath, and I had just reminded Red of how I'd been desperate to have him in my mouth. Recalling it, I felt a rush of heat between my thighs. "How was it for you when you first found out you had the virus?"

Red cleared his throat again. "It's a little different for me, Doc." His amber eyes flared gold, their pupils dilating.

"Your eyes—did they just—glow?"

"You have no idea how much I want your mouth on me again. How much I want to put my mouth on you. Ah, God." Red went up on his knees and wrapped his arms around me, and I could feel the waves of desire rolling through him, making him shake as my wet body soaked through his clothes. "Let me put my mouth on you." He kissed my damp hair, my forehead, and then he was kissing me on the mouth, a deep, ravenous kiss

that he broke off, gasping for breath. "Abra, oh, God."
He leaned over and took one of my nipples in his mouth,
suckling so strongly that I felt my response between my
legs. As if he knew, he switched his attention to the other
breast and reached down to touch me, his callused fingers surprisingly deft and gentle—more so than Hunter's
had ever been.

"You're so slick down there—ah, Jesus, woman," Red
said, and just as his light, skimming touch made me want
a deeper contact, his finger began to slide inside me. But
thinking of Hunter had broken the spell.

"Hey, hang on—slow down there," I said. "You're
moving too fast." Despite myself, though, my internal
muscles gave a little clench as he withdrew his finger.

"I'm sorry, Doc." But he didn't look sorry; he inhaled
my scent from his hand, and then, as if he couldn't help
himself, tasted me on his skin. His eyes were bright with
mischief and desire.

"It's just happening a little fast for me, Red."

He pressed a kiss to the top of my collarbone. "I got
you. You want me to help you out of there?"

"Thanks."

Red lifted me out of the bathtub, and I realized that he
was astonishingly strong, much more so than his wiry
build suggested. He wrapped me in a towel, and said,
"Do you want to see me do it?"

"Excuse me?" I wasn't sure what he was asking, but
assumed it had something to do with sex.

Red grinned. "What I meant was, do you want to see
me shift?"

"Oh." I felt myself flush. "Yes. I would."

"Okay. I can't quite concentrate like this. Do you have
any clothes here?"

"In the other room." I held the towel shut with my
hands and walked into the bedroom, followed by Red.
"That's my bag, over there," I said.

"How about this?" Red held up a thick red flannel robe.

"That's fine." I backed into it and let the towel drop. When I looked over my shoulder, I realized Red hadn't looked away this time.

"Jesus," he said, his eyes wide. I instantly recognized the expression in his eyes. It was what Lilliana had always called the "My God you're naked and a goddess" look, and I had nodded and pretended I knew what she was talking about. It was such a wonderful reaction that I didn't have the heart to chide him. I belted the robe.

"Can you concentrate now?"

Red turned around. "You're still very naked under that, but—yeah, I can handle it."

I sat on the bed, wrapping my arms around my knees. "So what happens now? We wait for the moon to rise?"

Red sat down beside me. "It's easier when the moon's full, like now, but I'm not a werewolf, so I can change at other times."

"What do you mean?"

"Lycanthropy's a virus. What I've got is more, ah, genetic in nature. I'm Limmikin—a shapeshifter."

"I've just accepted the idea that lycanthropy can actually turn people into werewolves—Unwolves—whatever. And now you're telling me there's more supernatural weirdness around?"

Red threw back his head and laughed, revealing canine teeth sharper than I remembered. "Doc, around these parts, I'm what passes for normal."

I felt my eyebrows rising up. "So prove it."

"Right here?"

"Right here. Turn into Red the coyote."

Red flushed his splotchy, hectic redhead's blush. "A wolf. A red wolf, not a coyote."

"I didn't mean to offend you."

"I know I may not be quite as big as some of the timber wolves . . ."

"Sorry, I just remembered that in Texas, some red wolves had interbred with the local coyote populations . . ."

Now Red narrowed his eyes. "Coyotes are tricksters, Abra. I am not a coyote."

"Okay, I believe you."

Red stood up so that he was looking down on me and the bed. The look on his face made my breasts tingle and my nipples harden. "A Limmikin doesn't require the moon," he said, his gaze dropping down to my mouth. "All that's required is that I be naked and in an ecstatic state."

THIRTY-ONE

◑◯◯ In a sense, all women are shapeshifters. But even though I'd thought I was pregnant until a short time ago, I had found it hard to imagine myself undergoing the dramatic transformation into moon-bellied hugeness. Picturing myself with an actual baby had been even harder. My mind had accepted it; my gut had not.

So even though I didn't think Red was lying, I couldn't quite wrap my mind around the image of him turning into a wolf, and imagining myself transforming felt even more outlandish.

Except that I still had the guilt-blurred memory of Halloween night, the sudden storm of intimacy between us, and the unexpected climax of that intimacy. My mother had always insisted that as a child, I'd had some sort of strongly empathic ability that I'd blocked out when I became a teenager. I would argue that I'd had a very good reason for embracing rationality as my religion, and in any case, doesn't every mother want to believe that her child is special, gifted, magic? Even when she knows she is only the absolutely plain and ordinary daughter of an extraordinarily vivid woman?

My defense had been to grow up and resolutely not believe in it, any of it—no to my mother's bags of aromatherapy herbs, no to her crystals and runes and astrology charts, no to her psychic dreams and votive candles and hand-painted leather voodoo charms.

Yet here was Red, telling me if he just shucked his clothes and, presumably, his inhibitions, he could turn himself into a wolf. And if he could, then presumably, I could, too.

The one thing I'd wanted more than magic, as a child, had been to be a dog.

With all these things running through my mind, I couldn't quite sort out what to say when I opened my mouth. But Red seemed to understand. Because he knelt down between my thighs, as if he were about to propose, and waited.

"What do you need to do?"

Getting up to sit beside me on the bed, Red reached over to cradle my head between his hands, then raked his fingers through my hair, tugging gently at the hairband until it came loose and my hair tumbled down my back. That almost familiar sensation his hands induced in me, a kind of mindless sensual relaxation, kicked in and I felt my eyes go heavy-lidded. "I need to take off my shorts. Anyone likely to come in here? Disturb us?"

I shook my head no. My mouth was kind of dry.

Red drew in a sharp breath. "Jesus, Abra, you smell . . . you smell like you want me."

I swallowed, with difficulty. "I do, Red. But I'm not going to make love to you." I couldn't. Not five minutes after believing myself pregnant with another man's child.

He nodded. "I just need to get a little—you know, reptile-brained. Instinctive. I can do it with the right ritual, or music, but that would take a while. Don't suppose you happen to have any pot?"

"My mother probably does but I have no idea where."

"So it might be quickest if you—if you let me kiss you."

"Just a kiss?"

Red's eyes crinkled with amusement. "Doc, a kiss done right is a pretty powerful thing."

"All right then. Just a kiss." As if I hadn't had my mouth on his penis a month ago.

Red pulled down his shorts. "One thing, though."

"Yes?" I tried to look away, but it was hard. I mean— well, yes, I guess I meant that, too. I hadn't been with many men, and I hadn't really thought much about size before. It wasn't that Red was that much longer than Hunter—it was just that he was, well, thicker. And I couldn't help but wonder how that would feel. I put my thumb and finger around him, trying to measure.

Red gave a sharp gasp and his eyes closed. "Just . . . just wanted to mention that . . ." I moved my fingers slightly, and he moaned. "Wanted to . . . Jesus, wait, I can't think when you do that . . ."

"Yes?" I took my hand away.

Red swallowed hard and opened his eyes. "In my other state, I might not be as, ah, restrained."

I nodded in mock-seriousness. "You think your dog-self is going to try to mount me?"

I guess the tone of my voice fell somewhat short of diplomatic. Red looked at me with something that was mostly amusement but ever so faintly tinged with an-noyance. "Oh, just shut up," he said, and kissed me.

At first it wasn't much, just a press of his thin lips to mine, just an angling of his jaw to set his mouth more firmly over my mouth, just his big hands cradling my cheek, my jaw. And then I became aware of his bare chest against my breasts, the red robe must have slipped down off my shoulders, and as I reached for it he took my wrists in his and held them captive, and that one small gesture did me in. I moaned, and the next thing I knew Red was biting his way down the side of my neck, sharp little nips like nothing Hunter had ever done. Red lifted one of my breasts, the skin underneath so sensitive it nearly hurt, and took one of my nipples between his teeth, sending a shock of painful pleasure straight down to my womb.

I grabbed ineffectually at his hair with my bandaged hands and he pulled his head away. "I thought you said just a kiss."

Red grinned, and his eyes were an intent, wolfish yellow. "I lied," he drawled, and buried his face between my breasts.

"Stop," I said, and he opened his mouth wide, engulfing most of one small breast. My thighs fell open, and Red made a strange groaning sound. "Really stop," I said, and tried bringing my knees together.

"Little pig, little pig, let me in." His hands parted my legs.

"Red. Red!" I was crying now, and he looked up, all humor gone.

"Doc?"

He came up until my head was level with his strong chest and pulled me into his embrace. "Ah, Jesus, Doc, I'm sorry. Please, don't cry. I stopped, all right? I stopped."

"Red." I cried his name into his mouth and felt his startle, and then his comprehension. He started kissing me again, and again I could feel that barely restrained wildness in him, sharp teeth leaving faint marks of possession, my heart thudding with fear and excitement. But when his eyes met mine, I could feel the strength of his love for me, holding his hunger in check. This time, as he slipped down my thighs and I started to cry, he understood and held my wrists all the tighter, and I finally let myself go and wailed as he found me with his tongue.

He did not ask me if I was all right, thank God, and when he closed his teeth on the tender bud of my flesh I lost that tenuous sense of self separate and apart. In the moment when I seized his coarse hair with my damaged hands, in the moment when need became savage and primal and fierce, I threw my head back and howled and howled.

THIRTY-TWO

◐○○ "Okay, so here's the problem—you're not a dog. Or wolf, or coyote, or any other canid form."

We were lying in bed, my head on Red's chest, one of my legs thrown over his hip. We were not lovers by Bill Clinton's definition of the word. But we were definitely more than just friends.

"Well, no." Red's fingers traced lazy patterns on my back.

"But you did say that all that was needed . . ."

"Was my being naked and in an ecstatic state. But here's the thing, darlin'—that was *your* ecstatic state."

I leaned up on an elbow and planted that elbow in the middle of Red's chest. "But you said—"

Red had begun kissing the inside of my elbow where it dug into him. "I'm in love with you. I'm part wolf. I want to eat you up."

I drew my knees in and sat up. "So why aren't I a wolf then, if I have lycanthropy?"

Red propped himself up on one elbow. " 'Cause the virus kicks in when it reaches a certain level in your bloodstream. If it kicks in—some are predisposed, some aren't. Also, it depends on the moon. And we're not within Northside's borders now—the town tends to have an amplifying effect on certain conditions."

"You watch my mother's movies, don't you?"

"We need to change your bandages now."

"Don't change the subject." But I held out my hands as he gathered the gauze and antibiotic ointment.

"Well, would you look at that." We stared at my hands as Red unwrapped the gauze. The skin was a paler shade of pink, the color I'd have expected to see in a burn two weeks old.

"Can you feel this, Doc?" He ran a finger over my palm.

I looked at his finger touching my palm. "No."

"You're healing this fast because of the virus."

I wiggled my fingers, then touched my knuckles. "I still can't feel anything."

"Maybe if there was a complete change . . . Do you want me to try to bring it on?"

The rush of fear left me feeling almost sick. It wasn't a rational thing. I knew that even as I heard the breath hiss out of my teeth. "I don't know. I don't think I'm ready."

Red gave me the kind of look I am used to in dogs: a look of perseverance. "I think you're readier than you know."

The fear was gone, leaving something darker and more difficult in its wake. "Oh, Red." I wondered if I was going to be able to love him back the way he deserved.

"How about this. Let me change. Then we'll work on changing you."

"Fine, do it."

Red raised one eyebrow. "This how you talk to all your gentlemen friends?"

I touched the side of his face. "Sorry. What should I say?"

He came closer, so close the tip of his nose touched mine. "Say, Hey, I never noticed how incredibly handso—" The phone rang.

We froze, looked at it. "Don't pick it up, Doc."

"What if it's an emergency?"

I could feel his sigh in my hair. The answering machine clicked on as I sat up. "You have reached Beast Castle, a refuge for abandoned, abused, and unwanted cats and dogs," said my mother's voice, incongruously sultry and dramatic. "We are currently tending to some of our animal patients. Please leave a message and one of our dedicated volunteers will get back to you shortly."

"I am an extremely patient animal," Red growled, getting up from the bed.

"Be quiet," I said.

"Pagan? I'm calling from the airport to tell you that I'm catching an early flight back." It was my mother, sounding more than a little stressed.

Red, moving more quickly than I would have expected, was there to lift the phone to my ear.

"Mom? It's me. Why are you coming back so soon?"

"Abra? Where's Pagan?"

"With her boyfriend. Mom, listen, I don't want you to get alarmed, but I have to tell you—"

"Wait a moment, they're announcing something—no. Abra, my flight should be in this evening, but they're experiencing some delays. I may be in late."

I was looking into Red's eyes as I spoke to my mother. There was a band of dark green, another band of gold. His lashes were tipped with gold, and I traced my finger along the fan of crow's-feet which deepened with his smile.

"Mom, before you get here, I wanted to tell you what happened. Hunter and I had a—we had an argument."

"It's the pregnancy. Hunter can't stand the thought of being tied down to anything. I've always told you that about him—he's an emotional sixteen-year-old. He wants you to be the home that he keeps leaving."

As I watched, Red's eyes began to fill with tears of mirth. I realized he could hear every word my mother was saying.

"Mom, I'm not pregnant. It was a false positive. And I've left Hunter. But there's something else you need to know."

"Wait a moment . . . Christ, another flight's been delayed. Abra, I need to get myself a drink before any more serious talking takes place. I just wanted to inform Pagan that I was coming back, not get into a whole emotional unburdening." There was a pause while my mother snapped at someone standing too close to her that she was having a private conversation.

"Abra? Are you there? Listen, I realize that you are the daughter and therefore filled with your own concerns right now, but it would be nice to actually hear you ask me why I'm coming home a week ahead of schedule."

I put my hand over Red's mouth to stop his snort of laughter, and he kissed my palm. "I don't need to ask, Mom. You're coming home because Grania broke up with you. She's emotionally immature and you caught her flirting with some other guest. Or spa worker. Male," I guessed.

There was a momentary silence. "You think yours is the only drama that counts, don't you, Abra?"

"No, Mom, that would be you. What I've been trying to tell you for the past ten minutes is that I just burned my hands and—" The phone went dead with a click. Red and I stared at each other.

"Well," he said.

"Meet my mother, the undead queen of psychodrama."

"I guess I'd better go fix some coffee. Something tells me that you need it. We can always pick up where we left off a bit later."

I didn't know what to say. I'd told him the truth when I'd said I couldn't just sleep with him—well, have sex with him, as I *had* slept with him. But then, lying on my back a few moments ago, I had rather lost my sense of boundaries. Had he pressed his advantage sooner, I would have said yes. Now that I was no longer aroused, however, I couldn't see myself taking the next step with this strange new man. But I couldn't exactly leave him stranded, either.

"Forget the coffee. Lie down on your back," I said.

"No."

"No?"

Red reached out and touched me on the side of my face. "This time I won't be able to keep control. If you do that for me—I can't promise not to take you. In any form."

I stared at him. No man had ever seen me as the kind of woman who would make restraint impossible. "What do you suggest, then?"

Red scratched the back of his neck, his arm and shoulder muscles bunching. "Well, I do need to prove to you that there's more to me than meets the eye. If it can't be sex . . ."

"It can't."

"Then it has to be beer and rock and roll."

Since beer and rock don't really sit well before eight A.M., we spent the day pilling a few cats, taking a shivering greyhound's temperature, and putting ointment on the fungal Burmese. I noticed that the animals had a strange reaction to Red: At first, a few of the cats hissed and arched, but after a moment all of them became downright affectionate, rubbing against him and purring loudly. Most of the dogs were relaxed after they'd had a chance to sniff him. To my relief, they sniffed his breath, not his rear end. The Akita, never a stable character to begin with, did a little mad barking dance, but Red crouched down and smiled a particularly unfriendly smile, and then the Akita rolled over and writhed.

"So dogs don't mind the fact that you're an Unwol . . . Limmikin?"

"Most don't. I've got a good way with animals, in any case." As if he were reading my mind, Red added, "You'll still be able to work as a vet, you know. During the time of month when you're transitioning, you'll smell like a cross between a menstruating female and one in estrus. But the animals aren't going to go white-eyed with terror—they'll just try to sniff your crotch a bit more than usual."

Something to be grateful for, I supposed. At four o'clock I rested and discovered that in the forty-five minutes I'd been asleep, Red had cleaned out one of the spare guest rooms so it no longer smelled as badly of cat piss and mold. I moved my things in and looked out the window. It was not my childhood bedroom—that was the room Pagan was using. It was the room my father had liked best, overlooking the garden in back.

Red composed one note for my mother and another for Pagan, explaining about the animals, my hands, and the sleeping arrangements. Red seemed to be assuming that after the upcoming evening of boozy rock and possible shapeshifting, I would want him to leave me back here with my mother. I suppose that was the best way to handle things. My mother could help take care of me until I figured out what to do with the rest of my life. Or maybe I'd turn into an Unwolf and my hands would heal completely. I couldn't really say which outcome seemed more likely. My mother hadn't been much good at taking care of me when I was little, but then, I'd never turned into a hairy monster before, either.

At seven Red brushed out my hair and braided it, his hands firm and deft as he formed the plait. Then he helped me into a button-down shirt and jeans. "I guess no makeup," I said, mostly to myself, as I looked in the mirror. I looked, in Hunter's words, nunlike.

"What do you need makeup for?" Red was buttoning the silver snaps on a jeans shirt.

"I just thought a little blusher, some lipstick . . ."

"Wait." Red came up behind me and put his hands on my hips so I could see both of our reflections in the full-length mirror. Then he leaned in and kissed me on the pulse in my neck.

"What's that for?"

"Wait."

He leaned in and turned my head till our lips met, and now the pulse between my legs throbbed. It seemed to take less and less for him to arouse me, as if I were becoming tuned to his frequency. When he released me, I looked at my reflection and saw flushed cheeks, red lips.

"You don't need artifice to look like sex, Abra. You look like sex."

Since Red didn't know anyplace local, he drove us a full hour till we were back in Northside.

"So where are we going?"

"Somewhere they serve beer and rock and roll and I feel at home."

"Oh, no. Red, you aren't taking me to Moondoggie's?"

"Yup. From what you said, your husband's going to be pretty busy stalking his mistress . . ."

"Very funny." Despite Red's assurances, I really didn't want to go there. What if we did meet Hunter?

But when we arrived at Moondoggie's, Red went and stood at the door and inhaled, a deep breath as if gathering his nerve, though I knew better. He was checking out the joint.

"He's not here."

How could he tell? All I could smell was beer and cigarettes.

The restaurant had a few elderly diners lingering over their turkey and yams, but the dark side of Moondoggie's was almost empty. The bartender tonight, I noted with pleasure, was a burly, middle-aged brunette, not Kayla.

Red turned to me, and I realized he smelled faintly spicy, like cologne. "What do you want, Doc? Beer? Wine?"

"Just a soda. No caffeine."

Red put his hand on the small of my back as he ordered. "Listen, Jelaine, mind if I put on some tunes?"

"You go right ahead, Red."

"I want to open up the back patio. That suit you okay?"

The brunette lady laughed as she handed Red our drinks. "Hell, freeze your ass off if you want to, Red. It's your ass. You want glasses?"

They both looked at me. "Not if we're dancing," I said, and they both laughed as if I'd been witty.

Red led me over to the jukebox, his hand on mine reminding me of high school dates. There was a lot of country western and eighties power rock, but Red seemed to know what he was looking for. He flipped rapidly from one selection to another, not asking my opinion.

"Come on, Abra, let's go."

The back patio, which must have served as a dance floor in the warmer months, was lit with two red and two pink floodlights. Red opened the doors and I wished I'd put on a sweater underneath my wool jacket. Red put his beer and my ginger ale on the table and the first song came on, an old tune about dancing in the moonlight, a fine and natural sight. Red caught me around the waist and started moving, and to my surprise I found myself following with ease. I'd never been partnered by someone who knew how to lead so well that my feet just sort of fell into place. My bandaged hand crept from Red's palm to his shoulder and my hips began to roll more fluidly. Red half-closed his eyes and we turned neatly, almost in a country two-step.

"This is fantastic, Red!"

"Your husband doesn't dance?"

"No, I'm the one who doesn't dance."

Red finished his beer and ordered another. The next song was faster and we moved apart, then together, and I threw back my head and laughed with the sheer delight of this kinetic flirting. Sweat was rolling down my forehead and between my breasts, but Red seemed impervious as the music shifted to something acoustic.

"May I?"

I walked into Red's arms as some band from the seventies crooned that they would believe in miracles if I would. We moved together, with only the hand on the small of my back guiding me. His breath smelled like yeast and hops. We were both sweating now.

"You ever listen carefully to the words of this song, Doc?"

I paid attention. There was a clear suggestion that the miracle in question could be achieved tantrically.

"We tried that, remember?"

Red playfully bit my ear. "We *almost* tried it."

"Are you going to change soon? Are you close?"

"Abra." He rocked me away from him, back into him. "Didn't you ever have some guy asking, Was that it? Did you come yet?"

"Oh, whoops."

After that I just forgot about why we were there and enjoyed the evening. Two more couples came in and joined us on the patio, younger than us, teenagers. I became so relaxed that I didn't pay attention to the small kisses Red pressed to the tip of my collarbone, to the pulse behind my ear. I let him pick me up in an exuberant show of strength before sliding me down the length of his body, and if I danced away from him I moved right back in, so close that I knew that this was foreplay, and not just for shapeshifting.

And then we just stopped moving and looked at each other, and Red was sweating and unsmiling and his eyes were burning a deep gold color, and I could feel how badly he needed to get out of there.

"Let's go."

He was following me so closely that he stumbled, and one of Red's friends called something out, but Red seemed sick, pale, and clumsy, and intent on me in a way even lust could not explain. He was following me as if I were the only beacon in a dark world.

"It's okay, Red, we're almost there." I was leading him out into the bar area, toward the front door, the parking lot, our car. There were a few locals drinking post-Thanksgiving beers, big, bearded, deer-hunting types. If I'd been thinking more clearly, I would have taken Red out of the patio straight into the woods. But I meant well. I wanted to lead him home.

"Hello, Abs."

I looked up at the bearded man with the fierce eyes, uncomprehending. And then I recognized him, despite the full black growth of facial hair.

It was my husband.

THIRTY-THREE

◐○○ I had last seen Hunter clean-shaven on Thanksgiving morning. Less than twenty-four hours later, he was standing in front of me looking like a mean Grizzly Adams. And suddenly this whole lycanthropy thing didn't seem quite so far-fetched.

"Hunter!" He was wearing a black sweater, dark jeans. He looked like some sort of bearded assassin.

"Hello, Abra." His nostrils flared, and I wondered what he was smelling on me. We became aware of Red at the same moment. I glanced behind me, hoping to see normal, watchful Red, laid-back and easygoing, hazel-eyed and cautious. And it was close. If you didn't notice the pallor, the yellow eyes, the patina of sweat. It was a good approximation of normal.

"Hello, Hunter."

"Hello, Red. Fucking my wife yet?" Hunter leaned close, inhaled. "Ah. Not yet, I see. But you'll keep dogging her until there's a weak moment, is that it?"

Red smiled, and it wasn't friendly. His canines looked particularly sharp. "Seems like you've been a bit of a dog yourself, now."

"She's got my baby in her belly."

"Hunter!" Other people were listening. Kayla's colleagues and friends were listening.

"No, friend, I'm afraid she doesn't. It's the virus kicking in. She has it, too."

"And what do *you* know about it, vermin catcher?" Hunter stood up, and I felt a cold wash of adrenaline sweep through me. I wasn't the only one sensing real violence in the air; the small crowd murmured and gathered itself for the coming fight.

"Take it outside, boys," said Red's friend from behind the bar, who seemed to be speaking *for* the bar.

"Red, don't do this." I held on to his arm. It didn't occur to me to hold on to my husband's.

Red glanced down at me and then lowered his mouth to mine. He brought his hand up to cup the back of my head and held me there while his tongue explored my mouth, and I tried to push him away. I could feel Hunter watching, feel the growing sense of excitement in the room. Lust and violence, now. "Delicious," Red said, and then looked up at Hunter.

A direct challenge.

"Outside, Red. Let's discuss boundaries."

Red grinned, and I could see a side of him I hadn't suspected. He was enjoying this. For him, there was a dark humor to the situation, while for my husband, there was nothing but fury and dented pride. "What, right outside, in front of all these folk?"

"You chicken?"

Red's eyes narrowed in what almost seemed like delight. "Well now, sticks and stones, Hunter, may break my bones, but name-calling, that's serious business. Your place or mine, sweetheart?"

"Mine." Hunter gestured at me with a sideways turn of his thumb. "But Abra comes with me."

"The hell you say."

I put my injured hand on Red's shoulder. "No, it's okay."

Red shook his head. "Don't do it, Doc."

Hunter laughed. "You don't know her very well if you think that's going to work. Come on, Abs, let's take a drive."

Thinking that I would have time to talk him out of this fight, I followed him out of Moondoggie's, shivering from cold and nerves. Red, just behind us, cursed under his breath. Overhead, the rising moon shone a spotlight on our little drama. "If you hurt her," Red warned Hunter, "I'll hunt you down."

Hunter looked over his shoulder. "I'm not going to hurt *her*, you moron." He unlocked his car and I opened the passenger-side door. As Hunter started the engine, I saw Red watch us for a moment, his hands balled by his sides and his body coiled with tension, before he sprang for his car so that he could follow right behind us.

Like me, Hunter was observing Red in the rearview mirror, and for a moment, our glances met. "What the hell do you see in that asshole?"

"He's the opposite of you," I retorted. Then, remembering why I was in the car with him, I said, "Tell me what the point is in you two fighting each other. It's not like he took me from you. It's not even that you want me back."

"He trespassed," Hunter said simply, turning onto a side road. "And besides, he wants the fight as much as I do." Then he smiled, revealing sharp canines. "At least, he does now. In about twenty minutes, my guess is your new boy toy will have changed his mind."

Hunter was right; he was bigger and stronger than Red, and this was not going to be an even contest. I wanted to plead, Don't fight him, but I wasn't sure that was even an option anymore. Somehow, I had gotten myself into a place where pangs of jealousy and possessiveness could become punches and bites that left visible wounds.

The moon seemed to follow us as we drove, sometimes dipping behind trees for a moment, then reappearing in a different position. I could see its light reflected in Hunter's dark eyes, and noticed that dark hairs had begun to sprout on the backs of his hands as they clutched the steering wheel.

I no longer tried to speak, and the silence between us felt so deep and weighted it seemed impossible that this was my husband, my old college friend, the charming rogue who'd singled me out and reinvented me as a desirable girlfriend after a lifetime of being the plain daughter.

If you are not Hunter anymore, I wanted to ask, then who am I?

The bearded stranger beside me parked the car at an angle and hopped down just as Red pulled up in his jeep.

"Doc, you'd better climb on up to the porch."

As I walked toward the steps, I felt the crunch of dried leaves and fallen twigs underfoot. Pulling my coat more tightly around me, I wished with all my heart that I could find a way to stop this before it began.

"You first, Texas. Let's see it."

Red took off his clothes and Hunter followed him, garment for garment, a kind of terse strip poker. Naked, my husband was taller, handsomer, broader. Red was more leanly muscled, hairier, balanced on the balls of his feet like an experienced fighter. He changed first, a ripple of movement through his muscles, then waves of transformation, spine curving, legs bowing, face elongating. Hunter was not so quick or so graceful about it, and I realized that his struggle was tied to the lunar phase. On this clear November night, the moon was so bright that you could see the details of her surface.

According to the calendar, we were one day shy of the full moon, but you could have fooled me.

When I looked back, Red was a wolf, a small one, short-coated, with a coyote's narrower muzzle and larger ears. He was not the great timber wolf of legend, but I hadn't been expecting that. I'd seen him this way before; I accepted it now.

But my husband writhed and screamed and panted, the change a painful one for him. And when it was done, he was a wolf man, like the creatures of B-movie lore. He hunched close to the ground, hairy and grotesque, clawed and splay-footed, and to the naked eye it looked as if there could be no contest. Red was a wolf. Hunter, my husband, was a monster.

Hunter stood there, yellow-eyed, breath fogging out over his fangs in the cooling night air. Red stalked toward him stiff-legged, his ruddy, gray-tipped fur bristling. From where I stood, safe on the porch, it looked like my husband would be having Red for lunch.

Then Hunter launched at Red, more like a man than a wolf, and the fight was over almost before it began. Red lunged up and snapped his jaws over Hunter's throat, and Hunter swung wildly left and right before dislodging his foe.

Like a good street fighter, Red took advantage of Hunter's momentary disorientation by darting in. He got a few good bites in to Hunter's flank and clawed hands, and I was clenching and unclenching my fists, worried now for my husband, when suddenly Hunter grabbed Red by the throat. Red twisted and writhed, and Hunter sank his fangs into the smaller wolf's side, missing his belly by only inches.

"Stop!" Galvanized, I tried to draw their attention back to me. "You're killing him!" But the creature that had been Hunter was beyond human recall. He would have disemboweled his rival then and there, except that the brief distraction had allowed Red to break free.

This time, as the opponents clashed, I could hear Red's whimpers along with his snarls. Though weakened and seriously injured, he seemed no less aggressive than before.

Knowing dogs, I could see all the signs of a fight to the death.

"Submit, Red," I whispered, but then he hurled himself at Hunter, biting hard at Hunter's calf. Hunter lashed out, catching Red right below one eye with his claw.

"That's enough! Stop!" Hunter was slashing at Red's belly again, and Red was refusing to back down. I had to end this *now*.

I ran down the steps knowing what might happen. You can't be a vet and not know the chance you take when you put yourself in the middle of a dogfight.

"Stop!" I planted myself between them just as Red lunged up. It was his weight that knocked me down, and though he was light for a wolf, he had used all his remaining, desperate strength to attack. As he tried to swerve, his teeth grazed my thigh. Hunter snarled and seemed ready to continue the battle.

Then both combatants smelled the blood trickling down my leg. In the long pause that followed, I think I saw Red ripple and begin to change, but I will never be sure, because it was at that moment that I heard the woman's voice.

"That is quite enough," she said. I had to admit, I agreed with her. I wasn't feeling at all up to any more.

And then she came out of the shadows of the porch and I saw her face, and realized at once who she was.

THIRTY-FOUR

◗ ○ ○ I knew one thing for certain: Magdalena Ionescu was not my husband's usual type. In the past, his girl-friends had always been pretty. Magda was not pretty. Magda ate pretty for breakfast and then looked in the mirror and admired how sleek and shiny she was from a diet rich in iron.

"You are bleeding?"

I looked up into her dark, almond eyes and wondered if I should lie.

"Never mind. Sit down, woman. I will examine you. I am medically trained."

"So is Red, and I prefer not to have you touching me." She'd just stepped out of the house, and it didn't take a master's degree to tell who'd been sleeping in my bed.

"He is indisposed," she pointed out, and I saw that he was still in his wolf form, injured and panting.

I looked at Magda and knew that if I pushed her away, the curtain would fall, and I would see the reality behind this little play of normalcy. So I sat down on an old wooden bench and let my husband's mistress look at the gash on my thigh. The fabric of my jeans was ripped and stained with blood, and her nostrils flared.

"If you get queasy at the sight of blood, you're not go-ing to be much help to me," I pointed out.

"Blood does not disturb me. Did you know you are

about to get your period? No, wait." Her nostrils flared again as I scrambled up off the couch. "It is not menstrual. You are about to shift." She didn't sound too happy about it. "Hunter. You did not inform me that your wife was also *pricolici*."

The wolf man—or Unwolf—that was Hunter made a grunting sound, not unlike the noncommittal grunting sounds he made in human form. Some things, I supposed, didn't change with the full moon. I noticed there was blood on his calf, and his bicep. I didn't particularly care.

I stared up at Magda. She was taller than I, larger boned, with full breasts beneath her turtleneck sweater and a tiny waist set off by a thick leather belt with a heavy, almost medieval buckle. A gold cuff of a ring adorned one hand, more like a weapon than a wedding ring. Her chic, boyishly short dark hair had a jagged streak of white shot through it. She had the kind of mouth that made men rearrange their underwear. Right now, though, it was frowning. "I thought you were not intimate with each other," she said, turning to Hunter. "That was why I came, because you said . . ."

"Guess he was cheating on both of us, huh?"

Magda's eyes were flat and dark, unreadable as she gazed down at me. "You will bleed now for a few hours. There is no stopping it, until you change. Perhaps you will die, though—not everyone survives the change."

"I suppose you missed the medical school course on bedside manner." I was talking tough, but I felt a wave of dizziness and had to put out a hand to steady myself on the bench.

"Better if you wait to stand." She reached out to steady me, and the touch of her hand sent a wave of discomfort down my back. "Perhaps you would like to clean up in the house?" She gave a meaningful look at my bloodstained jeans.

What a lovely hostess. "Actually, I'd just like to be on my way."

"You cannot drive like that. Your hands are shaking. And it is not my intention to kill you." She smiled. "We are all civilized people, no?"

"Fine." I wasn't going to thank her, but I walked into the house and headed for my bathroom. Getting my jeans off was the hard part, but the wound underneath wasn't too bad. Ideally, I would have stitched it up, but instead I washed it off, applied some antibiotic cream, and closed it with a couple of butterfly bandages. I found a pair of fresh panties and a sanitary pad and changed into a pair of loose sweatpants. On the bright side, my injured hands seemed to be in fine working order.

On the downside, Magdalena's toothbrush and makeup were all over my sink.

And her skanky wolf-bitch smell was all over my bed.

I limped down the stairs and saw Red, pale and human, sitting in the living room. There was a cut under his right eye, and bruising on his neck. He was wearing his jeans, but naked from the chest up. He was holding a wad of reddened pillowcase against his ribs.

"Oh, God, Red, are you all right?" I hadn't realized how badly he was injured.

Red smiled grimly. "I'll be fine, darlin'. You just tell this husband of yours that this is not a fight over who gets you."

I turned to my husband, who did not look quite right and seemed incapable of standing still. His eyes still burned yellow. His hairline seemed lower, almost meeting his eyebrows. But he was wearing jeans and a T-shirt, and, as I now realized, the clothes inhibited the change. "You can't go with him, you know," he said. "Not when you carry my child."

"Hunter," I said, "weren't you listening before? I am not pregnant."

Magda looked at him sharply. "She is not, my love. Use your nose if you do not believe me."

"And what was your plan if I *was* pregnant? Set me up in the guest room while you slept with Magda? Or were the two of us going to take turns?"

"I would never—" Magda began, but Hunter lurched over to me, his misshapen legs making him clumsy.

"I'm not completely insensitive. Magda came to make sure I could handle what was happening. She was here to help you."

I put my hands on my hips. "Funny she never came by before. Where did you stash her, at the local bed-and-breakfast? In the attic? And how did you have the energy for both her and Kayla? No wonder you didn't want to have anything to do with me!"

"Don't be such a child. If Magda hadn't been around, I would have damaged you. And I thought you were pregnant," Hunter went on, his voice roughened to a near growl. "Didn't you notice anything different, Abs? How blind can you be? I could have torn you in two. Magda was here to help me leash what I could no longer control."

Magdalena walked over to Hunter and placed a hand on his shoulder. Instantly, he quieted down. "The initial change is a very sexual time, Abra." Her voice was the voice of a seductive schoolmistress, something British mixed in with the Eastern European accent. "It cannot be gentle, controlled. It is a time of instinct and passion."

"Oh, and I'm supposed to thank you for relieving me of the duty? Well, no thanks, lady. You infected my husband, you've ruined my life—"

"Your friend here understands."

We both turned to look at Red, who flushed, though not as deeply as I would have expected. "Red?"

Magda smiled. "Your friend allowed me to stay at his house. It was nearby, and convenient for visitation."

"Red?" I felt a rush of blood between my legs. I wanted to sit down.

He started to get up, then winced as if his ribs were hurting him, and sat back down. "Listen, Doc, you have to understand. I knew what was going on. I knew there was a damn good chance that Hunter could kill you, playing slave and master or whatever the hell you were doing."

I didn't understand. How could he know this? I turned to Hunter. "What's going on here?"

Hunter smiled, and suddenly I saw his father in his face, arch and sarcastic. "Oh, come on, Abs. You knew. Do we really need to sit around explaining things like this is some kind of soap opera? Darling, Red here is therian and so am I. I had questions."

I looked back and forth between Red and Hunter. "Okay, I've heard about Unwolves, werewolves, shapeshifters, Limmikin, pricolwhatsit—now what the hell is a therian?"

"'Pricolici' is a Romanian word—in English you would say Unwolf, or werewolf, although the 'were' is Old English for *man,* so I would not call myself a werewolf. I have never heard of Limmikin. In my country we would call him a *vârcolac,* because he uses magic to control the change. And a therian is any being that can change into a beastly form," said Magda. "I see you haven't had a classical education."

"This isn't part of a classical education!"

Magda raised her eyebrows. "Well, it does help to know Latin and Greek roots."

I dragged my hands over my hair. "Okay, wait a minute. Forget the vocabulary lesson. Let me get the facts straight. Hunter, you told Red about me and our sex life—to ask him advice?"

"And to make him suffer, of course. It made him so unhappy when I described how much you liked me holding you down and treating you roughly," Hunter rasped. "And then, when I said I wasn't sure I could stop myself from getting really rough, he suggested I contact Magda."

There was a buzzing in my ears. "Red, how can you not have told me any of this?"

Red stood up and walked toward me. "I didn't think you'd believe me, Doc." He tried to draw me into his arms and I pushed him away. "Oh, no you don't. I'm sorry, but I am not happy with all these secrets you've been keeping from me."

Magda laughed. "Wait a moment—I think I do remember hearing something about the Limmikin. I believe my father once said that—"

"It's a Mohawk word," Red interrupted. "It means a shapeshifter."

"A therian," she corrected him. "Does it really? I thought the American Indians believed in skinwalkers."

"There are different traditions."

"And you have a wolfskin in your cabin, do you not?"

Red seemed irritated, and I understood that he did not keep it out in plain sight. "It ain't magic," he said. "I don't need it to change. But it is personal."

"Yet you keep it hidden and heavily warded."

Red looked at her, and I realized he didn't like her any more than I did. "I control the change," he said. "Not the skin. And not the moon," he added pointedly.

"Do you really?" Magda sounded truly interested. Then she slowly pulled her sweater over her head. Her generous breasts were not completely firm, I noted. She slid her long skirt down her thighs and stood there naked, a forty-five-year-old woman, muscular and confident. And then she smiled at Red, and stepped closer in to him. I wanted to say something—Stop, I suppose. Don't. But instead I just watched as she knelt beside him and began licking his wound. And as she licked, her nipples puckered and grew erect, and her fair skin flushed and darkened. Red's head went back. I could hear the moan gathering in his throat as she pulled his pants down. I retreated a step, toward Hunter, and heard the growl in Hunter's chest as he, too, stepped out of his jeans.

I turned back and Red was a wolf again, whimpering, smaller and ruddier than the dark, sleek female with the surprising arctic blue eyes. She continued licking at him, now at his belly, now lower still. She presented her back to him, lifting her tail. And then Hunter growled and shifted into wolf form. He paced back and forth, putting himself between Magda and Red until she raised her hackles at him: Keep to your place.

As the wolf Magda looked at me, I understood what she was saying: I am alpha, and I rule here. I will have both males as my mates and you will stand and watch, losing your husband, losing the man who would have been your lover.

Red had said the virus was in me. He'd said I could change. But would I? There had to be some predisposition. Did I have the right genes, the right mixture of magic and intuition? I watched as Red whimpered and turned back and forth, torn between instinct and something else, something strong enough to make him stop, trembling with the effort, with the scent of estrus in his nostrils.

Hunter had no such qualms. He lunged forward, gripped the ruff of the female's neck, and mounted her. Then he looked up, and there was still something human in his eyes. Something that found it amusing that I was watching.

I took off my clothes, feeling supremely self-conscious. Absurdly, I wondered if my stomach was pooching out. As I inhaled to flatten my belly, the dull ache of a cramp rippled through my abdomen. *Ignore it.* I closed my eyes and tried to awaken something. Rage. Grief. Jealousy.

Some tidal wave of emotion strong enough to wash through logic and civilization and the whole of my upright primate's sense of self.

But there were too many emotions, and the main thing I felt, standing there naked in Hunter's family's living room with all the ancestral Barrow furniture around me, was stupid. I was going to leave a stain on the carpet.

But then Red, loyal Red, came over and started to lick the back of my hand before taking my wrist in his mouth and gently tugging me toward the door.

"No, Red, I don't want to leave," I said. I was tired of being the good girl. I wanted my turn to be the bitch. But then he bit down harder, and I was forced to follow him. Growling and snarling, nipping at my bare fingers, he herded me outside.

For a moment, I felt relief to be standing inhaling fresh air instead of stale hostility. And then I realized that I was standing on what had been my front porch, stark naked in the moonlight. I had just lost everything to Magda, including the shirt off my back. *Shit.* Red sat back on his haunches, wagging his tail as if he'd just done something marvelous.

I rounded on him, frustration and inarticulate rage boiling up in me. "No! No! You stupid, mangy—bad dog!" I chased after him, too furious to care what kind of a spectacle I was creating, and Red bounded away. I had never wanted to swat a dog so much in my life. "Get back here! Come here this instant, you . . ." Red used the tried-and-true dog ploy of pretending this was a game, putting his front legs down and raising his hindquarters up in a puppy-play bow, his tail wagging optimistically.

"No, I'm not playing with you—this isn't funny, Red . . ." Now he was running from me, looking coyly over his shoulder. I lunged forward and grabbed his tail, but he slipped away, giving little mock growls and shaking his head from side to side, as if playing tug-of-war with an imaginary toy. "I'm. Not. Joking!" I bellowed, shaking with fury, and then I realized that I couldn't stop the tremors quaking through me, or the strange, icy sensation racing through my limbs, like the aftereffect of a powerful anesthesia. The first contraction took me by surprise, and I stopped in my tracks. Even with the odd, tingling numbness in my arms and legs, the pain was incredible. It felt like the worst menstrual cramp I'd ever had, magnified and attenuated, and I looked at Red, who was next to me now, his wolf eyes wide with concern. I tried to say, This really hurts, but no words came out.

The second contraction made the first seem like the edited-for-television version, and I dropped to my knees and screamed.

The third contraction felt like it was turning me inside out, and didn't so much end as bleed into the fourth, and then the fifth. All coherent thought ceased, and I stopped making any sounds, and then something ripped and I thought, I'm not going to survive this.

But after a while, the pain began to recede, and I opened my eyes, exhausted. Something was wrong with my vision, I thought, because everything looked grayed-out and blurry. I tried to stand up and realized that my body wasn't responding the way I expected. And then I realized why.

I was a wolf. I was a wolf!

And Magda, walking out to meet me, was a bigger wolf.

THIRTY-FIVE

◑ ○ ○ It wasn't a fair contest. I was smaller, weaker, new to this idea of running around on four legs. Magda was top dog. As Magda began to circle me, flanked by my faithless husband, I really missed the ability to form words. There had to be some way to communicate our feelings that didn't draw blood. Couldn't she just take Hunter, I'd take Red, and we could all go home and call it a day?

And that's what I told Magda. Or at least, that's what I thought at her. Out loud, what I said was, whimper, whimper.

Red looked at me, and his ears went back. Ears back—that's a signal. But what did it mean?

Magda lunged at me and inflicted a painful blow near my left shoulder that made me yip and dart away. Ears back meant protect yourself, I realized. Damn it, I knew that.

Magda stalked toward me, and as I moved toward the protection of a wall I felt someone behind me and skittered sideways a moment before my husband tried to take a bite out of my hindquarters. He had finally managed to get himself into full wolf form, although there was still something a little wonky about his hind legs.

I snarled at him, so incensed by his sneaking up on me that I missed Red's streaking out from my right side and grabbing Hunter right under the throat—a benefit of being smaller in stature. But Hunter swung his muzzle and knocked Red loose, and then Magda was on me, the ruff on the back of her neck sticking straight up, her head held low as she growled.

I didn't know exactly how I wound up on my belly on the floor. But then I rolled onto my back and began posturing faster than you can say "submissive." Magda looked like she wasn't going to be having any of it. She and Hunter kept nosing at me, trying to get me to stand up and take it like a wolf. But I did not want those Alpha Female fangs ripping my beta throat out, and my current posture of abasement seemed to be inhibiting her from doing just that.

Red was walking back and forth, head held low, trying to figure out what to do now that his teammate had chosen to throw the game. And that's what I was doing, I realized. Letting that bitch win. No sooner had my thoughts turned aggressive than I found myself in motion, rolling off the floor and launching my attack on the male—I mean on Hunter—while Red came in to distract Magda, the more experienced fighter.

We did all right for a few moments, Red and I, holding the other two at bay. And then I heard a particularly painful yelp from Red. When I turned to look at him, I saw that Magda had torn a chunk from his ear. I think what happened next surprised even me. I leaped past Hunter onto Magda, my teeth going for her ear. I wasn't thinking biblically, I swear. It was a purely bloodthirsty moment, a moment in which I just saw a vulnerable spot and went for it. I had her ear in my jaws and her pain was music to my ears.

"Enough." There was a woman underneath me. A wolf-woman. I couldn't understand it. And then I felt a man's hand on me, lifting my muzzle to face him.

"Abra." It was the kind-eyed, smaller male. He looked

at me as if he were trying to think of the right command to give me. There was no challenge in his gaze, but still, I looked away. There was blood dripping from the side of his head, and I wanted to taste it. "She's in trouble," I heard the smaller human male say to the wolf-woman. "This was no way to come at a first change."

"Take her out of my sight and out of my territory," said the woman. "And stay out." She also had a cut on the side of her head and looked very, very angry. There was another male with her, also human, but with a very canine scent. He was familiar, but when he looked at me, I caught a whiff of anger tinged with lust. The female scented it, too, and yelled again at my male. Something about getting me out. He said something back, about needing our clothes.

I felt the human male's hand on the scruff of my neck, and it was a comfort to me. He led me into the night, and then into a little metal room. A car: I remembered. He looked down at himself. He was bleeding from cuts on his side, ear, and forearm. I whimpered at him and he crouched down so I could reach him better. I licked the blood until it stopped flowing and then I licked the salt from the male's face. Red's face. I remembered that, too.

"Oh, Doc, if only you meant it." The human hands rubbed and stroked the muscles of my shoulders and then caressed behind my ears. In my strange state of gray-toned vision and Technicolor smells, I could sense how Red was bonded to me, almost as a mate. I thought this one was a good one. We could form a new pack. I tried to tell him this, but he kept trying to pull some strange soft cloth over my head. At first, I tugged at it, thinking this was a game, but then I could see from Red's intent posture that this was an important submission for him. So I allowed the cloth and then when the cloth was on I felt different.

"Doc? Abra?"

I was human again, human enough to be embarrassed that I was naked from the waist down. The wound on my thigh had almost healed, however, and the little cuts and scrapes on my arms were closing up as I watched. *Wow.* No wonder Malachy wanted to tinker with this virus.

"You with me, Abra?"

"Yes."

Red drove the car onto the road, and then, to my surprise, he stopped the engine halfway up the hill. Without the dashboard lit up, I couldn't make out his features. Turning to me in the dark, Red paused, took a breath. "I have to get my things from my cabin now. By morning, she won't let me back. My place is too close to Hunter's property. She feels threatened by us now."

"But it's your house. She can't just chase you off."

Red looked at me strangely. "Of course she can," he said.

It took me a moment. "Oh."

"Won't take me long, Doc. You can wait in the car."

"I can come with you. To get your stuff." My voice sounded quite matter-of-fact, I was proud to note. We stepped outside and I stumbled. Red took my hand and I walked in his footsteps through the woods, and when we reached the cabin he released me and I went to sit on his bed on the floor. I tucked my legs underneath me and tried to pretend I wasn't cold and bare-ass naked.

Red moved efficiently from place to place, throwing some small bottles and the tarot cards into a backpack. There was also some sort of pelt, wrapped with cords and scrawled with purple symbols. "Won't be a minute."

"Sure. Do you have a bathroom?" Because I hadn't seen one on my last, unofficial visit to his cabin.

The look on Red's face said it all. "The thing is, it's out back . . . I'm kind of off the grid here."

"With a CD player?"

"Batteries. Listen, Abra, I didn't mean to give you the wrong impression. I mean, it is an outhouse, but it's clean."

"To be honest . . . what I really need is running water. To wash."

Red cleared his throat. "I have a sink here. I could pump some water . . ."

"We have to rush, don't we?"

"I think . . . as long as we leave tonight . . ." Red's eyes dropped to my naked lap, then returned steadfastly to my face. "May I bathe you?"

Now I was blushing. "All right," I said. I watched him as he threw some logs in a small black woodstove and then turned to the sink, where he primed the pump before working the level over the sink. The room began to warm as Red set some water to boil in a kettle on top of the cast-iron stove. He fetched what looked like a huge roasting pan from a closet and set it on the floor.

"Is that a bathtub?"

"Well, it's what I use for one."

"I'm going to sit in that?"

"That's the idea."

It was all very *Little House on the Prairie*. Except for the look in Red's eyes.

"You okay for a moment? I'll chop a little more wood."

"I'm fine."

And I was fine. I loved watching him. I loved the easy, economical grace of his movements, the loyal caring tilt of his eyes. I loved watching his lean hips inside his jeans as he walked outside, the play of muscles in his arms and back as he turned a small log into kindling.

"You making sure I don't chop off a hand?"

"I'm just watching." How had I ever doubted his intelligence? He didn't need a PhD to prove himself to me. Red was wolf-smart, coyote-clever. He might read westerns and he might never impress my father discussing

Hitchcockian suspense techniques, but if Armageddon arrived, Red would lead you to safety.

"Abra?" He was crouching by the bath, pouring in the water from the kettle. There wasn't more than a few inches.

"Yes."

"The water's ready."

"That's not a bath."

"I'm in charge here, remember?"

I climbed in, still wearing the torn remnant of my shirt. Red removed it, and for a moment I just looked at him looking at my tightly beaded nipples.

"You sore?"

"No. I should be, but I'm not."

"Unless we're really wounded mortally, the change tends to speed up the healing process." Red picked up a flannel washcloth. "May I?" I nodded and he began to wash my arms. I leaned my head back and then Red lifted my leg, using the flannel on my calf and thigh . . . and then higher. I gasped with the shock of sensation. No way we could pretend *this* was part of a sponge bath. Red glanced up at me.

"I'm sorry. I know the rules—you're not going to make love with me. Guess I'd better stop this."

"Red, tonight I changed," I said.

"I know. I saw."

"The other thing, too. The part about falling in love with you. I changed that way, too."

Ah, the lovely light entering his eyes. "Abra."

"Please. Show me what comes next."

Red knelt beside the tin tub, his hands withdrawing from my flesh. "God, you have no idea how much I'd like to—but it's the first time you've changed and it's like you're drunk with it."

I silenced his mouth with my hand. "I'm going to kiss you now."

"And then there's the fighting . . ."

"We can do that, too."

Red's hand gripped my wrist. "Abra, no. It's not you speaking, it's the hormones. And it's kind of like I'm your teacher here."

I surged up and kissed him, ignoring the pain in my wrist. No, worse. Liking it. Liking the hint of something not so gentle in this gentle man. Maybe if I were not so gentle back, I thought. I could feel the heat between my naked breasts against his bare skin, my erect nipples brushing the furry mat of his chest hair.

"Abra." He lifted me out of the tub and onto the bed and was on top of me before I could draw breath. His hands were in my hair, his thumb moving down to graze the corner of my mouth as he rained kisses on my lips, my jaw, the corners of my eyes. But what I was feeling had plunged straight past tender, and I pulled his hair until his head went back and bit him on the firm wedge of muscle between shoulder and neck. I felt the ripple of desire go through him.

"I don't know what this is. Help me."

I watched his face change. "The moon's riding you. You need to change again."

"Oh, hell no," I said, recalling the agonizing pain.

"The second time's not so bad. And if it's the moon's pull, there are ways to make the pain . . ." He paused. "Pleasurable."

I stood up on my knees, grabbed the back of his jeans, and pressed him against me so hard I made myself gasp. "Do it," I said.

And then his eyes met mine and we kissed, a long, hungry, devouring kiss, a little too fierce, a little too desperate, conscious of the danger outside the door and the need to be quick.

Red seized my head in his hands, his teeth closing on

my lower lip, then moving to claim the pulse beside my ear, and then down lower, to trace the pulse in my neck. I sank my fingers into his hair as he bent to taste the hollow of my collarbone, then the space between my breasts, his mouth closing over one nipple so gently I wanted to scream.

I wanted to say, No, not like that, not human and considerate, just take me, take me hard and lift me out of myself. But suddenly Red looked up and his eyes flared golden, and then his teeth closed down on a breast and he was suckling me, hard, and still this was not enough, there was a wolf inside me raging to be set free. I yanked at his hair and he looked up, face flushed and dazed with lust.

"What?"

"Help me!" And Red, my tender Red, tore open the buttons to his fly, and grabbed my wrists hard, and I spread my thighs wide so he could shove himself inside me.

We froze for a moment, staring at each other, a little stunned to be here at last. I couldn't believe how good he felt, just stretching me. And then, holding my gaze, Red thrust into me. Once, twice, deeper, so hard I knew it had to hurt him a little, too. He thrust again, the corner of his jeans getting in the way, his face intent, unguarded, and I closed my eyes, bracing my heels on the bed by his hips. The pleasure was awful. I wanted it to hurt more. I needed the pain to ride the awful pleasure. And then Red lifted my hips and slammed into me and I realized what Hunter had meant when he'd said, I could have hurt you. This was not just a strong man making love full tilt. This was someone who could shift down to his bones, and there was preternatural energy trembling up and down his arms.

"Wait, I have to get my jeans off. It hurts." I watched him tug his pants down over his narrow thighs. Naked, he gave a shudder and closed his eyes as if he was fighting something back. "I can't—I can't keep going and not—you'd better turn over."

I didn't want to. I wanted to watch him. At some point during this endless night, he had become so beautiful to me that I couldn't bear the thought of not watching him as he came.

"Abra, this first time, I can't control it. You have to turn over."

"You don't have to control anything. Let go with me, Red."

His pupils narrowed in the luminous circles of his irises, wolf eyes in a human face. I watched him set his jaw so tight that a muscle jumped high in his cheek. "Abra, I'm too close. I won't be able to hold back much longer, and if one of us changes before the other, what we'll be doing will be illegal in this state."

"Oh." I let him turn me over, the wool of his Indian bedspread rough against my belly. Red positioned himself behind me, lifting my hips, and then he entered me very slowly, his arms trembling on either side of me with the effort. It was then, not looking into his eyes, that I felt what was happening—the surge of heat, the loosening of bones. Except this time the pain was all caught up with the pleasure.

"Are you okay?" His voice was hoarse.

I opened my mouth and found I could not speak, so I tried to tell him with my body, arching my back.

"I don't want to scare you, Doc."

I looked over my shoulder and met his eyes, and I could tell from his gasp that I looked the way I felt—already mindless, already somewhere where animal instinct ruled, except that down here where my muscles were reweaving themselves there was still the awareness that this was Red. Red, who loved me enough to fight for me.

Red cupped my chin in his hand and kissed me, a hard kiss, triumphant. "It's got to be now, Abra." I was amazed he could still talk, and I wanted him to stop. No words. Words reminded me of Hunter. Red and I didn't require the crutch of words in bed.

I felt Red brace himself more firmly, thrust in, thrust out. I lost my bearings. Forgot about the bed, the cabin, the dangers outside. Red began to pound into me, a steady rhythm that stopped all thought, and then he shifted his hips and now his thrusts were reaching that spot high up inside me that brought the feeling everywhere at once, into my breasts and nipples and belly and heart, and it was too much to bear, I had to reach the top of this or fall apart. And then Red leaned down to bite me on the back of my neck and as his teeth turned to fangs we both arched with the savage joy of release.

PART THREE

THIRTY-SIX

◖○○ "This is a definite drawback."

Red kissed the back of my shoulder. He was half-lying on my back, keeping some of his weight off me, and I was on my stomach, propping my face in my hands. It wasn't exactly a traditional postcoital position, but we weren't exactly in a traditional situation. Well, okay, it was traditional for canines.

"You mean being stuck together? It only lasts a few more minutes. I kind of like it."

"No wonder dogs look so embarrassed afterwards."

"We could always take advantage of the position," Red murmured, nibbling at my ear. He was lying curved around me, the bed a rumpled mess around us, and I could feel his radiant happiness at having me there, joined to him at last. I had never felt anything like it before, this drunken puppy sense of loving abandon. It was almost better than the sex, although the musky salt-sea odor of our coupling kept making me think I should get a second opinion.

Red must have been thinking much the same, because he began to swell inside me. I felt the prickle of change begin sooner this time, a gooseflesh sensation of the small hairs lifting all over my body.

I looked over my shoulder and Red's eyes met mine. He stroked the hair back from my face and we smiled at each other, wordless with the gift of love and sex. All this fun, all this remarkable, physical, mind-slowing, soul-searing fun, and it was ours for the having, free and clear. I'd always thought this kind of sex—the kind that sells cruises and canned soups and silk sheets and health club memberships—was some Hollywood invention. But it was real and it was mine.

"I sure hate to wipe that look off your face, Doc, but if we can, we'd better get moving. If we linger here too long, Magda's liable to take it the wrong way."

"What do you mean?"

"I mean, she said to take ourselves out of her territory. And I figure the sun better not catch us still here in easy walking distance."

"Or else?"

"Doc, if we discuss this any further in this position we'll be here till noon, if you catch my drift."

We tried to pull apart and, to my regret, succeeded.

"Well, that didn't hurt."

Red flashed me a slightly rueful smile. "Speak for yourself." I wondered whether or not he was joking. At least dogs didn't have to worry about what to say to each other afterward. Red pulled on his jeans and picked up one very small suitcase.

"You didn't take much."

"Just the important stuff."

We drove back, trying to be serious. Serious things were happening. But Red and I couldn't quite wipe the sloppy, happy grins off our faces. I was a wolf girl and he was a wolf boy and we were in love. Somewhere behind all of this giddy pleasure there was grief at losing my old life, but having Red to touch kept that pain at bay. We kissed at all the red lights, and some of the roads were so empty that we made out through two lights in a row. We necked our way up to Beast Castle's front door, his fingers hot against my skin despite the chill predawn air.

"I hope my mother's gone to bed already. I don't think I can wait till we get to my room."

"Ah, first change. There's nothing like it."

"You mean it doesn't stay like this?"

"Well, whenever the moon rides you, you'll find you're in the mood for a little bloodsport or sex. Sometimes both. But the initial metamorphosis is particularly—intense."

"So you probably can't keep up with me, huh?"

Red raised one eyebrow. "Careful, little girl. I've been doing this a mite longer than you."

I twined my hands around his neck. "So you think you can manage?"

My lover replied with a grin that revealed all his white and pointy teeth.

"I didn't know you could do that! You can change just a part of you?"

Red's eyes gleamed wolfishly. "It takes practice."

"Wow, I want to try."

"You'll probably be a quick study—it's unusual to change fully your first time, like you did—so, hang on." Red was still looking at me, but he wasn't paying attention.

"What is it?"

"I don't know yet. Shh." And then we both listened, testing the feel of the quiet darkness that was just beginning to lift in the east. Somewhere in the distance, a car's engine downshifted. Near us, a breeze blew leaves and a small rodent froze in reaction. Something was wrong.

"Red?"

He looked past me, out at the yard. "Aren't there dogs kenneled out here?"

"Of course there are. You helped me feed them—"

"They're awfully quiet."

"I don't usually hear them when I'm outside the kennel building."

Red's jaw tightened. "I do."

We walked over to the small outbuilding used for the Castle's larger and more obstreperous canine visitors. The door was still closed, but the lock had been broken.

"What is it, Red? Vandals?"

"Maybe." Once we stepped inside, I stopped thinking clearly. There was a tangle of limp, furred bodies on the hard cement floor—necks at odd angles, jaws frozen wide—and there was a lot of blood, the thick, ropy kind. The Akita had been killed near the front door, her throat ripped out. The rottweiler was in a far corner, his blood running in a thick stream toward the drain in the center of the room.

"What was it?" The smell of copper and flesh was so intense that I felt as if I were tasting it. I was still thinking vandals, some kind of animal, some hideous dogfight.

"Abra, maybe you'd better wait here while I check out the house."

And that was when I realized that, of course, it was Magda. Which meant that this was my fault, my responsibility, for seducing Red instead of leaving his cottage as quickly as we could. "Oh, God. Is this—is Magda punishing us?"

Red reached out and touched the back of my head. "Let's just take this one step at a time. Give me the key. You see if anyone here needs your attention. I'll be back in a few."

I had begun to crouch next to one of the mongrels, a sweet doe-faced female we'd called Happy, when I realized what had just happened. I didn't need to go to each victim's body. My wolf-enhanced hearing could detect that the only heart beating there was mine. Which Red would have known as well.

So the only reason for him to have gone in solo was to keep me safe. I stood up, my knees trembling a little in reaction.

The scream was sudden and high and unmistakably female.

Mother.

I ran to the main house and found the front door open. And then I stopped, waiting in the familiar Spanish foyer with its grand winding staircase, not knowing where to go. I had started heading for the stairs when I heard a metallic crashing sound, and turned back toward the kitchen. Remembering all the old cop shows I'd ever seen, I tried to ease myself along the wall so that I could see what I was getting into before it hit me.

"No good sneaking like that, Abs. I can hear you rustling around out there."

It was Hunter's voice. Surprised, I stood still for a moment, my hand to my mouth.

"Come on, come on out. Come on, dear, I can smell you. And what an interesting odor it is, too."

I stepped out into the light of the kitchen, and what I saw was so unexpected that I wound up just standing there in the doorway with my mouth hanging open.

Hunter, on the other hand, did not seem in the least surprised.

"Hello, Abs," he said, never looking up from what he was doing. "Still on the veggie kick, or in the mood for a little meat?"

THIRTY-SEVEN

◑○○ For one long improbable moment, I thought Hunter was cooking dinner or a really hearty breakfast, and the unexpected domesticity of it stopped me in my tracks. There he stood, bearded but dressed in a long-sleeved burgundy shirt and black jeans, chopping meat at the wooden side table while a pot of something bubbled on the gas range behind him.

"Hunter." I squeaked the end of his name, and he smiled.

"You took your time." His hands were surprisingly deft with the blade, considering how seldom he cooked. At first I thought he was carving up a chicken, then I looked again and thought, Maybe rabbit.

Or cat.

"What are you doing here, Hunter?"

The scream made me jump and turn, but Hunter simply raised the heavy French knife and sliced through a joint. "What was that?"

Hunter's eyes, when he looked up, were the ugliest shade of yellow I had ever seen. "That was a scream. As for what I'm doing here—well, I should have thought that was obvious. I'm making myself at home. This should have been my home, you know. And now it is."

By now I'd had enough time to notice the furry striped pelt which had been stripped from the carcass. Time to take in the amount of blood staining the old wood. "You bastard," I hissed. "Why are you doing this?"

The knife whacked off another joint. "Because you owe me."

"I owe you?"

Hunter's smile was pure malice. "Yes, Abra, you owe me. For all the years my father subsidized your fucking education, while your mother pissed all her money away on sick cats. You owe me. For dragging me down year after fucking year into domestic fucking oblivion while you refused to make any of the changes that would have helped my life, my career."

I was absolutely confused. What changes? What had Hunter ever wanted me to do that I had refused him? "Hunter," I said, "I have no idea what you're talking about. Do you mean my not asking my mother for money?"

Hunter moved around the side table, and now there was nothing between him and me and the big knife in his hand as he approached. "Oh, baby, don't forget your father. Did you ever once consider asking your father if any of his connections could have helped with my career? Did you ever do a single thing to help me get to the top?"

"He didn't like you. My mother didn't like you. What was I supposed to—" The knife flew past my face and shuddered as it embedded itself in the plaster by my head. Hunter braced his arms against the wall, imprisoning me between them. Then he leaned in close, his spittle flying into my face as he spoke.

"Maybe you didn't defend me very well. Maybe it served you to have mummy and daddy on one side and me on the other. Or maybe you just never thought about anyone but yourself."

This time the scream was cut off. I raised my knee up hard, jamming it between Hunter's legs, and then ducked under his arm as he crumpled. I took the stairs three at a time, stumbled, took them two at a time, and opened my mother's bedroom door so hard the knob slammed against the wall.

"Mom!" But it wasn't my mother. It was Magda, half dressed in a purple sequined Bob Mackie gown my mother had worn back in the early eighties. Her short dark hair, with its streak of white, looked oddly appropriate with the showy dress. She looked like a Disney villainess now, ready for her close-up.

"Oh, hello, Abra. Good—I *needed* someone to do up the back." Magda turned to me and smiled, and I saw that there was lipstick smeared at the corner of her lovely mouth. No, not lipstick. Blood. She had prepared this for me, part of my brain registered. This was a theatrical setup, and she was the star.

"Where's my mother?"

"Oh, that heavyset dyed blonde was your mother? I'm afraid your boyfriend's eating her." Magda gestured at the bed, where I could see what appeared to be a pile of discarded costumes. I looked harder and saw a mound of Piper LeFever's old movie star dresses lying in an ever-widening pool of blood.

"Where is she?"

"Some men just lose control when they change, haven't you noticed? Or are you so innocent that you thought it was just all fun and fucking?" Magda leaned in so close that I could smell the raw meat on her breath. I crouched there by the bed, hyperventilating, crying. "Hunter's gotten quite angry at you, hasn't he? The wolf in him has been waking up, bit by bit. And, guess what? Deep down, where instinct and passion rule, your husband has despised you for a very long time." I was breathing too hard, almost whimpering, but behind my panic and shock, there was that sober little nun voice inside my head, detached and still functional. She's doing this on purpose, the voice said. This is a production, and it's for my benefit. I looked up at Magda through a veil of tears and hatred. "I'm asking you again, Magda. Where is my mother?"

"I don't know where your coyote dragged her off. Follow the blood trail, I suppose. Or doesn't your nose work that well yet?" Magda turned in front of the mirror, admiring the way the fabric hugged her breasts. "Do you think I could keep this? In Romania, we didn't have much need for dressing up, but I can see that your husband and I might enjoy going out while we're here."

I looked at her and felt so much anger that my other senses kicked in. Suddenly I could smell the musk of her excitement. She wanted me to attack; she wanted to take me down. But I had caught the blood trail, and my sharpened vision caught the traces of blood on the dark wood and tile floor. My world had narrowed to the scent of my mother's injury, to the traces of dark blood splattered unevenly along the walls and floor.

I found my mother—lying naked on my bed, her skin far too pale—in my childhood room. Someone had tied a rough bandage around her right wrist, and my mother was cradling that hand to her chest. Red was huddled in the corner, as far from my mother as he could possibly get, incongruously draped in my mother's huge paisley caftan, a fringed bandanna wrapped around his head. Underneath her clothes he was clearly naked.

"Mom! Red! Oh, my God, what are you—"

"Abra." My mother's voice was faded, weak, almost unrecognizable. "He tried. To help me."

I turned to Red. "She's going into shock. Help me cover her and get her out of here."

Red shook his head as if he were pushing something away. "Doc, she took my clothes. This place is thick with blood and I've already changed twice tonight."

"Red, you told me that you're a shapeshifter. You can control this. I need you to control this."

"No. He can't."

I went over to my mother, and for the first time in our lives, I knew she wasn't dramatizing what she was feeling. I put my finger over the thready pulse in her neck. "What do you mean, Mom?"

"He's not my lover and he's not my family. Right now, all I am to him is fresh meat, and if he stands up, you'll be fighting to keep him from finishing me off."

I looked at Red, pale and trembling like a junkie. "Is this true?"

He smiled, and it was almost his old rueful grin. "Turns out your mother liked to research her roles. Knows a thing or two about wolves and men."

"But you said you were a shapeshifter. You said the moon didn't control you."

My mother lifted her good hand, and I could see the effort it cost her. "My daughter," she said, "does not believe in half-truths."

Red laughed, a hoarse little bark that turned into a cough. Or maybe it was the other way around. "They took my clothes and gave me a taste of your mother's blood, Doc. And locked us in here alone together. My control's good, but it's not perfect. Jesus," he said, shaking a little harder. "It's goddamn hot in here."

I watched in horror as he began shifting the dress farther down his shoulders. "You keep those clothes on!"

"I'm burning up."

"Red, don't take that off. You'll start to shift." Opening the door to my closet, I rummaged through a bag of old toys, throwing aside an old poster of Duran Duran and a pair of never-worn high-heeled boots.

"Abra," my mother said tightly, "this is not the time to clean out your closet."

"Oh, for God's sake, Mom." I finally located the safe and worked the combination. "I'm looking for the Telazol. I keep it hidden and locked away." With trembling fingers, I began mixing the powerful sedative.

"Typical. If you weren't so paranoid about drugs, you wouldn't have to waste all this time now—Abra, your friend here is taking off his clothes again."

"Red, please." I turned around, shaking the mixture in one hand while I tried to remove the cap from a hypodermic with my teeth.

"Don't worry, I'm fine now." Half naked, hairier than I remembered him, Red sat with his chest heaving in and out, panting for air. "I just couldn't breathe for a minute. You know what? I'll just open the window a crack."

"No! Abra," my mother called, "you have to stop him!"

Too late. I'd barely had time to take a breath of cold morning air before I saw the waxing moon hanging low in the twilight sky. Moonlight. Shit. I turned to my mother, and whatever I was about to say lodged in my throat because in the next moment Red was on top of her. And he wasn't human anymore.

THIRTY-EIGHT

◐ ○ ○ Panicked, I rushed forward, dropping the hypodermic. Cursing my own stupidity, I jammed my hand sideways into Red's mouth and for a moment there we all were, frozen in tableau: my mother silent and frighteningly cold underneath me, Red a hundred and seventy pounds of wolf above me. Then he twisted his neck to try to get free and I punched him so hard in the nose with my good hand that he rocked away from her and rolled off the bed and back onto all four feet in one smooth motion. For a second, I thought he was going to go for me, but there was something in his eyes, not so much recognition as lack of malice. He was like a dog on the scent of quarry, quivering with excitement and focused on one thing and one thing only.

Killing my mother.

I looked directly into Red's eyes, trying to challenge him, draw his attention back to me, when I heard them.

"Oh, look," Hunter said, and of course I turned to see him. His mouth and beard were stained with blood. "It's little Red and the mother-in-law."

Magda, still dressed in my mother's Bob Mackie, laughed that awful fake laugh women used to use with men, the kind you hear on old television shows. She turned and I saw that she had something in her arms, half hidden beneath the generous cleavage spilling out of the gown.

I had Red by the scruff of his neck, but his attention had caught on some new prey. Following the line of his vision, I saw what he was looking at: Pimpernell the Chihuahua, cradled like a baby in Magda's arms. Glad for the distraction, I managed to throw my mother's caftan over Red's back, and he shivered and changed. Trembling with reaction and paler than before, he remained crouched by my feet, a beaten man in a big dress.

"Red? Are you all right?" When I looked into his unfocused eyes, I could see they still gleamed a wolfish gold. "No, he's not all right, Abs." Hunter smiled at me, enjoying himself. "He looks like a frowsy red-haired fortune teller, for one thing. And he's hungry. Blood-hungry."

"Hunter, why are you doing this? If you wanted to leave me, then why didn't you just go? What does it gain you to be cruel?"

Hunter looked at me coldly. "Abs, you've spent the past ten years perfecting your little martyr act, but it's just not going to work anymore. My time with Magda helped me see your game. You pretended to be independent and fine with my work, and I never understood this undercurrent of guilt I kept feeling. You were reeling me in, trying to tie me down to the kind of life I loathe. Even when I tried to explain that I couldn't live your way anymore, you kept clinging to me, making it impossible for me to make a clean break without being a shit."

I could hear the echo of Magda's voice in this, and yet there was a strange, clunky ring of half-truth there, too. For the first time I understood that Hunter was filled with a kind of corrosive rage that had been eating away at whatever other feelings he might have once had for me. "So now you're okay with being a shit. Fine, Hunter. Great. But are you okay with being a murderer?"

"Don't be so melodramatic." Magda shook her head, and for a moment seemed again a respectable European scientist. "As far as I can see, the only person in danger is your mother. And the one looking to murder her seems to be your boyfriend." And that's when I looked up to see that Red had gotten right up close to my mother, and was sniffing her wrist.

"You've made your point by killing all the dogs, all right? So get him away from her."

"We set the dogs free, and they attacked us. It was self-defense. As for the cats . . ." She shrugged. "I am not a cat person."

"Are you willing to be an accessory to murder?" I tried to keep the panic from my voice. "You can't actually mean to let this happen, Magda." Out of the corner of my eye, I spotted the hypodermic that I had dropped earlier, lying half under the bed. I looked away, trying not to change my expression. "Back at the house, you said we were all civilized."

Magda narrowed her eyes. "That was before you challenged me. But fine. You want to save your mother? Go ahead. We won't stop you."

Red was kneeling by my mother and examining her wrist now. My mother made a low moaning sound.

"Hunter! Hunter, you can't let her do this!"

"Don't worry, Doc," Red said from across the room, "I'm not losing control. I'm just checking the extent of your mother's injuries."

My mother tried to raise her head. "What are you— Hey! Stop licking me. Stop . . ." Her voice trailed off as Red's eyes held hers, and she seemed to grow calmer. It reminded me of how wolves hypnotize their prey, giving some kind of predatory look that the wounded victim instinctively understands and accepts.

"It'll feel quite nice, actually," he said as he bent over her.

"Don't interfere," said Hunter, coming up behind me to grab my wrists. "I'm getting turned on."

I struggled, but Hunter's grip was like steel. "Red! Red, stop this! Please, don't hurt her, don't—try to remember who you are. Try to remember that I'm her daughter. Please, Red, stop."

Magda turned to Hunter. "Americans really love to talk everything to death, don't they? What a bore. Did she analyze your sex life, too?"

Hunter laughed. "She was too repressed."

"Well, I'm not." Magda lifted her chin and Hunter switched both my wrists to one hand and began kissing his lover openmouthed. The little dog whimpered as it found itself pressed between their two bodies.

And then everything seemed to happen at once.

Magda cried out, "Ouch, that little shit just bit me!" and dropped Pimpernell, who whimpered and then raced over to my mother. Bracing his little matchstick legs on her shoulder, he barked imperiously at Red.

I don't know what the little dog said, but it must have been convincing. The next thing I knew, there was a blur of reddish-brown fur as Red left my mother and his human form all in one lightning movement, launching himself onto Hunter with snarling jaws. For one wonderful moment, Hunter remained in human form and fell down. In that endless sixty seconds, I had time to dart forward and grab the hypodermic. And then Hunter changed and stood, a much bigger animal than Red, and far more aggressive. His hackles raised, and although Red did not back off, I could tell which was the more dominant animal.

"Don't forget me, Abra." Magda smiled, and it was like a baboon's threat of teeth.

"How could I forget you—the biggest bitch in the room?"

"Careful, little girl—I might just have to discipline

you." I could hear the snarls and growls as the boys circled and lunged at each other. How long did I have before Hunter took Red out?

I stood up and could feel my mother watching me from the bed. Make a scene, I thought. Make one worthy of Piper LeFever and maybe you can act your way out of this. "Oh, you mean I shouldn't mention that you're a little long in the tooth to be playing dress-up? Not to mention a little too old for whelping lots of puppies."

"I am fertile."

And that was why we were all here, I realized. I remembered Red telling me that not everyone who got bitten by a lycanthrope became infected. You needed to have some kind of predisposition. Maybe Magda had been looking for a mate for a long time—her own personal breeding program to save her own endangered species. "Are you? For how long, Mags? You're forty-five, forty-six? Fine for a woman wanting one or two kids, but you're aiming a little higher, aren't you?"

"I do not think the world needs more nearsighted, bucktoothed, asthmatic children who are allergic to peanut butter and require pencil grips for their clumsy little hands."

I moved closer to Magda. "Gee, I don't know. I was a little nearsighted, bucktoothed child myself."

"Precisely."

"Don't you believe in penicillin, or should we just let the sick work it out for themselves?"

Her snort of laughter was the first unpremeditated sound I'd heard her make. "Penicillin has bred a generation of weaklings. I suppose in your work you would like to save little mutant runts like that bowl-headed excuse for a dog. Dogs must be fast enough and smart enough to hunt and kill, or they should be allowed to die. And, yes, people, too. We need to bring out the best in our children, not settle for defects of the heart, the eyes, the brain."

"So you want to breed the strong, and I want to save the weak."

"Yes. That is why I—"

My bitch slap caught her completely off guard. I hit her on the right cheek, then harder on the left, and while she was falling back, I jammed the hypodermic I'd been concealing into her neck.

"What have you done!"

"I had to put a dog to sleep tonight," I lied. "It's sodium hydrochloride."

"How much?"

"Enough to put you down."

"Hunter!" She fell to her knees. "Help me!"

But Hunter was a wolf, and he didn't quite understand that bad chemical smell, although it scared him. He growled, and Red lunged at him.

"No, Red, down!" Magda tried to take advantage of my momentary distraction, but wound up causing me to jerk my arm, depressing the plunger.

"Oh, my God," she said. Her eyes were wide and terrified.

"Magda . . ." The syringe had actually contained only butorphinol, a sedative, and I wasn't sure how quickly it would take effect, or what kind of effect it would take.

"You are going to absolutely ruin the Unwolf species with your inferior genes," she said, and her eyes rolled back in her head. She had passed out from fear, I thought, unable to believe my good luck.

"I happen to like your inferior genes, Doc," said Red, who had changed form while I wasn't looking. "I'd be honored to mix them with my own."

I looked pointedly at my mother's caftan, which Red had wrapped around himself. "Not if you keep wearing women's clothes, I won't."

"Well, I did manage to subdue the wildlife." Red gestured to Hunter, whom he had muzzled and hog-tied with the fringed headscarf. "Now, let's see to your mother. You doing okay there, ma'am?"

My mother may have been half dead from shock and loss of blood, but you do not call Piper LeFever "ma'am." Her brows came together and she looked past him. "Abra," she said firmly, "get this redneck asshole out of the room. Get me my black gown. And for Christ's sake, call 911 before I lose consciousness."

"I love you, Mom."

"Then try to act like it sometimes."

I didn't want to kill her by trying to have the last word. I called the ambulance. But Red stopped me from calling the police.

THIRTY-NINE

◐○○ In the aftermath of violent change, you think you yourself are changed. And maybe you are. But after a while, things get back to normal. You start thinking about the fact that you need a new winter hat. You stop thinking about how you almost lost your mother and how she still has a thin scar on the inside of her wrist. You have that first argument when she criticizes your lack of a hairstyle. And then you remember that your husband and his new girlfriend killed her animals and are now on supernatural probation, which means they can't get furry unsupervised for a year. The sheriff, Emmet, turned out to be a gruff, taciturn, seven-foot man with hands the size of dinner plates and a sharp beak of a nose. When he shook my hand, I saw that there was dirt embedded deep in the wrinkles of his dry, hard skin, and when he tipped his long-brimmed Stetson hat to me, I saw that someone had carved crude symbols or letters on his forehead. I asked Red whether anyone thought the sheriff of Northside looked a little unusual, and he smiled and said that anyone who actually met him was already well-acquainted with weird.

At first, I'd thought that the sheriff had let Magda and Hunter off too lightly, but something about Emmet made it hard to argue. He did say that they'd have to perform community service, which in their case meant maintaining the cairns and wards all along the North-side town limits. I hardly thought this seemed sufficient, but at least they would have to wear bright orange jumpsuits when they did it.

And then I woke up feeling tired and cranky on the last day of the old year, with a cramp low in my abdomen. I could feel that it was that time of the month, but because I was in Pleasantvale and not in Northside, the pull of it was weaker than before.

My father had left just a few days ago after coming up from Florida, tanned and too thin, to celebrate our survival. He had wanted to bring his new girlfriend, but had finally agreed to leave her at home out of respect for my mother, who was still mourning the loss of her animals.

"She'll get better, Doc," Red reassured me. And at midnight, I saw him rescue her from my father, walking her underneath the mistletoe to kiss her gently on the cheek and whisper something that seemed to take her by surprise. She turned in my direction, and even from across the room I could see her eyes brighten. It was close enough to the full moon for me to tune my hearing in.

"So your bite wasn't infectious, but Abra's might be?"

Red whispered something else, and for the first time in over a month, I saw my mother's old flirtatious look reappear. She hooked her arm through my boyfriend's and walked him over to the buffet table, which was groaning with meat and pies and three different kinds of potatoes. I heard a noise and saw a bounding blur of large, curly dog. It was Morgan, a standard poodle who had broken out of the kitchen and was making a beeline for the roast beef. Red fixed her with a stern look and Morgan had the good sense to back off. He might not have been the biggest wolf around, but he was the biggest wolf around our house.

Except for me.

I felt him come up behind me, a full plate in his hand. "How're you doing, Doc?"

I leaned back into him and let him put a piece of chicken in my mouth. It's hard to be a complete vegetarian around the holidays. Especially given my lunar cycle of meat-hungry hormones.

I chewed while Red smiled at me. "You want to step on over here where it's quiet?"

I followed Red into my favorite spot in the house, a lovely little central hall area with a fountain in the middle of the room and a skylight overhead. The real El Greco house in Spain is open to the sky here, but this is as close as you can come in New York State. The others were still audible from the living room, but they seemed far away. From where we stood we could see out of two large windows, and I took a deep breath and felt better.

"I'm okay, Red. It's just—this is too claustrophobic for me." I hadn't been able to bear the thought of living in Red's cabin, so close to Magda and Hunter, who were still living in the Barrows' ancestral home. And, I suppose, I hadn't wanted to live in a place that had so much wild magic floating around. I didn't like believing in magic. I didn't want to embrace a lifestyle that meant losing control once a month—especially now that I'd seen where that could lead.

"Now, that's just what I was wanting to talk to you about. I know staying here at your mom's has been kind of rough on you, but I think I might have a solution in mind."

"I think I have one, too. I think I need to go back to Manhattan."

Red looked a little startled for a moment, but then he collected himself. "I guess I understand that. You thinking about the Medical Institute?"

"I'd like to finish my internship. If they'll take me back."

Red jammed his hands into his back pockets and whistled softly. "The city, huh? Well, as the good book says, Whither thou goest, honey, I go along for the ride."

I put my hand on his shoulder. "I'll be working almost all the time."

"Since you don't sleep much nights, I reckon I'll still get to spend a few hours with you after dark." Red grinned. With his hands still in his back pockets, he scraped the toe of one of his scuffed cowboy boots like a cowboy straight out of central casting. "Hell, after dark's the best time, anyways."

"You'd hate being in the city."

Red met my eyes, serious, all trace of the redneck act gone. "You might hate it too, Doc. You haven't been back since the change."

"Then I need to find that out for myself."

Red put his arms around my waist and we looked out the window together, at the dark night and the bare, brown earth and the skeletal trees. A glitter of white caught my eye.

"It's started to snow, Doc."

I nodded. I was crying.

"Ah, don't do that, Abra. I'm not going to let you get away. I've been looking for the right mate for way too long to let a little thing like an internship get in the way. I can wait a couple of years for kids—so long as you make an honest man of me now."

On the other side of the window, the snow looked powder-soft, and I watched it filling the air like a cloud. Behind me, I could hear the steady rhythm of Red's heartbeat. "So I'll commute for a while. A couple of years we won't see each other so much. That's not too bad, is it?"

I shook my head. I wanted to believe in what he was saying, but I'd lost the faith that had kept me with Hunter. Maybe Red would stay with me, driving back and forth whenever I had a day off. But I still remembered him huddled beneath my mother's caftan, fighting his own instincts. He'd said he controlled the change, that his initial attack on my mother and the subsequent wrist-licking had all been part of an elaborate trick, and I half-believed him. But that wasn't exactly comforting, because it meant he'd lied about what kind of animal he was. If Red really had been faking, then he was more coyote the trickster than he was admitting. In the Native American myths I'd heard, coyote was the card that always played wild.

So how could I trust him, knowing that duplicity was part of the package?

Which brought me back to thoughts of Hunter. I suppose I'd always known, deep down, that Hunter was capable of cheating on me. I may even have thought there was a chance our marriage might not last. But I never thought he would leave me so completely that he didn't care if I lived or died. I never thought he would tear me apart and then blame me for everything. My mother had warned me that I wasn't reading Hunter correctly. But who'd have guessed my lack of insight would nearly cost her life?

"Abra."

I turned to Red and discovered that he had dropped to one knee. Despite the submissive position, his smile held perfect confidence. Well, why wouldn't he feel secure? We'd spent the past month in a kind of extended recuperative honeymoon. "You haven't answered me, Doc. Suppose I ought to say it right."

I couldn't smile back. "Oh, please don't."

"Don't be embarrassed—I'm not. Abra Barrow, you are the cleverest, least pretentious, gentlest, and most passionate woman it has ever been my good fortune to know. I may not be quite up to the job, but I sure as heck would work at it. Take me on as your husband, woman, and I promise you won't live to regret it." He took the ring box out of his back pocket and flipped the top open. It was a lovely ring, a deep coppery gold set with a golden Topaz, the color of my wolfish lover's eyes. I thought about how much Red must have invested in this—time, money, the risk of my disliking the ring—or refusing him.

My face started to go, first the mouth contorting, then the eyes filling with tears. It wasn't pretty crying, and I knew it. "I'm so sorry," I said, and Red jumped to his feet in one graceful motion. His arms came around me and I rested my cheek against the soft flannel of his shirt. "I want to believe it could work. I want to say yes."

"Sh, Abra. I can wait."

"I don't know what's wrong, if I've lost faith or if it's just too soon after Hunter. But I'm scared of how people change. Even people who don't change." I sniffled, and Red stroked the back of my shirt. "I mean, if Hunter hadn't turned into a werewolf, would I ever have noticed he was no longer the man I'd fallen in love with?"

"I'm done with that kind of change, Abra. I'm not a man who needs to go finding himself anymore. Hunter still is."

"I know, you're probably right. But I still can't do it. I know in my bones that what I need now is to get my life together. You can't wait for that, Red. And I can't risk hoping that you will. I have to let you go now."

"Not now. Not tonight. Dump me tomorrow. Dump me the day after tomorrow."

At the edges of my consciousness, I could scent the tinge of Red's despair, and behind that, the desire in him, the desire that was so intermingled with love it never felt like a thing apart. The way it had with Hunter.

I leaned into Red and started to kiss him and the taste of him made me feel drunk with the change again, the pull of the other like the pull of the moon. I broke away.

"I can't do this, Red."

His hazel eyes searched my face. "Hold on to the ring for me?"

"I can't do that."

"Well, do it anyway." He pressed the ring into my hand, and I let him.

"This feels wrong."

"I won't let you go, Doc. But I'll give you the space you need to figure things out."

"I'm sorry."

Red walked to the front door, already unbuttoning his gray flannel shirt. "Don't be too sad. I'm coming back."

"Okay," I said, my voice breaking on the word. He walked out the front door and the cold night air raced in to take his place. I stared through the dark window for a long time, watching Red shake off his boots, unbutton his jeans, and then turn to look at me over his left shoulder, naked and unabashed. I thought I saw him wink, then change form between one eyeblink and the next. Four-legged, he bounded with astonishing speed toward the tree line. When I turned around to try to face the brightly lit room again, my mother was there.

"That was stupid," she said. She was cradling Pimpernell in her arms, and when he saw me, he wriggled with happiness.

"I know." I reached out my arms for the dog.

Placing Pimpernell in my hands, my mother put her arm around me, and for a moment, we just leaned into each other. "Well," she said at last, "I've done stupid things, too. Like your father. And look what came out of it."

I laughed, my forehead against hers. "The most stupid thing of all," I said, and my mother stopped smiling. Pimpernell barked, a shrill little reprimand.

"No," she said. "The smartest." And then, after a moment, she added: "Now, could I talk to you about the lycanthropy? Because Red had a very interesting suggestion . . ."

But as much as I sometimes wanted to, and as much as my mother longed to run with the wolves, I couldn't quite bring myself to bite her.

FORTY

◐ ○ ○ It was too cold for walking, but I needed the exercise. April is the cruelest month, the poet said, but my vote goes to March, which has the gall to call itself the beginning of spring, when it's really just winter in disguise.

I put on two layers of leggings, a turtleneck, and the faded flannel shirt Red had left behind. At first I'd tried to put it away, as I had done with his ring. But then there were all those long wakeful nights when I found myself searching for his things—his jeans, his Timex watch and worn cowboy boots—everything he'd left on my mother's front lawn the night he'd walked away. I didn't feel entitled to wear Red's ring, but it felt all right to try on his shirt. The ghost of his scent still clung to it, though fainter each time I wore it.

I was on the waitlist for a new internship at the Institute. Meanwhile, I was renting a room in Lilliana's East Side apartment, and had found a job spaying and neutering cats and dogs for the Humane Society. In my spare time, I was also working with Malachy, who had turned his Queens town house into a makeshift laboratory. I had contacted Malachy when I'd come back to the city, hoping he could prescribe something that would temporarily suppress the change.

Malachy seemed intrigued at the challenge, and had

come up with some foul concoction that I drank every morning. So far, three months had passed, and I hadn't changed. I also hadn't had a period, and my hair seemed to be falling out. But I couldn't see myself going back to Northside and letting my wolf run free without Red around to guide me. And thanks to my brilliant decision-making, Red was gone.

As for Malachy, his health seemed marginally improved, and he made it clear that what he really wanted was to continue his research—ideally, with me as a subject. Barring that, he intended to set up a practice in Northside as soon as he'd saved enough money. The idea that something about the town amplified certain conditions did not strike him as insane, which surprised me. But then, I had never been known for my ability to judge *human* character.

But I was back in Manhattan, and Lilliana and I were having a ball, cooking dinners together and watching the complete *Fawlty Towers* on DVD in the evenings. On the weekends, we went to museums and saw foreign films. So, really, I had nothing to complain about.

Except for the pain of losing Red. It wasn't going away, even though I'd started accepting that I really had lost him. I'd stopped calling Jackie and asking if she'd seen any sign of him. I'd stopped trying the cell phone number on his card. My mother had said, Listen, when a man is really ready to settle down, he settles down with the woman who's available. That's the reality. Red wanted a wife and family, and you said no. So give up on that and go start dating again.

But how do you tell a potential lover about this little medical condition you have which makes you hairy and homicidally horny once a month? And how do you content yourself with boring, safe vanilla sex when you've had the experience of complete surrender? I suppose I could have tried looking for bikers, but the kind of danger I wanted was wrapped in a package with love and respect and specific desire. I wanted a beast who believed in riding into the sunset. And every day that passed I seemed to want him more.

I walked west to Central Park, smelling the change in the season. Everyone seemed to be out today, and the Great Lawn was full of dogs and their walkers, which was nice—in general, I'd been exercising in a local gym, and I'd missed seeing other people in the street. I switched on my iPod and Helen Reddy sang that she'd been down on the floor but was much too wise to ever go down again. The air was cool enough for me to feel it in my lungs, and the uncivilized part of me whispered, Run. The part of me that needed the smell of the park like a taste on the back of my throat didn't want to just walk, it wanted to leap and race, bad knees be damned. So I let myself pick up speed. It wasn't until I moved past a slow jog that it happened. First the golden retriever to my left, tugging, breaking loose from the thin female walker, taking chase. Then the terriers, all three of them. Then the dachshund, pathetically moving its runt legs along.

"Hey!" She ran after them, reaching for their dangling leashes, but now there were other dogs joining in—a beagle descending from another path, a basset hound interrupted mid-sniff, suddenly bounding off—easily outdistancing their elderly owners. A black shepherd mix, puppy-eager, jumped a bench and barked his pleasure as he reached me ahead of the rest.

I looked down at his happy, floppy face, still jogging, trying not to lose momentum. It's not cardio exercise if you keep stopping. "What is it, boy? What's going on?" I patted his head as I moved on down the hill, and the others galloped along, the basset hound skidding to keep up.

"Come back here! Hey! Get back! Bad girl!"

For a moment, I thought the shouting was meant for me. Then I looked back up over my shoulder and saw, silhouetted against the pale, cold sky, a Pied Piper's assortment of breeds and mutts at the crest of the hill, all bounding along, freeing themselves from their leashes and owners, canines aroused by the irresistible, infuriating scent of wolf. I wasn't just another jogger: I was the friggin' call of the wild. Turning around, I tried to count. Ten now, including a Samoyed; a giant, dark, square-headed Bouvier; two collies; and a Great Dane.

And suddenly I understood why so many people choose giant hunting and herding breeds to roam their tiny Manhattan apartments. In a city this vast, you sometimes need a dog the size of a person to form a pack with. Except that it isn't always easy to convince these giants that you are top dog, even if you do bring home the Alpo.

I, on the other hand, obviously smelled like a leader. That, or they wanted to eat me.

I ran faster, nervous laughter bubbling up in my throat. I ran all the way through the park, up to Third Avenue, and back to Lilliana's apartment, where I had trouble getting my key in the lock.

The dogs went wild, barking, yipping, the shepherd managing a low approximation of a howl as I finally got the door open and slammed it in their eager faces. I ran up the stairs, still energized; well, I ran up the first two flights. At the door to the apartment, I stopped, trying to catch my breath. I braced my hand against the door, which I had locked not forty-five minutes earlier, and it opened.

The fear lasted only a moment, because I didn't have to look to know who had invaded my apartment. I could smell him. But I still couldn't believe it when my eyes located him, straddling a chair, regarding me with that familiar lazy smile.

"Did I wait long enough, Doc? I figured, April—she'll feel it by then. But I missed you too damn much."

I stared at him, conscious of being sweaty and unmade-up, my hair falling in a lank ponytail down my back. "How did you get up here?"

"Fire escape."

"But the windows were locked!"

"Jackie never told you? Right before I apprenticed with that shaman, I spent some time with a master thief."

I walked closer to him. He'd lost weight again, and there was grayish-red stubble on his chin. He was wearing a backwards baseball cap and a perfectly hideous green sweatshirt with a picture of a stag on it, and if I'd never met him before I'd have figured him as the type to hunt from the back of a pickup truck. But my stomach was coiled tight with excitement and fear, and I had to concentrate on my breathing. In and out, that's how it's done, I reminded myself.

"I've been calling and calling you, Red. But you never called back, and all Jackie would say was that you were out of town."

He unhooked his leg from the stool and stood up. "I know. Jackie told me that you'd talked to her a couple of times when I got back from Canada."

"How long since you got back?"

"Three days. It was easier to stay far away, you know what I mean? Since you sounded so damn sure of yourself on New Year's, I figured I'd better wait till it was really spring to come after you. Not that this feels like spring, but hey, it's coming. You can almost smell it on the wind."

I touched his face, tanned from a winter sun, and the shock of the contact raced all the way down my arm. "So what happens in spring?"

Red wrapped his arms around me and kissed me so hard my teeth hurt. Then he pulled back, laughed at my expression, and kissed me again, harder, his hands cupping the back of my head.

"How about this for a proposal: Come live with me and be my love and if you've got insomnia, hell, we can go chase sheep till dawn. No more lonely nights. That's my proposal."

"I've been pretty stupid about men up till now."

"I've been pretty stupid about women. Kept chasing after the ones who wanted to run away."

"I don't want to run away."

"Sure you do. But you also want to be caught."

And he grabbed my wrists and held them behind my back and we kissed again, till I could feel the rapid beat of his heart against my chest.

"Are you ready for a little adventure, Doc?"

"What kind?"

"Let me see. How about something that calls for you to hang on to the back of a motorcycle. We spend some time exploring out west. I'll show you where I grew up in Texas. Then, when it really warms up, we head for northern Canada, where my grandfather lived."

"And then what?"

Red traced my mouth with his thumb. "And then we go home." He kissed me again, and this time, his tongue found mine.

Maybe somewhere between complete surrender and total independence I could find a middle path. Maybe there was a way for me to forge a veterinary career that could bring me closer to Red, not distance me from him.

Maybe I was thinking below the waist and had completely lost my ability to reason.

But really, when you think about it, Manhattan is no place for anything on four legs. And certainly not for something the size of a wolf.

I pulled apart from Red, wanting to find the words to reassure him that my answer to all his questions was a most definite yes. But then Red growled and began circling me, and I let out a nervous laugh.

"What am I supposed to do now? Say, My, what big teeth you have?"

Red just smiled and didn't answer. And suddenly I really was a little frightened. For the first time, I was seeing Red with his guard down. Not careful because I was new to the change. Not cautious because he didn't want to frighten me off with his intensity. This was a man secure in himself, and as he moved deliberately around me, I could feel the balance of power between us shift and reconfigure.

I didn't know the name of this game, or the rules. In all the years that Hunter and I had made love, we had remained bound by certain unspoken guidelines. I like this kind of touch, not that; touch me here, not there. We were like those people who go on vacation the same time each year to the same room in the same hotel in the same place. When Hunter had first come back from Romania, he had crossed our unstated boundaries a little, but only a little. Maybe, deep down, Hunter had known that if he'd pushed too far, he'd have discovered the surprisingly deep reservoir of cruelty in himself.

But this was different. *Red* was different. I stood my ground as he closed in, forcing myself to hold eye contact, that primitive, dangerous intimacy which provokes all manner of animal desires. A shiver of anxiety raced through me and I recognized it for what it was: that age-old fearful longing to surrender and let passion consume you.

Red's teeth closed over my shoulder. I had finally met my fate, and it was delicious.